WILD SIDE

NATE TEMPLE SERIES BOOK 7

SHAYNE SILVERS

ARGENTO
PUBLISHING

Shayne Silvers

Wild Side

Nate Temple Series Book 7

Formerly published as The Temple Chronicles Series

ISBN: **978-1-947709-02–7**

© 2017, Shayne Silvers / Argento Publishing, LLC

info@shaynesilvers.com

CONTENTS

THE NATE TEMPLE SERIES—A WARNING

*N*ate Temple starts out with everything most people could ever wish for—money, magic, and notoriety. He's a local celebrity in St. Louis, Missouri—even if the fact that he's a wizard is still a secret to the world at large.

Nate is also a bit of a...well, let's call a spade a spade. He can be a mouthy, smart-assed jerk. Like the infamous Sherlock Holmes, I specifically chose to give Nate glaring character flaws to overcome rather than making him a chivalrous Good Samaritan. He's a black hat wizard, an antihero—and you are now his partner in crime. He is going to make a *ton* of mistakes. And like a buddy cop movie, you are more than welcome to yell, laugh and curse at your new partner as you ride along together through the deadly streets of St. Louis.

Despite Nate's flaws, there's also something *endearing* about him...You soon catch whispers of a firm moral code buried deep under all his snark and arrogance. A diamond waiting to be polished. And you, the esteemed reader, will soon find yourself laughing at things you really shouldn't be laughing at. It's part of Nate's charm. Call it his magic...

So don't take yourself, or any of the characters in my world, too seriously. Life is too short for that nonsense.

Get ready to cringe, cackle, cry, curse, and—ultimately—*cheer* on this snarky wizard as he battles or befriends angels, demons, myths, gods, shifters, vampires and many other flavors of dangerous supernatural beings.

DON'T FORGET! VIP's get early access to all sorts of Temple-Verse goodies, including signed copies, private giveaways, and advance notice of future projects. AND A FREE NOVELLA! Click the image or join here:
www.shaynesilvers.com/l/219800

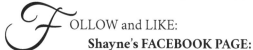 OLLOW and LIKE:
Shayne's FACEBOOK PAGE:
www.shaynesilvers.com/l/38602

I try to respond to all messages, so don't hesitate to drop me a line. Not interacting with readers is the biggest travesty that most authors can make. Let me fix that.

CHAPTER 1

I smirked at the man across the table, my face shadowed by a blue baseball cap that definitely didn't match my hot pink, furry cape. "He is a worthless bag of horse shit," I repeated. "Oh," I added as an afterthought, "and tell him I said *fuck Thebes*." The man's jaw tightened with barely restrained fury at my defamation of his boss's hometown.

I ignored Alucard's subtle shift in stance across the bar. His long, dark hair brushed his shoulders as his head swiveled about the room, watching for an ambush, but the dark sunglasses he always wore hid his eyes as he sipped his scotch. He was a Day-walking Master Vampire, actually gaining power from sunlight, and he was my backup in case the plan went sideways.

"Do you have a death wish, wizard?" the man snarled, shooting another frown at the game-table he had watched me set up a moment ago, before I sat down at his table.

I shrugged lazily. "I'm not too concerned about your boss, minion."

The man stood from the table, kicking his chair back to the ground, and the rest of the bar quieted even further. He stared down at me, shoulders heaving. "You're dead."

I chuckled, taking a slow sip of the ice water that I had ordered. "Not yet. But you should watch your tone. Run along, boy."

He stormed towards the back of the bar through a door, disappearing from view. Conversation slowly resumed, but it was significantly muted as everyone waited for the obvious reaction. I waited, appearing casual while shooting a meaningful look at Alucard to *wait*. He looked about ready to start a fight right then, just so he wouldn't be jumped in a few minutes.

Which was my plan. Picking a fight. Well, step one of my plan.

Because I was sick and tired of waiting. It had been the better part of a year, and the impending war with the unknown Greek God Indie had woken up had yet to materialize. I couldn't find Indie, Ichabod, or any of my Greek friends. This was the first time I had found solid intelligence of a Greek in town, and it was recent, so he must have just arrived.

The only reason I had even caught notice of him was because of the whispered rumors about a strange cloak that the man wore. One that should have still been locked away.

I had been housing my friends at Chateau Falco for a long time, waiting every day for the other shoe to drop, keeping everyone safe behind the magical defenses of my mansion's walls. Because a war *was* coming – an army of Greek monsters, warriors, demigods, and a genuine God to lead them, even though I didn't yet know *which* god. They were – thanks to Indie, my ex-fiancée – almost guaranteed to be pointed at me because, well, exes can be like that. And I was pretty sure they had already raided my Armory of its supernatural weapons of mass destruction – because Pandora, my librarian, was Greek, too – and I hadn't been able to enter my Armory since the horns of war started blowing after Indie woke up the unknown god.

The horns of war that hadn't resulted in any fucking war.

I had run to Kansas City a few times while waiting on the war to start, helping Alucard out with a small family problem, which had earned me a spot on a YouTube video at a stupid concert we had been forced to attend. It went viral, of course, much to my frustration. I had also met a pretty badass wizard named Callie while there, but that had been a different trip to the City of Fountains.

I needed to give her a call. And I had a proposition for her da—

The back door blew inwards – frame, door, and chunks of drywall flying into the room and peppering the nearby patrons with debris. I smiled at the mountain of a man who ducked through the opening, because even though he had torn a hole through the wall where the door had just been, he was still too big to fit through it, so he very literally had to slouch through the opening.

He was easily seven feet tall, had long blonde hair that hung loose, brushing his shoulders, and had three jagged scars down one stubbled cheek. His eyes were flecks of steel-gray, and they locked onto little old me. His neck was as thick as my waist, and his shoulders were easily five-feet across. I think you get the picture. He was proportionally huge, larger than even those Mr. Olympia contestants, reminding me more of the Incredible Hulk, but Greeker.

Hercules. Demigod. Son of Zeus.

He wore tennis-racket-sized leather sandals that went up to the middle of his shins. Even his toe-nails looked larger than mine. Three times bigger. I suppressed a covetous growl as I saw him sporting my fucking cloak around his broad shoulders. Well, technically, it *was* his, but it should have been locked away in my Armory. Safe. To prevent things like this.

The cloak was actually the fur taken from the Nemean lion he had killed. Sitting in the same room as the cloak removed any doubts in my mind. It wasn't a fake, but the genuine article, because I could sense the power coursing off it from here. So, Pandora had been loyal to her Greek origins and was handing out party favors from my Armory to my enemies. I tried not to imagine what else had been taken, because the stockpile held a lot of Greek artifacts.

His huge club thumped onto the wooden floor, silencing those who hadn't already shushed, perfect for my next words.

"Hey, bitch," I said. "Like my hat?"

I tipped it at him, and wondered if I would see sparks from his grinding teeth.

"*Make Greece Great Again...*" he growled, reading my hat. "For that alone, you shall die."

"Better idea. I challenge you to a game of beer-pong."

His eyes latched onto me like spears, and the ground literally shook as he stomped my way. "I'm going to squish you like a little bug," he said in a deep baritone. "Stay still for a minute."

"You aren't going to do shit but get your ass whooped by a tiny wizard," I said calmly, adjusting the cloak I wore around my shoulders. A faux lion-furred cape, but like one of those comical Anime versions with big animated eyes and a hot pink mane.

I pointed at the table I had set up, standing, and furling my cape in case anyone hadn't noticed the mockery of his Nemean Lion Cloak.

Old Hercules definitely noticed my cape and, judging by the unique shade of purple his face turned, he wasn't very happy about it. Especially not in addition to my hat.

My bodyguard, Mallory – who had recently admitted to actually being the Wild God, Pan, in disguise – had heard my plan for tonight, turned about as white as a sheet, and then given me some pretty potent alcohol from his private stash. The Wild God was good for that sort of thing. Knowing there wasn't enough light beer in the world to get Hercules hammered, Mallory had given me his prized homemade hooch, and had also cast a spell on me to protect the lining of my stomach from absorbing his alcohol for about an hour. So, I had to beat the demigod fast, hence my blatant disrespect of one who could quite literally, well, squash me like a bug.

To belabor this, he set his giant club against the bar, right beside Alucard, and approached the table, staring down at the cups – not Red Solo Cups – but big wooden steins.

"We drink these?" He let out a sharp laugh, shaking his head. "You don't stand a chance."

"Listen up, meat for brains. We take turns throwing these balls from across the table into the cups. If I make it in one of yours, you have to drink that cup. Then, it's your turn. The first one to run out of cups, loses. One grunt if you understand, two grunts if you want me to explain it again, slower, and with simpler words."

Hercules shook his head in annoyance, ignoring my jibe. "I'd rather just drink all of these and then club you to death for mocking the glorious city of Thebes."

That would cramp my style.

Luckily, Tory and Ashley sauntered in while he was speaking, wearing skimpy flowing toga-like tops and very short shorts. They also wore long leather-laced sandals. Hercules' eyes locked onto them hungrily as they sat down near the table, speaking softly to each other, smiling coyly at Hercules. "Oh, look! A game. What are the stakes?" Tory asked with a beaming grin, her dark hair glistening in the dim lighting. Ashley flashed a dark grin towards Hercules. Her red hair stood out in the crowd, and looked freshly curled. She also wore her librarian glasses. She was taller than most, and lithe like a blade. She turned to me appraisingly, then shook her head as she turned back to the giant, very pointedly stating her favor on the outcome.

I smiled towards them. Tory was a Beast Master – able to control shifters at will. And although only five-feet-tall, she could bend metal with her bare hands or smash you with a car as easily as wielding a hammer. She was... strong. And a good friend.

Ashley was fiancée to my best friend, Gunnar, the local Alpha werewolf, and she was hyper-violent when she chose to be. Life as a werewolf had only toned her muscles, which were evident with her current outfit. She definitely caught the eye. Another friend. And perfect bait for the Greek Frat boy.

I pretended not to know them. "Good evening, ladies. Maybe one of you would share a drink with the winner? He's trying to defend the honor of his shitty city, Thebes." I rolled my eyes. Hercules shoulders tightened, which seemed to threaten an avalanche of testosterone as he snarled under his breath. Then he looked back to the women, to the table, and finally to me. I held out my hands, waiting.

"Sure," Ashley said, smiling at Hercules.

"You're on, wizard. I'll consider doing this labor for the gods for free. Well, for a drink," he smiled savagely at Ashley and Tory, who egged him on with blushes and giggles.

"When I win, you owe me an answer, and your cloak."

Hercules rolled his eyes. "You cannot possibly win. So, I accept. But when I win, you die, and I'll drink to your death with one..." he met their eyes, "or both of them."

They shared a shy look with each other, and finally nodded, giggling.

I hoped Mallory's spell was good.

If not, the cavalry would need to swoop into the bar, Gunnar at the lead. To save the girls, not me. Because I would be a whack-a-mole casualty.

CHAPTER 2

I rolled up my sleeves, and prepared to play a drinking game with the demigod. I couldn't use magic, but I was hoping I wouldn't have to. I had experience with this game. I had been playing with Yahn – a chameleon dragon pal – since we had been holed up at my house for so long, waiting for the war. Still, I needed to get him drunk fast. But I had rigged the game in other ways, too. Making the cups a little smaller on my side than his. That had been hard to set up. First, to get permission to set up the game table, then to find a way to piss off Hercules fast so he might over-look it.

I had heard he wasn't too bright, and that he was very emotionally-driven. So I could play head games with the brute.

Also, Yahn and I had practiced with the much smaller cups at Chateau Falco. I hadn't told anyone my plan until tonight. Everyone had called it incredibly reckless, especially Gunnar, after Ashley volunteered to step in as bait. Herc had a thing for pretty women, booze, and all things fraternity-focused.

I used this against him. I pointed a finger at Alucard, an apparent stranger. "Ref." Alucard shrugged, his face mildly interested, and approached the table, nodding absently to himself. "There's more drink on the bar right there," I said, pointing. "A special home brew I think Hercules will enjoy.

Hercules looked instantly skeptical. I sighed, making it blatantly obvious how I felt about his lack of courage. I walked over to his side, took one of the cups, and then downed it, never lowering my eyes from his. This close, I could feel the power rolling off him. Not magic, but something else. He wanted to kill me. Slowly. And I was pretty sure he would enjoy doing it.

"No need to be scared, ya' big teddy bear," I said, shaking my head.

And I turned my back on him, half-expecting to die right there. That was the risk. I needed to mess with his head. I needed him emotional. Distracted. It was his weakness. He wasn't used to being ridiculed, only adored and worshipped.

The discreet laughs had the desired effect, because when I returned to my side of the table, I saw his face was that purple shade again. Alucard slowly approached with a jug of dark brown liquor and refilled the cup apologetically.

Hercules grunted, turning from the table to me. "Let's get on with this." His eyes roved to the girls. "I have other things to do this night."

"All you're going to be doing is wearing my cape, staring up at the ceiling, drunk off your ass."

Hercules' massive fists flexed, eyes flicking to my cape and hat. "That hat and cape will soon be shoved so far up your ass that you will briefly taste them. Before you die, that is," he said, letting out a deep laugh. No one joined him. "Enough words, tiny man. Let's pong ball."

Not too bright, the demigod.

I went first, sinking one easily. I motioned for him to drink. He muttered as he downed the cup, then blinked in pleasant surprise. "This is good. Even losing a little is fun."

I shrugged. "It's why frat boys play... pong-ball," I said drily, my eyes flicking to the slowly gathering crowd. They looked to be trying very hard to bite back laughter. "Everyone wins."

Hercules met my eyes as he scooped up the tiny ping pong ball in his hand. "Except when you die for losing," he grinned.

I waited until he was getting ready to throw, and then flung up one hand in a fake claw as I growled dramatically, "RAWR!" like I would at a toddler. My other hand flicked out my pink lion cape for emphasis. He fumbled, having expected a magical attack, and the ball bounced away. He scowled at me.

9

"Trickery will get you only so far," Hercules grumbled as both hands gripped the table, wood creaking beneath his fingers.

Alucard handed me the ball and I sunk one, despite Hercules waving his arms wildly to distract me.

Hercules was forced to drink the super-potent booze with almost every shot I threw. He sunk a couple, forcing me to drink, but was unsurprisingly clumsy with the game. And I had been chugging water all day and eating a ton of food just in case Mallory's spell wasn't as good as he claimed. Such a big guy, not known for his finesse, trying to throw a weightless ball as big as his fingernail was already difficult for him. But the booze was definitely strong, because it was hitting Hercules hard, making his coordination even worse.

He began boasting about what he would do to me. Then he directed his taunts to Ashley and Tory, letting them know he had very specific plans for them after our game. But his throws grew wilder, and he began to realize that although he was drunk and having fun, there was now a crowd, and they weren't cheering for *him*.

They were cheering for *me*.

The guy who had mocked his city, his country, and his achievements.

Very slowly, he lifted his eyes to mine, his lip curling up in anger. I flashed him a grin, and then I meticulously unclipped my cape, and set it down on a nearby chair, making sure it hung neatly, as if it was priceless. Then I stepped back up to the table, making a show to wipe sweat from my neck. Hercules grunted, taking off his own cloak and tossing it on an empty table, mocking me. He was also sweating, and had two cups left on the table before him. I fumbled my throw, missing, which earned a groan from the crowd as the ball rolled underneath a nearby chair. They knew that although I was winning, Hercules didn't have as much to fear from a successful toss since he was so much bigger than me and could handle the booze better.

Or so they thought.

He had to walk a few paces away to retrieve the ball, but he came back looking eager to end the game and get to the smashing part of the night. He nailed a beautiful shot, and I was beginning to realize that he played better drunk. That wasn't good. I drank, and even though Mallory had spelled me, I felt the alcohol beginning to slowly hit me. I set down my mug with a dramatic breath, and used the motion to glance up, sheepishly staring out at the crowd. I pretended not to notice the faint blur creeping across the back of the room. I shook my head violently, laughed, and then tossed the empty mug over my shoulder with a triumphant grunt.

Hercules was preparing to throw, and I used my peripheral vision to see the chair beside him was now empty. I barely hid my grin.

"Do your nipples have biceps?" I asked as Hercules threw again. He flinched, and the crowd burst into laughter as his shot went wild, bouncing off the wall behind me, and then...

Falling right into a cup before me. I groaned at the luck, but no one heard me over Hercules' hooting laughter. He threw his thigh-thick arms up into the air, encouraging the crowd. I took my drink. It hit me almost immediately and I began to grow nervous. The drinks were hitting him, but he was just so damned big. And I wasn't.

I was tempted – *very* tempted – to use my magic, but I feared he might be able to sense something like that, which would turn this place into a drunken brawl. And cheating was the last thing I wanted to do with an already emotional – and now drunk – demigod. Hercules was still holding up his arms, turning to accept the cheers from the crowd.

And he hadn't noticed the pink lion cape draped around his shoulders. Or that his real lion cloak was suddenly missing. I saw several confused faces, but most of those here were drunk, and simply accepted that Hercules had donned the cape in his drunken stupor simply to be funny.

None of his minions seemed to notice yet, too enthralled by the game, rooting for their boss.

I lined up, squinted with one eye as the room tilted, and threw as hard as I could.

I hit him right in the forehead with a wet *smack*.

Then I staggered, belting out a laugh as I overacted my drunkenness – which wasn't hard.

Hercules' face had instinctively shifted to violence at the blow, but as he saw me gripping the table for support, a slow smile crept back over his face.

He wiped his forehead with the back of a massive hand, and licked off the booze. Then he aimed, using his other hand to encourage the crowd to cheer louder.

"What's it like being Hera's bitch?" I asked right before he threw.

The ball almost took my head off – even though it was just a ping pong ball. I ducked and it hit a patron behind me. The ball splintered and he fell, momentarily stunned. His friends helped him up, staring at the red mark where the harmless ball had struck. The room was silent and I saw Hercules panting, eyes bloodshot as he stared at me with pure murder on his mind. I chuckled, turning to the crowd as if not understanding why they were silent. I shrugged, and accepted a replacement ping pong ball from a suddenly terrified patron. I think he was a werewolf, but I didn't recognize him.

"I am no friend of Hera," he growled. "Now, toss the pong ball, wizard. I grow weary."

I nodded. "Using your brain is hard. I get it." Then I stuck out my tongue and threw. The ball sunk into the cup like a magnet. The crowd went silent, unsure whether they should cheer or not. I smiled, motioning for Hercules to drink.

He stared down at the table in confusion, slowly lifting his hand to his forehead while the other gripped the table. Then he looked back up at me and calmly reached for the cup. In the process, he knocked over the last cup and I spun to Alucard, our referee, pointing. "Foul! He has to drink both! I win!"

Alucard looked very uneasy as he met Hercules' glare and nodded. "He's right. You… lost." Then my vampire pal poured another stein, and handed it to Hercules with a shaking hand, looking ready to bolt. Hopefully, he was just acting, and not really that scared.

Hercules downed both drinks, staring straight at Alucard the entire time. Then he walked over to the jug and began drinking straight from it, locking eyes with me, showing everyone how much of a badass he was, I guess.

He slammed the jug down, panting angrily, staring at me as if waiting for me to collapse. He began to frown when I didn't flinch, as if not understanding how I wasn't already dead from alcohol poisoning. "How?" he mumbled.

"I drink a lot," I said. Then I let out a hiccup. "I like your cape," I said, waving a hand.

Hercules stumbled a bit, then latched onto the bar. He didn't even glance at his pink lion cape, looking as if it took all his willpower to remain standing. "I must find your brewer."

I shrugged. "You might want to sit down. You really shouldn't have finished that off," I said, pointing towards the jug. Alucard was watching the two of us, as was the rest of the crowd. Hercules muttered something agree-able, eyes glazing over. Shit, he was about to pass out.

"Hey, deal's a deal. Who's in charge of the Greeks? Hera? Apollo? Who woke up?"

"Woke… yes. I think…" he stumbled, gripping the bar tighter. "I think," he said, falling to one knee, now. His eyes began to slide closed.

"Hey! Answer. You agreed."

"Right. Must honor…" Then he crashed onto his face like a felled tree. The room was silent for a moment, and then I began to hear angry mutter-ings from his crew – that they needed to restrain me until Hercules woke. So that he could *honor his agreement*, they said, but I was pretty sure my brief stay with his hospitable pals would involve pointy spears stabbing me. Politely.

I shot Alucard a look and reached into my pocket. Alucard took two urgent steps as if preparing to flee, attracting everyone's attention, and then he simply vanished into thin air. Everyone gasped in disbelief and began to shout, searching for him, momentarily forgetting about me. The girls had also disappeared, much to everyone's surprise. I bit the cap off the sharpie in my hand and drew a male… appendage on Hercules' forehead. I slapped my *Make Greece Great Again* baseball cap on his head, and leaned in to take a quick selfie.

Then I grabbed my glass of water and Shadow Walked out of the bar before Hercules' thugs could turn their attention from the vanishing vampire back to me.

CHAPTER 3

I appeared in an alley a few blocks away from the bar, and checked to make sure I hadn't spilled my stolen water. Seeing it was safe, I crouched down and instantly shoved my finger down my throat to throw up Mallory's magical booze. I continued until I was confident it was all gone, rinsed my mouth out with every last drop of the water, and then stumbled to my feet, leaving the glass on the ground. I studied my jeans and white tee, making sure I was still clean, and let out a deep breath of relief. I pulled out my phone, and chuckled at the picture as I started walking a block away to meet Alucard and the girls at our prearranged destination.

I finished my business and pocketed the phone with another chuckle. All in all, tonight had gone off about as well as could be expected. Especially Yahn, the only candy-painted dragon I had ever heard of. His skin had the ability to blend with his surroundings, making him all but invisible when he so chose. And he had used that to our advantage tonight.

He had been lurking in the bar, using his chameleon abilities to hide in plain sight and keep an eye on the situation, ready to swoop in and steal the Nemean Lion Cloak if the opportunity arose. But his most important objective had been to make sure my friends made it out of the bar in case things went to hell. Which he had, swooping in to hide the girls and Alucard. Because if he was touching you when he went incognito, you went incognito, too, instantly camouflaged. Alucard disappearing into thin air had really been Yahn grabbing a hold of him and then sneaking out while trying not to bump into anyone and accidentally revealing his trick.

I entered our designated alley to find the four of them staring in my direction, waiting nervously. The girls darted forward with a bag of fresh bagels and a bottle of water as soon as they saw me.

"You're alive!" Ashley belted out, shaking her head incredulously. "We thought something had gone wrong when you took so long to get here." She punched my arm, scowling. "Follow the plan next time," she warned.

I nodded woozily, still shaking off the watered-down effects of the Wild God's hooch. "Mallory's spell wasn't as foolproof as we had hoped. I needed to walk off the effects. And throw up. A lot. Herc handled his booze better than I anticipated, too," I added.

Tory nodded, waving the bag of bagels under my nose. "Eat. As much as you can handle."

I nodded, and began shoving the carbs into my mouth. "Great job tonight, Yahn. I only caught you at the end, but didn't notice you taking the girls or the cloak, and I was *watching* for it," I said between chews, not even bothering to cover my mouth. "You stole it right after he took it off, when he had to go pick up the pong ball, right?"

The tow-head beamed, grinning from ear to ear as he nodded. "I did toe-tah-lee awesome and stuff, yah? Dragon powah!" he squealed. Then he slapped a hand over his mouth in embarrassment.

I grinned at his enthusiasm. Yahn was the happiest son of a bitch I had ever met. Literally. "Dragon powah," I agreed between mouthfuls.

Alucard gripped my shoulders. "Did you actually do it?"

I nodded. "Pay up, Glowsferatu," I grinned.

He shook his head in disbelief. "We're all going to die."

I shrugged. "He was bound to try and kill us soon, anyway. Figured I would give him a legitimate reason."

He sighed, handing me a fifty-dollar-bill. He had bet me I wouldn't draw on Hercules. Or that I would even have the chance to do it. I turned to Yahn. "You have it? Safe?"

He nodded proudly, patting the satchel at his hip. He lifted the flap to reveal Hercules' Nemean Lion Cloak folded neatly inside.

"Well, we got the cloak, but no answers. Were you able to steal his club?" Alucard asked.

I shook my head. "No."

"Maybe if you didn't waste time drawing a wang on his face..." Ashley shook her head in disapproval. Tory looked torn between amusement and backing up Ashley.

I shook my head at Ashley. "It had nothing to do with that. I couldn't get close enough. His boys were waiting beside it."

Ashley sighed in defeat. "At least we have his blankie. What's so special about it, anyway?"

"Makes you super strong. It lets you shrug off more pain than your body could normally handle. Like an adrenaline shot." I didn't tell them that it should have been locked away in the Armory inside Chateau Falco, and that I didn't know how he had gotten it back out in the first place. I didn't need them staring over their shoulders, expecting an army of Greeks to come pouring out of the house. Besides, I had already set up precautions for just that possibility. Nasty precautions.

Tory let out a breath. "This is batshit insane. Did you at least find out which god it is?"

I sighed, plucking out another slice of bagel. "No. It looks like we move to phase two of the plan." I turned to Alucard. "You down?"

He slowly unzipped his jacket to reveal a shirt that said, *Sounds like a terrible plan. What time?* Then he zipped his jacket back up without saying a word, a smug look on his face.

"How about right now?" I asked, sharing a quick look with Yahn, who nodded subtly. I hadn't told anyone my timetable, or even my plan. Well, except for Yahn.

Alucard blinked at me, and then let out a laugh. "Why not?" He sounded resigned. Yahn would have held a pep rally for me in the vampire's place, but I couldn't ask Yahn. He had other things to do tonight.

"How long have you worn that shirt, waiting for the perfect time to use it?" Ashley asked.

Alucard smiled at her. "With him as a friend, the opportunity pops up often. I got this last week. Sooner than I had hoped, to be honest."

"Enough chit-chat. Let's move on," I said, brushing off my hands.

"Nate, you're drunk," Tory argued.

"Nah. And even if I was, it's probably the best time to do something like this. I don't have to use my own wheels for this," I said, pointing at my feet.

Ashley and Tory shared a look, silently discussing the futility of arguing with a drunken idiot wizard. I let them, and polished off my water bottle. Then I called my Uber driver.

Black lightning cracked the night, and a low rumble of thunder – like a passing train – reverberated off the walls of the alley. Twin points of fire pawed at the pavement a dozen paces away, and a murderous whinnying noise crawled across the night's shadows like hungry tentacles, making my friends shiver. Yahn disappeared with a muffled squeak on instinct, which he did whenever startled.

"Easy, Yahn. Grimm's a pal. You know that," I said reproachfully.

He reappeared, looking embarrassed. "Yah, I know," he admitted. "Just startled me." He fidgeted from foot-to-foot as he watched my unicorn approach. "He just looks so *stabby*."

Grimm snorted in pleasure at the compliment. "Ready to go see your brother?" I asked my murderous, pet unicorn – slayer of rainbows and all things happy in the world.

"Fuck yes," he snarled. Grimm really didn't talk much. But when he did, he sounded like a sadistic executioner. "Pegasus and I need to have words."

"Groovy. Yahn, is Camilla ready?"

Everyone turned to face him, stunned that he was privy to something they weren't. Yahn nodded after glancing at his phone for a second. "She's still there. Nothing has changed."

"Perfect," I said, nodding to myself. "Text her that we'll be there in ten minutes." Alucard looked anticipatory, but nervous. Probably excited to see the famed Pegasus, but terrified at the imagined *what else's* that usually popped up. Ashley looked to be planning on what exactly to tell Gunnar. Tory shared a look with Alucard, silently telling him to be careful and to look out for me. Then she held out a hand to Yahn. Ashley did the same, and the three disappeared. "Head to Chateau Falco, and under no circumstances are you to leave," I called out. "Keep the kitty blankie safe, Yahn," I added.

I heard him agree, and then they were gone. I knew they would pester Yahn to death, but maybe he would find a little backbone from this. We would see. It really wasn't that big of a secret, I just hadn't felt like sharing too much, in case I changed my mind. Grimm had first located my target, and then Yahn had helped Camilla keep eyes on him.

"Mount up, Sunshine."

"All this to find a name. Are you sure there isn't some magical, respectable way to find out which god she woke up?"

I slowly turned to face him, incredulous. "We're two dudes about to ride bareback on a fucking unicorn to meet Pegasus. How much more magical can you get?"

He cocked his head. "You really see things like that, don't you?" Then he shook his head and mounted Grimm, scooting back to give me room. I scowled at him before placing a hand on Grimm's horn – a gnarled, barbed protrusion of bone designed for one thing… removing blood from squishy things.

Like the other times I had touched his horn, I felt a low thrum of power call out to me. I ignored it, and Grimm seemed to chuckle under his breath. He knelt down slightly, and I climbed onto his back in one quick motion. I didn't like grabbing his mane to use as a handhold, because it was made of long, peacock-like feathers, and I always imagined that it might hurt him, even though I was sure it wouldn't.

"Let's ride, Grimm."

"As you wish, Rider."

CHAPTER 4

*W*e sat astride Grimm in the shadows of the park, staring out at an open field between the trees. "This reminds me of an action flick I once saw," Alucard murmured.

I frowned, turning to look at him. "I'm trying to be stealthy. What are you babbling about?"

"Brokeback Mountain."

I rolled my eyes. "Not my kind of action, I guess."

He grunted behind me as a figure entered the edge of the field, glancing both ways before crossing out into the open. A young girl, and she looked wary. Not scared, but alert.

The trap was set.

I patted my pet unicorn's feathered mane, waiting in silence. If the Four Horsemen were right, Grimm was much more than my pet. Because I had been volunteered to join their fraternity as the Fifth Horseman of the Apocalypse, with Grimm as my trusty steed. A midnight black unicorn of death with fiery eyes, and a feathered mane that flared out when angry. Like those venomous dinosaurs in that first Jurassic Park movie. But Grimm's feathers resembled that of a peacock – if peacocks had inky black feathers with red orbs on the tips.

Grimm was a killing machine.

And he was brothers with Pegasus – the immortal winged stallion from

19

Greek legend. But Grimm didn't have wings. He had wings when I first met him, but I had never seen them since, and I wasn't stupid enough to ask him about it. Pegasus was always depicted as white, elegant, and sporting beautiful wings, but Grimm was midnight black, and looked to have been designed by scraping up tidbits of nightmares, and then tossing in a stabby forehead just to drive the point home. He wasn't going to cameo in any children's books.

I had a small place in my heart for the little psycho. Alucard grunted behind me, and I turned to see him touching one of the red orbs on Grimm's feathered mane. He held his hand up to the moonlight and I caught a crimson glow on the tips of his fingers. He pointed at the orbs. "They're wet. With blood. Is he injured?"

Grimm whinnied. "They're always bloody," he replied, as if announcing that the night was dark and full of terrors.

Alucard grew very quiet. But before I could add to the pleasant conversation, Grimm's attention suddenly riveted to a darkened section of woods across the clearing from us, just beyond the girl, who was still walking along the dirt path. Something moved in those trees, and Grimm scraped a hoof across the earth in anticipation. I patted his neck. "Not yet."

An arrow flew through the night, a whispering hiss. The girl dodged it with a snarl, and then disappeared. I heard a grunt and then galloping hooves as a figure entered the clearing, searching for the girl. "How about now?" Grimm asked drily.

"Now," I agreed.

Before we could move, Alucard leapt off the horse, and then disappeared in a blur to intercept the hunter across the clearing. I heard a horse neigh and then a man grunt before something crashed into the tall grass.

"What is the meaning of this atrocity?" a very officious voice sounded, reminding me of Eae the Angel, for some reason. It wasn't him, but it had the same measure of authority to it.

I nudged Grimm with my heels. He snorted, but he sounded satisfied to hear that part of the work was already done. We trotted forward to find a large white horse with alabaster wings folded back neatly, looking as elegant and pristine as the lingerie models who wore fake wings in those fashion shows. He had not a mark on his white hair, and his wings looked as soft as... well, a feather. Sleek, but still soft. He was beautiful. Up close, I saw that he had dozens of thick rings braided into his mane, and one of them held an ornate, ebony bow.

Grimm snarled at him, and the white horse shook his head angrily, the rings clacking together as he danced back a step. He looked disgusted, nervous, and furious, all at the same time.

"Hey, bro," Grimm growled.

Pegasus let out a disdainful sniff. "You are no brother of mine, beast."

"Looks like we both have riders. Have you finally been tamed, or do you care for a race?"

"I will *never* be tamed. And I don't desire to waste my time playing with such a despicable offshoot of my noble bloodline. Not after our last encounter," he said, chomping his teeth.

I hopped off Grimm as his feathers began to rattle against his back, splattering me with crimson drops. I had honestly never noticed it before. The red orbs were actually blood. Unless he had killed someone on his way over to pick us up and hadn't told me about it. Either was likely. "Looks like you two have some catching up to do. I'm here for Ballerina, anyway," I said, walking over to where Alucard had an older man under guard on the ground.

"It's Bellerophon!" the man snapped angrily. "And I am a famous hero! You will show me respect—"

"I'll show you whatever I damned well please," I muttered, staring down my nose at him. I was surprised that my little plan had worked so easily. Thanks to Alucard. Bellerophon had close-cropped gray hair, and an angular face that had once been youthfully handsome. Now, he looked to be in the prime of his life, maybe his mid-forties, although he was obviously much older than that. He had bridled Pegasus thousands of years ago, after all.

He had once been a hero in ancient Greece, doing all sorts of favors for the Greek gods and goddesses, earning their praise. Then that human emotion we all know and love stepped in. Arrogance. He tried to fly Pegasus up to Mount Olympus to meet his pals directly, but Zeus decided to throw a speed-bump at him. Pegasus had bucked, tossing Bellerophon from his back, and the hero crashed back to earth to wander the rest of his days as a cripple. Although I couldn't see much of that now with him on the ground. He looked to be healthy.

Before that, one of his more notable accomplishments was killing the ancient Chimera. He kind of hated them, so I had set him up tonight.

As if on cue, Camilla stood from the tall grass, and the Greek scowled. "Tricksy bitc—"

I cuffed him with a bar of air upside the ear, rewarded by a very disapproving sound from Pegasus, but then Grimm snarled at the winged beauty and Pegasus quieted. Unhappily. I heard Grimm continue to taunt him as I approached Camilla, ignoring Bellerophon entirely.

"Thanks for waiting here, Camilla." Because she was a Chimera – one of those fabled Greek monsters that could shift into a hybrid beast of ram, cobra, and lion – and her kind had plagued Greece in ancient days. Camilla was just a young teen, though, and was still learning to master her abilities. When the Greeks were called to war, or whatever the hell had happened when Indie woke up a god, Camilla hadn't disappeared like the others. I guessed it was because she wasn't actually Greek, but just a shifter who happened to turn into an old Greek monster.

Camilla nodded. "He almost got me with that arrow."

I shook my head. "Yahn gave you the ward, right?" She held up the marble in one hand, nodding. The marble was one of my creations from my new company, Grimm Tech – where science and magic had sexy time together. It instantly disintegrated any incoming projectile if moving fast enough. "So, he must not be as good of a shot as we thought."

"I'll have you know that I am an *excellent* shot—"

I didn't even turn to look as I heard Alucard kick him in the chest, cutting him off. I nodded at Camilla. "I'm glad he took the bait, and that you were able to help me out tonight. This next part might be best if you were gone." She nodded, a sickened look on her face. "You and your dad ready to get the hell out of town?" I asked.

"Yep. He's waiting a few blocks away, like Yahn told him to. Car's already loaded." She looked suddenly embarrassed. "You sure you don't want us to stick around? We could help—"

"I know you could. Trust me. But with your flavor of shifter, I don't want to take any chances. I have no idea what's coming, or if being a Chimera could put you in further danger."

She sighed, nodding stubbornly. "Okay. I just wanted to try one more time."

"Get out of here, kid. Have a nice break. When you return, maybe you and I can spar."

That earned a grin. "Right. Thanks for letting me help."

"Thanks for being a target," I winked.

She jogged away from the field to join her father – a wizard-turned-Chimera – on a vacation far away from St. Louis. It wasn't that I didn't want their help. Chimeras were worth their weight in gold in a scrap, but with their heritage, I didn't want to suddenly find them switching sides against their will in the middle of the war. And I didn't want any of my other friends to have to kill the two in self-defense.

CHAPTER 5

I finally turned to Bellerophon, studying him up and down. Alucard stood with his arms folded, like a bouncer, watching the field, the horses, his prisoner, and me. He looked hard. Like a piece of polished marble. Despite all his time in the sun, he didn't tan all that well, still, compared to most vampires he looked like an Oompa Loompa. Weirdly tanned.

"You worshipped the Greek Gods," I said, taking thoughtful steps towards the Greek. "Sacrificed for them. Performed tasks for them. And all the while, they were setting you up to fail. But you overcame. And like Icarus, you tried to fly too high in their eyes, and they—"

"I am nothing like that spoiled brat, Icarus!" he seethed.

I held out my hands in a soothing gesture. "Be that as it may, your stories are not dissimilar in that regard, right?" He shifted to a more comfortable position, and I finally noticed his badly mangled leg. Not unusable, but no doubt painful, like the result of a horrific fracture that never quite healed right. His face grimaced and he nodded woodenly in resignation.

"You two tried to fly to Mount Olympus to at least meet those you worshipped..."

Pegasus snorted at the memory, still angry. Bellerophon nodded, glancing over at his black bow on Pegasus' mane. It was flashy, as if designed by Apollo himself, with horses carved into the wood.

"And look at you now…" I said in a mild tone.

His face tightened. "They are different now."

"Stockholm Syndrome. I've seen it a hundred times," Alucard said softly.

Bellerophon bristled, but then looked up at Alucard and saw that his face was not mocking, but instead showed pity. He frowned, and then shifted that frown to me.

"The Greeks have never loved you," I pressed. "At least not the gods. You did some truly incredible things for them, and in the end, they still showed you pettiness, striking you down from the skies when all you wanted was to meet your idols – those you worshipped, those you had bled for."

He glared back. "You think I don't know that?"

"One of those gods has come back, and now they want a war." I scratched my chin, frowning. "Well, I *thought* they wanted a war, but all I've seen so far is the communication lines cut and all my Greek friends disappearing about ten months ago." I let the silence build, and I could tell by the look in his eyes that he was torn, knowing full well what I would ask next.

"Give me a name. A date. A plan. Something. People are going to die. And some of those people will be my friends. And to be honest, I don't think I've done anything to piss this god off, other than pissing off the one who woke him or her up." His shoulders sagged. "Please."

He smirked, a bit of his fire returning. "Fine. What's in it for me?" His eyes flicked to his mangled leg. "Because *this god*," he teased, "gave Pegasus back to me." The beast snorted at the indication of ownership, but Bellerophon didn't acknowledge him. Oddly enough, I began to pick up that the way he looked at Pegasus was as property, not as a partner. Interesting. "Otherwise, I would still be shuffling from town to town, ranging from forest to forest with my bow, a laughingstock."

"*This god* gave you a pair of new legs," I mused, nodding my head to Pegasus. "Or wings, I guess." Pegasus stomped a hoof, but Grimm clicked his teeth in warning. "I can't beat that," I admitted. "Because I wouldn't give a slave to someone to earn their loyalty."

Pegasus went very still, and Bellerophon began to growl incoherently. "She will win."

I managed to hide my surprise, and simply arched an eyebrow at him. *She*. That was the first solid information I had received. That narrowed the field significantly. My mind began to race.

"Kill me, as is your due," Bellerophon spat, snapping me out of my thoughts.

I rolled my eyes, tempted to comply with his wish. "I didn't come here to murder you. I came here for answers. To end this. Whatever this is."

"Then I guess it's time we go our separate ways," he said smugly.

"Nah," I said, staring off into the distance. It was obvious we were done here. He was either too terrified to speak, or he literally couldn't speak. Forced to obey. But I had gotten something from him. The enemy was a Goddess. But who? I heard him spluttering, so finally turned back to him, deciding to play a card. "Oh, right," I said, feigning embarrassment. "You said *she*. You gave me exactly what I needed. Now I know who it is. Think she's going to be happy with you for that?" I chuckled as he began to stammer and argue. "No, you're probably right. You've tasted their happiness firsthand," I muttered, indicating his leg. "Well, we need to get back home, and…" I turned to stare at Pegasus pointedly, hoping I was right, but keeping my face a mask.

Pegasus suddenly let out a violent shiver, his wings flaring out. He whinnied in pain for a few moments, and then let out a nervous, but satisfied snort. Grimm blinked.

"I'm… free of him," the horse murmured, sounding shaken.

I nodded in relief. It had worked. "Thought so. Let's go, boys," I said to Alucard and Grimm. "Oh, you can come, too, Pegasus." But there was a loud snap to the air, and I looked up to see Pegasus hauling ass from the field, embracing his freedom without a sliver of guilt.

He had forgotten to give Bellerophon's bow back, which was just cruel.

"Huh. Loyalty these days, right?" I asked, turning back to Bellerophon, who looked stunned.

He finally looked up at me, rage replacing his fear. "You will pay for this. And for what you did to Hercules…"

"You know where to find me. I'll leave the light on out front. Might want to start hobbling now. Might take you a while to get to Chateau Falco on one leg." I turned my back on him, motioning Alucard to join me. Because I had just been proven right. The Goddess, although unseen, was watching, and had immediately punished Bellerophon for his slip, taking Pegasus from him, because I had so cleverly made her think I knew who she was.

When really, I had no clue. I had ideas, but nothing concrete. But now I knew she was *listening*. It was time to get back home to Chateau Falco. To warn everyone. The place was currently a hostel for many, many Freaks. For almost a year, I had been trying to keep anyone with ties to me safe, letting them occupy rooms or camp out on the lawns. Patience and fear had recently begun to ebb and fray, and they were now wondering if my warnings were little more than crying wolf. Now, I had proof, and had kicked over an anthill. Two anthills. Hercules and Bellerophon. The Greeks would have to come, now. To save face.

I had wanted my people safe... at first.

Now?

I could live with a few of them not being so safe. Before our unity died of starvation.

I ignored Bellerophon's shouting, pleading, and begging. Alucard stepped up beside me, staring at me in disbelief. "He will give you anything, now. Why are we leaving?"

"I came here to be a bully to save lives. Not to kick a man who already gave me his life. His boss isn't going to be pleased, so we should probably skedaddle," I said, glancing up at the sky.

Alucard bit his tongue in sudden shame, lowering his eyes. He nodded slowly to himself, and then looked up at me, a look of surprised approval in those depths, but he didn't speak. He climbed up beside me in silence, and even Grimm was quiet. I opened a Gateway, then stared at it for a few seconds. I stacked a few more Gateways on top of it so that we would touch down in three different geographical places all over the world before entering my warded home.

Chateau Falco.

Now a War Base.

For a war that hadn't happened yet. We stepped through the three portals in half a dozen steps, listening to Bellerophon scream behind us. Then I closed the Gateway, abandoning him to his fate, because I was confident that the Olympian HR Department wasn't known for having the cuddlies.

CHAPTER 6

I turned us around to stare back towards the city of St. Louis where we had left Bellerophon. Grimm abruptly stiffened, and a pillar of grey light hammered into the earth in the distance. I could have sworn I heard a scream, but it was lost as the strange pillar of light winked out.

Bellerophon had finally met his goddess.

"Go check on everyone. I have some work to do." I climbed off the unicorn, petting his nose. "Be nice, Grimm. You'll get to play soon enough." He whinnied hungrily before he and Alucard rode off towards the gargantuan white tree on the grounds. It climbed over a hundred feet above us, the limbs branching out to form a decent, but not impenetrable canopy. Dozens of tents and bonfires dotted my property now, even though there was still plenty of room inside the mansion. Everyone liked to be spread out after living together for so long. And it made tactical sense as well. Constant rotation, and we could guard the entire perimeter of the property this way – in case we were invaded.

Eyes followed me as I walked towards my house, some saluting, others cheering, and still others with thoughtful frowns. I plastered a simple smile on my face and waved a few times, anxious to get out of their sight and inside Chateau Falco – my seventeen-thousand-square-foot mansion. The house seemed to purr as I neared, welcoming me as I stepped into her mouth.

Soon, I would enter her heart, or her brain, to see what secrets I could find before any of my friends decided to check on my activities for the night. Namely, Gunnar. My well-intentioned best friend, and local Alpha werewolf of St. Louis.

But I needed some *me* time right now.

Two Ravens flew in through the front door right behind me – before it could close. They landed on my shoulders, and despite being so large, they didn't weigh much, and I was used to their unwelcome advances by now. Maybe they magically adjusted their weight so it wasn't an added burden on my already taxed shoulders.

One of them chattered at me, the one on my right shoulder. I still wasn't very good at telling them apart, even after a year. Hugin and Munin, Odin's Ravens – otherwise known as *Thought* and *Memory* – had decided I was important enough to be graced by their presence. Whether I wanted it or not. "Hercules *and* Bellerophon!" he cawed. "My, what great, big, calloused stones you have, Temple." Hugin or Munin?

The other piped up as if not hearing his pal. "The Allfather sends his regards. We've seen nothing alarming, but something is coming. Soon. The Father of Storms calls for it."

"Hugin, right?" I asked, not looking at him.

"Aye," he cawed, ruffling his feathers self-importantly. "War is coming, Rider."

I continued walking, used to their familiar chatter now.

Although I had never met Odin, his lackeys apparently dug hanging out with me. And were even depicted on my family crest. I glanced down at the brand burned into my palm – now healed – but still a perfect rendition of my family crest. I wondered for the thousandth time if there was a bigger reason for them being a part of the design, or if it was more the symbolism behind their names that were important – Hugin and Munin – perched on the butt of two speared weapons crossing the crest. The two ravens would never provide a straight answer on that, and my parents had never mentioned it.

"You two are more than welcome to tag along."

"So polite," Hugin squawked.

"Yes. Very," Munin agreed.

29

I grumbled under my breath as I continued on, walking towards the passageway that led to the secret library under my house known as the Sanctorum. "You two would just come along, anyway. This way I get to pretend I have a choice."

Munin began preening his feathers proudly. "Wise."

"The Wolf King wants to speak with you," Hugin said.

"Later," I muttered, not wanting to talk to Gunnar until I had some time to think. What was I going to do with this new information? I had pissed off Hercules, hoping to get a name, or at least anger him into accidentally letting something slip. I had succeeded with that part, at least. Also, I had wanted to rule out Hera. If Hercules was in the game, Hera likely wasn't. Unless she took pleasure in making Hercules work for her.

The problem was finding something solid. Actionable.

"Give me some space," I said, jerking my shoulders.

They didn't, simply digging tighter into my flesh with their talons. "Are you always this fussy after you kill an ancient hero?" Munin asked, head tilting in my peripheral vision.

I turned my neck to glare in surprise and anger at him. His beady black eyes were large enough to reveal a reflection of my face. "I didn't kill anyone."

"You may as well have held the blade. He died for what he let slip, and the lie you led him to believe. Led *her* to believe." I shot him a surprised look. "Yes, I know, and no, I can't tell you."

I grimaced. The bastards knew which Goddess had awoken. "I'm not causing this war. She is. I want nothing to do with it. Bellerophon spoke on his own. I just exploited it," I argued.

"After you set a trap, and after your vampire mowed him down. You saying you wouldn't have forced him?" Hugin chattered, sounding amused. We were a dozen paces away from the door leading to the Sanctorum.

"I suddenly have the urge for fried chicken," I said, licking my lips. "You guys hungry?"

They stiffened on my shoulders. "I think we'll just fly ahead. Or behind. You smell."

"Whatever," I said, striding forward as they launched off my shoulders towards one of the two Medieval armored sentinels on either side of the hall. One figure wielded a scythe, and the other was gripping a Fauchard –

or a spear with a curved blade on the end. The weapon had different names depending on the culture or country it was made.

The ravens rested on the weapons, not the knights.

Just like they did on my crest.

And they watched me with hyper-intelligent eyes, amused.

I just shook my head. I never knew when they were simply teasing me or trying to tell me something important. They thought very differently from humans. Or at least this human.

CHAPTER 7

I entered the Sanctorum – Latin for *big-ass secret library*, and frowned to see I wasn't alone.

I had always known that my personal bodyguard, Mallory, held a secret, that he was something – or someone – more important than just my driver. But to find out that he was actually the Wild God, Pan? And that he had made an oath with my father to keep me safe? Yeah, that one had messed with me.

I watched as Pan hurled a Nerf football all the way down the massive open space to my friend Gunnar, at least a hundred yards away. Gunnar, the Alpha Werewolf of St. Louis, caught it, and Pan threw his hands into the air, bleating triumphantly. Because Pan was in his natural form – a bipedal goat, complete with curved horns – rather than his human disguise, Mallory, the weathered, old sailor who loved to drink and fight when he wasn't driving me to my appointments. He didn't necessarily look scary, but he did look... intimidating.

Hugin and Munin flew up into the air, since the space was easily fifty feet high, and settled on one of the bannisters on the third of the five balconied tiers that contained row upon row of books and other bric-a-brac that made up my Sanctorum – a centuries-old depository of knowledge built by an unknown ancestor of mine. The ravens stared down at us as if watching a science experiment, or maybe recording details for Odin. I shivered at that, and then let my eyes drift past a noticeable open space near a large waterfall to my left. A magical round table rose up from the floor if I walked too close, and I had obvious questions about its origins. Fanboy questions. The space smelled of fresh mist and old books, and power hummed in the air.

Pan and Gunnar finally noticed me, and then shared a significant look. Gunnar jogged my way, dropping the ball as he approached. He stopped before me, leveling me with a glare, and then pulled out his phone to shove it in my face. It was his social media newsfeed, and it showed a picture of my selfie with Hercules.

I grinned, nodding. Gunnar's one-eyed glare – because he had misplaced the other eye in a fight against the Brothers Grimm – tightened. Then he pointed at the number of likes. I squinted down, and blinked. "Twenty *thousand?*" Then I doubled over laughing. "That must be a record!"

Gunnar grimaced, pocketing his phone. "That wasn't part of your plan."

I straightened with a sigh. "I've had a really long night, Gunnar. Ease off for a few minutes."

Pan looked concerned. "How much of my booze did you ingest?"

"More than I hoped to," I admitted. "But I got some food in me and threw up what I could."

He nodded, but still held out a hand as if checking my body for sickness. Because he could do that. He was surprisingly good at the whole healing thing, whereas I had never mastered it. I felt the cool tingle of his magic coursing through me. He finally let out a breath I hadn't realized he'd been holding. "That's good."

"Why do you look so concerned?" I asked nervously. "And if you're so concerned, why am I only just now hearing about it?"

Pan blushed. "You said you would return immediately after. But you didn't. Then Yahn showed up to drop off the girls, and disappeared without saying anything other than *Nate will be back soon.*" Pan didn't sound pleased, but I felt a small surge of pride for Yahn showing some backbone. "You use him too much," Pan continued. "He's still new to all of this."

I nodded. "Plans changed," I lied. "But Yahn is solid. His skills help me accomplish things without a fight. His stealth is *helpful.* If things ever get dicey, he knows to just disappear."

Gunnar patted the phone in his pocket, changing the topic. "This just made things worse."

I sighed. He wasn't going to drop it. "I needed him off balance," I said tiredly.

Gunnar shared a look with Pan, but didn't speak for a few moments. Pan abruptly shifted back to his human form – a meticulously-groomed, gray-haired man, fully clothed in an immaculately tailored plaid suit and expensive loafers. He dipped his head, his beard brushing his chest, as if nothing had happened. The suit only emphasized the lean, corded muscle beneath. He wasn't as bulky as Gunnar, but he was close.

"The weregorillas finally left," Mallory said, changing the subject.

"Damned dirty apes," I growled. "They finally did it..." I lifted my head, closing my eyes, imagining Hercules kicking down the gates and all my friends running away.

I turned back to them, burying the thought, to find Gunnar nodding, studying me with his one critical eye. You could say that the fight with the Grimms had started the mess in the world right now. Or that it had at least been a catalyst. Many lives had been lost or... changed by that fight. And I wanted this fight to be about *me*. I didn't want my friends hurt this time. That's why I was trying to keep everyone at my home. Keep them safe. Or safer.

But if the gorillas had left...

"Anyone else?" Mallory shook his head. "I could almost hope that they get attacked," I said under my breath, more to myself.

Gunnar's lips tightened under his beard. "How... compassionate of you."

I frowned at him. "If they were attacked, perhaps the others wouldn't be so eager to flee the safest place in town."

Gunnar shrugged. "All they know is that they've sat here for ten months in fear of an assault that hasn't happened. No one can even *find* a Greek."

"I did. I found two Greeks tonight. Three, if you count Pegasus."

Mallory's face paled. "Pegasus? Who else?" he asked.

"Bellerophon. I'm pretty sure he's dead, now."

Gunnar actually growled. "Bellerophon? Who is that? And... you *killed* him?"

"Bellerophon is the hero who saddled Pegasus," I explained. "Killed the first Chimera that was slaughtering people in Greece. He tried to fly to Mount Olympus and was struck down by daddy dearest, Zeus. I didn't kill him, but I think his boss did. For what he let slip."

"And what did he tell you? *Talk*, man! This is the first solid piece of information we've come across!" Gunnar urged hungrily, just as eager to have this over and done with as me.

Mallory finally let out a breath. An uncharacteristically shaken breath. So out of the norm for him that even Gunnar paused to look at him.

Mallory met my eyes. "I need to see you."

I frowned, and then turned to Gunnar, who looked just as confused. "Have you been sampling your own booze again, Mallory? You're seeing me. Like... right *now*."

He shivered, then wiped a hand across his face. Was he coming down with something? A godly flu? "Sorry, it happens like that sometimes." He composed himself and spoke again. "My *brother* needs to see you. Promptly."

"Shit in a can of ambrosia," a new voice purred from the shadows. I flinched at the unexpected voice, and then locked eyes on the huge furred cat swaying my way, tail flicking back and forth as it neared. Sir Muffle Paws, the cat I had saved during a fight with Baba Yaga a while ago. Back then, I had thought he was a Maine Coon, but he was *so* much larger than that breed, now. And, of course, I hadn't known back then that the cat could freaking talk, and that his form was really just a disguise. His true identity was still, apparently, above my paygrade, even though I sheltered, fed, and cleaned up after him. He was a violent, cold-blooded, feline, but intelligent, and I knew he wasn't in my life by happenstance, no matter what I had originally thought when Indie had convinced me to keep him. Mallory nodded at Sir Muffle Paws as if in answer to a perfectly acceptable statement.

"I think I missed something. Mallory went senile, and you're talking about shitting in a can."

"So observant," the cat mocked in a lazy tone before turning back to Mallory. "You want to take a blind man into the badlands? That festering shit-storm of refuse, deceit, blood, and claws? I have no desire to go back home."

"A vacation. This sounds appealing to me," a new voice spoke in a gentle hiss.

I flinched. "How many assholes are down here?" I cursed. Gunnar was grinning at me.

An albino lizard-man stepped out of the shadows of a reading nook. He was covered in crisscrossed strips of leather and had twin bone blades over his shoulders. He claimed his weapons came from the bones of his victims. His head looked like a snake, but he walked upright on two booted feet.

Underneath the oddly-shaped boots were talons like a dragon. He was an Elder, a race that had been banished from our world for eating people. A *lot* of people, because every brand of Freak had teamed up to get rid of them.

That was pretty much the extent of my knowledge on Elders. And his name was Fucking Carl.

And, of *course*, the place Sir Muffle Paws had so eloquently described sounded appealing to him. Because he was unbelievably creepy.

It wasn't that he was hungry for violence – even though he was – it was that the description very likely *had* appealed to him. On a personal level.

"Again, what exactly are we talking about? Context. Makes the world go 'round," I muttered.

"Let's get comfortable. I have drinks ready," Mallory said.

With no other choice, Gunnar and I followed Mallory to a depression in the ground that was full of pillows. I sat, letting out a breath as I rolled my shoulders. It felt so nice to sit down.

Mallory passed out drinks, even a bowl of red-tinted milk for Sir Muffle Paws. It was either strawberry milk, or Mallory had added a dabble of blood to it. Judging by how voraciously the feline attacked the drink, it could have been either, but I was pretty sure it wasn't strawberries.

Mallory cleared his throat. "It gets confusing sometimes. My brother is not happy with me, but he is me, and I am him."

Sir Muffle Paws let out a sound that sounded suspiciously like a chuckle, but continued lapping up his bloody milk. Then he looked up. "There is no place like home," he said in a distant voice, as if quoting something he had once heard. He shot me a brief look and then turned back to his bowl.

Mallory frowned. "I *must*. No, *we* must. The Invitation cannot be refused. You know this."

The feline grunted, but didn't offer further comment.

"Right," I said, still confused. "Where is home, and what does it have to do with your family problems? Are you in danger?"

Mallory hesitated, debating how to answer. "We are all in a very great deal of danger. And we need your help. Or... you need ours. Same thing, really."

I blinked, turning to Gunnar, who merely looked constipated. Him having only one eye really messed with my ability to read his facial expressions.

"Okay. You've helped me out enough in the past. What do you need? I guess we need to go talk to your brother? I can get us there quickly, but we need to get back soon so we can prepare for the upcoming war with the Greeks. Hercules isn't going to take tonight lying down, and I might have news to share with everyone soon. But we can take care of your brother tonight if it's urgent."

"Take care of!" Sir Muffle Paws blurted, wheezing with laughter.

Mallory scowled before turning back to me. "Not tonight. But soon. Very soon..." he said, staring up at the ceiling as if reading the sky beyond it. "Two women must join you."

I frowned. Then turned to Carl. "Are you a woman, Carl?"

"My swordplay is legendary among my people," he said without batting an eye or curling a lip. Not even joking. Just being incredibly literal in a way that made others uncomfortable.

"Right. Okay. Why do we need two women again? I can have us there in a few minutes. Just us. Right now," I pressed, wanting to get it over with.

Mallory shivered. "That would be... cataclysmic."

I frowned, and then threw my hands up. "Will you speak plainly?"

Sir Muffle paws stretched out. "Too close. Too close and too far. We must go where the wild things are," he said with a mirthless chuckle.

Mallory rubbed his temples, eyes distant. "Too close. Too close..." he said, repeating Sir Muffle Paws' words in a hollow tone. I felt the hairs on the back of my arms standing on end.

"Okay. What the fuck is going on here?" I snapped. Gunnar was propped up, no longer leaning back into the cushions, and he was frowning at the two of them. Or he was still constipated. Hugin and Munin cawed from high above, but when I glanced up, they simply stared down at us, heads cocked slightly as if trying to listen more intently. I muttered under my breath and turned away.

Sir Muffle Paws began cleaning one paw, revealing very long, sharp claws. Much longer than I had seen him reveal before. "He is channeling his brother, or his other form, his other mantle, so he is having difficulty speaking plainly."

I stared at the cat for a long moment, and then I slowly turned to Mallory, who was suddenly watching me with an alien gaze I had never seen before. Like his body and soul had just been replaced by a force of nature. A slow, ravenous smile began to stretch across his face.

"Fuck me," I breathed. "Your brother is—"

Mallory interrupted me, nodding. "I am my own brother, Manling. And I request your presence in my domain. Bring four, but two must be women or all hope is lost. The queens haven't forgotten your slight. Refuse the Invitation, and sacrifice the world. Love must die."

Hugin and Munin shrilled loudly, startling me. Then Mallory passed out, spilling his drink all over himself.

Gunnar jolted, staring over at me. "What the *hell* just happened?"

I stared back at him, mind scrambling. "I think we just talked to the Goblin King."

Gunnar stared back at me. "David Bowie?"

I couldn't even smile. "The King of the Fae. Of the Wild Hunt. I think he and Mallory are… the same person. Or something. And I'm pretty sure I have to go to the Fae World."

Gunnar's face paled.

I downed my drink.

And Sir Muffle Paws kept right on licking his crimson-stained paws like there was no tomorrow. "It sharpens the claws, it softens the skin, it drinks the blood of all known kin… With dreams and hopes of waking the wild within…" he murmured as if reciting a lullaby to a child.

"This sounds fun," Carl agreed with Sir Muffle Paws excitedly.

"I don't think that word means what you think it means, Carl," I whispered.

CHAPTER 8

I sat on the roof of my house, a flat terrace of sorts that my mother had often used for sunbathing. I stared out at the silent grounds. Other than the roving guards, everyone was asleep, and the campfires were only smoldering coals. It was early morning and the sun would be rising soon. If I scanned the area around Chateau Falco quickly, it looked dystopian. Post-apocalyptic.

I realized I was twirling my coin over my knuckles, and quickly pocketed it.

But it wasn't just a coin. Not really. That was just what I had transformed it into, for ease of concealment. It was a Mask.

The Mask of Hope. One of my ancestors had given it to me for my birthday, in case I one day chose to take up the mantle of Horseman of the Apocalypse. The Fifth Horseman.

I had chosen to actually wear it only one time. And no one who had been there wanted to talk about it. My friends had tried to get me to show them, but I had stubbornly refused. After seeing the horrified reactions of those who *had* seen it on me, I had decided I wouldn't be able to handle my friends looking at me with that same level of fear.

I hadn't asked for the Mask, or the offer to join the A-Team, because I was generally opposed to anything Apocalyptic-y…

But the Four Horsemen – Death, War, Pestilence, and Famine, as they were most notably known – seemed eager for me to mount up beside them. They also told me that I might be able to use the Mask a handful of times – they weren't sure exactly how many times – before I would be forced to make a choice: to remain as I was, or to ride at their side in the End Days.

As the Horseman of Hope.

I shivered. "No thanks."

"It's not all that bad, really," a gruff voice said.

I practically fell off the roof. Well, the lawn chair I was sitting on. I glanced over to see a robed figure sitting beside me. He wore a Mask of fire, but through the flames I could see what looked like one of those ancient ceremonial Samurai masks. I had seen it change in design several times, as if it was fluid, ever evolving, adapting—

"That's the art of war," the man nodded, reading my mind. And he would know.

Because he was the Horseman of War.

He tugged off his Mask and threw back his cowl to reveal a scarred, red-haired, older man. He didn't look scary, but he was rough around the edges, like the stereotypical biker that was just as comfortable with a giggling grandchild on his knee as he was in the middle of a knife fight. "Sorry. You get used to wearing it," he said. "Stops a lot of fights before they start." He pocketed a small amber plaque the size of my finger. His Mask also transformed for ease of carry.

My pulse slowly returned to normal as I nodded absently, wondering exactly what I wanted to say to him. I wasn't too pleased with my adopted Brothers. I had asked for their help almost a year ago, and they had declined. Very adamantly. They hadn't necessarily avoided me since then, but had let me know in no uncertain tones that the upcoming Greek War was not their concern. And that it wasn't mine either, whatever that meant. But they had no problem helping me out with other things, or randomly popping in to say *hello*.

"What do you want, War?"

He chuckled. I had never been able to faze him. He simply took the world as is. Good, bad, violent, pleasant. It was all the same to him. Was that a result of his Mask? Or had he always been so even-keeled?

"I came to see my Brother. We haven't spent much time around each other." He held out a hand towards the tents and bonfires and my property.

"And places like this call to us. To me, especially." He inhaled deeply, a nostalgic smile creeping over his scarred features.

I grunted. "War calls to you," I repeated flatly. "And it smells like a bouquet of roses."

He nodded without shame. "Aye."

"How can you do that? Be so calm about war. Death. Destruction? Is that why you were chosen?" I wasn't condemning him. I genuinely wanted to know.

He thought about that in silence for a few moments. "For most, blood runs hot in war. In battles. But my blood is always cool. Calm, even. Especially as the carnage increases. When others panic, I feel peace," he said with a shrug, trying to put words to his thoughts. "This serves a man better in war. Rationality." He held up a hand, wanting to add something. "War is wild, but one must know *when* to be wild, and *when* to keep calm. Too cold, and you become calloused, brittle, and breakable. Too hot, and your emotions rule you, stealing your control. But to be strategically ruthless? Analytically wild? In a General, these qualities are priceless. For everything else, there's soldiers," he added with a smirk.

I rolled my eyes at his crude humor, but his points were solid. "Is that what you are? A General?"

He grunted dismissively. "I am the Horseman of War."

"Right. I guess I should have realized that when I told you and your brothers about an upcoming war and you so boldly agreed to help me," I mumbled without thinking.

He gripped my arm suddenly, and I glanced down to see fiery claws holding me. Inches-long bone claws of fire and smoldering coals. "We told you. This isn't our war. It isn't even *your* war. And this isn't me trying to recruit you. Horseman or not, I will still gladly call you friend, and as a friend, I'm telling you we would *never* extort you. We want you *willingly*. Or not at all." He released my arm, and despite the living fire of his hand, I hadn't been burned.

I frowned, because he had me dead to rights. That was exactly how I had taken it. "Oh."

You could say that after recent events I was possibly overly paranoid by reflex, and you would be absolutely correct.

Because my fiancée, Indie, had transformed into an entirely different person, hungry only to wake a god so she could destroy the Syndicate – a group of shady wizards who had been secretly gathering power for hundreds of years – because she thought they had killed her mother. Now, I'm not a Syndicate enthusiast or anything, but I was understandably against calling in the nuclear option – a god, because them folks were tricksy, power-hungry, and merciless.

Every Greek friend I had ever made – who had joined me in the battle to try and stop Indie – had disappeared about five minutes after she succeeded in waking a god.

I had immediately gone to my Armory, fearing the worst, because Pandora – also a Greek – was my head librarian. And I found the door locked. And then today, I had discovered that something that had previously been stowed away inside that Armory had been draped across Hercules' shoulders. Which made it pretty obvious that party favors were being handed out to the people who were intent on killing me and anyone else who stood between Indie and the Syndicate.

With no other options, I had approached the Horsemen for help, expecting to hear a heartfelt and enthusiastic *Hell Yeah!* and been denied. Stunningly.

"Did you really think we declined to help you out of spite?" he asked, sounding genuinely surprised, maybe even hurt.

"I don't know," I admitted. "Maybe a little? To be fair, I assumed that you weren't *allowed* to help me until I made a decision," I said, pointing a finger up at the sky meaningfully. He shook his head, looking frustrated, as if we were speaking two different languages.

"Tell me, Brother. What is this war about?" he asked absently, still staring out at my people in their tents. His eyes scanned the camp, and something about the way he did it told me that he had just assessed the strengths and weaknesses, and that he had already determined how to break my army in the quickest way possible. I almost shivered, because he did this absently, with no apparent effort on his face.

"Indie using the Greeks to destroy the Syndicate. And anyone in their way," I finally said.

War yawned. He fucking *yawned!* "That's a surface view of this struggle," he said.

I decided to let him elaborate, because I was obviously boring him with my tiny brainpower.

"Indie is fueled by vengeance, true. That is just a spark, though. This is bigger than that, now. This is about who will stand up, and who will cave. The world will watch this, and the world needs to see that your allies do not need you. That they have teeth of their own..."

I stiffened. "You mean... I should stay out of it? While battle rages on my front lawn, I'm supposed to, what, sit up here and watch my friends *die*?"

He sighed empathetically. "Sometimes we must do things we find... painful, or even distasteful for a later, more important victory. Does not a mother bird let their babies jump from the nest? I'm speaking of risks, gambles, not that the ends justify the means," he clarified, likely sensing my budding argument. "But that sometimes one needs to pay a great price to obtain a great reward, and that not paying that heavy price can result in ultimate failure for all, later. Sometimes, hope requires a figurative sacrifice of something we cherish deeply..."

He stared into the distance, letting me digest his words. We hadn't really spent much time together, so this was kind of a jump into the deep end of the pool moment for me. War, the Rider I had thought to be the most ruthless of the Horsemen, was actually more like a philosopher.

I stared at him, feeling as if two conversations were happening, but that I was missing one of them. It teased me, whispering too softly to hear. He saw my face and nodded sadly. "The burdens of being good at my job," he admitted. "I see things... differently. Strategically ruthless. Analytically wild, remember?" he asked, reciting his earlier statement. "It may seem I am heartless, but I swear I have more heart than anyone you have ever met..."

I nodded very slowly, mind racing with the implications. Stand down? Do nothing? Let my friends fight without me? I didn't think I could do that. Even if for the greater good. I couldn't watch as Gunnar died, even if it meant saving people I didn't know in the future. These people on my lawn were my family.

"Compared to what is to come, this is just a bar fight," War said softly.

And the hair on my arms stood straight up.

War noticed that with a chuckle. "*That* is why we want you, Nate. Not..." he waved a hand at the tents again, dismissing them. "Not for this. This is a testing ground. To determine who will still stand during the *true* war. Who can be trusted. Who cannot. Who is strong. Who is weak." His excitement seemed to grow as he spoke, filling him with an inner fire. The Great Game. "This is where men earn their names. And women," he chuckled. "Some women will definitely earn their names here," he murmured, eyes glazing over at something only he could see.

I studied him thoughtfully. "You know how it will all play out."

He snorted. "Don't be ridiculous. I can see more than most, but no one can know the full outcome of a battle ahead of time." He turned to me and I almost shied away at the sudden intensity of his gaze. "This battle is for *them*. And must be *fought* by them. Wrapping them up in swaddling now will only suffocate them in the future. You will kill them with your love, and all will be lost." He shook his head in resignation. "I speak too freely."

"Yes, you do," a familiar voice spoke from behind us.

CHAPTER 9

I turned to see a robed figure in a nightmarish bone mask staring down at the two of us.

The Horseman of Death. And if he was wearing his mask, he wasn't here for a tea party. He was usually a pretty cool guy to have around. Not what I had initially expected from a man named Death, but he had gone to bat for me a few times.

But...

One could argue that him going to bat for me – saving Indie from death – had incited this whole Greek thing. War's words suddenly took on new depth. Death had gone out of his way to do me a kindness, protecting Indie, but in the long run, that act was now threatening to get everyone I cared about killed. I knew there was still more to his words that I was missing, but this alone was a... well, a revelation.

I glanced at War, shaking my head. "You two should write a book."

"We're already in one book," Death said drily.

Right. The Bible.

I studied Death, because I still felt like I was missing a larger piece of the puzzle. Something about Indie's transformation didn't add up to me. She had been... feral when I last saw her. Obsessed. Vengeful. Finally revealing that the Syndicate had murdered her mother.

But I had checked with a Syndicate contact – who I thought was pretty high up in the pecking order – and she hadn't heard anything about Indie's mother. I guess she could have been lying to me, but I was a pretty good judge of liars, and her reaction hadn't fit the bill. Which meant that either someone even higher up the Syndicate food chain had placed a hit on Indie's mom, or there was a third party who had wanted to make her *think* the Syndicate had done it…

But which was it?

To be honest, it didn't really matter anymore. She had a goddess in her back pocket now.

And to some extent, the goddess was obligated to help Indie achieve her task.

I met Death's eyes, but he didn't react. Just stared at me through his aged bone Mask. Nicks and scratches marred the surface. Even a few high impact craters as if from bullets. To be able to deflect a bullet with only a small indentation proved that his Mask definitely wasn't just bone.

It made me think of the coin in my pocket. My own Horseman Mask, if I so decided. But I wasn't a fan of that plan – becoming beholden to an authority figure. Forced to ride at the End Days and participate in demolishing a fraction of the population.

Sanctified genocide.

No thanks.

When I looked back up, the two Horsemen were gone.

I sighed, deciding to let my conversation with the Horsemen simmer on the old backburner. I had other things to see to. Mallory needed us to go to the Land of the Fae. And I needed two women – for whatever reason – to join me on my quest. My mind raced with possible candidates. How long would we be gone? Who could best take care of themselves?

Also, I hadn't told anyone, but I had felt a light strain on my magic lately. Nothing very alarming yet, but to me, *any* restraint on my power was deeply concerning given the present circumstances. Because it could rapidly get worse, and at the worst possible moment.

I was pretty sure it was the result of a promise I had made, and hadn't upheld.

I had sworn to grant freedom to a powerful Beast I had trapped in my old cane, unleashing him upon the world to do as he would. Later, everyone had been horrified to hear about that promise, but I didn't have much of a choice in the matter, now. If I didn't live up to my agreement, I would lose a chunk of my power. I needed to make good on it.

Which meant I needed to visit my ancestor. In his white world. Because he held my cane.

But I also wanted to try getting into my Armory. I had tried dozens of times to no avail, but tonight had been the first time I had run across a Greek since they all disappeared, so maybe my Armory was back online. Or that I would at least be able to yell at Pandora through the door or something.

My other item was a brunch date, even if it was a group meal. I had been looking forward to it for some time now, because this Kansas City wizard was pretty damned cool, and I wanted to introduce her to my friends.

Callie Penrose.

CHAPTER 10

I decided to forego sleep and tackle the Armory first, since it wouldn't require any magic, just a quick check. Well, unless the door was still locked, and I tried to huff and puff and blow the door down. But there was always the chance that now that I had at least seen a Greek, that maybe everything would be like normal again and I could simply walk in.

I needed to find out how Hercules had gotten his cloak back. The one he had made after he skinned the Nemean Lion in his glory days. I reminded myself to check on the cloak, that Yahn had secured it somewhere no one knew of. I couldn't have that disappearing again. Not after what I'd done to the brute.

I strode through the halls, blessedly alone, which was a rare occurrence these days, what with all the guests living here now.

Sir Muffle Paws was likely hunting for vermin, or small children.

Hugin and Munin were probably debating the finer points of Aristotle or Kant, or feasting on the remains of Bellerophon – if there were any remains. Perhaps they were doing both.

The old Greek Hero had at least confirmed that I was dealing with a Goddess. It narrowed the field considerably, but there were still so many potentials, and I knew that Indie was clever, so she would likely pick someone I didn't expect, someone with a hidden power I might overlook, not one of the obvious ones. I sighed in frustration. *Unless she wants you to think that.*

I idly wondered what would happen to Pegasus now, and if I needed to be concerned about finding Hercules riding him into the battlefield.

Depending on how my talk with Pandora went, perhaps I could put it back in the Armory. I stepped into my office, and—

"Nate!" An octopus latched onto my body, trapping me in her death tentacles of affection.

"Othello, calm down. I'm not going anywhere," I said, smiling as I pried her hands away.

She leaned back, staring at my face for a few moments, searching for something in my eyes. Satisfied with whatever she found, she abruptly pinched my ass.

"The world would be a darker place without an ass like that to see every now and again." And she winked before turning on a heel to go back to my desk, which had pretty much become her desk lately. It now held five computer monitors, and a congestion of other electronic devices I couldn't even pretend to understand. She sat down in my chair, and then kicked up her bare feet on the desk. She wasn't wearing pants, just lacey underwear under a long tee that said *SensualAF*. She had raided my closet. Again. Living with Othello in the house had quickly taught me that what was mine was, in reality, hers. Full stop. Absolutely no sense of privacy.

Then again, she was a world-renowned hacker.

She smiled wickedly, and then crossed her legs. "You don't get to stare at my toys anymore," she teased.

I rolled my eyes. "Didn't you just say you get to stare at my toys?" I pointed out.

"Of course," she said, waving a hand as she scanned her screens briefly. Then she looked up. "Like my new tech?" she asked.

"Looks complicated."

She shrugged. "To a caveman, maybe. But I am Othello."

She said this in a tone that would have justified saying GOD.

I grinned, sitting down in one of the chairs before the desk. "It's come to my attention that you have effectively evicted me from my office."

"You were never fit for an office."

"That's true," I admitted. She was right. I was a field guy, not one to be kept sequestered. And I didn't follow orders too well. It was in my blood. "How's Plato's Cave?"

She waved a hand. "Sales are up."

I stared at her. "Aren't you supposed to be, you know, running the place for me?"

"What do you think I'm doing?" she frowned, pointing at the monitors on the desk. "Expenses are down. Sales are up. People like the griffin… *animatronics* you built to walk around the store and play with children."

I smiled, pleased with myself. Othello shot me a very warm smile. They weren't animatronics, but Guardians, like the ones protecting Chateau Falco. Full-sized griffin statues that were technically alive, or at least sentient. I had sent some over to Plato's Cave to keep the store – and the patrons inside – safe in case anyone decided to attack.

"Thanks. I don't know how you do it, but—"

"Stop. Repeat that last part."

"But," I said, deadpan. She scowled, waiting. I sighed. "Fine. I don't know—"

"*There* she is. That's all I needed to hear. You admitting your weaknesses. Feels good to be humble, doesn't it?"

"Only when someone points it out. Often. I think it's the repetition that really makes it special."

"Hemingway stopped by," she said, studying my reaction, hands placed on the table.

I nodded. "Yeah, we talked. Kind of."

She watched me. Because she was kind of dating Death, or Hemingway, as we called him when around others. It was funny to see such a cute pixie of a young woman dating a seemingly much older man, but she had been surprised when I had pestered her about it. Apparently, she saw someone entirely different. When I told her about the old man I knew as Hemingway, she had burst out laughing, describing a much younger, muscular, dark-eyed, bad boy. We had even called him in to hear it. He simply smiled, not explaining.

Which meant he could look however the hell he wanted. The rat bastard.

I changed topics. "Any word from the London crew?"

She shook her head. "Nothing yet, but I haven't heard from them in a week. I'll give them a call. Also, Raego's out on patrols for the rest of the day, so let me know if you need me to tell him anything. To look out for anyone in particular," she added, hinting at Hercules.

"Alright. I need to take care of a few things before brunch."

Her eyes sparkled, and she leaned forward eagerly. "Do we finally get to meet her?" she asked in the same tone as *can I eat some of the candy in your pocket?*

I rolled my eyes. "Relax. She's just a friend."

Othello leaned back, squinting suspiciously. "Hemingway tells a different story…"

"Yeah, well, Death fucking lies. He's a lying, dirty liar who lies."

She smirked. "Fine. Shoo, shoo. I'm trying to work here, Romeo."

I muttered under my breath as I stood. "You really shouldn't talk to your boss like that."

She snorted. "I'm thinking about forming a Union."

"You should read about how well that worked out for Robert E. Lee."

"That was a Confederacy."

"I know, but they're really just different names for the same thing," I said touching a handle on the fireplace. I was gone before she could respond, and found myself in a stone corridor. I cast a ball of pale white light before me and began to walk. Then I froze, staring at the light, feeling uneasy. I had meant that to be blue, not white. I shivered, the coin in my pocket feeling like a hunk of lead. I changed the light to blue fire, and continued on, pursing my lips.

The white color had been creeping into my magic lately. My spells, my whips, everything. And it had something to do with the Mask in my pocket. Then again, I had met another wizard with the same problem. And she wasn't a Horseman. But she had other ties to the same management structure. Even if neither of us knew exactly what or how that was possible.

I slowed my breathing, forcing deeper pulls from my lungs, measured and relaxed. Satisfied, I finally rounded the corner to see a large wooden door before me. The Armory. It was carved in a nature-scape, complete with one large tree, a pond, tall grass, and other trees in the background. The carving was full of life as well – birds, fishlings, and even a wolf.

I cursed. The damned wolf was hiding behind the tree again, out of my reach. That pretty much gave me my answer. The birds flitted happily from branch to branch, and I watched as the fishlings darted back and forth in the pond.

Because the carving was alive. The leaves swayed back and forth as an unseen breeze moved them, and the creatures lived their lives in that wooden door as if it was their entire world. Which it was. I scowled at the wolf peeking out from behind the tree.

"Here, boy!" I cooed, but the wolf immediately ducked away again. "Goddamn it," I cursed. The wolf was the key to the door. Petting his fur opened the door to the Armory.

Which meant that Pandora still wasn't allowing visitors. Or, judging by Hercules' recent fashion sense, she had gone Greek.

I might have lost my cool a bit, because I realized I was holding as much power as I could handle, and that my fists were crackling with blue energy. A bed of thorns surrounded my feet – long, twisting black barbs, inches long, and shining from the glow around my fists. The coin throbbed in my pocket, but I ignored it as I stared at the door.

The wolf whimpered behind the tree, but I ignored him, too. He was just doing his job.

I studied the door itself, and began to probe it with my power, searching for an opening. I had tried simply blasting it open in the past, but that hadn't worked. Still, the surrounding stone walls were scorched from the explosion, now blackened with char around the pristine door.

I mentally dove deep into the grain of the wood, searching, questing, listening, seeing, like a thief picking a tumbler on a safe.

Strange magic danced around me, alien, yet distantly familiar. Like owning a dog, but never seeing a wolf before. This was in the same family as my domesticated pet, but wholly different.

Elements danced against my senses – whispering, arguing, fighting, shouting, attacking, welcoming, defending, pressing, relenting, over-whelming me – like an army of souls.

I gasped, stepping back as I suddenly noticed the sharp pain in my ears. I lifted a hand to touch one and it came away bloody. My vision swam for a moment, and pinpricks of light twinkled in my peripheral vision. I stared down at my fists, which were still crackling with blue light. Then I glanced down at the thorns to find them smoking, but they were longer than they had been a moment ago, in a thicker tangle, too. They didn't touch me, the vines growing around my legs, but coming as close as possible to my flesh without actually making contact.

I frowned. I didn't understand the thorns. They weren't a conscious effort on my part, but I had seen them the last time I used the Mask in my pocket. I stared down at my fists again, and they suddenly flashed white, the blue vanishing as if it had never been.

And the door screamed in fury.

Not the door, but the magic living inside the wood.

The nest of thorns at my feet began to grow before my eyes, expanding into a wider circle, the barbs growing thicker, sharper, longer, at least two feet tall, now.

I stared at the door's surface, and the wolf howled in terror.

I pressed against the door again with my magic, this time white instead of blue, and the elements evaporated like smoke, as if I was probing an entirely normal door.

I pressed deeper, and found myself surrounded by darkness. Like velvet soaked in blood. A deep laugh echoed up from the depths of my mind, and my eyes began to throb as I pushed against the blackness. The laughter grew louder, and my eyes began to ache, not just throb. I felt blood dripping from my ears now, and finally pulled back with a gasp, panting.

The bed of thorns at my feet fairly smoldered now, smoking and stunted.

And I knew – somehow – that without that bed of thorns, I would have resembled them, my body smoking and charred. The thorns had protected me somehow. Not enough to prevent me from harm, as my eyes felt like they had just survived a long stint in a smoke-filled room, and my ears felt hot. I used the tail of my shirt to wipe the blood away, and stared down at my fingertips. The power was gone, and the tips of my fingernails were blackened and burned, although I felt no pain. At least it wasn't my flesh. I stepped back, and the surviving thorns let me pass. I sat down with a groan, bone-weary. The thorns disintegrated into gray ashes, and I saw the wolf nervously watching me. The birds and fishes were watching me. I also saw an owl tucked away in the branches, watching me with too much under-standing.

That tweaked my attention for some reason, but I felt numb.

The white magic had helped me get further into the door than ever before, and I knew I had been close, but it still wasn't enough. Was it because I wasn't fully accepting my mantle? If I indeed became a Horseman, would I have the strength to break such a strong, wild barrier of power? Or was it because of my unfulfilled promise with the cane? I weighed that in my mind, and decided that the tiny drain I had noticed wouldn't have made a difference here.

I shook my head, glancing down at my watch. I had a few hours, and I still had something I wanted to take care of before brunch.

I groaned as I climbed to my feet, stumbling against the wall. My fingers gripped the charred stone as I steadied myself. Confident I wouldn't fall on my face, I pushed off, glancing down at my fingertips. Black soot from the walls painted my fingertips.

I stumbled on through the hall, not even bothering with a light this time.

For some reason, I never found myself actually needing one. Perhaps I had been here often enough that I remembered the path without my sight. Like when you try to creep through your room at night as a teenager, trying to sneak out of the house. You know where everything is by memory and don't need a light.

I found myself hoping Othello wasn't in the office. She would take one look at me and call someone for help, and I didn't have time for that.

I sat down in the middle of the darkened hall, right before the opening that would take me back to the office. If I reached out, I could touch the space that would Shadow Walk me there. I wondered if a reaching hand would be enough to transport me back.

Not wanting to risk it, I scooted back a foot instead, and closed my eyes, focusing on a very familiar place, and forcing the pains of my body deep down where they could be ignored for a short while.

Did I really want to go to this place?

Nope.

But I needed to. Before things got any worse.

Because if my past was any indication, *worse* was always on the dessert menu.

My soul exploded from my body like a phoenix rising from a pile of smoking ashes.

CHAPTER 11

I opened my eyes to see I was sitting on a white leather divan. One of those old school, gentleman's club type pieces, freshly waxed with arrogance and elitism. I was holding a white martini glass with a white liquid inside. It looked like milk, but I could smell the alcohol.

Because everything was white here.

I stood, glancing down at my clothes. I wore a white seersucker suit. I held it up to the light spilling through a window to see that the stripes were neatly embroidered to say *Team Temple* in tiny silver letters, too small to see without leaning close – and the fact that the silver thread was on white fabric also made it difficult to read.

Still, I found myself grinning. I wore white boating shoes and white pants that matched my coat. I wore no shirt underneath, revealing my tanned, lightly furred chest. I blinked at that. No shirt?

But that was par for the course here. I walked over to the window and stared out at a white landscape of an immaculately maintained garden complete with white roses, white grass, and neatly manicured white shrubbery.

I blinked.

A silver peacock strutted along a path of white stone.

Silver. Not white.

I glanced up at the sky. Then out at the milky white sea beyond the grounds. Then back to the peacock. Another emerged from beyond a bush, fleeing from yet a *third* black peacock, his train flared out to show an impressive fan of black feathers with red orbs at the tips.

My heart might have skipped for a moment.

Just like Grimm, my unicorn.

Then the three birds were gone, and I heard the door clicking closed behind me. I hadn't even heard it open. I turned to see Matthias, or as he had referred to himself for quite some time, the Mad Hatter.

He wore a white fedora, a crisp white dress shirt with a silver ascot, and white shorts. He was barefoot. I looked up to find him smiling at me, his ginger beard slightly obscuring the silver ascot. My eyes still latched onto it for a moment before finally rising to his eyes.

He nodded slowly, a faint smile on his face.

"Changes…" he said, waggling his fingers dramatically.

And I was suddenly very, very concerned.

He had been banished here – unjustly – to live in this white world by an enemy, a man named Castor Queen. Hundreds of years ago. They had formed the Syndicate together for all the right reasons, a check of power against the Academy – the ruling body of wizards. But when Matthias decided to hunt down the Brothers Grimm, his old pal Castor Queen framed him as collaborating with them while simultaneously recruiting the Brothers Grimm to work for *him*.

Matthias suffered the consequences, and was banished here to live in a white world, like the *white hat* philosophy he stoically defended – since he had stated that doing the right thing was paramount – being a white hat as opposed to a black hat – one who let the ends justify the means.

He had taken the fall, and survived the last few hundred years in this white realm. He had gone slightly insane during his captivity, and thanks to Death giving him a book to pass the time, had spent a good portion of his imprisonment actually believing he was the Mad Hatter.

So, was he insane?

Yep.

Was he dangerous?

Double yep. He was a Maker. A Tiny God. A Deus Ex Machina. One of the last. It meant he harbored a Beast, shared his body with it, and that

Beast granted him the power to *Make* things. You might think being a Maker and a Wizard were the same, but I'll rectify that really quick. A Maker was to a Wizard what a Wizard was to a non-magical being.

He could literally create things out of thin air just by believing in them. A wizard would have to use magic to decide which elements he needed to make each piece of something, and then use magic to assemble those pieces into the final product. But a Maker...

He just thought about what he wanted, and *whammo*. He had it.

Like he had done when he gave me my Mask for my birthday last year.

Since he was admittedly insane, and a Maker, you could say he was the equivalent of a leaky nuclear uranium core.

And I was sipping a martini with him.

Because, well, he was my ancestor. The last true Master of my home, Chateau Falco – which harbored a Beast of her own. The last time a Maker had decided to free his Beast, they had been forced to build my mansion around it in order to contain it – since that was the only non-living entity strong enough to house a spell that could trap the Beast.

And I was here to...

Ask for my cane back. So that I could free my own Beast I had trapped inside it. Because I had very briefly been a Maker, too. But through circumstance and opportunity, I had been able to remove it from my soul, anchoring it inside my cane. But only after agreeing to let the Beast go free as soon as I had the chance. And since I hadn't yet done so, my magic was now having hiccups. Warning hiccups.

Matthias had warned me that releasing my beast in near proximity to Chateau Falco – my home – could result in them mating, and producing a baby Beast. To be honest, even I had trouble wrapping my head around my reality sometimes.

But I had made a promise, and I had to live up to my word, or no more magic.

"How are things?" I asked lamely.

"Less white than usual," he said with a lazy grin.

I swallowed. "Yeah. What gives?"

The Hatter leaned forward, a mad gleam in his eyes. "Like your jacket?"

"It's very... elegant," I offered.

"Arrogant, you mean," he corrected.

I smiled. "That, too."

"It's how we Temples roll," he said, leaning back slightly.

"Rule, you mean."

It was his turn to smile. "That, too."

We watched each other for a few moments. Then he finally spoke. "I smell madness."

I blinked at him. Then I sniffed myself. "Pardon?"

He scratched his gnarly beard thoughtfully, as if weighing me with his eyes. "Maybe not madness, but a..." he waved his fingers in the air as if trying to grasp a feather. "Wildness, perhaps." My drink splashed over the rim, and his eyes latched onto me with a predatory grin. "You're finally doing it!" he whispered excitedly. "Good man!"

I carefully set my drink down. "Doing *what*?"

"Going on Walkabout. Tasting the wild. Feeding the soul. Quieting the mind. Quenching your instincts," he said, patting his thigh excitedly.

"I honestly have no idea what you're talking about."

"You received your Invitation! It took me a minute, but I recognize the smell. Death told me they had stopped Inviting us. For hundreds of years, now. But... you are no longer a Maker..." he leaned back in his chair, thinking. "That is most... unusual," he said, idly stroking his beard. "But your life is forever about to change. The world will change colors. Your life will never be the same. Welcome to the... well, you'll find out the name soon enough. No need to get ahead of ourselves. You have to survive first, after all. Now, what is it you wished to see me about?"

I stared at him, a bazillion questions suddenly filling my mind. Matthias waved a hand at me, and mimed covering his ears. I blushed. He could read my thoughts, so he must have suddenly felt inundated with all of them at once. I took a firm grip of my thoughts, no less troubled, but more in control. He let out a breath of relief, and then waited.

"I... need to make good on a bargain."

"Smart."

"And I need your help to do so."

He waited. I made no effort to hide my thoughts, but he refused to let that suffice. He wanted me to say it out loud. I let out a breath.

"I need my cane. To be honest, I'm surprised the effects haven't hit me harder, or sooner than now. I made an oath, and I have yet to fulfill that bargain. I am suffering for it."

Matthias nodded, scratching his beard contemplatively. "The Americas are still a capitalistic place, no?"

I began to agree, then thought about recent events. I finally shrugged. "More or less."

Matthias chuckled. "It has always been so. You need something from me. And I refuse to lend favors. They have only repaid me with pain in the past. You know my price. Tell me if it is acceptable."

I forcefully relaxed my shoulders, considering. This wasn't a new thought, but hearing it out loud, realizing that it was no longer just a fear of mine – but an actual potential reality – helped me rationalize the consequences more objectively.

"You want your freedom," I said. He nodded slowly. "I don't know if that's possible." Matthias' eyes tightened, but I held up a hand. "Read my thoughts. I'm not saying I don't want to." He arched a brow at me. "Okay, fine. Filthy cheater. Of course I'm scared of the outcome, but that doesn't mean I'm trying to spite you. I don't know *how* to get you out of here."

Matthias watched me for a time, face thoughtful. Then a stunned smile slowly spread across his face, revealing an opening of white teeth buried under the mass of beard. It was a decidedly scary look. "Well, well, well. One would almost think this to be design, but I long ago gave up believing in Serendipity..." He must have noticed the look on my face, so leaned forward companionably. "Think on it. We will meet again soon. After your trip. In the meantime, we will both prepare to fulfill our parts of the bargain." He spat on his hand and extended it my way.

A small, but very loud part of me began to shout. He was asking me to make a pact with him in order to fulfill another pact. But I didn't have a choice. Quite literally. "I'm not promising I will do it. I'm promising that I'm agreeable to the terms we discussed. Your freedom for the return of my cane. I won't be held accountable if I'm unable to find a way to make this happen, you understand?"

He blinked. "Oh, that is *very* clever of you. The thought hadn't even crossed my mind, but if it had, I definitely would have used it against you. No offense," he added behind another grin. "Good move, boy. Our pact could have quite literally implied that. Fine, we will speak it. I, Matthias Temple, the Mad Hatter, titles ad nauseum, do agree that I desire to give you your cane and her trapped Beast in exchange for my freedom and release into your world. Given this option becomes available and possible for us to achieve, but not holding the other party responsible if a way cannot be found."

I nodded. "I, Nate Temple, do agree that I desire to free you from this prison of a world in exchange for reclaiming ownership of my cane and the Beast within – as it was when you took possession of it. I will try to find a way for this to be achieved, but cannot promise I will succeed. If a way is possible, I will make it so, as long as the power required causes no direct harm to the life of any loved ones." I didn't specify loved ones *to whom*. You never knew when loopholes would work in your favor. Of course, as I thought this, I had my mental barriers up all the way so that he couldn't read me. It was taxing, but I had gotten good at it after spending so much time around the Mad Hatter.

So, if he agreed, I could factually argue that any person at risk was someone's *loved one*, because I hadn't limited my oath to *my* loved ones.

Too clever by far, he caught it anyway. "Nice touch at the end. I believe you have an *out*, now." I smiled guiltily. "Now, it's time for you to prepare, and to find our solution to this puzzle. I believe the color white is no longer in season for me. Ever."

I smiled at that. "Understandable. Just don't go black."

He winked. "You understand that not going black is what got me here?"

"That's exactly why I'm saying it. Jumping to the opposite end of the spectrum will be no less pleasant than your current situation. Just a different prison."

He watched me for a moment. Then simply said. "Take your… coin with you."

Then he was gone. I let out a breath, thinking back on the peacocks and what their color might imply. Because nothing had color in this place. Other than myself sometimes appearing in grays. But I had never seen anything *from* this place in any color but white. I pondered Matthias' odd reaction to our agreement, and how we would successfully complete it. He had sounded as if he knew something, speaking about design and serendipity.

I sighed, shaking my head, feeling my lack of sleep creeping up on me. I focused back on my body at Chateau Falco, connecting my soul to the anchor of my physical body. Astral Projection was cool, but it was exhausting, and my body was already wrung dry.

As my soul collided with my physical body, the pain I had been ignoring hit me like a blow, and I found myself gasping as I lay on the cool stone. My nose was bleeding – well, it was crusted over with dried blood, as were my ears.

Christ. I could have died sitting there. I hadn't realized how much pain I was in from trying to break into the Armory. I closed my eyes and let out a breath.

"Foolish bastard," I groaned, trying to convince myself to stand.

"Aye," a voice repeated beside me.

I flinched, scooting back on instinct. Mallory stared at me from across the hallway, also seated on the ground. He was in human form, but his eyes glinted at a small glowing orb in his palm. "You… how long have you been here?" I rasped, surprised I hadn't noticed the light immediately.

He shrugged. "Twenty minutes. As soon as I sensed the surge of power down here. I couldn't do anything for your injuries while you were gallivanting about. But now I can." He waited for me to nod, and then scrambled closer, a wary grimace on his face as I felt a cool wave of magic pour through me, delving deep into my body to assess for damage. He grunted. "Foolish, foolish, foolish…" he mumbled, and a complicated web of glowing light began to form between his fingers, as if he was making the world's most complex design of Cat's Cradle with his fingers. Hundreds of strands, a geometric beauty.

My mind began to grow fuzzy. "Thanks for inviting me, bonehead…" I mumbled, feeling very sleepy.

"Shit," he cursed, hands moving twice as fast, blurring.

"This isn't my fight. I'm just going to hang out down here while you guys take care of it… Unicorns… Callie…" I trailed off, suddenly laying on a blanket of storm clouds that rumbled beneath me. Chariots of fire raced past me, horses screaming, lightning cracking, and thunder grumbling like an oncoming freight train.

"Fucking Temples. Pig-headed Masters of the universe. Think they're goddamned Time Lords or something. That will have to do," he snarled, and slammed his web over my face like he was trying to suffocate me with a swath of saran wrap. I just watched him, wondering why the chariots weren't running him over, and how the hell a horned goat had gotten up in the clouds with me. His web of light struck my nose, and then wrapped around my entire head, and a dozen spikes of ice shattered my mind.

I screamed, unable to breathe.

The last thing I saw was Mallory staring at me with tears running down his cheeks. The tears were bloody, and he was cackling.

CHAPTER 12

I opened my eyes to find a beautiful, cherub face above me. Angry, crystal blue eyes with faint purple flecks studied me. Her long, wavy white hair brushed my cheeks, and a pleasant lavender scent washed over me. Despite her hair color, the woman was younger than me. I tried to smile, but her face hardened into fury.

"What the hell were you *thinking*?" she snapped.

I tried to speak, but my throat felt raw. I cleared it and tried again. "Hey, Callie. You here for brunch? I'm starving. Been waiting for you forever," I rasped.

Her eyes tightened as if reading a hidden meaning in my words, but I was still fuzzy from sleep, and didn't have the energy to dissect my comment. Women were strange. No use trying to learn their language. She sniffed before walking away. Mallory replaced her, taking his turn to study me. He no longer looked like a demon, as he had when I last saw him in the dark hallway, but I was pretty sure that was just a hallucination along with the other stuff. "No ill effects, thankfully," he finally said after the familiar tingle of his healing magic washed over me.

"I'm fine," I pressed, feeling my strength and wits slowly returning. "Thanks, Mallory. Food will probably help a lot. I just overtaxed my magic, and then stupidly decided to Astral Project before taking care of my body."

Mallory blinked. "You almost burned away your soul."

Callie gasped. "Astral Proj— Wait, you can destroy your *soul?*" she hissed, incredulous.

Mallory nodded very seriously. "If one has just the right amount of stupidity and recklessness. Darwinism usually sorts those ones out early, though," he added with a straight face.

I swallowed, but the sensation sent me into a coughing fit. "Water," I gasped.

Callie handed me a glass, looking concerned.

Mallory placed a hand on her shoulder, patted lightly, and then withdrew it, long enough to impart shared concern, but brief enough to not make her feel uncomfortable. Mallory was pretty intuitive. "He's fine, child," he told her. "Although it might have served him well if there had been consequences," he added as an afterthought.

Callie nodded her agreement, arms folded over her chest, concealing the words on her black t-shirt. She wore matching tight black jeans and biker boots, which only emphasized her bright hair and sapphire-blue eyes.

Callie was a wizard from Kansas City. She trained with the Shepherds – an arm of the Vatican that was shrouded in mystery and secrecy, almost as if they didn't really exist, because I had asked my hacker friend Othello to do some digging, and she had come up with zilch – to hunt down monsters. There were twelve of these wizard Shepherds, and they typically roamed the earth like gypsies, never staying in one place too long before moving onto the next country and the next urgent call from one of their churches.

Except, while in Kansas City, one Shepherd named Roland had met Callie at a very young age, saving her from some monsters in a dark alley. Discovering she was also a wizard, he had decided to stick around and train her.

She wasn't a very churchy kind of gal, but had still agreed to his tutelage, which involved learning how to use her magic…

And an insanely rigorous curriculum of hand-to-hand combat.

She was a badass of the highest order, even if she was still coming to grips with her magic, and her place in the world. Because she had made one thing very clear. She wasn't sure if she wanted to be a Shepherd.

I had met her a few months ago on a case involving the Spear of Longinus – the spear that had stabbed Jesus Christ on the Cross – when Roland had been injured. Some demons, werebears, vampires, and werewolves had tried to take her out, and Callie had learned some things about herself –

about her parentage – that had shaken her to the core. And sent her enemies scurrying.

But we didn't talk about that.

Still, it seemed like we both knew how to draw power from the same boss – the Big G. Because her magic was also tainted white on occasion, like mine. We might have let our hormones get in the way of our professionalism – not that anything had really happened – but *something* had happened.

We didn't talk about that, either.

And we were both okay with that. For now. I had invited her here to meet my friends. Because Callie was one of the coolest women I had ever met. And that was good enough for me.

For now. But we both liked to tease each other. Flirting for flirting's sake. I think.

I rolled my legs out from under the sheets and realized I was naked. Callie arched a daring eyebrow at me. I stared down at my feet for a few breaths, and then said, "You're welcome," as I plopped myself out of bed and walked over to the dresser, flashing my ass to her and Mallory.

I heard Mallory chuckle, but Callie was very silent. I smiled to myself.

I found a pair of light, comfortable jeans, tried to put them on, and almost fell on my ass. I quickly lashed out with my hand, snatching onto the dresser. With the added support of the antique furniture, the notorious, deadly, all-powerful wizard succeeded in dressing himself.

I finally turned back to the two of them. "Let's go eat." I stumbled out of the room ahead of them, ignoring Callie's grumbling protests. I casually grabbed a hold of the bannister, and made my way to the stairs, nodding at a few patrolling griffin statues that walked this level, tails lashing back and forth as they sniffed the air, keeping us safe. I heard Callie laughing lightly behind me and glanced over my shoulder to find her crouched down, nuzzling cheeks with one. I smiled, and then turned back to the sudden obstacle currently trying to thwart the infamous Master Temple from saving the world. Stairs.

I stared at them with a very doubtful expression that was cleverly masked as brave stoicism.

"How dare they," Callie murmured in my ear. I grunted agreement, but was caught off guard when she suddenly grasped my elbow and began carefully guiding me down the death trap.

I relaxed, and found myself smiling. We reached the base of the stairs, and I paused, staring up at a painted portrait of my parents with a nostalgic smile. Callie followed my gaze.

"Your dad had good genes," she admitted. I shot her a look to find her grinning at me, obviously teasing me to get a reaction. I sighed, guiding her around a corner to a new hallway.

And I suddenly stopped, staring in surprise.

A small golf cart stood before me. Gunnar was behind the wheel, smirking at us. He waved at Callie. "Good to see you again."

"Likewise," she smiled.

"You did it," I whispered in awe.

He nodded. "Get in, Tiny Tim."

I grinned as I climbed inside, relieved I wouldn't have to walk the rest of the way, even if it wasn't that far. And let's face it, driving a golf cart inside a house was pretty cool. Callie hopped on the back with an excited giggle, but Mallory appeared at the bottom of the stairs behind us, shook his head, and then walked past us. Gunnar stepped on the pedal and we soon passed him.

"Did Dean see you sneak it in?" I asked.

"Nope," Gunnar beamed as Callie clapped her hands delightedly behind us.

Even though golf carts weren't that fast, it felt dangerously so since we were inside a house and driving past cabinets of priceless artifacts and knickknacks. I could just imagine Dean's apoplexy when he saw.

Gunnar eased on the brakes as we reached the dining room. The last time I had used the table had been for Thanksgiving over a year ago. I led the three of us into the room to find the rest of my friends seated. Ashley patted the chair beside her, and Gunnar obediently joined her. Callie remained standing beside me, smiling politely. They returned the favor, but my attention was suddenly drawn to the back wall, where Dean was glaring at me, lips pressed tightly together. "Laziness breeds weakness. Or so I've been told," he offered in a flat tone.

I shook my head. "It's not laziness. It's a sport utility vehicle. Maybe we can start a Polo club," I added, pleased to see his horrified reaction. "And it's a good practice vehicle for everyone to learn on before they try the ATVs outside. Everyone needs to know how to drive them, in case we need to transport injured people around the property. Especially the kids."

Dean stared back. Those at the table watched in silence. "You are going to let the children drive... inside the house?" he looked as if I had told him I wanted to try sacrificing puppies.

"Well..." I began, thinking about all the priceless items decorating the hallways.

"They will learn how to drive the ATVs *outside*. Where they *belong*." It wasn't clear whether he meant that the kids or the vehicles belonged outside. Callie folded her arms, grinning.

"Um, what about Polo?" I reminded him.

Instead of answering, he stormed through the swinging doors into the kitchen to get our food.

Mallory entered the room behind me, shaking his head before taking a seat at the large, black chair on one end of the table. Callie followed, aiming for the empty chair nearest him. I cleared my throat before she took her seat. "Everyone, meet Callie Penrose. Callie, meet everyone." Before they could speak up and startle the living hell out of her, I indicated the animals – Hugin, Munin, and Sir Muffle Paws. "Stray pets," I told her, pointing them each out by name as I gave them warning looks. Sir Muffle Paws lounged on top of a china cabinet, watching lazily. The Ravens perched beside each other on another cabinet, blinking as they shifted from foot to foot, watching. I was grateful that Eae the Angel wasn't there. What with Callie's... abilities, I wanted to postpone that meeting as long as possible.

Gunnar dipped his head at Callie, drawing her attention, but Othello's overly dramatic nod of approval – thankfully out of Callie's view – distracted me. "We briefly met in Kansas City a few months ago," Gunnar reminded her, "when Nate stuck his nose into your demon business." Ashley smiled warmly as well.

Callie returned the smile, remembering. I was about to glare at Gunnar when I realized the room had turned uncomfortably silent.

Because of Carl.

He was staring at Callie, very directly, but not speaking. Her face was completely blank as she met his eyes. His tongue flicked out like a snake, and then he began thumbing one of his blades, squinting at her, now. Faces slowly turned to face him, wondering why he wasn't speaking.

"She smells like you, Master Temple," he finally said. "I approve of you two mating." My face flushed red, and Callie abruptly sat down, taking a big drink of water from the nearest glass.

Alucard burst out laughing. "Fucking Carl..." He shook his head, still laughing until Tory smacked him in the chest.

"You may have missed it, Callie," I began, "but he politely introduced himself as Carl. Creepy Carl. I didn't hear him say anything else." I didn't make eye contact with her.

Carl frowned at me. "She smells like you do when you sleep," he added, sounding confused.

If possible, my face flushed even darker, and I desperately wanted to dump some ice water over my head. Gunnar stared openly at Carl. "How do you know what Nate smells like when he sleeps?"

Alucard leaned over to the Reds, pointing a thumb at Carl as he whispered loud enough for everyone to hear. "He knows how to fucking party." The Reds were trying not to fall out of their chairs with laughter.

Carl cocked his head, the openings of his reptilian ears contracting. "I watch him sleep, of course. I protect him." He turned to Callie. "I will protect you, too, if you wish."

Callie cleared her throat, politely deflecting Carl's offer to watch her sleep. "Nate gave me a stuffed animal and a book. Maybe that's what you smell?" she asked in a helpful tone.

Carl shrugged uncertainly. "Possibly," he said, looking frustrated. "I don't understand you people. It was a compliment. Master Temple smells pleasant when he sleeps."

"Right," I butted in quickly. "Carl, please raise your hand if you want to say anything else."

"I don't see why I'm the only one..." he began, then let out an angry breath. "Fine." His tongue flickered again, this time looking hostile.

Tory piped up. "I'm Tory. I run Shift, Nate's school for wayward children." She elbowed Alucard next to her. "This is Alucard, my secretary. Daywalker Master Vampire on the side."

Alucard scowled at Tory, but nodded begrudgingly. "Pleasure," he said, flashing Callie a courteous smile. "Heard you kicked some serious ass a few months ago, but Nate wouldn't share the details."

"Just some carebears and a few demons," she replied humbly, shrugging with a smile. Alucard studied her more intently, nodding absently, wanting to hear more.

The Reds, Aria and Sonya, piped up, staring at Callie as if they had found their new role model. "We're dragons. We help out at the school, and

Alucard's our stepdad. Not officially, or anything, but he's the best we could ask for."

Alucard squinted at them suspiciously, likely wondering if that had been a jibe, but I was pretty sure it wasn't. Alucard and Tory had stepped in to look after the Reds after their mother had been killed, and the two teenagers thought the world of him. Then again, the two weredragons also had mind-manipulation abilities, and were still learning when it was acceptable to tap into that. Like calming an angry stepdad after he was called a secretary, for example.

It was a good thing that Tory was a Beast Master, able to control shifters at will, because anyone else would have been wrapped around the teenagers' fingers.

Callie gave the two a mischievous grin. "I *love* your hair. Dragons, you say? I've never met a dragon. Maybe you can show me your stuff after brunch? Perhaps we can go play outside for a spell." The Reds beamed, loving the fact that they had not only received direct attention in a room full of powerful adults, but that the newcomer had basically shown them the most interest.

Callie then turned to Tory. "Shift... such an interesting name for a school. But, of course, they aren't just wayward children, are they?"

Tory's eyes flicked to mine, and I gave a subtle nod. "True. Nate saved a bunch of shifter kids from a monster who was using them for an illegal fight club. Nate shut it down, and we took them in, hoping to rehabilitate them into society. Give them a normal life."

Callie shot me a considering look that I pretended not to notice. It hadn't just been me that saved the kids. Everyone here had helped. "I take it many of them were... mentally damaged as a result of their captivity..." Tory nodded sadly. Callie leaned back, looking pensive. "You're the one Nate was talking about. Able to control shifters..."

Tory again checked with me before nodding.

"I'd like to speak with you after brunch, too, if you can spare a few moments. But maybe I should clear it with your secretary..." she turned to Alucard with a teasing grin, and I knew that Tory and Callie were going to get along just fine. Alucard rolled his eyes, smiling.

Tory smiled. "He's really not that good of a secretary. I'd love to chat if Nate can spare you for a few minutes."

"I'll somehow manage," I added drily.

Othello leaned forward. "My name's Othello, and I think you and I have a lot to talk about," she said, grinning conspiratorially as she not-so-discreetly pointed her head in my direction.

Callie nodded. "That sounds positively... ominous," she grinned as if the two were speaking in code that only they understood. "Tell me when. I think I've got some questions for you, too."

Othello leaned back, looking satisfied. What the hell had that been about?

Callie turned from face-to-face, tapping her chin with a finger. "This is fun. But I think I like Carl the best." Which earned very different reactions from each person present.

I bit back a laugh, because that statement right there proved how clever Callie really was. I wasn't sure if I had ever met anyone as deft at manipulating people, or reading groups, motivations, and fears of those around her. She was like a Chess player in that regard. And she won over Carl as easy as that. And piqued the interest of everyone else. "No offense," she added to the others. "You're all better than Nate, if that's any consolation." And she won the rest of them over with that comment.

I shook my head. "This is going exactly as I hoped. Let's eat."

I sat opposite Mallory in a gaudy white chair that was taller than the rest as Dean began bringing in platters and trays of savory foods. I listened absently as everyone began to talk back and forth. I answered when addressed, but for the most part, I let them get to know each other. Because I could feel Sir Muffle Paws grinning at me from his perch atop the cabinet. He was eating a mouse, ripping out the internal organs as he stared at me with golden, unblinking eyes.

I turned away, not wanting to ruin my appetite, and found Hugin and Munin staring at me. They weren't eating, but they looked very... focused on me.

I turned back to the table, hoping to get sucked back into the conversation, ignoring both the furred and feathered psychotic beasts, and found Mallory staring at me.

His eyes flickered with golden fire, and his face was entirely expressionless, the face of a creature unfamiliar with his surroundings. His mouth opened to speak, but no words came out.

I could still read his lips, though.

Tick Tock...

I shivered, and turned my eyes down to my plate. I ate mechanically, refusing to look at any of them after that. When the meal was finished, and everyone was saying their goodbyes, I pulled Tory aside. "Do you have a second?"

Her eyes roved past me to where Callie was patiently waiting by the stairs with the Reds. She looked up and our eyes met. We smiled at each other, and then she turned back to the dragons, who were staring up at her as if seeing a Rock Star. They led her towards the front of the house, no doubt to go show off their skills and impress their new best friend. But she cast one more look at me before she left, and it was curious. Was I talking to Tory about her?

Truth was, it had nothing to do with Callie, but—

"You should totally hook up with her. She's a fox."

I blinked, realizing I was still staring at the space where Callie had been standing. I turned back to see Tory grinning at me, Alucard smiling in agreement.

I shook my head. "Thanks. But romance is kind of what put us in this pickle." Their smiles faltered and died at that. "Look, I need to ask you something, and it's probably good that your secretary is here for it." They grew instantly serious. I scrubbed a hand through my hair, wondering if there was a specific way I should phrase my question. Mallory was gone, so I couldn't just ask him.

"Okay. I need to go help Mallory with something soon. And given the location, I think it might be a good idea to offer you a ticket on the bus."

Alucard's shoulders tightened, not sure what the words meant, but not liking the sound of them. Tory furrowed her brow. "Okay. No need to be cryptic. What's up?"

"I'm going to the Fae. To help him. Or... help his brother, I guess. Sir Muffle Paws and Carl are also going," I said before I really thought about it, realizing for the first time that I had subconsciously decided to bring them. "I need two women to join me, and since you have unfinished business with the Fae, I thought this might be a great opportunity to settle some accounts, especially since we'll be helping Mallory's brother, who I believe to be an important person over there. Maybe even enough to get the Queens to listen to him."

"I'm going, then," Alucard said quickly.

I shook my head. "Love the sentiment, and if it was up to me, we would all go, but someone needs to look after the kids at Shift. That's you. They trust you. Gunnar will need to look after the army while I'm gone," I added, feeling nauseated at the sudden thought that Gunnar might permanently be in charge of the war if I did as War had advised.

Alucard shook his head. "If you need two women, why not take Callie and the Huntress."

Tory shook her head. "The Huntress told me that she would never, ever go to the Land of the Fae. No matter what. I think she must have done something unforgiveable over there, because she isn't scared of anything. Besides, she's doing something mysterious for Nate in London. With Van and Baba," Tory added, studying me. The fact that she knew about that at all was a little concerning, because I had only told Othello about it. But even she didn't know the reason.

"All the more reason Tory shouldn't go," Alucard argued. "They already want her."

I ignored Alucard. "This is completely up to you. You don't have to go, but I thought with the rest of us already going, and to do a favor for Mallory's brother, you really couldn't ask for a better chance to rectify things with the Queens. Remember, they have no love for me, either. At least you two didn't directly piss them off…" I smiled weakly. "It's not like either of you drop-kicked them in the boobs, or pinned one to a wall like a butterfly in a science exhibit."

They nodded, but didn't smile. Because our brief encounter had left them entirely enthralled to the Queens. Being wise and adept at social interactions, I didn't remind them of that.

"Just think on it. I'm not asking Callie. She's a badass, but she still has some things to learn, and I need anyone going with me to be a bit more jaded, cynical, and ruthless. The Land of the Fae would eat her alive." Tory arched an eyebrow at me, no doubt taking it as an insult against women in general. "And this trip has nothing to do with her. She isn't one of us. She works for the Vatican… kind of. And lives in Kansas City. I don't want her dragged into our problems unless we have to."

"Who else were you going to ask?" Ashley asked from directly behind me.

I flinched, so engrossed with my conversation that I hadn't even sensed her approach.

I turned to her, considering. "Well, to be honest, I hadn't decided yet."

"I'll make it easy on you, then. If Tory goes, I'll go, too. We girls need to stick together."

"Go where?" Gunnar slipped out from a side hall, approaching us. "Because it sure as hell isn't the Land of the Fae…" he growled.

"This doesn't concern you, Alpha. It's not pack business."

His lips actually curled at that. "Then as your fiancé, I say *no*."

She leaned into him, planting a quick peck on his bearded cheek. "It's so cute that you think our relationship works like that. No man tells a woman where she can go." His lone eye squinted, veering my way as if to take it out on me.

I held up my hands. "I didn't even *ask* her!"

Ashley saved me. "Look at it this way, Gunnar. I'm either facing war with a God here, or a quick trip through the woods with a powerful Fae backing us up over there. How long is this trip?" she asked, turning back to me.

"Two days. Tops." Because that would be a requirement of mine. I couldn't risk being gone longer than that. The defenses I had set up here could last quite some time without me here to help. But at some point, they would weaken without me here to juice them back up. Two days was perfectly safe.

Gunnar grunted, but Ashley wrapped her arm through his, calming him. Then she looked up at me. "Let me know when. I'll be ready." Then she was leading Gunnar away.

He shot a cold look over his shoulder at me, and I did my best to look apologetic and innocent, because I *hadn't* asked her to join.

But deep down, I knew that she would have been my second choice, and that if she hadn't offered, I would have likely sought her out about ten minutes after asking Tory.

Alucard began to pace. "I don't like it. Let's both go."

Tory shook her head. "No, Nate's right. Someone needs to be here to watch over the students, and the house, and… the Reds."

Alucard froze, face growing angry. "Not fair. You would use them against me?"

"No. I thought I was asking my dearest friend to watch over the two most important things in my life while I'm away. Even though you did such a splendid job last time," she added teasingly.

Alucard sighed, shoulders sagging. "Doubly unfair," he muttered. Then he looked up at me. "You better keep them safe, Nate. Or else." I nodded solemnly. The two weren't romantic, but you would have thought they were long-lost brother and sister, or something. And they cared more about those troublesome Reds than any parents I had ever seen, despite neither of them being blood related to them.

Rock-solid.

Alucard called out over his shoulder as he led Tory down the hall. "The Reds can't afford to lose two mothers, Nate..."

I swallowed, feeling sick to my stomach at the thought.

Mallory had said I needed two women or all hope was lost. Normally, I would have simply brushed off Mallory's request at this point. We had more important things to focus on. Like war.

But then the Hatter had chimed in, and making it sound like this quest might just be the most important thing in the world to me, even though I was going in blind.

We were going to meet Mallory's brother. Or Mallory's other self. To do him a favor.

And the Hatter thought I had something to learn from it, something important.

Thinking back on my conversation with War, he had seemed troubled, like he was desperately trying to make me understand something. Was it related to this or the war? Because Matthias had said that Death was at least aware of these Invitations, so War must know about them, too. Was this some ancient rite of passage that everyone knew about, but wouldn't share with initiates?

I had been kicking ass for years now, even taking down some pretty heavyweight bad guys.

So...

Why did I feel like it was suddenly my first day on the job?

I turned to find Callie staring at me from the shadows, having returned from outside. "Show me your lair, rascal," she said playfully.

My heart skipped a beat both at seeing her there without warning, and her words.

Then again, I knew she was a master at manipulation, even though I was pretty sure she wasn't entirely aware of her gifts in that area. Still, she subconsciously knew how to mess with people's minds, and how to use that to her advantage.

So those words messed with me.

Or maybe it was just because it had been a long while since a pretty woman asked me to show her my lair from the dark shadows of a hallway after everyone had left.

I smiled, nodding.

CHAPTER 13

e strode through the halls of Chateau Falco, and I watched Callie study everything like a kid at her first museum. Sometimes I felt like her older kid brother, and then other times...

She bent over to pick up a cat toy on the ground, then jingled it playfully at me.

Yeah, other times...

I nodded innocently, smiling.

"Your cat doesn't seem that friendly," she said absently. "Didn't really give me the playful vibe," she said, inspecting each painting we passed.

"Oh, I don't know. He just has to have the right toys to play with." *Like a fluffy, white magician's rabbit in front of a crowd of screaming children.* "Once you get to know him, he's not that bad." *For a sociopath.*

She nodded, continuing on, not really waiting for me to guide her, but choosing her own path. I let her, watching her all the while. I really wasn't sure how I felt about Callie Penrose. We had met a few months ago when I was in Kansas City for an auction. I had jumped in to help her on a case with a stolen artifact since her mentor had been injured. To be honest, I wasn't entirely sure why I had offered to help. Well, she had needed it, and I wanted to be sure that the stolen artifact didn't fall into the wrong hands, but something else had pushed me to help her. I wasn't sure if it was attraction, or protectiveness.

Because Callie, although dangerous in her own right, was also very naïve to the dangers of the world. Pleasantly so. She wasn't as jaded. She had a spunk to her. A fire of life in her eyes that made me happy to be around her. Her shirt very accurately portrayed this, saying *I'm mostly peace, love, and light, and a little go fuck yourself.*

We might have let our hormones interfere a little in Kansas City, but nothing had really happened, and I wasn't sure how to feel about that. Neither of us had rejected the other, but we had... danced back and forth in the romance arena.

And, surprisingly, I liked that.

And I think she did, too.

I let those thoughts evaporate as I focused on simply being with her, here, now. Enjoying myself. No war. No angry Greeks. No vengeful ex-fiancée. No Fae. Just two friends exploring a dusty old house. A smile crept onto my face.

"Falco, SPEAK!" I shouted. Callie whirled, eyes wide, surprised by my sudden outburst. She saw me grinning, arms folded.

And then the house began to purr. More of a grumble really. Callie's widened eyes shot to the ceiling, the walls, the floor, and then back to me.

"Thanks, Falco," I said, looking up at the ceiling. The house quieted, and I turned back to Callie with a big grin. "Cool, huh?"

She stared at me for a few seconds. "The house is... *alive?*" she whispered.

I shrugged. "Kind of."

She stared at me longer this time, and then a slow smile began to split her cheeks. "That is..." she trailed off, studying the walls as if she had never seen them before. "So *cool!*" She walked up to one of the walls, glanced over her shoulder at me – catching me subconsciously appreciating her posterior with a quick smirk – and then petted the wall. "Hi, Falco," she said. "I'm Callie."

The house purred soothingly, and Callie giggled.

I shook my head, amused, and embarrassed at her catching my wandering eye. "Let's go."

She danced up beside me, and casually twined her arm through mine like I was escorting her to a dance, head darting back and forth to take everything in: each painting, table, artifact on a shelf, and antique piece of furniture. Her appetite for beauty and exploration knew no bounds.

She was voracious.

Remembering her father's home, I had a sudden understanding of why. This was a palace to her, and it was the little moments like this one which constantly brought me back to reality.

My sense of *normal* was entirely different from others'. Her family had worked their asses off to make ends meet.

I had lived like a king my whole life.

Showing her something that made her smile felt like the best gift I could offer, and watching her reaction made me realize I had been missing something for a very long time. Genuine joy. Not a triumphant victory over evil, but basic, simple joy. Being happy about the little things.

And I liked seeing that smile. It was just so pure.

It wasn't even romance. It was just seeing a beautiful, kind-hearted woman so deliriously happy. And I liked making people smile for pleasant reasons. Those little things add up.

"I want to show you something," I said.

Without missing a beat, she said, "As long as it's not your bedroom."

I blinked, and began stammering an argument. She squeezed my arm, eyes twinkling as she let me fumble around with my words. I finally sighed, shot her a scowl for good measure, and then led her onwards.

A short time later, we stood before the door that led to the Sanctorum. I placed my palm against the door, and it dissolved into a waterfall of sand, revealing an opening. Callie gasped, then grabbed my hand. She turned it upwards to see the crest branded there, and frowned thoughtfully. "I saw that once and thought it was something else."

I frowned, but she dropped my hand and tugged me through the opening, not waiting to let me lead. I grinned at her back, allowing her to drag me through my own house.

When we finally exited the hallway to enter the massive Sanctorum, Callie grew very still, dropping my hand. Then she began to spin in a slow circle, taking it all in. She squealed when she saw the waterfall, running up to it to let the water splash over her fingertips. She laughed, a great, chiming sound, and I found myself chuckling. It was like watching a puppy.

She danced over to the desk, eyes fixing onto the carving on one of the legs for a brief moment before studying the intricate carving of the desk itself. Then she moved onto the bookshelves, studying them quickly as she strode past.

Her eyes locked onto the concaves carved into the floor, and noticing they were filled with pillows, she jumped into one of them. She furrowed a brow at the fireplace until it burst into purple flame. She looked up at me, patted the pillows beside her, and then rested her head on her palm, waiting.

"What if the fireplace was rigged to blow up or something?"

She frowned. "Why would anyone rig a fireplace to explode?" She patted the pillows again, and I found myself shaking my head as I joined her. She was silent for a few moments, leaning back into the pillows as her eyes trailed up to the ceiling, studying the constellations depicted above – with genuine gemstones.

"Did you make this?" she asked.

I shook my head. "No. One of my ancestors did. He built the whole place."

She murmured unintelligibly, and then turned to face me. "He must have loved beauty," she said, staring right through my eyes and into my soul. I swallowed, but managed a nod.

That was the other thing about Callie. When she looked at you, she *really* looked at you. She did it to everyone, and probably didn't comprehend the intensity of those blue eyes.

Or maybe she did, and used it as a weapon, only feigning innocence.

She slowly swiveled her head, taking in the room. "A house built by an ancestor. It talks. And this room is obviously full of magic because none of the books are damaged by the water." She jerked her thin chin at the blank space opposite the waterfall, where a hidden Round Table could be raised. "And there is something seriously weird about that section of the room," she said absently, before turning away. "Is your house a trapped angel? Or demon?"

I blinked, opening my mouth, but found I was unable to answer, because I wasn't sure of the truth. It took me a few moments, and she didn't turn my way as I clamored for a response. "I don't think it's a demon. But it's alive. Sentient. Have you ever heard of a Maker?" I asked.

She shook her head lightly. "According to my boss, there is only *one* Maker," she said with a smirk. I smiled back, nodding. Because she worked for the Vatican.

"Well, a Maker is… hmm. A Maker has the ability to make things. He can literally think of what he wants, and make it so."

She turned to me, frowning. "How is that different from a wizard, and why haven't I heard of them before?"

I arched an eyebrow at her. "Maybe because you work for the church?" I teased. She gave me a very dry look in response. "Okay. A wizard – if he wanted to make... that book catch fire, for example – would need to find a way to make fire from the elements around him, and then how to fuel that fire for a short period, and then how to send that fire at the target, and then how to make it stick. This is all done very quickly, but he has to take steps."

Callie nodded.

I waited until she looked at me. "A Maker would simply think *burn* while looking at the book." I leaned closer. "And. It. Would. Burn."

She digested that in silence. "I take it there aren't any Makers anymore?"

I shrugged. "A handful. Most were hunted down."

The room was silent for a few moments. "Are you a Maker, Nate?"

I shook my head, deciding not to elaborate on the topic. I wasn't. Not anymore. I had a brief relationship with the power, but that was now finished, so that was all that mattered. She also didn't need to know that my ex-fiancée and my ancestor both had Maker abilities.

"So, someone in your bloodline was a Maker. They made this place..." she said softly.

I nodded. "You could say that the power a Maker wields is what makes this house sentient. I've heard it referred to as a Beast, and one of those Beasts lives within the very walls of Chateau Falco. In fact, the Beast's name is Falco."

She stared up at the ceiling again, scanning the place in a whole new light. "I see," she said, her mind far away. I leaned back with a sigh, thinking about Mallory and his quest. About my Beast. How to get Matthias out of his prison. And Hercules. About my failed attempt with the Armory.

"Enough about you, let's talk about me," Callie said. I blinked to find her staring at me from only inches away.

I nodded. "Dazzle me."

"Our powers. They are similar." I nodded, knowing she was talking about the strange white color our magic sometimes displayed. If I wanted fire, really wanted fire, the fire was white. If I wanted ice, really wanted ice, the ice was white. But it hadn't always been that way. I was pretty sure my power change was a direct result of getting tangled up with the Horsemen of the Apocalypse.

But Callie didn't know about that. And she wasn't a Horseman. But she did have some tie to the church, so it was possible that the white power was related to Heaven somehow. Or at least something Biblical.

"I don't really want to get into details. Not yet. But I wanted you to know I was aware..." she said in a soft voice. "I'd rather figure a few things out on my own, first." I nodded, and the room grew silent. "About Kansas City..." she began.

I held up a hand. "We'll talk about that some other time. I'd rather you did a little digging, soul-searching, and learning about your place in the world. I'll be here to talk whenever you're ready." I cut myself off, not wanting to say more.

Her eyes latched onto me as if I had said something incredibly stupid, ignorant, or... incredibly profound. I pretended it was the latter.

Then an idea hit me. "I might need your help in a few days, though," I said, my mind running with the idea. "Regarding our similar powers, actually."

She nodded curiously. "Sure. As long as it's not for anything criminal. Or this war of yours."

I smiled, shaking my head. "We'll never even leave Chateau Falco, and we'll only be touching something that belongs to me."

Her eyes twinkled in amusement, and too late, I realized how it had sounded. "Right. I'll take your word for it," she said drily. I opened my mouth to clarify, but she placed a finger on my lips. "I'm not feeling up to Shadow Walking home right now. Do you care if I stay here for a little longer?"

I blinked. "Um. No. That's fine."

"Good. Because I'm a big fan of naps. And I feel a nap coming on. Care to join me?"

I stared back at her. What the hell was this? Was she being literal or using her feminine wiles against me? I nodded at her, unsure what else to say.

"Good. Talk to you soon," she said. Then she curled up on the pillows, reached back with her hand, grasped mine, and placed it around her waist. "I'm cold," she murmured. I didn't fight her, simply rolled with it, and soon found myself spooning with her, feeling like a middle-school-aged boy all over again.

The estrogen was strong with this one.

But something magical happened. I wasn't sure if it was related to my injuries, or if it was simply her, but as I debated what this all meant, I soon realized that I was dreaming, with Callie tucked in neatly against my chest.

Then again, maybe I wasn't dreaming at all, because that was exactly what was happening in the waking world. Maybe I was still awake and hyperaware of my situation.

I didn't question it.

CHAPTER 14

I woke suddenly, gasping as I sensed something. I lifted my head, stared up, and found Mallory gazing down at me curiously.

I blinked a few times, but he didn't speak. I was still pressed up against Callie, and she still held my arm over her stomach as if trying to use it as a blanket. Mallory nodded happily, but I scowled up at him. Callie must have sensed his presence because she suddenly woke up. She groaned as she stretched her arms above her head, smiling with her eyes still closed. She opened them to find me staring down at her. She arched a brow and I realized my palm was still resting on her stomach. I jerked it away as if burned, and her smile grew wider.

She turned to Mallory. "Well, I got him to take a rest, I guess."

Mallory nodded. "Thank you, child. It really is time for us to be leaving, Master Temple. Everyone is waiting."

I blinked first at Mallory, then at Callie. "Wait. That... you tricked me into taking a nap?" I asked in disbelief. Not angry, just... baffled. I pulled out my phone. "Six *hours*?!"

Callie shrugged. "Mallory told me you needed rest for something you had planned, especially since you almost burned away your soul earlier," she added with a stern look. "He knew you would only argue about it, so asked me to help. I really did want to see your house, and knew we would likely pass your room at some point, where I could use my feminine wiles to get you into bed," she winked suggestively. "But then you took me down here, just the two of us, to your cozy lair, and the rest just kind of fell into place," she shrugged, watching me. "Don't be upset."

I just stared at the two of them, unsure whether to be angry... or feel genuinely appreciative.

Mallory began to laugh, pointing at me. "That face. Priceless."

I scowled at him. "Well, thanks for being an asshole about looking after me." He bowed his head as if at a compliment. Then, when Callie wasn't looking, he jerked his head at her, asking a silent question of me.

I shook my head. "No, not Callie." I felt her studying me, knowing she had missed something.

"It is time," Mallory said. "Everyone is waiting by the tree. Dress natural. No iron." Then he left.

Callie slowly climbed to her feet. "Just when I was getting comfortable. Who knows what could have happened next," she said offhandedly, and I felt my face flush again. What the hell did *that* mean? But she was staring up at the books, as if wanting to go explore. Maybe she was alluding to that.

Goddamned Mallory.

I climbed to my feet and stepped up beside Callie, holding out a hand. She took it without looking, squeezed once, and then allowed me to guide her from the room.

"Until next time…" she said sadly to the room.

I wanted to kill Mallory. Just a little.

CHAPTER 15

*W*e stood beside the giant white tree on my property. Hugin and Munin watched us from the branches and Sir Muffle Paws sat at my feet, scowling at everyone with a level of lazy hatred and disdain that only a cat could manage. Callie had left me after the Sanctorum to go find Tory while I changed. Not knowing what to make of Mallory's cryptic advice, I had dressed in jeans, boots, a t-shirt that said *I don't believe in Fairies*, and a distressed leather jacket I found in the back of my closet – because it was early evening, now, and the temperature was cooling down.

I had also grabbed a few magical items I had been tinkering with for the war – some old, and some new – just in case. With a brief explanation, I had given one to both Tory and Ashley. My coin was now a small wooden disk with a hole in the center, and tied to a leather cord around my neck. I hadn't wanted to risk carrying a metal coin into the Land of the Fae – because I could have subconsciously included iron in the coin. Who knew? I certainly wasn't a metalsmith of any kind. I had just thought *coin* and it had become a coin.

Each of us had received small packs from Dean with a few water canteens and some travel food – jerky, dried fruits, and the like. Things we could eat on the go so we didn't have to try any Fae takeout food. Because everyone knew Fae food could be lethal, like shady Thai food trucks at an innocent farmer's market – magically enchanting with their Demoncraft scents, and bright colored vehicles that you couldn't turn down. But you would still try it, knowing full well that you would be on your knees later, praying to a god you might never have prayed to before, begging for *the end*, or at least for the pain in your *guts* to end.

Callie was standing beside Tory, speaking softly out of earshot, and when Tory came back to stand beside Ashley, she looked thoughtful, but didn't share. Neither of the girls had weapons, preferring their natural talents, and like me, wore jeans, boots, and a t-shirt.

Gunnar and Alucard scowled at me as if this were all my fault.

Carl grinned from ear to ear, caressing the blades at his hips. Two more rested over his shoulders like an X, and he wore his leather armor that consisted of dozens of straps and buckles. He didn't seem aware of Alucard and Gunnar's anger. Or he simply didn't care. He looked like a kid on his first trip to a zoo to see the elephants.

Callie watched us for a few moments, standing beside Sonya and Aria. She held their hands in support, but I could see the question in her eyes. She didn't know what was going on. The Reds were trying very hard to look tough, but I could see through it. They were terrified. Of losing another mom.

But I wouldn't let that happen. I shot them a warm, comforting smile, and some of the tension faded from their faces. Callie nodded appreciatively at me.

I turned to Mallory – who was standing by the tree – and nodded. It was time.

He merely nodded back, not speaking, and then blew a quick tune on a pair of pipes I hadn't seen in his fist. The world flashed with green fire, and I saw every single person nearby burn to green ashes between one second and the next.

Then their ashes were blown away to the wind.

I gasped, trying to shout, but no sound came out.

Because I was also green ash.

Sir Muffle Paws let out a dark laugh and I heard Carl join in. I don't know how they were able to make sounds, because I felt like a wandering soul with no physical presence, just awareness.

Then I was solid again.

And Stonehenge stood before us. *The* Stonehenge. But we hadn't Shadow Walked.

I heard the girls gasp in surprise, but Sir Muffle Paws and Mallory simply approached the stone columns. And as they did, fiery blue Druidic carvings began to glow from deep within the stone pillars.

Each of them.

The rest of us hesitantly followed as the light increased in intensity, bathing the sparse grass around us in a silvery blue glow. When each of us had reached the center of the ring, wild lighting crackled between two of the stones, connecting them. Then another pair was connected. And another. Until each was connected by a ribbon of crackling, untamed electricity, surrounding us, effectively preventing us from leaving.

"Don't lose yourself. Welcome to the Trial, Master Temple," Mallory said, staring at me very intently. Then his face began to change, and I stared, transfixed, unable to ask what he was talking about. The skin of his cheeks and jaw slowly morphed – twitching, stretching, and narrowing – until it almost looked like I was seeing an ancestor of his. A harder, darker, feral version of the man I had come to know. He sliced open his forearm with a sudden slash of a bone dagger I hadn't seen, and before I could react...

The world exploded with a technicolor splash of light.

The light faded after scant moments, and I grasped my knees, panting. It was nighttime, and we stood beside a massive slab of stone. A different Druidic symbol was glowing on the stone, but the light slowly faded as I watched. When the light was gone, I saw the symbol still there, but painted in blue by a crude hand.

I assessed our surroundings, and my pulse began to race.

Because I was pretty sure I was tripping balls.

Nearby trees glowed with neon light. Three moons hovered in the sky, all in varying phases. One crescent, one half moon, and one full moon – and each was at least twice as large as the moon on earth.

And the moon on earth wasn't pink, orange, or blue.

We stood in a small clearing that butted up to a horseshoe-shaped line of massive sagging trees, like weeping willows back home, but each leaf glowed a bright blue, and giant pink berries the size of coconuts hung from their thin branches, weighing them down to the ground. Chuffing noises could be heard in the near distance almost like we were surrounded by a troop of monkeys, but no one bothered us. Two choices: the neon forest or the rolling fields in the other direction.

The green grass looked normal, but crunched underfoot, emitting a sharp, savory smell.

The air felt wet and thick, carrying a dozen traces of perfume from the glowing trees. The scents mingled together in harmony, reminding me of a fruit smoothie, but different. Strong, but not overwhelming. The night was warm, here, and I began to regret bringing a jacket.

I glanced over at my friends to see how they were faring, to make sure everyone was healthy and present. That no one had been left behind.

My jaw dropped when I saw a bipedal, black werewolf staring back at me. Ashley. She had on only a heavy pair of boots and strange leather pants – not the jeans and t-shirt we had each been wearing – that were crossed with straps, harnesses, and dozens of pockets. Her belly and chest were coated in a very short, thin layer of fur, revealing the taut muscle beneath – a genuine six pack. Her arms were covered in thicker fur, and she wore a band of colored cloth over each bicep. A bone bracelet adorned each wrist, and they were carved with symbols in a harsh angular script I had never seen before. Her head was obviously that of a wolf, but her eyes were too intelligent, and the fur was much longer than I had ever seen on her. It even sported metal bands that bunched pieces together to form what appeared to be random dreadlocks amidst the ruff of her neck, but doubled to keep it clear of her eyes and snout.

She saw the look on my face and glanced down, frowning. Then she gasped. "Fuck me," she blurted, patting herself down as if it were a hallucination.

"Don't say that too loudly," I heard Sir Muffle Paws say from behind me. "Very literal creatures, here," he chuckled. Instead of turning to the cat, I saw myself studying Tory with equal astonishment. She remained, more or less, human.

But wore a fur bikini. A furkini. With Gladiator-styled, knee-high, leather sandals.

Her hips sported a wide leather belt lined with primitive-looking daggers, and she wore a long, matted fur cape with the hood drawn up. The hood was actually the gaping maw of a once-living beast that pretty much proved that, at some point, a saber-toothed tiger had boinked a gorilla.

Tory, noticing something in her peripheral vision, yanked back her hood, and then tore off the cape itself, staring at it in stunned disbelief. Her head was shaved on the sides, and a dozen braids were tugged back into a ponytail, reminding me of those Viking warriors. Although her face was still familiar, it looked thinner, harder, as if she had survived on an island by herself for a year. Her skin was pale, and her veins had a luminescent, golden glow, like that one time I had briefly seen her under a revealing spell at the Vaults, a supernatural bank in St. Louis.

The two women huddled close together, talking softly and inspecting the other with approving compliments, like this was the first day of a very twisted summer camp of death. Ashley helped Tory put the cloak back on, nodding in approval.

I glanced down at myself, fearing the worst, and blinked. I...

Hadn't changed. At all.

Jeans, leather coat, and a t-shirt, still.

"This place sucks," I complained.

"Maybe you're scary enough as it is," Carl said cheerfully. I looked up to see that Carl also hadn't physically changed, although he did look more relaxed. At peace. I shook my head and turned to Sir Muffle Paws, prepared to begin demanding answers.

And I almost fell on my ass.

A five-foot-tall, reddish-brown werecat stared back at me, wearing a pair of velvet boots, leather chest armor, and a kilt. He gripped a white polearm – like a spear – that was taller than me with a long, slender axe blade on one end. The hair on his face looked freshly cut, making his head more angular and predatory. Fangs as long as my fingers peeked out from his lips, where his fur turned white, resembling a well-groomed beard. His ears were shaggier, longer, and thinner, pointing backwards like horns, and had a few golden rings dangling from each lobe. He hissed at me. His eyes were now silver, mercurial.

And the little bastard had hit the gym, because he was proportionally as stout as Gunnar.

"It's rude to stare. And rudeness grants death, here, wizard," Sir Muffle Paws said. "I go by Talon the Devourer in this cursed place. Remember it." He thumped the base of his spear into the ground aggressively. Carl burst out laughing, and Talon's neck fur instantly began to stick straight up. We turned to look, only to find Carl laughing loudly as he spun in slow circles, holding his two swords high above his head, not looking at us. His laughter sounded different, too. Unrestrained. Like the first real laugh after a hundred years of silence. He wasn't laughing at Talon, he was laughing with... joy.

Talon muttered unhappily under his breath, turning back to me. I gave him a respectful nod. I'd never heard of Talon the Devourer, and had assumed I would learn he was the Cheshire Cat, or a Malk, or something obvious. Not... *this*. Whatever *this* was.

"This feels like home..." Carl murmured after his laughter died down. He sheathed his blades, and lifted a scaled claw to the air with a nostalgic look on his face. He turned to me, tongue flicking twice before he smiled. "Can you not feel the death? The blood? The primal urges?" He shivered like he had just received a happy ending at a massage parlor. "Like wisps from a distant campfire on a cool night..." I nodded slowly, turning to Mallory.

But he was gone.

I whirled, suddenly tense. The sounds around us quieted, and Sir Muff – well, Talon the Devourer – began to laugh and purr at the same time as if at some great, big joke.

"What the fuck is going on... Talon?" I asked, almost using the wrong name.

He licked his paws absently, wiping back his whiskers and grooming his beard. "He is unable to join us. He can't very well meet *himself*, can he?"

I cursed myself for not thinking of it sooner. It made perfect sense. Thinking on Pan, I still wasn't sure what to make of the revelation that he was also the Goblin King. Or something very close to it. But he still should have warned us. Red-hot rage began to roll over my shoulders in euphoric waves. "Well, I don't know what the fuck we're doing here, or where we're supposed to go, and our guide just slipped out faster than a guy hearing the breakfast call after a one-night stand."

Carl exhaled loudly. "Paint your blades in blood, brothers and sisters. Or as Nate might say, *I think we're about to have a party.*"

And the forest erupted with the sound of hooting and breaking branches.

CHAPTER 16

*W*hips erupted from my palms – one fire and one ice. Ashley howled, and Tory shouted.

But Carl and Sir... Talon the Devourer?

Those two nutjobs just cackled as they sprinted forward into the oncoming wave of shaggy, four-armed, headless monsters. The creatures did have one huge yellow eye and a double row of stained brown fangs in the center of their chests, though. Just nothing above their shoulders. Their limbs were splashed with bioluminescent paint, like we had accidentally stumbled onto the last stretch of a color run race.

And the racers wanted to eat us.

Rather than taking the time to study our attackers in more detail – because I really didn't want to get *that* close – I dove straight into the fray and began my ribbon dance of death routine. Because there were just so many bodies to hit.

At first, I was concerned I might hit a friendly, but as I swung, lashed out, and swiped with my elemental whips, my friends managed to dodge without any real effort. Like a sixth sense. Now, I knew this wasn't our first rodeo, but something felt different this time.

It wasn't like a hive mind between us or anything, but... well, I guess it kind of was.

When I swung at a nightmare of tooth and claw, Tory was instantly ducking out of the way, only to dart back in for the kill the moment my whip was out of range of her. Ashley was suddenly airborne, pouncing on a creature trying to tear out my throat as I spun to slaughter a new threat that I shouldn't have seen creeping up behind me.

Talon the Devourer – I would really need to talk to him about shortening that name – was liberally dripping with blue blood, cackling madly as he swung his great big pole-axe, hamstringing, stabbing, and slicing in one continuous whirlwind of kitty power.

Carl moved like a snake, slipping past attacks with effortless ease as if his body contained no bones, and he bellowed excitedly, as if cheering on his favorite team at a rugby match.

I found myself grinning as I slashed wildly, losing myself in the rhythm, inhaling the blood in the air, and enjoying the dying screams of our enemies. This was how it was *supposed* to be.

It swept me up.

And I danced.

Releasing all my anger, fears, and concerns. And I felt something wake up inside me with a faint *click*. I let it come out to play, shutting off my conscious mind.

I cut loose, letting instinct take over.

And it was so… *therapeutic*.

I wasn't sure how much time had passed when I realized that no one else moved, and that I was leaning on a knee. My boot rested on a small pile of the dead creatures, and I was panting from the exertion. But it was a satisfied exhaustion. Like sex.

Tory and Ashley skipped around the perimeter, singing, laughing, tallying the number of foes they had taken as they danced past the corpses, and taunting anyone still within earshot in the forest to join the party.

Carl stretched his arms behind his back, letting out a pleased sigh. "Oh, I *needed* that," he said, staring at me, eyes dancing with joy.

I nodded back, grinning.

Whispers in the back of my mind kept trying to kill my mood, warning me of something Mallory had said, but I ignored them, shoving them away like a cloud of gnats. Talon was dipping a paw into the gaping wound of a fallen monster, using it as a palette. He withdrew the bloody paw – a viscous, blue substance coating the pads – and began carefully drawing a swirling design on his chest armor.

He reached back to his palette, dipping back into the blood again, and resumed his drawing.

I nodded to myself absently. This felt right.

I began to walk through the mounds of bodies until I found my pack. I reached inside and withdrew a water canteen. I took a big sip, and then poured a little over my head. It tickled my chin rather than washing it clean, which was an odd sensation. I reached my other hand up to wipe it away and was surprised to find a short beard rather than scruff.

I stilled, the whispers in my mind pressing harder, straining to be heard.

I shook my head and took another drink.

"Gather," I commanded.

Everyone complied. Instantly. Talon nodded at me, a calculating gaze in his eyes, but I had the feeling that he was just like that, like I somehow knew him better, now. Before, he had been a housecat. Then he had let me know he could talk. Then I had seen him *act*.

And in that last action, I had learned more about him than I had in the last year of cryptic comments. It was like learning a thing from practice rather than text. Reading about it was all well and good, but *doing*... that was where true mastery lay.

I dipped my head at Talon, then the others in turn. "Well met," I said in a low, rasping tone, as if I hadn't just had a drink of water. They nodded, and I turned back to Talon. "What were we doing before the celebration?" I asked him, not remembering.

He watched me for a moment. "Conquering. That way," he said, pointing. I followed his motion, staring out at the wilderness before us. A world of possibilities waiting for me to take what I would.

I nodded greedily. "Let's move," I said. "Gather your things." I frowned as a whisper seeped out from deep within me. "Do not eat or drink from this place..." I frowned thoughtfully, not sure why that was important. We lived off this land. They each nodded, not catching my inner quarrel, and obeyed me. As they should.

A few minutes later, we were off. I pointed my hand in rapid succession, and my warriors ghosted to their positions. Talon the Devourer, my old friend, acting as guide. Elder Carl bringing up the rear. Beast Master and...

A whispered voice abruptly pressed against my mind, fighting me.

That's not her name. No, no, NO! Don't lose—

I finally shoved it back down with a growl, stumbling a step. No one noticed. As I looked back up at my trusted canine companion, her name finally came to me. Wulfra.

Wulfra and Beast Master took either flank. I strode in the center, wondering what pleasures we would discover on our way to... wherever we were going.

I couldn't remember where that was, exactly.

But I was smiling, excited to conquer it.

CHAPTER 17

*W*e walked in silence for a few hours, the night never really changing. The moons had shifted slightly in the sky, and the smells had just recently begun to grow sharper, muskier, like home. We had left the light willows behind long ago, and now walked through rolling hills of pleasant, tall grass. I saw the usual bone-bark trees in the distance, but as we travelled, they, too, faded away. No one had dared attack us, but some had tracked us. I had let them follow me like the whipped dogs they were. But they had quickly faded away, apparently deciding to pursue easier game.

My coat was tattered, and as I glanced down at it, I realized I didn't know where I had picked it up. From a fallen foe? I shrugged absently. It was made from the strange, polished and cured skin of a beast I didn't remember eating, so I must have taken it as a spoil of battle. It was well-crafted, I just didn't understand the point of the senseless brass buttons and straps that seemed to have no purpose. I had long ago torn off the strange thin shirt I had been wearing, feeling suffocated by it. I had seen no tactical advantage to the fabric, so had abandoned it. Of course, I had burned it before continuing on. No use leaving a trail.

The warm breeze now caressed my bare chest under the open coat. This was better. I would keep the coat, because it was thick enough to maybe protect my skin from a slicing blade. The strange blue pants I wore held no memory for me, either, but they were also functional, even if tighter than I would have preferred for battle.

I fingered a pocket, reading out loud. "Levi…"

Then I laughed.

Beast Master arched a brow at me from her position, but didn't speak before turning back to her scouting. Her question had been plain. We didn't have to use our *voices* to communicate. How uncivilized. We were all one family. A Band of warriors with me at their head. We *knew* each other. To our bones. We had bled together. Still, sometimes it did feel nice to talk.

"Perhaps I can add a new name to my belt," I answered her out loud, for fun. "The Levi Slayer." I shook my head, chuckling, as we topped the hill. Talon stood there, his poleaxe propped up beside him, waiting for me. Blue gore dripped from the pale weapon.

A shelled corpse twice his size lay before him, blood saturating the grey dirt. It had horns and antlers, both, but they were only a sword-blade long, so the Rarawk must have only been a fledgling. A full-grown Rarawk would have been much bigger, the horns the size of small trees.

Not that it would have mattered to Talon. He had always loved hunting them when younger.

Talon's head snapped up at me, silver eyes flashing in the moonlight. He looked… wary. I dipped my head at him, acknowledging his tiny victory in defeating the baby beast. He continued watching me for a time, then nodded, not even glancing down at the carcass. Why would he? It had only been a baby.

"There," he said, pointing. He licked a few drops of blood from his paw as he waited.

I stared ahead, and my eyes grew feverish. "I desire it as mine."

The hilltop was silent for a beat. "Then you shall have it… Wylde," Talon murmured. I frowned, wondering why he had hesitated to use my name, but before I could ask, he cocked his head, glancing over my shoulder. "Has the Honorable Elder Carl spotted our fly again?"

I heard him answer behind me. "Yes," he hissed. "But he was gone when I tried to catch him. He held up two fingers rather than one finger this time. I don't know what the devil he's up to."

Talon nodded thoughtfully, then turned back to me, waiting.

I frowned. The strange, rusty-haired Fae had been following us. We'd seen him twice now. But he neither attacked nor approached. Almost as if greeting friends from afar, but to do so twice? And the odd motion of showing us his fingers from a distant hilltop was baffling.

None of us had understood the bizarre motion. It was uncivilized. I dismissed it, staring back at the mountain Talon had pointed out just ahead. My mountain. Talon sighed. Respectfully, as always, but something was troubling him. He would tell me later, when no one else was near enough to overhear. He would not shame me in front of the others with criticism or advice. He knew better. But I had always valued his opinion.

Beast Master grunted, gaze calculating as she stared at the cavern fortress before us. Green fog slowly began to eddy around her feet as she lost focus. I coughed, and she grunted in embarrassment, the fog dissipating in a heartbeat.

I touched my temple with one finger, a dismissal of her shame. *No harm done*, it said.

She returned the gesture, slightly different, with two fingers. *Thank you.*

A cavern lay at the base of a large mulch-coated mountain that sparkled with precious-metaled trees. Neon-blue frost-water coated the peaks, and the copper trees glinted in the light of the different moons, frostcicles hanging as long as swords from their branches.

Wulfra sniffed the air, then began panting eagerly, likely thinking of food over conquest. I snapped my finger and she shifted to a whine, the ruff of her neck flaring a bit in both shame and instinctive defense. I nodded, dismissing her unintentional slight. Wulfra was exceptional in the hunt, but needed to be restrained more often than not. She was too wild, at times.

I began to laugh.

Weren't we all?

Shaking my head, I began walking. Talon stepped up beside me, his velvet boots making not a sound as they deftly stepped from rock to rock, never leaving a trail. Because his boots were designed for just such a skill. A gift he had once received.

I wished I still had some of my gifts. I could almost remember them…

But until then, I would just have to acquire some new ones.

My eyes latched onto the cave entrance ahead. Those caverns would be deep. And if the gem seeds reflecting the moonlight on the mountain were any indication, treasures galore filled the belly of the mountain.

And it would soon be mine.

I glanced back at a muttered curse and saw Elder Carl frowning as he tugged at the back of his neck. I made a chuffing sound, and everyone stopped, turning to look.

Elder Carl tugged harder at the base of his neck and ripped free a large swath of dead skin. As he held it out before him, inspecting it, I suddenly laughed, pointing at his neck.

Where he had torn away the old, dead skin, a scaled fan of horned flesh now flared, making a shielded crest around his neck, like a mane of scales and horn. He reached back to touch it and gasped. A stream meandered through the ground beside us, and Elder Carl quickly dropped the hunk of dead skin and darted up to the water to catch a view of his reflection. I left him to it, resuming our walk beside Talon.

Elder Carl hooted behind us, obviously appreciating his evolution. It had been about time. I had known Elders half his age with a crest. Late bloomer. But I also hadn't met an Elder of any age with even half his level of skill in the Dance of Bones – what his people called their sword forms.

After a short while, we reached the mouth of the cavern. Talon hesitated, sniffing the air.

The land was barren around the entrance, no metal trees, no serpentine vines, and no walking rocks. None of the usual life that nested near mulch-coated mountains.

I lowered my hands to my sides, suddenly anticipatory.

"A welcome, I think…" I murmured, sensing a presence approaching.

Talon purred beside me, fingering his poleaxe as a dozen green creatures crept out of the shadows of the cavern. Their unblemished skin shone in the moonlight, and yellow teeth greeted us as they grinned politely.

"Welcome, Wylde. Our Master has been expecting you…" one said in a low tone.

I leaned closer, sneering. "I *am* the Master…" And something about the name felt right, like it was mine. Just like Wylde. Was it a name I had forgotten, something tied to my old gifts? I hid my confusion, not wanting to show weakness here – to the green creatures *or* my Band. The goblins shared a look, not afraid, but considering. They must have heard that name of mine before, *Master*. Then they placed their palms flat on their chests, a symbol of servitude and peace. I nodded. "Lead on, goblins."

They did.

And my Band followed me into the darkness.

CHAPTER 18

*W*e didn't walk long through the wide caverns of white, shining stone. The white stone was fairly standard for a mulch-coated mountain, where the soil was not full of clay and gravel, but long, thin strips of bark that grew from the ground like weeds. But the gems peeking out of the stone walls were *not* common. Not anymore. They pulsated with light as we neared, then faded away as we passed. And there were hundreds of them.

Stonelights.

This place would definitely have treasures for me. I hadn't seen a mulch-coated mountain – or wooden mountain as some called them – still retaining its Stonelights in a long time. They were usually mined at first discovery.

As we walked, I tried to recall where I had left my gifts, and why I had chosen these strange clothes over my usual shadow armor and cloak. Maybe the absence of my gifts was causing the strange sensations inside. Forgetting my Names. That voice trying to tell me that something was wrong.

But that would all change in moments. I would build a new Name in this place. Rebuild my reputation. My core. Because that was important. A man needed to know his own Name.

And his enemies needed to know it, too.

Or else we... faded.

I shivered at that. The only thing that I was truly afraid of.

The goblins leading us filed to either side of a massive stone door, lowering their gazes as we walked between them. They held out an arm to the door, the other arm placed palm down over their chest in submission. I grunted, disgusted. Too much submission was sickening. Weak.

I assessed the door, appreciating the beauty of the rippling stone. It reminded me of when I had been a youngling, staring out at the oceans of rock – rippling and undulating for leagues and leagues beyond the shore of my home. I had even heard that the stone shifted to white *water* at some point in the far distance. An ocean... of *water*! How *ridiculous*! Everyone knew that true water could only collect *inland*.

I had also heard that an island sat in the middle of that white water. A white island. With a white palace perched on a cliff. And that a true monster of a Manling lived there...

But those were just myths, of course. Manling Tales. Stories the Fae told their children.

I shivered involuntarily at some whispered inner thought. *I am a Manling.*

I didn't let my surprise show, but I suddenly felt very confused. How had I been a Manling in the Land of the Fae? And how had I forgotten such a crime? I carefully scanned my Band, wondering if they knew this about me. Or if they had also suffered some version of memory loss. Surely, they would have slit my throat while I slept if they knew I was a Manling. A monster.

Only Talon was staring at me. He nodded one time, and then placed his open paws against his chest very deliberately.

I curled back my lip, a challenge, but he continued pressing his paws into his chest, silver eyes pleading. He *knew*. Knew I was a vile Manling, and still obeyed. That... that didn't make any sense. I brushed three fingers from lips to chin in a flippant gesture, warning him for good measure. He nodded, then flexed his paws, his claws biting through his armor and into his flesh, drawing blood. A sign of undying loyalty. I almost embraced him with two pats to the belly for that, but I knew he wouldn't appreciate it.

His kind never did like more than one pat.

Elder Carl sniffed the air suddenly, sensing the fresh blood, but his gaze latched onto the goblins as he settled into an aggressive stance. Talon lifted a paw and lapped at the blood, then wiped the resulting saliva across the shallow wounds on his chest. They instantly closed, and I saw Elder Carl sniff the air with a nervous frown. I hated that his saliva couldn't do that for others. It would be a handy trick for battle, being able to cure wounds with a lick.

I dipped my head at Talon, letting him know I had heard his message, but that I would remain wary. It was a sign of respect. Talon grinned suddenly, approving of my compliment. I snapped my fingers and Elder Carl flinched. His shoulders only relaxed after he saw no concern in my eyes, and then he turned his attention back to the door.

Whatever the blood had been, The Master had just told him it didn't matter. Wylde had spoken. So, it didn't matter to him any longer.

Blind trust. And respect.

But as I turned back to the still rippling stone door, watching the tides of rock and gravel splash back and forth as if under a raging storm, I found myself very troubled. How had I forgotten such a thing about myself? Being a Manling? Forgotten my past? And what about this place had made me suddenly remember it?

The memory of that cursed rust-haired man showing us his fingers from a distance troubled me. I growled to myself, throwing out a hand, because when I was troubled, I broke things. Decimated things.

The blast of power from my hand struck the center of the door like a piece of wood thrown in a stone ocean – the two elements incompatible. The center blasted forward under the pressure, and ripples exploded out from the blast, splashing onto the walls, spraying the goblins with droplets of gravel. They screamed as the razor-sharp stone ripped those in front to shreds. The others didn't move, merely waited.

The door broke under my blast, and an avalanche of sand and gravel splashed to the floor of the cavern, sinking into an unseen grate before it could splash over my Band. Of course, I wouldn't have let it do so, but it was nice that I didn't have to concern myself with it.

Haunting, piping music drifted to our ears from beyond the opening, and without further thought, I strode through. The goblins followed at a safe distance, eyes downcast as Beast Master and Wulfra snarled a warning. They kept their hands to their chests, and never lifted their eyes, looking meek and subdued, even though everyone knew goblins considered pixies to be delicacies and murdered everything else for fun.

We entered a vast auditorium large enough to fit a palace inside without touching the ceiling. Wave after wave of goblins sat on the floor, facing us, eyes downcast, also with hands to chests. I didn't slow, striding down the auditorium in a path between the two masses of goblins, like a royal carpet.

Ahead of me sat a throne.

And on that throne sat a king.

Great antlers like that of a White Stag protruded from the sides of his skull, easily two sword-blades tall and wide, and *dozens* of points on horn. And they were stained brown, but with white tips. The antlers seemed to grow and shrink at random, like a nest of serpents.

A white-spotted goblin stood beside the throne, glaring at me. He looked bigger than his brethren. Not by much, but he also wore nicer hides, with a bit of blue fur lining the edges. I dismissed him. He was beneath my attention, even if this king obviously valued him above others.

The king wore the oddest clothes I had ever seen, but they fit him perfectly. Then again, he was a king, and could wear whatever he pleased during his season of reign.

Until a new season was born, and a new king emerged...

The cloth of his ensemble shone, not a loose thread in sight, despite the harsh environment of a cavern. Surely, it would have torn against stone. But it was crisp, precise, and had nary a wrinkle in sight. The pants had a sharp folded crease down the center of each leg, and his feet were bare. A blinding white shirt was tucked into his pants, and a glaring red strip of fabric hung down from a similarly-crisp folded collar buttoned close to his neck. The red cloth seemed to look like a very meticulous knot at the throat. Was that a subtle challenge? To wear a noose around your throat, daring your enemy? Over the shirt was draped a well-fitting coat that matched the pants, and a band of gold adorned his wrist.

I noticed a faint, repetitive ticking, and cocked my head, the sound familiar for some reason.

A watch. A suit. Armani, most likely... I barely managed to hide my gasp as the voice struck like a whip. Was it trying to tell me the man's name? Armani? But the voice was gone.

I jerked my head, staring the king straight in the eyes. His face was entirely normal, like mine, but not a whisker marked his jaw. Entirely clean shaven. Which was unheard of. Who wanted to look like a woman?

Except... Fae did unusual things like that. In the Royal Courts. *This man works for the Queens...* I found that I was snarling in disgust.

The king took one look at me, and then began to laugh.

My Band instantly bristled at the challenge, the mockery.

I readied myself to redecorate the halls of my new throne in blood...

Kingkiller would be a nice, fresh Name to start with...

CHAPTER 19

The king held up a hand before I could move. "My, my, my… That took a hold of you rather quickly, didn't it?" he said, eyes twinkling.

I opened my mouth to shout for my Band to attack goblins, and to leave no survivors.

The king was mine. And I wanted that shiny band on his wrist. It looked… appealing.

But the king flung out an empty hand, and a wave of power washed over us.

We collapsed to our knees, gasping, shivering, and huddled together in a tight mass.

"Stop!" a voice commanded. I peeled open an eye to see a horde of goblins staring down at us, licking their lips hungrily.

"What the *fuck?*" I shouted, scrambling to my feet, prepared for an ambush. My eyes darted about wildly, and I saw that Tory and Ashley did the same, both utterly naked, hair a mess of sweaty tangles as if they hadn't brushed it in a few weeks. Or washed it. Hadn't they looked different a minute ago? They locked eyes with me, looking terrified, confused, and very, very concerned at the army of goblins staring at us like we were grilled steaks.

Where the hell were we?

I turned my head to see Carl shaking his head as if at a bad smell. He had a horned crest behind his neck, and it was currently clicking like a rattlesnake. He didn't look as bewildered, but more as if he had woken from a pleasant dream. I turned to look for Sir Muffle Paws... No, that's not right. He had asked me to call him...

"Talon... the Devourer," the same voice I had heard a few seconds ago said as my eyes locked on my... cat? But he wasn't a cat. He looked right, as if wearing his favorite clothes. In fact, he stood as I had last seen him – a bipedal warrior feline. He held out his hands in a peaceful gesture. I blinked at him, shaking my head. Then I turned to the voice that had spoken.

And I saw the antlered man on the throne. I slowly began to remember, feeling as if I was two entirely different people. The man nodded slowly, hands in his suit pocket. "We have much to discuss..." he said after a long silence. "But first, we should clothe your friends." His eyes glittered with amusement. "Unless they prefer their current state?" he asked with a leer.

They instantly stammered that they wanted clothes, covering themselves up with free hands as best they could. Oddly enough, everyone still had their packs.

"You... You're Pan," I said in a whisper, my mind juggling two realities. Two worlds.

The man shrugged. "I prefer Oberon, here. But, yes. We are..." his eyes grew distant, considering, "the same, Manling."

"Master," I mumbled, correcting him for some reason.

He grinned back. "Yes. Master Temple. Is it coming back now? You've had a taste of our lands. If you had taken any longer to get here, I might have grown concerned. Then again, it's all part of the invitation. Still, it would have been disappointing. To fail so soon. You have so much potential, you see..." he began to laugh to himself.

My mind raced as bits and pieces began coming back to me. Almost as if I was watching a movie of a different group of people. We had traversed the Land of the Fae like reunited, nomadic conquerors. A tribe. A band of killers. And we had relished in it. Because it had been our lives for years, almost since childhood. We had drifted apart for some time, and then suddenly been reunited this evening. No, that wasn't right...

I shivered. What the literal fuck had Mallory brought us to?

"You did well, boy. You almost earned a new Name, but you skated past it. Like reaching for something on ice. By the time you missed it, you were already too far away to try again. That's why I pressed us here faster. To see *him*," Talon said in a respectful tone.

I glared at him, remembering that doppelganger of me, controlling my actions, my thoughts. It was... unbelievable. "That entire time... you *knew?*" I growled.

He nodded. "It is why I came. To watch your back."

"Why didn't you stop me. Stop us?" I shouted. "We just got blind-sided, believing in a reality – an entire *life* – that never *existed!*"

"Actively stopping you would have meant failure. I can only guide. Reminding you *why* you must proceed, or warning you why you must hold back will destroy the world as you know it." He sounded ashamed, but resolute. "He has something for you, but you must earn it. It is an honor to be Invited. Even though you might not know it. Hundreds of years have passed since the Invitation has been given."

I frowned at him, having no idea what he was talking about.

"Right. Well, I fancy something green, tiny, and medium-rare, so unless someone starts talking, we're about to have a cookout," I hissed, turning to glare at the goblins behind us.

Oberon snapped a command, and the goblins were instantly gone.

Entirely.

Leaving us in an empty room with him.

I whirled, stunned. "What the hell?" I saw that the only remaining goblin was the bigger, white-spotted one with the blue furred armor. His attendant? His General? I pointed a shaking finger, furious. "Fuck you, in particular," I snarled, preparing to blast the white and green shithead into the throne.

"I would rather you not decimate my people, Master Temple..." Oberon said. "Kaba, here, is my voice. My... right hand, you could say. Since you don't speak goblin, I'll leave his full name out of the conversation. It's over..." he furrowed a brow, as if pulling up a statistic from the very edges of his mind. Or, like asking his counterpart, Pan, to tell him something. Oberon's eyes finally cleared, and he nodded. "Over seventy syllables long."

I grunted in disbelief. "Kablooie, it is. Today's your lucky day. I won't kill you. Yet."

The goblin's lips thinned, and I got the feeling he didn't like me changing his name. Good.

Oberon spoke. "That is most kind of you, Wylde— I mean, Master

Temple." He let out an amused laugh. "Let's go get settled, refreshed, and then we shall talk. Then you shall receive the details of your Invitation. And in successful conclusion of that, hopefully learn your reward."

I frowned at that. "Earn, you mean... Not *learn*."

Oberon just fucking grinned. Kablooie also looked satisfied.

"I like Pan a whole helluva lot better," I muttered. He laughed out loud at that, and then snapped his fingers. A pair of goblins appeared, palms to chests, not meeting our eyes.

I shivered, remembering how I had communicated like that only minutes ago. A feral, primal sort of communication. Then the details of our fight, our battle, our journey, and the world we had traveled came back to me in bits and pieces. I was momentarily overwhelmed as I remembered seeing a stone ocean, having memories as a child, hearing stories about a white island.

The Hatter... He was *here*. In the Land of the Fae. Well, kind of. It seemed he was a myth to them. A... Manling Tale instead of a Fairy Tale. The Fae apparently viewed us much as we viewed them. A frightening enemy. A menace. A disease. A danger.

So, why in the living fuck had Mallory brought us here and then abandoned us? What was this Invitation? I shook my head and looked back up. The two goblins had politely handed folded piles of clothes to Tory and Ashley. They looked like canvas togas of sorts, with belts to cinch around the waist, earning a zero on the sexy factor of the two usually-stunning women.

They didn't look happy about this fact, and I very wisely didn't speak my thoughts.

Because I was too busy remembering how they had looked only a short time ago. I hadn't even called them by their names. Tory had been Beast Master, a wild tribeswoman with glowing veins. Ashley had been Wulfra, which meant Wolf Queen. And she had been a Shaman-looking bipedal werewolf.

I glanced down at myself, remembering that I hadn't changed like them. Well... My hand reached up to brush a thick beard. Other than that, I was the same. But it had only been hours since we first arrived, since that first battle. Not long enough to grow a beard.

And who had that man been. The red-haired human waving his fingers at us? Something about him seemed familiar, but I hadn't gotten a close look. Just a twenty-something ginger.

I turned back to Oberon, considering. Oberon was the name of the Fae King.

But there were still a few Fae Queens I was suddenly nervous about.

Because they didn't really like me, or Tory, and we were deep in their world, now. With no idea why we were here in the first place... Except we had an Invitation, whatever *that* meant.

I found Oberon suddenly sitting in a large wooden chair at the head of a table with enough chairs for my crew.

Exactly enough chairs for my crew. Not one more seat available. I shivered. Had he just imagined it here? I was beginning to realize I knew very little about the Fae and their abilities. But I did remember using the strange power against his front door.

"What's going on, Oberon? Why did you summon me? What is this *Invitation?*"

He thumbed his lip as I sat down. My friends joined me, eyes furtively checking the room for threats. "Doesn't feel very nice, does it?" he asked.

I frowned. "What?"

"Being summoned somewhere without knowing why. Grates on you, doesn't it?" I nodded. "Yet you humans have done this to creatures for centuries. Since you figured out how."

I leaned back in my chair, and finally nodded. "True," I said. "So, am I being punished for all the humans? Is that why I've been dumped here with my friends?"

He shook his head, grinning with amusement. "No, I just like pointing out Manling faults. Makes me happy." He leaned forward suddenly. "The Queens don't like you very much, I'm afraid." Then he chuckled. "But that's okay. I'm your friend. And I don't like *them* very much."

I ground my teeth, wanting him to get on with it, but he seemed content to poke and prod me. "Can we skip the cryptic stuff? I get it. You're different from humans. Now—"

"Yes, you had a taste of that not too long ago, didn't you? We are *very* different from humans. From Manlings, as we call them." He turned to the girls. "Even the women are referred to in such a way. Like you call us the Fae, we call you the Manlings. Was it fun to taste our way of life?"

Tory and Ashley shivered, but Carl spoke up. "Oh, yes. Delightful!" Talon looked bored.

"Not really my cup of tea," I said, scowling at Carl. That fucking guy...

"Well, you might need to acquire the taste if you want to survive, Master Temple."

I frowned at him. "And why would I do that?"

"It's the only way to kill a god."

The room grew as still as a winter night during a snowstorm. "Becoming Fae will let me kill a god?" I finally asked in confusion.

He waggled his fingers dismissively, as if I had missed the entire point. "We'll get to that later. I have a request of you."

"That's funny. I have a request of you, too. Send us home, Bonehead."

His smile disappeared, and Kablooie hissed, hand darting to the hilt of a dagger on his belt. Oberon punched him in the jaw with absolutely no effort. Kablooie went flying to strike the wall with a grunt, and then collapsed bonelessly to the floor.

No one moved. For about thirty seconds.

Kablooie finally climbed to his feet with a few groans, dusted off his hands, checked his head for wounds, and then respectfully walked back up to Oberon, head bowed. "Sorry, Master."

Oberon nodded absently, and then turned back to me. I closed my mouth. Wow, with servants like that... "I have more lenience than most of my kind," he said, leaning forward, "but it is not infinite. Not even close, *Manling*... I'm. Not. Pan." I could feel a cyclone of magic whirling around him. But it wasn't like any magic I had ever sensed before. It was like... trying to grab the ocean with your hands, throwing starlight, licking fire with a tongue, drinking stone. I shivered. His magic stick was bigger than my magic stick. "Best you remember it," he growled.

I held up a hand, a peaceful gesture, because he was obviously certifiable if he would strike his own right-hand-goblin for defending him too well. "Please explain it. To my tiny, Manling brain," I added, self-deprecating. "Why did you ask Pan to extend an Invitation to me. To us."

"I have a test for you. Someone has been taken. One of yours. To get them back, I require a favor."

"You took one of my friends?" I snarled, the wood crackling underneath my fingertips. I squeezed and the wood disintegrated to ash, but I wasn't really sure how. It wasn't fire. It was... something else. Something just at the edge of my knowledge. Something… just like I had felt when my mind had been overridden by the Fae allure. When I had obliterated his door.

Oberon studied me. "Actually, I did not take your friend. A friend of yours took another friend of yours. To encourage your… motivation. They have a vested interest, it seems. I would have Invited you to the game anyway, but they doubted your resolve. Well, not *resolve*. Let's say they placed high value on your disdain for authority, for anyone trying to manipulate you without leverage."

A friend had betrayed me? *Again?* I needed to incorporate a test or something before I gave anyone a *friend* card in the future. Unless… Oberon was lying. Or bending his words. My friends felt tense, ready to throw down, but they didn't look too hopeful about it. Except Talon. He looked bored, watching us with his silver eyes.

"Speak. Plainly. Or we all die here. Or at least we die *trying*," I whispered in a very low tone, feeling the alien tendrils of power calling out to me from the land beneath my feet. I wasn't exactly sure what to do with them, or even if I could do anything with them, but I could sense them, which was startling.

And I saw it in Oberon's eyes. Fear, but also… anticipation. As if he was anxious at the fact that I was at least partly succeeding in… something. Whatever that something was.

"The Queens hate you. Succeed in my request, and I will grant you safe passage home. And in this request, perhaps you will learn something useful for back home."

"How to kill a god…" I breathed. After a long pause, he nodded. "What is the request?"

He leaned back in his chair, crossing his legs. "You've heard of Changelings?"

"Stealing a human child and taking them into the Land of the Fae. You replace the stolen child with a Fae lookalike. I presume you gain twice in this endeavor. Your Changeling can learn more about our world, and the stolen human also teaches you of our ways. But you can also brainwash the child to become a hybrid of sorts… Believing like the Fae, but possessing human blood."

Oberon nodded in approval. "The Queens do this often. *Picking up a new pet*, they call it. I had chance to see an acquisition of theirs some years ago. A bright young Manling."

I wanted to snarl, but took a deep breath. Just one more reason to hate the Queens. "And?"

"The Queens have decided to kill him as retribution for their Changeling being murdered in your world. I desire them to fail. This Manling made..." he tapped his lips thoughtfully, "an *impression* on me. I don't wish him harmed for a crime he did not commit."

I watched him for a few silent moments, and then turned to Talon. "What do you make of this?"

"Lord Oberon speaks the truth," he said, idly sharpening a claw on a small pocket-sized sharpening stone, like a human would smooth out their nails with a file.

I turned to Ashley and Tory. "A child is in danger. What do you want to do?"

Their eyes were hard, merciless. "Have some fun," Ashley said.

Tory nodded. "Make an example," she added.

I didn't smile back, but instead turned to Carl. For some reason, he still had the crest around his neck. As if noticing me looking at it, it suddenly folded flat against his neck. I blinked. Huh. He really *was* like that venom-spitting dinosaur in that dinosaur park movie. "And you?" I asked.

He shrugged. "I don't really understand the first part about the child, or why we should care about him. But if you're asking what I want to *do*, in *general*," he said, shrugging, "murder sounds satisfying."

"Fucking Carl," Talon chuckled, shaking his head.

Carl turned to him, frowning, not understanding.

I sighed. Some things never changed. I turned back to Oberon. "We retrieve the boy, and you let us go back home? What am I missing? I didn't hear anything about my so-called friend being kidnapped. And I don't understand what you get out of this. If we save the kid—"

"You can bet your ass we're not leaving him with you," Tory snarled, basically reading my mind.

I nodded at her. "What she said."

Oberon frowned. "I don't want the boy. What would I know about raising a Manling?"

I wanted to lay my head on the table and scream. So, now I had to save him, keep him alive, and then... what, return him to parents who thought him *dead*?

Talon, or Sir Muffle paws, rather, sensed this. "Just tell him. We've been here long enough, already. Sir."

Kablooie grimaced at the delayed title, the lack of respect, but Oberon nodded. Talon must demand some heavy respect around here to speak so openly among the Fae. And ol' Kablooie didn't like it. But the thing that concerned me most? Talon had shown *me* – or *Wylde*, at least – more respect than anyone today, and he was openly disrespecting Oberon.

And I remembered *knowing* Talon. As a young feline. What the fuck was that about?

Oberon cleared his throat. "The Queens will be most displeased with you absconding with their prize. That is my reward. Their fury is my ecstasy. But I also require you to steal their high-heeled shoes. They each have a colored pair. One blue, and one red."

I blinked.

Ashley roared with laughter. "*Shoes?*" she finally hooted. "You want us to steal a woman's *heels?*"

Tory was shaking her head. "We're all going to die."

"Okay, that's pretty random," I said, not liking this one bit. "But what about your leverage? My alleged kidnapped friend? Who is it? And surely you could have found someone else to do this task. Someone familiar with this world. To steal some shoes."

Oberon was shaking his head. "We do not work that way. Open war, yes. But other than that, we keep our hands clean."

I sighed, remembering. "Cat's paws."

"Easy, wizard…" Talon murmured darkly.

I wanted to scream again. "This isn't just about what you've told me out loud, is it? What else is up for grabs? I doubt learning how to be a shoe thief is going to help me back home."

He snapped his fingers, and a strange fruit suddenly sat before each of us. It looked like an orange, but blue. "I almost forgot. You'll be wanting to eat these before you try to rob the Queens. Disguises. Otherwise, you won't make it past the gates."

I studied the strange fruit as if it were a rattlesnake. But I shoved it into my pack, as did the others. "You haven't answered my question about the friend," I growled.

He snapped his fingers again in agreement, as if happy for the question. "This is your *Invitation*. Every Invitation needs a quest, and it's been so long since we've extended one to a Manling. This will be *fun*! Like a Manling Tale. Save a child, find your friend in the wild, steal some shoes, and return home to kill a god," he chuckled, entirely too pleased. Kablooie nodded his agreement, folding his arms.

"What do you mean, *find my friend in the—*"

Oberon interrupted me. "Remember what you learned here so far. *Control* it, but *savor* it. Like a fine wine... But you mustn't let your friends get too drunk. They need to find a... *driver* to get home," he said, eyelids growing heavy, as if about to doze off.

"Driver? How *do* we get home? Return here?" I asked urgently.

"Love is fire. For some it strengthens. For some it destroys. History, knowledge, fire..." he trailed off, yawning. "Only savage hope can quench a heartflame, but only love can conquer savagery. One coin, two sides," he chuckled, eyes a million miles away. Talon began climbing to his feet, nodding at Oberon as if listening to something. Love? Fire? Was he hinting about this place, or back home? The war. Aphrodite was a love goddess. But fire could be attributed to a lot of people. A female version of Prometheus, maybe? But Hope... that could be Pandora. Was he saying...

"What—" I began.

But we were suddenly in a moonlit glade, and Oberon and Kablooie were gone.

And we were all back in the forms we had taken before meeting Oberon.

A tribe of maniacal beasts with their packs on their backs. They turned to face me, eyes expectant. And there was nothing human about those eyes. They were all savage, all Fae, all wild. And they stared at their leader, Wylde, awaiting orders.

I groaned inwardly, because I had somehow managed to retain my sense of self, but I could feel that darker shadow over my shoulders, watching me, urging me, baiting me. Wylde wanted to play with his friends. And I had a feeling I needed to let him, while somehow keeping him in check. Because I needed to figure out what the hell Oberon had meant about many different things. Fucking Fae, speaking in riddles while asking for help.

This was going to be un-fun.

CHAPTER 20

I faced them, and tried to think and look like Wylde, hoping I could sell it. "Discuss," I growled.

They frowned at me. "Kill?" Carl asked.

Tory – or *Beast Master*, as she went by – nodded slowly. "Of course."

Ashley – Wulfra – stared back at me with eyes like diamonds. Her voice was rough, a low feminine growl. "Kill and eat. Harry our quarry."

I nodded, feigning consideration, but only half-listening. They weren't answering the question I had hoped, because they didn't really remember it, I was guessing. I tried to remember some of the hand motions that had seemed so second nature to me, but couldn't come up with one. Talon spoke up. "Perhaps Wylde needs a few moments in private to collect his thoughts after privately meeting with Oberon…" he offered.

I turned to him sharply, noticing that my tribe looked suddenly interested, as if they hadn't known I had a private moment with Oberon, but that it could promise great things for them. They nodded enthusiastically.

"Yes," I said, staring off in the distance, trying to gauge where we were in relation to where we had been. I didn't recognize anything. "Talon, a word," I said, turning away from my tribe, expecting Talon to follow. I called out over a shoulder. "Perimeter!" I snapped.

Grunts answered me.

I didn't hear Talon creeping along behind me, but I could sense him.

Once out of earshot behind a large tree a dozen yards away, I stopped, speaking out loud but not facing him.

"What the fuck is going on, cat?"

"If you want my assistance, you better start calling me Talon. Or the Devourer. Or Talon the Devourer. Not fucking *cat*, Nate."

I shook my head at his arrogance, and even though a small part of me was happy to hear him address me by my Manling name – meaning he wasn't brain-washed like the rest – I still had too much on my mind to be happy. "I *remember* you. From a young age. What the *hell*?"

He sounded very troubled as he tried to answer. "I… don't know. But…" he shot a nervous glance my way. "I felt the same connection. I remembered hunting with you… here."

I shivered. "Right. Okay. Well, that obviously didn't happen, so we should think on that. But it's not our biggest problem. What am I supposed to do with them?" I pointed. "Why are they back to psychopath-mode? Why am I *not* back to psychopath-mode? Fucking *Wylde*? What the hell kind of a name is that? And how do some people know it," I leaned closer, "if none of it ever really *happened*? He doesn't really *exist*!"

Talon scuffed a rock with his velvet boots. Even this action didn't leave a trail. The rock he scuffed fell into another smaller hole, looking as if it had been there for a thousand years. I shook my head in disbelief, staring at his boots. Couldn't even kick a rock in anger with those things.

"I remember you getting those. I think…" I whispered softly, shaking my head in disbelief.

Talon flinched, staring at me before recomposing himself. "That's… impossible."

I shrugged. "My question stands. How am I supposed to control them without becoming like them, and without them getting wise to the fact that I'm a… Manling? Not their precious Wylde."

Talon shrugged. "I will help how I can. I can mention, offhandedly, that in order to abduct the child, Oberon asked you to act like a Manling, to get in touch with the Manling Tales from your youth, so that the child will listen to you."

I nodded slowly. "That's… actually a really good idea. Might cover up any slips."

Talon grimaced. "But that's not the full answer. I think… you need to learn to become a little more like *them* at the same time. I think this is the real test. You need to teach them to be a little more human while you need to learn to become a little more… wild. A little more Fae."

I sighed. "But why?"

Talon shrugged. "Just a guess. I can help guide, but I don't have the answers. And if I did…"

I frowned. "That's what Oberon told you at the end. What you were nodding about." Talon might as well have clenched his butt cheeks together, as fast as his lips tightened. "Who did they take?"

"I don't know. But I can tell you he wasn't lying. Someone was taken and they are here. I think they're here alone, not as a captive. Well, not in a jail, but a captive of the Fae World nonetheless…" he added.

I blinked. "They can't leave. Someone scooped them up, dropped them off, and then disappeared. All to motivate me to do this… thing. Save a kid. Steal some fucking shoes."

Talon shrugged, staring out at the fields before us. I could see hills in the near distance. We were in a valley of sorts. "Perhaps," Talon said.

"Does that mean we need to be on the lookout for a wanderer? Like that guy with the red hair? Because I didn't recognize him. Maybe they do this regularly. Drop off a mortal in their world to feed the Wildfae."

Talon nodded absently. "Perhaps. I've been away for… some time. I'm not up to date on their sporting events."

I shivered at that. Kidnapping was a sporting event? "What *are* you, Talon?"

His fur bristled up as if I had rubbed it the wrong way. "A cat. Leave it at that, or I walk."

I almost held up a hand to calm him down, but caught Ashley studying us from a distance. Such a motion would not be used by Wylde.

"Fine. I'll drop it. But after, we'll talk. Or no more cream at Chateau Falco. No more birdies to play with, either," I added, referring to Hugin and Munin.

Sir Muffle Paws looked genuinely alarmed for a moment before he saw my smirk. "Fucking wizards," he yowled softly.

"Maybe this person, this friend, really is a captive in a prison. Like the Queens' prison. Where the kid is." I frowned. "Wait. The Queens have different palaces, right? Which one has the kid? And how far apart are their castles? I thought this was going to take a few days. That's what Mallory said."

Talon nodded. "The Queens are hosting a dinner. To celebrate the boy's execution."

I groaned. "That's convenient. And not. It means everyone will be watching him. He's the star of the show…"

Talon grunted affirmation. "But they're all in the same place, at least," he said, carefully.

I sighed, taking a few steps forward, pretending to scan the horizon. "Well, it's still night. We have time. It's only been a few hours."

"True."

"How far away are we?"

He stared at the land before us, thinking. "Half a day's hard jog."

I thought about that. "Well, the land is crawling with monsters, so let's call it a day." A day of hunting wild monsters with my own Band of murdering monsters. All while trying to become monster myself. I was scared of that.

How I had felt as Wylde had been so natural, so right. I saw. I wanted. I took. No middle steps. Why on earth would I need to learn how to tap into that? And what had Oberon been talking about with all his cryptic words? Fire, love, history, coins, hope, ancestors. Was he trying to confuse me? Or was it relevant? And if so, was it relevant for *here*, in the Fae World, or back *home*, with the Greek war?

The wooden disk at my throat felt suddenly tight, constricting.

"Go back to them," I said. "Tell them we will move soon. I'll be there in a minute, and will think while we march. The constant vigilance will give the others something else to focus on."

"Yes, Wylde," Talon purred, then slipped away without a sound, leaving me alone in a glade of what looked like glass trees for chrissake. What the hell kind of world was this? Wooden mountains, glowing trees, three moons, oceans of *stone*?

I remembered that all too brief sensation of magic with Oberon. The wildness of it. The utter irrationality of it. It defied everything I knew about magic, and I had about as good a chance as breathing water as I did understanding it.

Let alone *pretending* to have it mastered.

But I really didn't have much of a choice.

A poor kid and an incompetent friend needed my help.

CHAPTER 21

I had thought long and hard on my situation, and had come to the conclusion that it sucked.

Hard.

But I persevered. I was a wizard. A Temple. Master Temple. I would get through this, somehow. Being able to remain silent for longer periods actually helped me. With my band of psychopaths, talking wasn't really a priority, and was considered unnecessary most times.

The best way to think about it was that silence was common to them. Like animals. A pack didn't constantly yap at each other. They made occasional sounds, but the rest of their communication was silent, with subtle motions.

As long as I kept my face broody, everyone thought I was normal. I could talk, but I couldn't be chatty. Which gave me time to think, unmolested, which was a new experience for me.

But I still felt like I was walking on eggshells. Like I was different from them. A sheep hiding in a pack of wolves.

I spent the first hour of our walk towards the distant palace carefully dipping into that darker side of me, trying to recall the communication gestures Wylde had used. It felt like cautiously reaching into a calm pond, and never knowing if the Loch Ness Monster had chosen that moment to be in the exact spot you were reaching toward, ready to grab you and pull you into the depths to turn you into sushi.

Since I had actually *lived* as Wylde for a short time, it was fairly easy to remember the ones I had already used or seen earlier tonight.

One finger to the temple meant *no harm done.*

Two fingers to the temple meant *thank you.*

Palm flat to the chest meant *servitude*, or *peace.* Flexing your nails to break skin while doing it meant *undying loyalty.*

Brushing three fingers down from lips to chin was a *warning.*

But other stuff?

I tried making a world in my head for Wylde. A construct of a home. I imagined him as a solitary, bearded sage living in a cave at the top of a cliff. I filled his cave with spoils – food, drink, women, and fire. And I gave him a club to hit things with. It was actually kind of fun.

With his home complete, I remembered my brief lesson with Ganesh, when I had been attempting to awaken my Beast, to dominate it, and initially felt like this would be easy.

I was wrong.

I approached the fire outside his cave, not locking eyes with the wild man sitting on a log. I noticed his shoulders bunch up, and his fist clench his club aggressively, but I was sure to keep my eyes down and my palms on my chest, a symbol of *peace.*

He had jumped to his feet, roared at me, and then swung his club dangerously close to my face, missing me by inches. Then he promptly grabbed two women from his cave and disappeared from sight. I sat by the fire, heart racing, and waited.

It was a long time until he came back out, and he exited his cave like a deer stepping out into a new field at dawn. Or like a wolf creeping up on that deer. My arm was metaphysically sore from keeping it placed on my chest the entire time, in case he had decided to watch me from the cave. He took ten minutes to walk to the fire, and then cautiously sat down.

I grunted at him.

Silence stretched for a few moments, and I began to grow wary of that club I had stupidly given him.

But then he grunted back, begrudgingly.

I had managed to keep a smile off my cheeks, and simply sat in silence with him.

I thought, and thought very loudly, trying to let my body naturally move to match my words, in what I hoped would be decipherable to him.

You're stronger than me.

Wylde grunted self-importantly.

I have need of your knowledge.

He was silent for a very long time, then slapped his knees twice in quick succession. *Price.*

I stopped myself from nodding back, and decided to act more like I was at a zoo, trying to talk to an animal. I wouldn't nod my head at a lion. I would try to stare him in the eyes and let him know I agreed, wrapping danger around my shoulders, hiding any sign of weakness.

Life, I thought at him, squeezing the palms placed against my chest, a sign that if I had claws, I would be bleeding, emphasizing that my word was not a threat.

He grunted, but it sounded different, like a question.

We are hunted. Enemies surround us. He jumped to his feet, gripping his club. I thought hard. *Not here. In another place...* Wylde clenched his jaw, looking frustrated, and he let out a light snarl of confusion. I split my mind in two, and let him see what my real eyes saw, walking through a crystal-clear glass glade of what looked like grass. I let him see each of my Band, and then imagined myself as I was now. *Here.*

Wylde howled in alarm, looking up at the sky, and then down to me, and then back at my vision, which was apparently to his right. I knew he wasn't merely viewing our surroundings, because something was off with his eyes. They were focused on a big picture a foot ahead of him, where technically only empty air was visible. Like he was staring through a window.

We are the same. We share a body. A mind. A heart... I thought with as deep a meaning as I could muster. I felt sharp pings in my temples at the strain of maintaining two worlds – one fake, and one real, as I followed my merry band of killers through the Land of the Fae.

All while creating, maintaining, and trying to occupy an entirely imagined world with a part of myself that had been deeply buried for eons. Since the dawn of time. My primitive self.

Wylde slowly turned to look at me, and gave me an awkward nod.

I blinked, slowly nodding back.

My thoughts were bleeding back on him, and he was trying to speak to me in *my* language.

He hooted triumphantly, and curled his lips back in a horrifying snarl. It took me a moment to realize he was trying to smile at me. I very dramatically, and very slowly, let a smile creep onto my face.

He watched, studying me, and then duplicated it in a less nightmarish fashion. I nodded back slowly, encouraging him. *Yes. Just like this. You can feel me, now?*

He grunted, and then ran back to his cave, shrieking like a banshee.

I groaned, letting my imagination close like the curtains of a play. My mouth was dry, and my vision swam. Talon glared at me, then quickly commanded everyone to hurry up and move.

Because they were all frowning at me, looking confused. Concerned.

I tried to act like Wylde, and growled warningly at them. Very literally growled.

They flinched, and their shoulders began to relax as they obeyed Talon's command and increased their pace. I did the same, despite my exhausted mind and body.

It had worked! To some extent. I had established communication with Wylde. We jogged for ten minutes, and the physical exertion helped me, surprisingly. I reached into my pack, and chewed on some jerky. I wondered if I would have the time to learn what I needed before we reached the palace.

Because it was on the horizon, now.

Talon called for a halt, and I grunted affirmatively. Then I strode up to Ashley, shoved her with a shoulder, and sat on the rock she had been about to occupy. The wolf growled subtly at me as she strode away to another rock, but I could tell she felt affection for me. A sense of pride in submitting to one as great as Wylde. That she was important enough for me to want to take her seat.

Any other time I would have simply shaken my head in disbelief. The real Ashley would have eaten my face for acting like that. Which was odd to consider. Me being feral to her here made her more docile. Me being feral in the *domesticated* world would have made her more violent. Talk about confusing.

But it was beginning to feel normal, which had me concerned. I needed to get close to that person I had temporarily been. Wylde.

Without becoming him, in fact.

Or else none of us would even *want* to leave. We would simply want to *hunt*.

Talon strode up to the clearing, and clicked his tongue a few times, signifying we would take a rest for an hour and then double-time. The others instantly rolled onto their backs, and went to sleep. I didn't.

I watched the night around us, silently marveling at the strange woods around us. Metal trees were just ahead, glinting with what looked like golden fruit. No more neon glow surrounded us, but the shine from that metal was intriguing. Like a forest of treasure. The ground was covered with golden brush, like any other forest would have twigs and leaves of wood.

Confident that everyone was asleep, I very carefully reached out to my magic.

The world fought against me, urging me to touch *her* magic, not my basic, elementary world's magic. I blinked, listening to it for a few moments. Not obeying, but listening. Because it really was like a conversation... but a conversation that I couldn't translate back into words.

It was astounding. The world around me called out, whispering, seducing, sensing me like a sentient being.

A furred paw slapped me across the jaw, only slightly diminished by my thick beard. Talon was glaring down at me. His eyes flickered to the sleeping forms, then back to me, making sure they were all asleep. "Not yet. You're not ready, yet. It would have taken you," he whispered.

I nodded, feeling cold sweat down my spine. He was right.

I could practically feel the frustrated claws of ethereal beings snarling with anger at the near miss. I reached back out to my magic, and carefully wove a web over Ashley. Those voices fought me, but I managed to overpower them. Barely. And much like I had done to speak to Wylde, I made a world with my mind. But this world was based on real memories.

With Gunnar, his pack, their pet-supply company, Thanksgiving Dinner at Chateau Falco, friends, loved ones, and drinks at a bar. I made that world *real*, and then slowly connected it to Ashley – or Wulfra – and whispered a single word in my mind.

Same...

She stirred, and I saw Talon's arms tense, ready for her to wake and attack. But she continued to sleep. I let out a shaky sigh, and turned to Tory. Talon began a soft, soothing purr, that sound that instantly made humans sleepy. Tory and Ashley settled even deeper to sleep. I don't know exactly how I knew this, but I could sense it.

Weakness... take her... a voice whispered in my mind.

My hand was reaching closer to Tory, as if to do just that. Talon still purred beside me, but had a restraining paw on my wrist. It was shaking as it fought me. Carl was sitting up, awake, watching us with a grin. That look made me stop in an instant. If Carl thought it was entertaining or a good idea, I should probably not be doing it. I shoved off Talon's paw with clenched teeth that Carl was sure to see, and Talon visibly wilted, as if expecting a blow. Carl snorted, frowned at the two of us, but then went back to sleep, looking bored.

I shivered noticeably. What the fuck? Carl had wanted me to take advantage of Tory in her weakness. He didn't consider it taking advantage. Just a good round of fun. And deep in my mind, I thought I knew that Tory would also find it fun. Sex was just something that needed to be quenched. It didn't mean anything. Just a need to be sated.

What the hell, Wylde? I said to myself, imagining the bastard in my mind.

For a slip of a second, I saw his face nod back. Then he ran away into the darkness, snarling at one of his cavewomen as if to take out his lust on them since I had forsaken him.

I focused back on Tory, making sure to keep my guard low, but not entirely down – so that I could hear him if he wanted to make contact, but shut him out if he became too intense and tried to force my hand again.

I created a world, and in that world, I placed two red dragons. Teenagers. And a memory I had of Tory with their mother, Misha, on a couch in Chateau Falco, right before she died in battle. I had found the two cuddled up, and Misha had urged me with her eyes not to wake Tory as she snuggled against her lover. I imagined that scene in as much detail as possible, leaving out the heartache of loss, and then built more memories.

Her school, Shift, the wayward home of shifters we had saved from the brutal circus.

And I imagined the Huntress, solely for the fact that she also seemed to love Tory – even if from afar – and I desperately wanted Tory to understand love. Something beyond feral to attach herself to.

I laced the world up like an intricate cloth, and then gently placed it over Tory, as if tucking her into bed. She whimpered, snuggling into the earth, but to my eyes, her hands gripped that imaginary cloth like a toddler with her blankie.

I smiled, and then promptly collapsed from exhaustion. I squinted my eyes, enough to see, but pretending to be asleep as I saw Carl sit up abruptly at the sound of me falling off my rock. He scanned the surroundings, and then went back to sleep after a quick glance at Talon.

Talon walked away, as if merely making his rounds on patrol.

I let myself fall asleep. And dream about my magic making a difference in this cruel world.

CHAPTER 22

A boot nudged me, and I jumped to my feet, lashing out with my hands. I grabbed a fistful of my attacker and yanked them to my face.

I was holding Ashley by a grip of her dreadlocks, and had my teeth pressed into her throat before I realized what was happening. She whimpered submissively.

And... suggestively.

I paused for a second, squeezed down with my teeth, and then released, shoving her away.

The thing I didn't let show was that releasing my teeth might have been the hardest decision I had ever made in my life. The rest of the crew chuckled good-naturedly, and then went back to whatever they had been doing. Tightening straps, boots, and checking on weapons.

Ashley sat on her haunches, well, crouching on her toes. All that fur made it confusing whether to use wolf parts or human parts to describe her motions.

And she was staring at me, panting. I touched a finger to my temple, granting her forgiveness.

She nodded, and then froze, looking very confused for a moment.

I bit back a smile as I saw a flash of the very human Ashley behind those eyes. A crystal-clear moment of her realizing something was wrong, and that this Wulfra wasn't her. Not really. What settled over her face next was very satisfying, because a little of both remained. I pretended not to notice.

Tory, on the other hand, looked angry. Storming about the clearing, muttering under her breath. Talon snapped at her. She lifted her head, and I realized her eyes were red, that she had been crying.

Talon took one look, opened his mouth, and then froze as the breeze shifted all of a sudden. His ears perked back, against the wind, and he took a big ol' sniff.

Then he was racing away from us, bounding from rock to rock on all fours now. Straight towards the golden forest I had seen before falling asleep.

I shouted at him, chasing him. I heard my group pounding after me, shouting eagerly, as if expecting a great big battle, and that the Devourer was leading us to victory, so excited that he couldn't even warn us. He disappeared into the golden forest a dozen paces ahead of us.

I shoved branches from my face as I tore after him, making sure my pack was still attached to my shoulders. And what sounded like a million chimes erupted around us. The golden fruits on the branches I pushed fell to the ground, jingling with the apparent golden seeds inside, and as the fruit hit the golden detritus on the floor, it clanged like steel on steel.

This was amplified by the fact that I was still running, shoving away branches, and pounding across the forest floor of metal, which sounded as if I was racing across a pile of coins, clattering, clanking, and rolling across each other.

Also, my other companions had the same concussion of sound around them from their own motions. Talon disappeared from sight, not making a single fucking sound.

His velvet boots, I thought to myself, *don't leave a trail...*

What could be here to leave a trail for?

I got my answer.

About fifty silver spiders suddenly descended upon us, the size of beagles, dangling from butt-ropes of silver webbing. The wooden disc around my throat suddenly throbbed in warning, as if urging me to use it. No fucking way was I falling for that.

"Kill everything!" I shouted.

Every single spider turned an ear to me, and I realized that their faces were all flat. Now, when I say flat face, I mean that they had a mouth of razor blades, but above that?

Nothing. No eyes. No nose. Just a smooth silver expanse on the front.

And big silver ear holes that were currently locked onto us.

They began swinging towards us, each gripping their butt ropes with two legs, cutting it, and swinging closer, somersaulting before spewing more silver butt cables up into the golden trees, and repeating the motion.

They swung through this golden jungle like our friendly neighborhood webslinger.

Of chrome death.

"Elder Carl, get Talon!" He obeyed, weaving past the hanging spiders with idle bats of his bone blades, killing some along the way. But he was fast, and the spiders must have decided they had enough here for a meal without chasing down the albino lizard.

"Wulfra! Scale!" I shouted, hoping to god that she remembered what I had given her.

Her hands moved to her pack, but she had a slight frown on her face, as if wondering why she was moving them. She slapped a silver scale against her chest, and armor washed over her like a wave of quicksilver, unfolding, rolling, and clicking into place over most of her body.

Like Iron Wolf.

It didn't cover her completely, but it was better than nothing. I had designed it to work for anyone, rolling over their body in skin-tight armor. I had made it a very long time ago when Raego had given me a truckload of silver dragon scales. The one I had killed over the Eads Bridge when first encountering the damn reptiles. I hadn't known at the time, but I had been using my Maker's ability, something stronger than a wizard, and had been prone to tinkering since nightmares had plagued my mind.

I had locked it away in Plato's Cave, in the third projector room that held secrets I almost wanted to keep from myself.

And that wasn't the only one I had made. Tory reached into her pocket and did the same, slapping it over a thigh, right before the spiders reached us.

I didn't bother. I reached out to Wylde, and gave him a gift.

Temporary control. A peace offering.

I heard a pleased chuckle, and then I watched as I began killing things.

All the things.

I grasped a moonbeam, ripped it into shards, and threw them with a shout and a stomp of my boot. Blades of lunar liquid splashed over the spiders, and they erupted in purple flames, howling with agony as they were burned alive.

I spun in a circle, holding my hands out, and whispered foreign Names.

The golden branches below me came to life in dozens of tiny stick figure men, and began ninja-flipping through the air, hammering and stabbing into the spiders as they swung. The crazy fuckers grabbed the golden leaves on the ground and began flinging them around like saw bladed playing cards. They screamed through the air, whining as they sliced through spider or butt rope, sending the unlucky spiders to the ground, where the golden stick men rolled over them like an army of zombies, eating them alive.

I glanced over to see Tory laughing as she punched the spiders like speed bags, her fists denting, shattering, or sending the arachnids flying into each other or into the tree trunks where they made a *splat* noise like bursting melons.

Wulfra, on the other hand, looked very uncomfortable, and hopped all over the place. She had a golden tree branch in either hand, and batted them away when able, but other than that, she looked kind of pathetic.

Then it hit me.

Silver. Werewolf.

She was *afraid* of the bastards.

I couldn't help it. I began to laugh, and flung out a hand towards her. My stickmen raced her way, flipping, shouting, and yelling as they cartwheeled up into the air, using her knees and chest as jumping off points to reach the piñata spiders to get their candy.

The forest soon quieted, and I heard dozens more of the silver spiders fleeing into the trees, where they were pursued by my golden stickmen. I grabbed Tory by the back of the hair, and had almost began shoving her mouth to mine in a triumphant celebratory—

No, I commanded Wylde, lashing out with the last scrap of control I had left to me.

I shoved Tory away, who looked both hungry for my touch, and bewildered at being hungry for my touch. I breathed deeply, wrestling control away from Wylde, and watched him snarl back at me in outrage.

I regained composure, and without turning, said, "Good job. Let's find the filthy feline."

Ashley laughed abruptly, and just as abruptly, the sound cut off. I glanced over a shoulder to see Tory staring down at the ground as if searching for something. But I was pretty sure what she was searching for was deep within her.

What I had almost done with her had felt wrong.

But also, *right*. She was remembering herself. Even if in just a tiny way.

But Wulfra beginning to laugh and then abruptly cutting off, made her look up, able to hide her confusion by pointing out the odd behavior of another. Projecting.

Because some part of Ashley had found humor. Not humor at an enemy dying, but at an idle set of words. *Filthy feline*. Like, well... a human. Or Manling. They hurriedly unclipped their scale, and the armor evaporated in a puff of light mist, leaving only the silver scale in their hands. I had coated the scales in a substance that would protect the skin from silver, knowing I would someday hand them out to werewolves. Still, Wulfra looked sick to her stomach as she tucked it away.

I could tell they were disoriented by the conflicting emotions. The fact that I had cemented my wakeup call to their own memories was wreaking havoc on them. I just hoped it wasn't too much havoc, and that I wouldn't break their sanity before we got the hell out of here with the kid.

I stomped through the golden underbrush, following the direction I had seen Carl run.

CHAPTER 23

We found them. Carl was staring openly at Talon, who was hanging upside down on a thick branch of a very normal-looking tree. Except that the bark was bright red. Other than that, at least it looked like wood, even if the leaves were black. His knees were tucked over the thick branch and he was batting at a dangling pod from one of the branches playfully, giggling.

"Wheeeeeee!" he yowled, purring excitedly.

Carl stared up at him, disgusted, horrified, and utterly bewildered. He heard us behind him and turned to me with fear in his eyes. "I..." he began, swallowing audibly as he saw the anger on my face. "He's broken. Giggling. Playing. I think he's trying to mate with it..." he said, wonderingly. "Should we leave him be?" I ignored that for a number of reasons, but mainly because I didn't want to teach Carl where babies came from.

"Stay back!" I shouted at the girls.

I walked closer, frowning at the odd sight, watching as Talon swung back and forth, laughing at us. "You look gorgeous, Wulfra!" he hollered, meowing at the end. He flipped from the branch, reaching for one of the pods, missed, and latched onto another branch, cackling madly. He skittered across the branch sideways on all fours, back arched. "Beast Master! Will you scratch my back later?" Then he dropped from the branch, using his tail to swing upside down like a possum, batting at another pod.

The girls stared in horror, already confused by their own inner turmoil. But to see Talon act like... a playful child? A drunk?

I noticed dozens more of the pods up in the trees, but saw another, older one, on the ground, partially decomposing and dried up. I picked it up, and sniffed it cautiously.

I slowly lifted my eyes to stare at Talon, then back down at the pod.

And I began to laugh. I slapped my knees, genuine tears coming to my eyes as I watched the murdering nutjob play with a pod of...

Catnip.

Talon swung, did a somersault, and then landed lightly on his feet. "Oh, I *needed* that."

He pimpwalked up to us, strutting like the only rooster in the chicken coop, and winked at the girls. They grinned back at him.

"Gunnar is going to laugh his ass o—" Ashley slapped a hand over her mouth, eyes wide.

Without missing a beat, I nodded. "The one-eyed bastard sure will, and so will porcu-shine." I shrugged at them, keeping my tone and face casual. "But we have to get home, first," I said. Then I turned my back on them and began walking in the direction I thought the castle would be.

Talon skipped up beside me, chuckling as he slightly redirected my course, and murmured, "Well played. Casual agreement, use of words, and idle dismissal. As if it was totally normal and acceptable to think of the stupid mutt."

"I'm sure your actions back there were also rationally calculated, and not that you lost your tiny brain for a quick fix. The Ravens will *love* to hear this one."

"You wouldn't dare..." he said, sounding terrified.

"Oh, I definitely will. Unless you help me more. Start using more speech here and there. Enough to get them more comfortable with it. I know we all know how, but something about this place encourages us to go primitive, first. Also, remind them that this is practice so that we can win over the kid's trust. He's a Manling. And we need his trust if we want to take him. Take, not rescue. Be sure to use that word."

Talon nodded slowly, and did a cartwheel for good-measure for the trio behind us. "Very clever. Appeal to both natures. The wild and the domesti-cated..." he purred. "You're doing surprisingly well. For a Manling..."

I grunted, knocking him over as he tried another cartwheel. He fell on his ass and hissed at me, back arched and everything. I continued on, barely pretending to notice. "No thanks to you. We almost got killed back there."

Talon sauntered back up to me, and I could see his tail was tucked between his legs for show. To prove his submission for the others. "What?"

"The spiders that descended on us."

"That was very impressive," Carl agreed, suddenly on my other side. "I've never seen you use magic like that before. Why not?"

My stomach gurgled as I slowly turned to face him. Carl's face was expressionless, as always. I grunted.

He frowned at me. And then flicked his tongue at me, hitting my nose. Then he faded back to walk beside the girls.

I almost fell over, having no idea how to handle the tongue thing. Was that a sign of disrespect? Or was it like a high five of some kind?

"Fucking Carl," I whispered under my breath.

Talon nodded. "He is very strange. I can't quite figure out what to make of him. He seems… the same. But different."

"I think this place just appeals to him. I don't know if he's fully feral like we all were in the beginning, or if he's something like the girls. I didn't have time to send magic at him."

Talon looked like I had hit him in the groin. "Goddamned don't!" he hissed. "Are you *insane?*"

I blinked at him, but made sure to continue walking. "What's wrong with you? You saw me last night, helping the girls with memories."

Talon was practically shaking. "You want to show him some of his *memories?* You want to fuck with an Elder's *mind?* Are you batshit *nuts?*"

"Well, I was going to show him memories from around *us*. His *new* family," I argued.

Talon ground his teeth. "Promise me you won't try such a thing. No one messes around with an Elder's head. Why do you think we banished them so long ago?"

I blinked. "They have some kind of mind power or something?"

"No. Anything that tries to get inside their heads without the proper protection simply ceases to exist," he shivered.

I let out a breath I hadn't realized I'd been holding. "That's… very concerning."

"Damn skippy," Talon muttered nervously. "I thought you knew.

Thought you just did the girls for that reason, and purposely avoided tampering with Carl for the obvious reasons."

I shook my head. "I had no idea about that." Silence stretched as we neared the fringe of the red tree forest. It was still night, but the moons hung very low on the horizon ahead of us.

"Good fucking thing we had this chat, then," Talon snarled, as if backing away from a cliff. "You should probably keep me informed of any ideas you have in the near future. I thought you knew... well, a lot more than you apparently do." He shook his head in disbelief. "Honestly, I don't know how the hell you made it this far. It's baffling."

Then he strode ahead of me, exiting the forest.

I followed, and stared down the hill before us.

The Palace was surrounded by a city of wooden huts and two-story buildings, like we had stumbled into the Medieval Era.

The Queens.

The kid.

Some stiletto heels.

It was time to tell them my plan, because I had been thinking lately on a Chinese guy named Sun Tzu. But I would need a little help from Wylde, first.

CHAPTER 24

I let go of my control, giving Wylde a chance to help. I needed to know we could work together. *Speak with them. Danger ahead. Planning now.* I felt him wrestle control from me, even though it was unnecessary since I had given it to him, and he threw my fist up in the air. I heard everyone halt behind me. My fist twisted, and everyone slowly backed into the forest again, out of sight from the palace not an hour away.

I turned to them, grimaced, and then cocked my head. "Bathe. Foresee the battle plan." I felt fingers dig deep into my brain as if searching for something. It hurt. Then it suddenly hurt a whole lot more as something was yanked away and thrown at each of my Band in rapid succession. But my body didn't move. It just *gave* them my plan. The plan that I had silently devised over time, remembering a book I had read a few times, *The Art of War*. Wylde grabbed my plan, read it, and passed it on like a flyer for an impromptu kegger in the school hall.

Bam, bam, bam. The three warriors stared back at me as they received their individual orders for the upcoming attack, and then nodded before setting up a small camp. Carl chuckled as he built a fire.

I took control of myself again and walked away from them, towards the stream.

Safely away from prying eyes, I settled down onto a rock and spoke with Wylde. *Thank you.*

… *Yes*, he replied awkwardly.

What do you think of my plan? I thought at him.

Could be better, he finally said in halted words.

I frowned. *Show me*, I told him nervously, remembering all too well what had happened when I let him use his own magic with the spiders.

My mind launched into the air like a bird taking flight, and I was suddenly sailing out over the valley below, racing towards the palace. Kind of like Astral Projection. In no time at all, I swooped down lower, and buffeted my wings, hovering over a particular section of the palace that was separate from the rest. *Manling*, Wylde murmured. Then I was flying again, scanning the courtyards, and circling the buildings a few times. It felt as if Wylde was thinking. Creating plans and then discarding them, although no words were spoken between us. And none of these thoughts were directed by me.

But I could tell I was smiling, thirsty to spill blood, take over the castle as mine.

No, I shivered. *Not invade. Steal and escape. Evade*, I corrected, realizing that his natural instincts to plunder had taken over. He stubbornly fought me on that for a moment, washing me in visions of the palace burning, Tory and Carl dying, Ashley and I sitting on a throne, bloody, but triumphant. I saw myself rip open her shirt and— I pressed that thought down and away, repeating my demands for the operation.

Begrudgingly, we began circling the air again, and in a much poutier tone, he pointed out three other locations. *Distraction. Conquest. Escape.* Then he was gone.

I sighed, letting out a deep breath. My vision swam, whether disoriented by Wylde himself, or the odd bird-in-flight experience, I didn't know.

Then I began to laugh. *Yes, that plan is much better*, I thought to myself as I rubbed my beard eagerly. Maybe there would be a little time for plunder and destruction.

Just a little. A few dying screams…

I jolted, shaking my head. *No*.

Distraction. Kid. Theft. Escape. That was the outline.

I made sure I was composed before returning to camp, but I could feel Wylde watching, no longer needing a direct request to participate. Just happily sitting on my shoulder, waiting for the right time to strike.

And for the life of me, I didn't know why I let him stay there… but I was kind of looking forward to him showing his hand, if necessary. Maybe even if it wasn't entirely necessary...

CHAPTER 25

*I*t was still dark, but the sky had a slightly pinkish hue to it now, as if dawn was approaching, but I saw no sign of the sun on the horizon, though. The sky was simply brighter than it had been. Enough for me to see clearly. It was a weird place, folks.

My merry Band of murderers stalked down the hill, nearing the town below. Except if I hadn't known better, I would have said we were all strangers.

Because none of us looked the same. We had eaten Oberon's strange fruit. It had the consistency of meat, but the flavor of fruit punch laced with sulfuric acid.

And the moment we swallowed, we each transformed into different people. Ashley was now a young, pretty woman with pointed Fae ears, looking nothing like normal. She had taken one look at me, dropped her jaw, and then licked her lips hungrily. I wasn't sure if that was part of her disguise, or if I looked that delicious.

I hadn't seen what I looked like, but the rest had simply shrugged upon seeing me, so I guessed it wasn't anything fancy. Just a Fae dude, or something. But my clothes were gone, obviously. My mortal threads would give me away in a heartbeat. So, the only thing different about me that I could tell was that I wore refined leather, with what felt like over a hundred different straps and buckles. The material was worn, but not beaten. Just used and properly maintained. Like armor should be. I wore knee-high boots with a red sash around the calf, and thick bracers on either arm, leaving the rest of my arms bare.

And those arms were banded with tribal blue designs. Remembering that much of the blood I had seen in this place had been blue, I was assuming that color was purposely chosen when Oberon came up with my disguise. My hair brushed my shoulders, and my beard was still there. But I felt bigger, stronger, and my arms were definitely corded with more muscle than usual.

Ashley continued to watch me, but I thought I saw pain in her eyes now, too. I pretended not to notice, hoping to appeal to the Fae part of her, letting her know that her reaction was inappropriate.

Tory was a tall warrior woman in leathers. Carl was an almost unnoticeable man with a bow across his back and a quiver of arrows at his hip. Sir Muffle Paws, or Talon, was a goblin. A tiny green goblin.

And he wasn't happy about it. If I looked closely, flickers of their true selves were visible, but when I had asked Talon about it, he simply shrugged. "You are a Manling. They cannot see it."

We entered a small thicket just beyond the town leading up to the castle, and a small piece of gravel hit me in the forehead. Then a triumphant hiss as a glittering pixie assaulted me.

Ashley darted back nervously, seeing only silver dancing around my face, slapping and kissing me in equal measure. I had almost lashed out to destroy the threat before noticing the silver glow. And then I saw the ebony figure at the edge of the thicket watching us.

"Barbie," I said, shocked. "Good to see you, but we're trying to maintain our cover."

She zipped in front of me, placing tiny fists on her hips. Then she began tapping a foot. Even though she was hovering in midair. I grinned at her. Talon licked his lips, eyeing her. I held out a hand, shaking my head at him. I remembered the last time he had seen these two, and chased them out of Chateau Falco.

"We know you," she said in a warning tone, and despite being nude, she still oozed authority.

I nodded. "Uh, yeah."

Her foot began to tap faster. "Your disguise didn't stop us," she elaborated.

I frowned, suddenly nervous. Had Oberon tricked us? "That's not good."

She nodded satisfactorily, and Ebony zipped up beside her. "We also *don't* know you."

I had forgotten how annoyingly obtuse they could be. "Please explain that."

"You stink of us. Yet you do not. It... changes," Ebony said distractedly. Barbie nodded her agreement.

"He has tasted our world and adjusts. This is good. He is becoming civilized."

Before I could speak, because I suddenly felt very self-conscious with my friends hearing this, Ebony continued. "Your disguise will work on those not yet acquainted with you, but the Queens know you as well, and will see through your subterfuge," she said.

I quickly reconsidered my plan. It could still work. We didn't intend to run into the Queens.

"Okay. Thanks for the advice."

"You're here for the Manling child," Ebony said, frowning thoughtfully.

"Yes. We need to take him home."

"Who told you this?" she asked curiously.

I hesitated, not entirely sure who I could trust.

Barbie waved a hand. "Doesn't matter. Does Hope Ride?"

I stilled, feeling the eyes of my friends on me. I glanced at the nearby houses. People walked here and there, most appearing normal, other than the pointed ears. But none had noticed us, thanks to the thicket.

I turned to Barbie. "It's a possibility..."

She nodded happily. "The fun begins. We must go. Our absence must not be noticed." Then she dove straight at the ground, rolled around in the dirt, and then zipped back into the air. Ebony fluttered closer, took a big sniff of Barbie's rear, and then nodded.

"The scent is gone," she said satisfactorily.

I blinked. "Wait. You're talking about *my* scent? It's that strong?" I asked nervously. Hell, our disguises wouldn't matter if they could smell through them.

Barbie rolled her eyes. "We will be attending the Queens. They know you," she said, as if that answered everything.

I began to realize that I was becoming used to their way of talking, because her words did make sense to me. "Well, now you're covered in dirt. Put some clothes on to cover it up if you can't bathe in time."

She frowned at me, and then turned to Ebony, as if asking for help. Ebony shook her head helplessly. Barbie turned back to me. "Others will believe I've already been bedded, so will go after another at the royal table. And none wear clothes at the royal table. They only get in the way of the Takings."

Then they disappeared. What had been the point of popping in like that? Barbie and Ebony had helped me out a few times in the past, in my world. Risking their loyalty to their Queens. They were – although frustrating – good friends. But why had they stopped to chat? And how had they found us?

I frowned down at Talon. "The Takings? What's that about?"

He nodded. "Orgies or blood feuds. Either. Both." He shrugged nonchalantly.

I sighed, and pressed on, exiting the thicket and entering the city. Of course, orgies or blood feuds. What else did you do at parties? The palace loomed ahead, looking like a giant reaching out to embrace us.

I hid my trepidation, keeping my face calm, relinquishing a small part of my control to Wylde in order to better blend in. My friends did the same. Or, it was probably more accurate to say that they ignored those odd sensations they had been experiencing lately. Memories of a different world with loved ones.

Right now wasn't the time to embrace that part of themselves. We would get back to that after we got the kid. "Everyone remember what to do?" I murmured in a low tone.

They grunted affirmatively, and then peeled off into the crowd of Fae heading to the castle. Those not attending – looking like farmers and poor merchants – snarled at Wulfra and I. We snarled right back, and they cowered. A few Fae ahead of me chuckled with amusement.

Monsters of all sorts lined the streets as we neared the Palace, speaking in a low hum, or snarling at each other in guttural tones. I saw a few ogres, sans clubs, looking twitchy without their maul of choice. I watched as one of them snatched a pixie out of the air, and guzzled it down in one fell motion.

The pixie had been trying to cut in line. A trio of other pixies hissed at him, and their teeth were all needles like a carnivorous plant. Part of me shivered, but Wylde simply grinned with amusement. Ashley stuck by my side, appearing casual, bored, and avoiding looking at me for personal reasons, nothing to do with our plan. I really needed to catch a reflection to see what was bothering her about my disguise.

Talon and Tory had gained a few spots ahead of us in line, and were also acting nonchalant, snarling occasionally at those who offended them. Talon looked to be struggling not to lick his paws, which would have looked odd from a goblin.

Carl was nowhere to be found. I hoped he was successful, or we were all dead.

It took an hour to reach the guards at the gate, and our time in line was not uneventful.

Merchants hawked their wares in garbled voices, trying to sell us locks of Manling hair for virility, or a stone to ward away humans. He didn't outright say it, but it sounded like the stones were to prevent human children from invading their homes. I wanted to shout, laugh, and tell them humans – for the most part – didn't even believe in fairies, let alone want to invade them. Especially not children.

Judging by the agreeable nods the merchant received, this comment wouldn't have been received well. All in all, I counted enough locks of hair to make a full body cloak for Bigfoot. Another thing I noticed, was that every one of these bloodthirsty savages was hungry to watch the Manling boy tortured. Their eyes danced with anticipation, and this made for hot blood.

A young Fae swaggered up to Ashley and promptly grabbed her breast with a lecherous grin. Well, where her disguise *looked* like a breast, because Wulfra wasn't flaunting cleavage in her Fae form. I tensed, wondering if physical contact would break the disguise, but it sure as hell looked like he had a pleasant handful and was happy about it. "You are mine," he drawled possessively. "Let's step out of line for a moment."

She glanced down at his hand, which was still gripping one of her love pillows, and then looked up to him, grinning. "Are you royalty?" she purred.

He sniffed in disdain. "No. I'm much better th—"

And she decapitated him with her dagger, her grin never slipping. She nudged his head with a foot, kicking it towards a small group of goblins who immediately began laughing, kicking it back and forth playfully. "Good. I detest peasants," Ashley muttered with a bored yawn.

I bit my tongue as I saw his friends off to the side, snarling at us. But they also looked crestfallen, as if she hadn't actually done anything *wrong*. They just weren't happy about it.

But the larger contingent of Fae in line with us simply chuckled.

Needless to say, I didn't think she was going to have any more suitors approaching her.

I used my boot to flip the body out of my way and advanced a few paces. "Fucking waste of space is holding up the line," I snarled, not even glancing down. We patiently stood in line, a few paces beyond the dead body as the commotion and interest seemed to die down.

I glanced warily at Ashley to see a flicker of disgust in her eyes. And fear. "You okay?" I murmured, pretending to readjust her weapons belt for her.

She nodded, still wearing a mask of disinterest, but she whispered a word. "Gunnar..." I swallowed and gave a subtle nod. She met my eyes briefly, and I saw the pain again. "You look like his twin brother right now," she whispered.

I managed not to flinch at her words. I looked like Gunnar? No wonder she was acting so strange. I suddenly feared that she might not be up for this, that seeing Gunnar standing beside her might make her act like a human, giving us away. I squeezed her shoulder. "We'll get back to him soon," I whispered. "But right now, I'm a bloodthirsty warrior, and you are my equally bloodthirsty killer. Got it?" I asked, realizing that this was the first time I had directly acknowledged that this feeling she was having was entirely normal, and not a mental malady.

And that I was Nate, not her tribal king.

She nodded, her cold mask falling back over her features. I gave her belt a firm adjustment, and stepped back, grunting approval. I spoke louder for those nearby to hear, and spotted the handsy Fae's friends dragging the body out of the line, shooting angry but nervous glances at Ashley out of my peripheral vision. "How long does it take to walk through a door?" I complained.

"As long as it takes," a richly-dressed Fae said just ahead of us. I acknowledged him with a grunt, and he glanced over his shoulder. "First time in a Palace?"

I grunted again. He was a very handsome man, and although not clean-shaven, he didn't have a beard, either. Just light scruff. His long auburn hair was tied back in a tail, and his face was long and narrow, with wide, thin lips. His eyes glittered with mischief, like a noble's son.

"One of *those*, eh? The Marauders," he chuckled. "You can speak here, you know. No need to act like a Barbarian Manling." He glanced behind me at the puddle of blood. "Although, it is nice to see every now and then." He grinned politely at me, extending a hand. "Robin. Robin Goodfellow. And you are?"

I stared down at his hand, suddenly nervous. I dared not risk telling him my name, but I also didn't want to touch him, in case he knew of me. But I really didn't have much of a choice.

Because Robin Goodfellow was also known as the Hobgoblin.

Or Puck.

A trickster if there ever was one.

And probably the worst person to associate with, because he was known to be conniving and heartless, and I didn't know what side he might fall on. Probably his own side.

But I didn't really have the option of ignoring him.

"Wylde," I growled, staring at his hand suspiciously.

He studied me curiously, and then chuckled, withdrawing his hand. "My reputation precedes me, it seems."

"I only touch things I kill. Or things I take," I replied in a gruff tone, smirking at him.

He belted out a laugh. "Oh, I *like* you!" This caused a general stir among those nearby, but I could sense they wanted to keep a safe distance from the famed Fae. Ashley pretended to ignore us, but I could sense she was listening to every word.

Then again… there was always the chance that Puck wasn't famed here. What I knew of the Fae and what they knew about themselves could be entirely different. Hell, he could be considered a hero, here. Or a nobody. I had to be careful.

I slowly turned to him. "You do this often?" I waved a hand at the surrounding mayhem.

He nodded. "When the occasion calls for it," he said, watching me thoughtfully. He began touching his lips absently, as if thinking, or planning, or maybe I had given myself away somehow.

That was the thing. I had no idea. Even Wylde seemed apprehensive speaking with Robin.

"We should share a table at the feast," he finally said.

Inwardly, I groaned. But I had no way out. It wasn't like I was batting down offers for dinner, and I didn't know any names I could casually toss out to try and deter him. I also couldn't tell him that I wasn't going to the feast, because that might sound odd. Why go through the trouble of entering the city to not partake in the feast?

I couldn't just tell him, *because we will be long gone by then, running away with the kidnapped Manling you all want to watch die.*

"Thank you," I finally said. "That would be… entertaining."

He nodded. "Get you back in practice of talking, too. You'll need it to dance with the Queens. To catch their eyes."

I blinked at him. Seeing my confusion, he chuckled. "That is why you're here, correct? To ask to bed one of the Queens. Or her attendants?"

I hesitated, using the moving line as an excuse to stall. How the fuck did I respond to that? Back in my world, one didn't attend a party to try to bang a queen. Unless they weren't particularly attached to their head.

But here?

Barbie and Ebony had mentioned the Takings. Was it some kind of traditional fight? Whoever wins gets to sleep with a Queen?

Robin shook his head in amusement. "She does like her consorts rough. Perhaps you have a chance," he said with a shrug, "if you ask nicely. Anyway, best of luck. Everyone tries."

I shrugged, trying to look guilty. "Thought it best to keep it a secret," I chuckled. "The Taking," I added, grinning.

Robin froze, completely turning around to face me, looking stunned. And I instantly wanted to run away. Shit.

CHAPTER 26

*R*obin continued to stare at me, and I saw Ashley slowly reaching for her dagger. Before she could act, Robin spoke. "I thought you were trying to gain their attention and get an *invitation*. But you intend to *Take* one of the queens?" he whispered in a tone so low that only I could hear.

I hesitated.

He shook his head in disbelief. "Sweet sylph… You really are one crazy bastard…" he said in an awed tone.

I carefully relaxed my shoulders, nodding in gratitude of his compliment. "I aim to surprise."

He was nodding agreement. "That you do. That you fucking do. You should probably keep that between us. I don't recall the last time one of the Queens was Taken, or if they had ever *been* Taken, but that will surely be a nice surprise. Keep that to your advantage. And if that interferes with our feast arrangement, good fucking riddance to you," he said, smiling from ear to ear. "But you must tell me all about it, after."

I nodded, and then placed a finger to my lips. He turned around, shaking his head, and I realized we were at the front of the line. The stone walls of the palace climbed above our heads for fifty feet or more, and that was just the wall. Several towers rose even higher, but I couldn't make out the entire layout from here. Not that I needed to. I had flown over the whole palace earlier, getting a better idea of the grounds than I ever could have by walking through it.

A dozen guards in armor stared us down with perfectly hairless jaws. Their armor was made entirely of leaves, sticks, and vines, but somehow looked as elegant, pristine, ornate, and serviceable as any I had ever seen.

Simply put, they looked stunning. I even spotted a few women among the guards, relieving some tension I hadn't noticed I'd been carrying. I wasn't sure how the Fae considered women – other than the obvious royalty – and had been concerned that Ashley and Tory might raise eyebrows.

Robin was quickly ushered through with a familiar nod from a female guard. I noticed her satisfied grin, even though she tried to hide it, meaning that she and Robin were already well-acquainted. Robin called out to her. "Those two are with me," he winked.

She glanced at us, studying us from head to toe, and then shrugged. "A friend of Robin is a friend of mine." Then she leered at me suggestively. "Perhaps I'll see you around after my shift. You have a touch of nature to you, and I miss having a rough hand in my bed."

Robin scowled at her, but I could tell his heart wasn't really in it. She glanced at him over a shoulder. "Oh, I'll have plenty of time for you, too, my sweet. Dessert."

Robin nodded greedily. "Divine," he said. He rubbed his knuckles on his fine velvet suit, looking like he had stepped out of the Renaissance Era. I hadn't really looked earlier, but with his attention on the guard, I had the perfect opportunity. His clothes were perfectly tailored, and in various shades of green. I hadn't really read much on him, but something about him felt wrong, like I should know him.

"What about me?" Ashley said, studying the woman before her. "I have an appetite as well."

Robin burst out laughing. "These two!" he chuckled.

The guard nodded at Ashley. "That sounds… quite intriguing. Find me." Then she looked at me. "Both of you. I, too, have an appetite."

I grinned back at her, trying to make my face look like I was gazing at a piece of sizzling steak. Ashley stretched her hands above her head, displaying her body for full view. "You won't be hungry for long…" she said as she strolled by.

I heard the guard purr in response, but didn't glance back as we rejoined Robin. He nodded at us, and then held out a hand behind him, revealing a tunnel in the stone walls that led deep into the heart of the Fae. "Welcome to the palace, where all your dreams may come true…"

CHAPTER 27

*W*e had about an hour before the festivities began, which should give us ample time to find the kid, kill the guards, and get the hell out of here. Ashley shot me a questioning look, and then glanced at Robin's back, politely asking if we should just kill him.

I shook my head, and her face grew concerned, as if to say, *then what the hell are we going to do?*

I had no answer to that. We followed him through the tunnel, towards bright lights just ahead. Let me just tell you that I wasn't really sure what to expect, even though I had spent some time in the Fae by now. This is what I had learned so far – some trees were alive, sentient, and could kill you.

Eight-legged pests in our world were chrome killers here.

Everyone I had met wanted to screw, kill, or eat anyone *they* met.

Except for Robin, who seemed… maybe not *normal*, but close.

Which made me a little nervous of the opening just ahead. Because Robin's version of civilized still had some very dark undertones. I stepped out into blinding light, squinting.

It was daytime. What the hell? That quickly? The sun was fully overhead now, shining down on us as if it were noon, revealing a tapestry of life and wealth that made my head spin. Flowers, bushes, and stands with merchants selling fruits, meats, and charms filled the stone courtyard. A fountain stood nearby with several nude Fae splashing each other while giggling. A few had skipped the foreplay and were simply going to town on each other. Hungry males watched them with wicked intent.

Giant cages swung from the branches of two giant white trees, as thick around the trunk as an SUV. Inside the ornately gilded cages were groups of Fae, wildly dancing, kissing, painting each other, and getting it on. In no particular order, and much of it happening simultaneously.

The only thing that made me glad was that I didn't notice any inter-species play. I wasn't sure if I could have handled that. An ogre and a goblin, for example, would have simply made me run screaming in horror. Every one of the participants was vaguely humanoid with pointy ears. Their skin seemed to glow with glitter, and they each wore jeweled collars around their throats. Property of the queens, I guessed. The geometric designs they painted on each other were savage, making them look like we had stumbled onto the Wall Street version of Burning Man.

The cages swung back and forth in great swooping arcs, but none of the Fae inside stumbled, either used to it, or the cage was enchanted so that they simply didn't slam into each other, ruining the sex show with broken limbs.

Silk ribbons hung from the bottom of the cage, and every now and then, a Fae on the ground would jump to snatch one. They tore away easily. I watched as one successful Fae took his silken prize, and looped it around another Fae woman, who rounded on him with an angry glare. The moment he tugged on his sash around her waist, her face changed into lust, and she willingly danced into his arms. She grinned, ripped off her top, and pressed her body against his. Their embrace devolved from there, encouraged by rounds of applause from the other young men, and scowls from the young women. I kept my face blank, turning away. A date-rape ribbon?

Several trolls lay on cushions beneath the swings, eating great roasted legs of meat that must have come from a bison or something. Pixies on delicate leashes zipped around their heads, picking out filth and bugs like you might see those monkeys do in the zoo. Once finished, another set of pixies swooped in and began to braid the ogre's matted hair, tying in shells, bones, and trinkets.

The pixies looked exhausted, and defeated. I saw that a lot of the ogres in the area had already been fancied up, and then I saw the long line of ogres behind those being serviced. It seemed they all wanted a quick clean and upgrade, and the tiny sprites were all but spent. I knew for a fact that no matter how tired they were, they wouldn't dare stop any time soon. Because a hungry troll held a fistful of chains like one might hold a bouquet of balloons. Except those silver chains each led to one of the pixies, rather than a balloon. They were prisoners. Slaves.

And I saw that the troll was cleaning his teeth with a pixie-sized bone that still had some flesh attached to it. I pretended not to see this, too, or else I would have had to kill him. And then an army of guards would hunt me down for being a buzzkill at their civilized party.

I saw Talon watching me out of the corner of his eye, a dozen paces away. Even though he looked like a goblin, now, I could see through his disguise if I focused. He gave a subtle shake of his head, and then he and his tall warrior woman – Tory – drifted into the crowd, heading away from us.

I let my eyes roam, trying not to focus too intently on any one facet, because it was all so much. Sensory overload. A band of musicians played nearby, a haunting melody that sent the nearby crowd into applauding sobs. As they stopped, another tune seemed to melt out of it from another band, seamlessly transforming the end of their sad tune into a merry dancing jig.

The only ones nearby who didn't dance were the several trios of guards marching in small pockets, giant halberds at their shoulders. Their faces were hard, hairless, and beautiful, like polished ivory.

I watched them, while pretending not to, and counted their number in the several groups I could see, trying to learn their rotation. As I did this, I realized I wasn't entirely sure what they were supposed to guard against. Everything I had seen so far was pretty much a felony in my world. What could be considered worse than servitude, murder, bondage, and date-rape ribbons?

I got a decent idea of the timetable we had to work in, and the number of guards we needed to look out for – at least in this area – and turned back to Ashley. Robin stood beside her, holding her wrist, and smiling at me. Before I could get all territorial, he waved me to follow.

I walked up to them slowly, glanced down at his hand on her wrist, and then back to his face. I didn't show any anger. I just *looked* at him. He casually released her hand, and I nodded.

"I think we'll take a walk before the feast. Clear our heads," I said, casting a subtle wink at Robin. A smile crept onto Ashley's cheeks, and she slowly reached out to grip my wrist subserviently, licking her lips as she studied some of the more amorous guests.

Robin chuckled, shaking his head. "Insatiable beasts…" He sighed. "Well, find me before the festivities. I'll make sure to grab a table near… your next conquest," he said to me in a cryptic manner. Right, the Queens. Because he thought I was going to try to take one of them in some triumphant rape scenario that everyone seemed to be casually open to.

This place…

I grinned, dipped my chin, and then began walking away with Ashley. She let out a soft sigh when we were out of earshot. "Nate?" she asked.

"Hmm?" I said, studying the flow of bodies, looking for an opening that would lead us towards the kid. Then I froze. I jerked Ashley into a nearby stoop behind a stand selling fruit, acting as if I was suddenly interested in a little hankie-pankie. The crowd took no notice, used to this. I stared into Ashley's eyes from inches away.

She swallowed, licking her lips. "Nate, where are we?"

I let out a long breath, and then an exuberant smile. She had called me Nate. That was a first. She was remembering. "It's okay, Ashley. We're here to save a kid, remember?"

"It's like a dream," she whispered. Then, realizing how that sounded, she shook her head. "I mean, this place is like a nightmare. But it also feels *normal* on some level. What feels like a dream is those *other* thoughts. Gunnar…" she said, her eyes taking in my disguise. "What's happened to us? Why is everything so confusing?" she asked, sounding on the verge of tears.

I broke it down for her, telling her everything that had happened, and how everyone had been acting, that the Fae world had been changing us, somehow. After a long silence, she slowly nodded. "I feel crazy," she whispered.

"Just remember which one is the real you. Don't block out the other you, the one this place made, because we need that person for a little longer. Okay, *Wulfra?*" I gripped her chin gently but firmly. She nodded uncertainly. "But. Don't. Forget. Gunnar," I said, pinning her with my eyes. "Use him as a totem. That's the real life. Gunnar. Remember that, and everything else will fall into place."

She nodded, studying my face – my cheeks, chin, jaw, everything. "You look so much like him. It's… I think it's what finally snapped me out of it." I nodded, not sure if this was a catastrophic turn of events or a good one. Here in the palace, it could be the worst thing imaginable. Unless she could keep track of that primitive side – Wulfra – now having a better understanding of how important it was.

"It's affecting all of us. Even me. I just snapped out of it sooner. Talon's aware, like us. I'm not sure about Tory, but I tried to use my magic to help you two remember the truth. You were asleep, but I think it's helping. But we can't assume. We can't let on that we know something is wrong. We have to guide them to it. If we dump something like this on them now, when they are in this savage state, who knows what could happen?"

She nodded. "It's so hard being both. But I'll try." She paused, thinking. "What about Carl?"

I shrugged. "No clue. He's still extremely creepy, but I think I'm beginning to realize he's a lot more dangerous than we ever thought. Talon is terrified of him on some level."

"Fucking… Carl," she finally said, as if it exhausted her to recall the words.

I grinned. "Fucking Carl is right. Now, can you keep it together? Act like a bloodthirsty psycho, but on your best behavior for the party?"

She nodded. "I'll do my best."

"Keep an eye on me. I'll try to guide you if I think you're doing anything wrong. Otherwise, just act like the merciless werewolf you are. They seem to dig that here."

She shuddered, but gave me a nod. Then she kissed me on the lips, grabbing my ass in the process. She peeled herself away, breathing heavily. I couldn't move.

"Um, Ashley?"

She looked down. "It felt like something Wulfra should do. They were watching," she mumbled, indicating a few watchers behind us. I didn't turn to look, but nodded at her.

"Okay…"

"And…" she added, squeezing my wrist affectionately. "I wanted to kiss Gunnar. To keep me grounded." Her eyes slowly lifted to mine. "If he ever hears about this, I'll rip your face off."

I nodded, unable to hide my grin. "I don't think you'd get to. He already would have killed me by the time I got halfway through the story."

She smiled, nodded, and then took a deep breath. "Damn right. Let's go."

I tugged her out from the alcove and we continued on through the crowd. I kept my palm on her wrist, letting everyone see she was mine.

Wylde grumbled his approval at that, but he had been oddly silent while I was talking to Ashley. Not much I could do about it. I was sure he had heard every word, and that he didn't exactly know what to make of it. But I was sure it had bothered him.

As we wandered through the crowd, I reached out to him. *How are we doing on time?*

I felt a swirl of strange sensations inside of me, and then felt Ashley's arm tense under my palm. But nothing obvious happened. We stood near a bend in the street with an open doorway tucked behind a bush a few paces away. We were in position.

Then something exploded far away, past the area where we had first entered the palace. Then another blast rocked the palace in a slightly different location, but still near the first one. I shoved Ashley out of the way as a handful of guards spilled out of the open doorway behind the bush.

They raced out, halberds down, using them to smack lazy Fae out of the way if they didn't move fast enough. Most were well clear, as if familiar with their chances. The funny thing was that although everyone turned to face the explosions, watching the smoke rising up in the air, none of them looked particularly concerned. They looked... excited.

I tugged Ashley through the open doorway before anyone had a chance to notice, and we pressed ourselves against the cool brick wall of a dimly lit hallway that was significantly less ornate than the courtyard and streets had been.

"Let's be quick," I whispered.

Ashley's eyes glinted in the weak light, looking like an animal, no trace of the woman I knew.

CHAPTER 28

We crouched behind a stack of barrels in an underground storage room between hallways, waiting. We hadn't run across any guards, managing to hide just before being noticed, thankfully. I could sense Ashley's agitation, so I placed my hand on her thigh, squeezing.

"Wait," I whispered.

She nodded, breathing deeply, looking as if I had told her to wait while a table of fresh barbecue sat two feet away.

We didn't have to wait long. The ground rocked, and the barrels above us groaned in their stands. That explosion had been much closer, on our side of the city, and likely only fifty feet away, but located in the streets, under a merchant's stand if Carl had done as he was told. Which sounded stupid, but really wasn't.

If Carl made his explosions and distractions on only one side of the city, someone was bound to consider why attention was being drawn away from the other half.

Of course, this only mattered if one of the Fae guards was intuitive and particularly devious, but judging by my time here, I had assumed this to be the case. Fae weren't very trusting, and with so many tricky, deceitful stories about them, I had figured it kind of ran in their blood.

"Find them and kill them," a voice bellowed from the other side of the barrels.

Boots pounded away, tearing down the hallway we had just exited.

"So, the first explosions weren't to lure us away…" a new voice said in a respectful tone. "Is this a full-scale assault, then, Sir? And why?"

"That's the question, boy. Why would someone attack, today of all days?" the first voice growled, not sounding pleased that his initial assumption was apparently wrong – that the first explosions had been used to lure guards that way. Of course, he had been exactly right, but Carl's latest explosion had been to dissuade that assumption. Cause confusion.

"The Queens…" the second soldier offered to his Captain or whatever they called superior officers, here.

"Perhaps. Or one of the guests near the Queens. Gather the men. I want a full Vine of Hatchetmen at the Feast. Now. But be discreet. We don't want to cause a panic. The Feast and the Taking must continue as planned. Nothing out of the ordinary for the guests to notice. Not even the Queens. Look for any loners, those standing apart from everyone."

"Yes, Sir." He paused before leaving. "Forgive me, Sir, is everything alright? You seem… different."

"Get out of my sight, boy. And don't presume to know your betters, or how they think."

"Yes, Sir," the boy said, sounding terrified. Soon I heard him shouting in the distance, and then hundreds of boots racing past us through yet another hallway.

The hallways grew as still as a tomb, and I couldn't be sure if the Captain had left or not. The silence stretched, and just as I was about to have a look, I heard a very soft, muffled moan from the barrels to our right. Ashley flinched, then turned to look at me. I shrugged, glancing at the shadowed stand of more barrels.

We crept closer, hands at the ready, and then froze as we saw it. A Fae was tied up and blindfolded. He wore military clothing like we had seen on the other guards, and had thorns on the shoulders, likely signifying rank of some sort. His clothes were crisp, clean, and well maintained.

An officer. What the—

"Master Wylde?" a voice whispered from beyond the first barrels, where we had heard the two soldiers speaking. I shared a confused look with Ashley, and then crept closer, leaving the hogtied officer where we had found him. I reached our hiding spot and then risked a glance over the top of the barrels.

And froze.

Robin Goodfellow was neatly folding a set of clothes on a table before him. He sat there, patted the pile, and then lifted his eyes to mine. He nodded politely, and then held out his hand for me to join him.

"What is this?" I asked, suddenly wary.

"I told you I would find a table near your conquest," he said, watching me intently. He didn't look mad, upset, or betrayed. In fact, he looked somewhat anticipatory. And thrilled.

I stood to my full height and stepped out from the shadows, scanning the hallways. "How did you know?"

He shrugged. "I didn't. You obviously weren't who you said you were. Looked like a couple of virgins in a brothel, to be honest. Then again, maybe I'm just perceptive. You seemed to have the others fooled well enough." He tapped his fingers on the table, keeping them in plain sight. "If I wished you harm, I wouldn't have sent away the guards." He glanced down at the folded clothes before him. "Or subdued two officers, stolen one of their uniforms, and then impersonated him to give you a better chance. I simply would have strolled in, pointed at the barrels, and told them where you were."

I nodded slowly. "But how? And why?"

"I followed you," he said simply. He glanced up at the ceiling, leaning back, twisting to encompass the entire room. "This place can be so boring at times, whereas you excited me. I have a knack for discovering interesting things."

"So, what, you're just going to wish us good luck?" Again, something about him nagged at me, on the verge of memory. But I couldn't grab it.

Robin nodded. "Why not? I don't know what you intend to do, but it seems infinitely more interesting than your ridiculous idea to Take one of the Queens," he said, laughing lightly. "May I ask—"

"I'd really rather you didn't," I said politely, even though I was cutting him off. "Better this way." I hesitated, then flashed him a guilty grin. "But it will definitely be memorable. Especially if you have front row seats at the Feast."

He tapped his lips, thinking. "Will I be seeing you at the Feast?"

"Not likely," I said.

"I see," he said, sounding disappointed. "Well, have fun, then." He stood, brushed off his hands, and then began to whistle as he strolled past us. He called out over his shoulder before rounding a corner. "That guard was quite adamant about wanting you dead." Then, he was gone, and the hallways returned to silence. I cocked my head, expecting to hear a battalion of these so called Hatchetmen storming to our position. But nothing happened.

"Let's move," I said. Ashley unfolded from a stack of chairs behind the table in front of me – where she would have been perfectly positioned to launch a knife into the back of Robin Goodfellow's head. I nodded approval, not realizing she had moved to cover me. She sheathed a set of knives, and then ghosted towards one of the hallways, arching a brow at me. I nodded, and she disappeared around the corner.

"Clear," I heard her whisper after a minute. I followed her into another hall that led directly to a set of stairs. I looked at her. "I checked at the bottom of the stairs, too, Wylde," she said rolling her eyes as she emphasized my name. "What do you think of Goodfellow? Do you trust him?"

"I don't trust anyone, Wulfra. Let's hurry. Just in case I'm right."

We dashed to the bottom of the stairs, careful to be quiet in case any guards had decided to pop in for tea after Ashley cleared the area. We peered around the corner. Two guards were slumped against a table, heads resting in plates of food. I arched a brow at Ashley.

"I took care of them," she said with a shrug.

"I thought you just checked to see if any were here?"

She just grunted at me in response. Hearing no one else, I stepped out into the area, scanning three different doors on the opposite side of the room from the stairs. Ashley had either knocked out the guards, or killed them. It really didn't matter at this point. If she had killed them, it didn't change our priorities, and I couldn't afford to waste time chastising her for it.

I stepped up to the closest door, took a breath, and then opened it.

A narrow hallway stretched into darkness, with cages for prisoners lining the walls. I waited for my eyes to adjust, fearing what kind of criminals I might view after seeing what the Fae considered civilized.

I frowned, suddenly feeling my hair stand on end. The cells were empty. All of them. I met Ashley's eyes and saw they also looked very troubled.

I left the hallway, closed the door, and tried the next one. The kid had to be in one of them. If he had been taken to the banquet, Talon would have set off a fourth explosion before rushing to continue his task with Tory. But there hadn't been a fourth explosion, so the kid should have been here, in the dungeon.

I opened the second door only to find more empty cells. No prisoners. At all.

I raced to the last section of doors, not caring about stealth any longer. It, too, was empty.

"Fuck," I muttered.

"What now?"

I debated. No kid. The only thing left to do was meet Talon and see what the hell was going on. He was supposed to be heading to the royal chambers right about now, or already on his way back with his shoes. Or I could do like I was supposed to, and flee the city.

But I didn't have the kid, which was the whole point in risking our lives today.

Just then, a very deep horn blew, sounding very far away, as if outside the city gates. But to be heard from the dungeons, it had to be very loud indeed. We shared a look, and then raced up the stairs. We rounded the corner to return to the room where we had seen Robin Goodfellow, and instead, we saw the two Fae Queens, sitting at the table, the officer we had seen tied up lying on the table between them.

Except he wasn't alive anymore.

He looked to have been stabbed to death with an antler that one of the Queens was currently licking blood from. This blood was red. So, only some creatures had blue blood, I thought to myself, trying to ignore my sudden terror.

The Queens turned to look from me to Ashley, frowning.

Things can always get worse.

CHAPTER 29

I lowered my hands, staring at the two Queens. They looked much like last time I had seen them, except this time they weren't pretending to be dressed. They had abandoned the lingerie and stood in all their feminine glory, which was currently liberally splashed with blood.

The Winter Queen had pale, pale skin, like the world's most translucent sapphire glinting in the sun. She didn't have fangs this time, but her pointed ears were still coated with wild frost, and her eyelashes had tiny little icicles. She absently touched her bare breast, not even seeming to realize it. Certain parts of her anatomy were the color of frozen raspberries – use your imagination – and her dark hair glistened with purple undertones.

In contrast, the Summer Queen looked like a California girl, pleasantly tanned, and hair in shades of red, yellow, and orange. She smelled fresh, like fruit, and a light patina of sweat slicked her skin, just begging to be touched… I shook my head, frowning at her.

I remembered another thing. Last time I had seen them, the Summer Queen had been wearing heels that resembled molten lava. They were both barefoot now, but was that the pair of heels Talon was trying to steal? I couldn't remember seeing a pair on the Winter Queen.

They did not like failure in their soldiers, obviously. Poor bastard had been kidnapped and tied up by Robin Goodfellow, and now he was dead, having his own Queens drink his blood.

The Summer Queen strolled around the table in slow, languid steps, a cat hunting two mice, considering me hungrily.

But I wasn't a fucking mouse.

I was Wylde.

I stepped forward, unbuttoning the strap closest to my throat, tugging it loose so I could show off some skin, but also a little of something else.

Her eyes latched onto the skin with a hungry purr, which suddenly transformed into a rictus of unease and confusion. Her eyes darted to my face, my body, and back to my throat.

Where the wooden disc hung on a leather thong.

"My Queens…" I said, licking my lips. "I'm here for the boy. Let's not replay our last encounter. As fun as that was," I added with a shit-eating smirk.

She took a step back, and even though uneasy and stumbling for a Fae, she still moved like poured molasses compared to most humans, luxurious, smooth, and flowing.

The Winter Queen stood, placing her hands on her hips in a universal sign that commanded children to obey their parents.

"You've put on some weight since we last met," I commented.

She snarled, opening her mouth wordlessly, face furious, but also not having anything she could actually do. Because her eyes consistently locked onto my necklace, now, too.

I reached up, thumbing it absently. "I'm not sure what a war of succession would look like here, but my Brothers did tell me that I need to get some practice time in. Riding a horse, killing, butchering, causing general mayhem. You know," I waved a hand. "Apocalyptic-y stuff."

The Summer Queen actually snarled at me. "How did you *get* here?" sounding both stunned, amused, and anxious at the same time.

"Well, I walked through a fucking door, believe it or not. Where is the kid?"

The Winter Queen leaned forward, scraping her nails across the wood, actually digging up curling ribbons of wood, which immediately frosted over. She sounded angry, but slightly satisfied at the same time. "I don't know how you got here, Temple, but it just might have been the stupidest thing you've ever done. The boy is *gone*, running through the forests." She seemed to be suddenly realizing a delicious chain-of-events that no one else saw.

I frowned. "But you intended to kill him. Why would you let him go free?" I asked, keeping my tone threatening.

The Summer Queen folded her arms, pressing up her cleavage – which had likely impressed many people in the past. Not me. Fae boobies were not as fun as they looked. I knew she was a monster. All monsters were pretty. The prettier, the more dangerous. And ruthless. "Did she say we freed him?" she asked, amused. "Perhaps placing him in the wild was only the first stage of his torture…" she grinned hungrily. "The start of the game. A game everyone has gathered to watch. Every pixie, troll, barrow hag, and nymph will see this, from every reflection of water, we will *see*. From every drop of blood, the show will reflect to us. We watch that most hallowed tradition among our people…"

My mouth turned dry, and I shook my head. "That… doesn't make any sense."

The Winter Queen nodded in satisfaction, slowly licking her lips. "From your surprise, I take it that Oberon himself had something to do with your arrival." She let out a delighted laugh. "Oh, my. You had no idea what you were walking into, did you? I'm inclined to let this play out. Much better than killing you now," she chuckled. "Naughty, *naughty*, kings. Can't be trusted a finger, because to kings, one finger *always* means two…" she added with a lustful grin.

I shook my head, ignoring the sexual innuendo. This couldn't be true. Oberon had sent us here to get the boy. Why would he lie to us? Only to…

The Summer Queen laughed delightedly, clapping. "Oh, dear. Were you *Invited* here?" She rounded on her sister, who looked suddenly ecstatic, nodding. "How very clever of him…" she added, shaking her head. "Alas, your game is over now, Initiate. You have failed. Your death approaches on swift feet, but not by our hand. This is *so* much better than what I had planned for you."

"You are beginning to see the depths of the game played upon you, Temple. You were misled. Oberon hunts the boy even now, as we sit here," The Winter Queen said, grinning.

"What is she talking about, Wylde?" Ashley growled, and her words snapped me out of it.

"The Wild Hunt, Wulfra. Oberon commands the Wild Hunt, and he's going after our prey."

Ashley grunted, sounding unimpressed. "You knew this already. It doesn't change anything. That child is mine. Oberon was just a means to an end, anyway. You used him as much as he used you," Ashley muttered arrogantly, putting on the best show I had ever seen. I went with it, ignoring the sudden confused, calculating looks on the Queens' faces.

They had, of course, assumed correctly. That Oberon had sent us here to get the kid, double-crossing us. But Ashley was making it sound like we had been here to get the kid anyway, and that we had simply used Oberon to get a better shot. This would make them wonder why we wanted the kid, and would effectively remove any blame from Oberon. Well, not that. But it would make the Queens forget about any kind of permanent collaboration, which meant they didn't truly understand where they stood.

Thinking I had been duped by Oberon gave them a sense of control, a reason not to kill us.

Hearing that we had been using Oberon the entire time gave them a sense of unease. What surprises had we yet to reveal? If Oberon was just a convenient happenstance, what had been our true plan? And I saw fear in their eyes as memories of Manling Tales danced in their minds. Those deceitful, evil little Manlings.

Create fear and plausible doubt, even if unfounded, and then let the enemy stew in it.

Ashley was either using her skills as a Corporate Executive, or some unknown law of the jungle that she had garnered from her savage side. It was both the same, really.

"True," I sighed. "Oh well. We'll stick with our original plan, then," I told Ashley, nodding. Then I turned my back on the Queens. "Let's go, Wulfra. I'm not sure what it is about seeing Fae women naked, but maybe the instant disgust just drives me to the arms of a real woman. Let's go have some fun before we pick up the kid. We've got plenty of time, after all. Oberon has no idea what's coming." I growled hungrily, eyeing her up and down. "And my eyes want to feast on some real beauty after all this..." I glanced back at the Queens, grimacing with distaste, "Overcompensation." Then I reached down and pinched Ashley on the ass.

Ashley shot me a fiery, passionate look, and a slow, promising smile split her cheeks. Then she paused. "What about the two crones?" she asked.

I shrugged, glancing back at them again. Their faces were red with outrage. "I guess we can leave them. It's not like they can do any harm. Let them have their feast, I guess. It will make for a good story when we get the kid back and their entire kingdom witnesses their failure."

And I turned away again as they began to shout, threaten, and curse – screaming for guards. No longer content to let Oberon's Wild Hunt take us down. The first wave of Fae soldiers rolled into the doorway in front of us. I remembered my first conversation with the Queens, when we had been grabbed into their world while fighting in the Circus. They had mentioned balance. *Dark and Light. Glamourie and Grammarie. Beasts and Masters. Fire and Ice. Life and Death...* Could that pertain to here? With Wylde and I? That we needed to find that balance, that give and take. Not one over the other, but an agreement between them.

I smiled hungrily, and embraced Wylde, not even slowing my steps. *Time to play*, I told him.

I wasn't sure what I did, how I did it, or if I really wanted to know.

I pulled deep from the shadows on the wall, and rolled it over the soldiers like a lead blanket. They suffocated under the weight, choking or crushed. I stepped over them as the next wave stormed in. I brought their armor to life with a whisper to the earth, calling her Name, bowing down to her will, and asking her to usurp these Fae who had killed her children only to wear their carcasses as armor.

She screamed in motherly outrage, and I realized I was laughing.

Their armor burst to life – vines, wood, and leaves squeezing, strangling, and piercing the dozen men. They died horribly and instantly, painting the hallway with their blood. The earth let out an appreciative sigh, and then thanked me for granting her retribution, paying her tribute.

I dipped my head, and stepped through the doorway into the courtyard.

Robin Goodfellow watched from a nearby barrel, discreetly nodding his head in approval, but also looking ready to bolt in case I tried to kill him. His eyes flicked to the right, and I noticed a fist of soldiers glaring at us from two dozen paces away. I heard the Queens shrieking for the guards to halt and leave us be, sounding frightened at both the sudden violence and the fact that I hadn't used my *Manling* magic, but their *Fae* magic. This terrified them.

And their soldiers obeyed.

I didn't cease walking. Robin subtly pointed his chin down the courtyard and I followed it to see Talon and Tory standing beside Carl, hiding in the shadows as they watched the nearby soldiers. They didn't look scared, but they didn't look eager, either. As I strode past them, I looked straight at them. They immediately stepped in behind Ashley and I, strolling with us as if we were on a casual morning walk. Guards stood in small pockets, here and there, flexing hands on their weapons, and guests of all species stared at us with cold, hard eyes. I kept a smile on my face as I continued to walk. Then I waved a casual hand over our group, and our disguises disintegrated, revealing our true forms. Well, our true forms while we had been here. Those wilder, more primitive versions of ourselves.

As we entered the courtyard with the swinging cages, I saw that no more fun time was happening, but that they were all staring at us. I held up a hand and my group stopped. Alone, I walked right up to the troll with the pixies and held out my hand.

He blinked at me in disbelief, and began to snarl.

I punched him straight in the face, snatching up his fistful of leashes with my other hand. Wylde must have juiced up my fist, and I was so deep within, that I didn't even notice him do anything magical. The ogre went flying into another ogre, knocking him down – which in turn, knocked down another ogre. I grunted, spat on the ground, and returned to my group clutching the bouquet of pixies in a fist. They flapped their wings, whispering to each other nervously, wondering what horrible fate awaited them now that they were in the hands of this psychopath.

We strolled out of the tunnel leading back into town, and no one harassed us, even though it would have been the perfect choke point.

But I had made a strong impression. And a bottleneck like that could easily go both ways. After all, one man could hold off dozens in such a small space.

We walked up to a stable, picked a few horses while Carl watched our backs, and then climbed on. The stableman stood there, wringing his hands, shooting furtive glances at the guards, who refused to do anything to help. I turned back to the guards, the ones in charge of letting people into the city. I saw the cute Fae who had let us in.

I grinned, licked my lips, and then mouthed *later*. She blushed, but kept her reaction hidden behind her visor where her fellow soldiers couldn't determine which soldier I had addressed.

We rode out of town in silence on our horses. Amazingly enough, they were your everyday horses – no tentacles, or wings, or anything odd. I began to laugh at the insanity of it all.

I saw a pair of stiletto heels strapped to Tory's saddle, and another pair strapped to Talon's saddle. I let out a sigh of relief, even though I wasn't sure why. Oberon had lied about the kid. Had he also lied about my friend and the heels?

Why had Oberon Invited us to come here to save the kid, but not told us that he was intending to hunt the child with his Wild Hunt? Was his purpose really just to get his hands on the Queens' shoes? Did he have a foot fetish of some kind? Or was this all some great, big, pointless game?

I couldn't do anything about it, now. We exited the thicket where we had met Barbie and Ebony, only to find them waiting on the other side. They took one look at the bouquet of pixies attached to the chains in my fist, and grew very still. I motioned for everyone to halt, and then strode up to her, holding out my hand with the chains.

I closed my eyes, focused on the chains, and with the help of Wylde, the metal leashes evaporated, and the cloud of pixies began flapping in earnest, zipping back and forth until Ebony and Barbie got them under control with harsh curses in a language I did not know.

It took her a minute, and as she did, I scanned the surrounding hills. I saw a black mass a few miles away, like a shifting ocean. Then another horn blew, coming from that direction, and the mass suddenly surged forward.

I slowly swiveled my head to Talon, motioning for him to guide us. He trotted up, swallowed audibly at the Wild Hunt, and then said, "Shit."

"We need to find the kid. Now."

Barbie zipped up to land on my shoulder, and I felt the air vibrating as her companions followed. "He went that way," she said, pointing away from the Wild Hunt. "Right after you entered the city."

I cursed under my breath. If we had just waited to enter the city, we might have run right into him. And an army of guards, no doubt. Still, it was frustrating.

"Find him," I said to her.

"For what you have done for my sisters?" A devilish smile split her cheeks. "We will shake the very pillars of creation," she snarled. The cloud of pixies burst ahead like a shotgun blast, covering a wide arc. Talon surged after them, yowling excitedly.

I grinned. "We ride!"

"Fucking right, we do," Carl hissed, giving me a meaningful look before he burst ahead to join Talon.

I followed them, feeling good to be riding a horse again, wondering exactly what Carl had meant. Ashley and Tory brought up the rear. Ashley was speaking softly with Tory, who was frowning thoughtfully. I didn't know how fast the Wild Hunt moved.

But I was betting it was pretty damned fast.

CHAPTER 30

We followed the swarm of pixies into a deep valley full of weeping willow trees. We had to be close. The boy couldn't have gotten far on foot. I doubt they had given him a weapon of any kind, and a young boy couldn't last long in this world. Not when everything wanted to kill and eat him.

We didn't want to ride too fast and wear out our horses, but we also couldn't move too slowly, either. Those blasted horns continued at random intervals behind us, and each time they did, I felt the icy breath of death at my back. I found myself reaching out more and more to Wylde as we rode. Or maybe I just listened to him more. Sought out that partnership, that balance the Queens had once spoken of. I extended him my trust.

He didn't always speak. I was just very aware of his mentality, now, the lines between us more blurred. He accepted our predicament with a calm detachment. Hunt or be hunted. It was the way of the world. Finding yourself on the losing end of the spectrum wasn't necessarily a bad thing. As long as you could maneuver your way out. A test. A proving ground.

It was just the way the world was. Nothing to get upset about.

Wylde was a charming fellow.

My thoughts drifted to Robin Goodfellow. Was he an enemy? Or had he helped us? How had the Queens found us? Had he led them to Ashley and I?

And why hadn't there been a stronger guard presence? An army against five, no matter how strong the five were, really shouldn't have been a question.

Thinking of that sent another sensation down my spine. Not an icy chill, but more like a searing thrill. I had tapped into the magic of the land and used it as simply as I breathed. Not a conscious effort, really, just using the world around me. No more than if I had seen a sapling nearby and decided to carve a switch.

I had tapped into this crazy world, felt a connection, and then used it. To do some pretty insane magic. I wasn't even sure if what Wylde did was considered magic, because although I had slaughtered a good number of soldiers, I hadn't broken a sweat. Not really. Not like I should have. To be honest, it began to make me feel nervous. As if I had found another Demon – like the Maker's Beast I had ripped from my soul. That Beast was currently residing in my old sword cane, which was in the possession of the Hatter.

Who was in this world. At least... someone from this world had seen his prison and brought the story back to the children as a folk tale.

I wondered if he was even aware he was so close to the Fae. Thinking about that, I recalled him once mentioning something about the Queens pestering him, but that had been a long time ago, and I had dismissed it as him being insane.

Because he was.

He had said a lot of things that were better left forgotten, and knowing his imprisonment had made him slightly unstable, I had found myself purposely forgetting many of the things he uttered. To save myself from future nightmares.

Regardless, my Beast was somewhat safe with him. I didn't need to worry about teaming up with the life force of creation, or whatever the hell the Maker's Beast was. I had heard the Cliff Notes version of it and – thanks to a unique opportunity – had been able to successfully get rid of it and take back my wizard's gift.

But it had cost me.

I had promised to free my Beast from the cane.

And that unfulfilled promise had begun to tax me. I frowned to myself. Well, it had taxed me in my world. None of that seemed to matter here.

But I wasn't planning on making this vacation permanent. In fact, I wanted to get out of here, stat. Even though Oberon had betrayed me somehow, I knew there had to be a sliver of truth to his request. That in order to escape, I had to get the kid, the shoes, and my kidnapped friend.

Even though he was a big fat liar on many things, possibly even those things, there was no way in hell I was leaving a kid in this place. Not happening.

But I had plenty to occupy my time back home. Namely, a freaking war against the Greeks. I had snubbed the nose of Hercules and inadvertently killed Bellerophon. And even though it had been less than a day in the Fae world, I knew time was funny between our two worlds. It could end up being twenty minutes in earth time.

Or...

A week.

Surely one night couldn't be more than that. I had spent about an hour here before when I first met the Queens, and the time change hadn't been too bad.

Still, it made me uneasy. I had made a mess, and then left.

Now, I found myself fleeing from the man who had asked me to come here in the first place. Mallory's other half, so to speak. Oberon. And he was apparently the Goblin King as well, leader of the Wild Hunt. It made me really wish I could just sit down and connect dots, jotting down who was who in my world, because I was beginning to see that these legendary people usually had more than one hat, and that the world at large thought they were two entirely different people, when in fact, several gods and myths seemed to be neatly wrapped up into one sadistic individual. Like the world of magic was really just a group of people with multiple personality disorders.

The usual stories that most read about the Fae are kind of contradictory, and although I had read most of them, I hadn't expected anything like this. I had expected a sophisticated court of royalty. Deadly, sure. But not this... primitive.

Then again, primitive didn't sound right. That implied they were backwards, uncivilized, impractical. But they were the opposite of that. They were cunning, ruthless, and savage. But they also seemed... enlightened, maybe? At one with their surroundings.

At least, judging by my relationship with Wylde.

But that opened up a whole 'nother can of worms. Who was Wylde, really? I had memories of him as a freaking kid, for crying out loud. And memories of spending time with Talon the Devourer – my pet cat. And Talon said he had memories of me, as well. Wylde even looked like me, where my friends had drastically changed appearances in this place. Was Wylde a version of myself? Like Pan, Mallory, and Oberon were kind of the same person?

Or was he real? His own person. Was I simply inhabiting his body? Possessing him? I shook my head as I thought about that. It didn't make sense. Because Wylde was a force of nature. A conqueror. A… Marauder, as Robin Goodfellow had said. And Robin had acted like he'd never heard of me. If Wylde was a real person, surely the Queens would have at least acted confused, wondering how Nate Temple was possessing the body of one of their subjects. Or they would have heard of him, because Wylde seemed like the kind of bro that might have earned a name for himself. Judging by how efficiently he slung magic around. How casually he used his powers.

Then again, he wasn't really using *his* powers. He was using my powers. Or the powers in the land. Simply asking them for the occasional assist. Like borrowing starlight. Or asking the dead branches to exact a little vengeance against the Fae for wearing their carcasses as armor.

I sighed, shaking my head.

I needed to get the kid, and get out of here. Then? A drink.

I looked up at my surroundings, scanning the trees, making sure none of them were about to eat me or my friends. Everyone seemed fine. They each had weapons out and were alternating between riding and walking beside their mounts. Like experienced horsemen.

But I knew for a fact that none of them were experienced horsemen.

Yet… they rode, maintained, and cared for their horses as if it was a normal part of life.

Because this damned place had affected them as well. Changed them. Brought out that darker nature inside them. The raw instinct. The carnal thirst. The bloodlust. The heart and soul of a survivor.

Well, Carl had already had that, and had been learning how to become *civilized* like my other pals in my world. Maybe coming here truly was a jaunt back home for him. But I knew for a fact that at least Ashley was in the same boat as me. Aware, and struggling against her new self.

I had yet to spend much time around Tory, but that was next on my list. I just wanted to think for a minute. Give them a task to accomplish, keep them occupied so I could think unobserved. Because if any of them grew suspicious of why their leader was acting soft as opposed to harsh, I was pretty confident that I would be placed on a spit and cooked for dinner.

Hopefully, Talon the Devourer, would help me with that. Stick up for me.

He was an asshole. But the little fuzzy bastard had grown on me. And not just because he had upgraded to the rated R version of Puss in Boots. Over the last year, I had found him to be a confidant. He didn't share much about his past, but I had often spent time talking with him in the Sanctorum. Much like I would have talked to, well, my dad.

He knew things. Or at least understood me when I brought up things. I had smart friends, but none of them truly understood me when I went off on magical tangents. They trusted me, so they nodded affirmatively and went along with it.

But Sir Muffle Paws? He challenged me at every turn. As did the Ravens. The three beasts had an unspoken truce of sorts. Maybe truce was too strong of a word, because I was sure one would attack the other if they thought they could get away with it.

I idly wondered if Sir Muffle Paws would remain as a cat once we got home, or if the time for disguises was long past. Or maybe he had sacrificed his current form to come to my world. Part of a bargain.

I sighed, scanning ahead again. Tory and Ashley hunted in a pair, watching our left flank, leaving no stone unturned. Because if I had been a kid fleeing for my life, I would have immediately sought out a hidey-hole. Carl was on the right flank, doing the same, using his superior senses to his advantage. The pixies had given him the boy's scent.

Speaking of, the pixies scouted ahead in a confusing cloud of flashing lights. Sparkling like Will-o'-the-wisps. They led our party, with Talon hot on their trail in his velvet boots that didn't leave a trail.

I whistled sharply, and saw a silver form peel off from the cloud of pixies. She zipped right up to my face, waiting patiently. "Barbie, go check on the Hunt. I need to know what they are doing."

She nodded. "They're likely hunting, Rider."

I scowled at her, but she had already turned away.

I glanced up at the ridgeline to our left, knowing it would lead back the way we had originally traveled. Did we need to return that way after we retrieved the kid? Was that even an option? With the Wild Hunt breathing down our necks, we might not have time to spend hours traveling back to where we had first appeared by that stone.

That was… if we even could return. Because Oberon, the man leading the Wild Hunt, had been our first friendly encounter in the Land of the Fae, and I wasn't really sure how to get back without his help. Mallory had brought us here. Did Oberon have to return us? Because that meant we simply needed to let the Hunt overrun us. I glanced at the other ridgeline, and froze.

A tall, red-haired young man in hunting leathers stood limned on the crest of the hill, staring down at me as if he had been waiting for my attention. It was the same fucking wanderer we had seen earlier. To prove this, he held up a sword, letting the broiling sun above reflect off the copper blade. I grunted. No steel in this world. Then he stabbed his sword into the ground and held up both hands, revealing three fingers on each. Six total. Then he lowered his hands, grabbed his sword, and turned away.

Carl saw me looking over his shoulder and followed my gaze. As he looked, the man had already disappeared over the hill. Carl turned back to me, frowning. I pointed up at the hill, urgently. "It's the fingering Ginger! Find him!"

CHAPTER 31

*E*lder Carl jumped onto his horse, sensing my urgency, and galloped up the hill. I watched him disappear over the other side, and waited. The others took turns watching me and the hill.

Talon glided up to me with his horse, the stiletto shoes he had stolen clacking against each other as the horse moved. They glistened like frost, and I had heard him more than once ask if anyone else was cold. "Fingering Ginger? Is that really the first words that came to mind?"

I shrugged. "He's a redhead. And he waves his fingers at us. He's obviously stalking us." I turned to look at the feline. "Do you think he works for Oberon? Part of the Hunt?"

Talon thought about that, and finally shook his head. "I don't think so. He doesn't look like anyone I remember, but I guess it's possible. I've been gone a while."

Carl reappeared at the top of the hill and held out his hands in the universal *I didn't see anything* gesture. Then he trotted down the hill, resuming his search for the kid.

I shared a look with Talon, who shrugged. "If he didn't see anything, there was nothing to see. But I can go have a look if you want," he offered.

I growled. "No, don't worry about it. We need to get the kid. That's all that matters. Leave the Fingering Ginger to the Wild Hunt." Talon chuckled before rejoining the sprites.

Several times so far, different pixies had returned to report to me. Each one of them had still looked tired and drained, but beneath that weariness had been a spark of hope. It had tempered my frustration. I had done something good, at least.

Hope…

I realized I was fingering my necklace and slowly lowered my hand. Tory was approaching, leaving Ashley to scout alone. I watched her approach, glancing at the stilettos affixed to her horse's bridle. She had been sure to tie them so that they rested on leather, not the horse's flank. They shifted as the horse navigated a large rock, lifting away from the leather. I saw that the material was darker where the shoes had rested, as if burned.

I waited for her, maintaining the cool detached nature of Wylde.

She walked beside me, not speaking, but I could tell something was on her mind. Something to do with Ashley, I bet. Once it became obvious she wasn't going to speak, I leaned over my saddle, checking a strap, and spoke casually.

"I wonder what the Reds have been up to…" I tugged the strap, patted the horse, and clucked at him in a soothing tone. I ignored Tory's flinch.

"How…" she whispered, glancing at me out of the corner of an eye. "That was a dream. You heard me sleep talking."

I snarled at her, a warning for her to watch her tone, and her shoulders slouched instinctively.

Then, unexpectedly, she began to straighten, and turned to glare at me. "You think that a beard is going to make me listen to you, Nate?" she snapped.

I didn't respond, merely let my face smile as I continued to walk.

But she wasn't beside me any longer. I held up a hand and motioned her to rejoin me. Because she had stopped right after saying my real name. I waited patiently.

A full minute later, she slowly clopped up beside me, studying me anxiously. Her eyes darted about, verifying we were alone. "What is going on? Why do I keep imagining these things, Wylde? Why did I call you Nate? And why is Ash—" Her words cut off for a second. "Why is Wulfra speaking of a man named Gunnar. What have you done to us?"

"I did nothing," I said, not looking at her.

She chewed over that. "Is this Oberon's doing?"

"You could say that," I said after a short pause. Then I nodded. "Yes, you could say that he has made you think you are someone you are not. Someone strong enough to survive this place."

She went very still atop her saddle. "You mean he has given us visions of weak creatures. To distract us."

"I think I spoke clearly, Tory. Use your cop skills."

She flinched as if struck. And then left, muttering under her breath about cops. She chose to watch our rear rather than return to Ashley.

Ashley gave me a very thoughtful look, but I pretended not to notice.

I really had to play a fine line here. I couldn't abandon Wylde. He had something to teach me. And that meant it was more than likely that the others had something to learn from their darker sides. Forcing them to abandon it would defeat the purpose, and those savage tendencies had kept us alive so far.

And Oberon had called this an Invitation, me coming here. Something that used to be common practice. I kind of believed him. As big of a dick as Oberon seemed to be, he and Pan were the same guy, and Pan never would have convinced us to come here if it was a frivolous trip. Or a trap. Especially not during a pending war.

I was missing something.

But what?

Oberon had told us to get the kid – forgetting to mention that the child was to be hunted down and killed by his own Wild Hunt.

He had told us to get the shoes from the Queens. Then a bunch of cryptic statements with words that made me shiver, because I didn't know if they related to the Land of the Fae, or the war back home, or me, specifically. *Hope, love, fire, savagery*, and a handful of others.

The Four Horsemen had once joked about me being the Horseman of Hope. I wasn't really a Horseman, even though they had repeatedly tried to recruit me. Sure, I had a Mask – currently disguised as the wooden disc on my necklace – but I hadn't actually accepted the mantle of the Fifth Horseman – if it was even possible to have such a mantle.

And there was a glaring lack of love in this shithole world.

The shoes…

I reached out to Wylde, preparing to give him a summary.

Talk, talk, talk. That's all you do in your head. Feel, don't talk. Experience, don't ask, he muttered, sounding grouchy, not even giving me a chance to speak. I blinked, not having thought that he had the Nate radio station playing the whole time.

What are the shoes? I asked him.

The most important thing in this world.

If he had been corporeal, I would have grabbed him by the shirt, demanding him to explain. Sensing this, he chuckled in amusement. *What do you mean, the most important thing in this world?* I asked.

He didn't respond in words. He simply sent me mental images. A baby looking up at his mother. A child staring back at his dad before jumping off a cliff. A rabbit fleeing a fox, diving into a hole at the last possible instant. A young girl crying into her father's shoulder. A boy kneeling in the grass, bloody, and a wooden practice sword lying at his feet while the father looked on with an encouraging look. A silhouette staring at a hut from the shadows of night, smiling at the light inside. An injured man returning from war, beaten, bloody, and staring at a poor wooden hut with a woman standing outside, smiling at the man as she held out her arms, crying.

More visions flew by in a blink. A montage of *life*. Then Wylde laughed triumphantly as he ran back to his cave, leaving me in confusion. The bastard was insatiable, having to go club a new woman every five minutes before dragging her back to his cave to do as he would.

I pondered the message, wondering what it could mean. Family? Love? Protection?

"We should rest the horses. Eat. Wash. And the sparkly mosquitos need a break."

I flinched, shocked to see Carl staring at me from a few feet away. I had been so lost in my conversation with Wylde that I hadn't noticed him approach. I quickly replaced my mask of authority, and grunted, flashing a few hand motions at him to signify agreement. He cocked his head, watching me curiously, and then turned away without a word.

I had to stop myself from panting in relief that he hadn't stayed a moment longer.

Because I realized that I had used a few gestures that I didn't know.

Not consciously, anyway.

Wylde cackled in the caverns of my mind as I heard Carl announce a quick break in our search.

What was happening to us, and why had Carl looked at me so oddly?

Had I messed up the gestures? I drew a strict rein on my connection with Wylde, deciding that I needed to keep him on a close leash moving forward. I couldn't risk the bleed over becoming so easy, even though I feared that I needed to do just that.

I might just lose myself in this place.

CHAPTER 32

*T*he naked pixies lay in an exhausted pile, sleeping. As I approached, I heard Ashley and Tory arguing with each other. A combination of words, gestures, and guttural sounds, as if switching from their darker natures to their human natures.

I watched, to make sure they didn't kill each other, but otherwise left them alone, pretending it wasn't happening.

Carl strolled up to me, grinning wide. "This is fun."

The two women heard him, and immediately turned their anger on him, snapping, snarling, and shouting. The last thing I heard from them – that I could decipher, anyway – was, "too good to use your body to talk. Want to act like a sniveling Manling to feel high and mighty?"

Carl calmly turned to them, eyes narrowing.

"Elder Carl," I began in a warning tone.

He didn't even look, holding out a claw to stall me. "This will only take a moment," he hissed under his breath.

Then he began a Shaman rain dance. Well, it looked that way to me, but it was more the sudden passion that went into his flurry of emotions. I watched as an explosion of snarls, claps, growls, snarls, hisses, and wild hand motions assaulted the two women. And he spun, squatted, stomped, and jumped at the same time.

The anger drained from their faces, and they fell to their knees, slowly curling up on themselves until they finally sat bunched in a protective ball, hands over their heads, and whimpering submissively.

I stared, jaw hanging open.

I slowly turned my head to find Talon grinning openly at Carl, who was breathing heavily through his nose, his albino scales shining in the sunlight. He waited until the women peered up at him, finally moving their hands out of the way.

He slowly lifted a hand, joined his thumb and forefinger together, and began to make small circular motions with the tips of his claws. This washed the blood from their faces. He cleared his throat, halting his motion very deliberately, as if it meant something. "I will speak as I please. I am an Elder. There is no harm in using words rather than this," he said, emphasizing the last gesture that had terrified them. "A warrior practices with all weapons available to him, and isn't scared to learn new skills. Stupid fucking children," he spat on the ground, and his saliva sizzled.

Everyone stared at *that*, even Carl.

Then, he turned on a heel, disrobing as he moved. "I'm going to bathe in the stream." The women watched me, but I simply turned to Talon, bewildered. Carl continued to undress, leaving a trail of white leathers on the way. I saw his white, scaly ass walk into a stand of reeds before he disappeared. I continued to stare. He had done better than Talon had in convincing the women to start speaking. In private, they had both come to me, admitting their odd memories in different ways, but once joined back together, had reverted to their instincts, and had apparently gotten into an argument. Likely over these strange visions they were having.

Carl had just solved the Rubik's cube by taking a shotgun to it. Gordian Knot style.

Talon seemed to be smirking as he licked his paws.

"That would have gone so much better with a saucer of cream," he said between licks. "Or blood, I guess," he added.

CHAPTER 33

*I*n Carl's absence, the women were oddly silent as they disbursed food from their packs. They didn't act confused to be handing out small bags of trail mix in Ziploc bags.

I didn't comment on that, just accepted the food as I sat down on a rock.

I had spent a few minutes rubbing down my horse, more for something to do than anything else. We hadn't ridden them that long, but even such a small dose of affection would go a long way in establishing a bond between us.

I was lost in thought when I saw something out of the corner of my eye. I turned to see Carl standing before us, the wad of his leathers in one fist. I had a sudden idea, and acted on it without thinking.

"Snake!" I shouted, pointing at his crotch in horror.

Carl glanced down, frowning. "No, that's just my dic—"

I interrupted hurriedly, like old times. "Yeah, I know what it is. I think I even have one," I said drily. "Last time I checked, anyway."

Carl studied me, looking confused, but I ignored him. It hadn't been for his benefit. My outburst had the desired result. Tory and Ashley began to giggle. Then giggle snort. Then it became uncontrollable, and they were grasping at each other, crying and sobbing as they laughed their asses off. I found myself smiling from ear-to-ear, leaning back against my rock. "Fuck-ing… Carl!" Tory gasped, panting. Ashley joined in, and soon they were chanting it back and forth, supporting each other as tears ran down their cheeks.

I let out a breath, and closed my eyes for a full minute, smiling. That was a win. I opened my eyes and studied my surroundings. I didn't want to rest too long, because the kid was still in danger, even if not currently from the Wild Hunt.

A pixie suddenly flew straight at my face, stopping a millimeter from my nose, and flicked me in the eyeball.

"Ow!" I snapped, rubbing my eye.

Barbie grinned at me. "They sleep."

It took me a few seconds to understand. "The Hunt?"

She nodded. "A wise man would take that as a compliment. They need rest in order to face a Rider."

I grimaced, both at the long-term thoughts of them coming at us refreshed, and the title she had used for me. But I didn't dissuade her.

"But a clever man would see this as an *opportunity*," she added.

I nodded, turning to the group. They were watching me, even though the girls did shoot very studious glances at Carl and his snake while he tugged his leathers back on. "The Hunt rests. Let's stretch our break a bit longer, but not too long. This is an advantage."

"I'm not tired," Tory said, frowning.

I nodded slowly. "That's what concerns me. Neither am I, but we haven't *really* slept since we came here. We should be exhausted." It was a gamble to say it like that, but I wanted to gauge their reactions. Wylde wouldn't have said *since we came here*, and if they were still savage, they would have picked up on that, sharing considering frowns with each other.

They did frown, but in a way that signified they were suddenly wary... about not being tired. *Good*, I thought to myself. Because the thought had recently hit me. We had been here for one night and part of one day, but it felt much longer. Which made my skin crawl.

Time was different in the Land of the Fae, or so everyone said.

Barbie sniffed, and then darted into the pile of naked pixies. None of them stirred as she sprawled over them to catch some sleep herself.

Ebony wasn't sleeping. She stared at me from across the camp, nodded, and then drifted off to circle the camp, making sure we weren't falling into a trap.

I couldn't sleep either, so I sat there, resting my eyes, thinking, planning, scheming.

How did one evade the Wild Hunt?

CHAPTER 34

$\mathcal{I}$ rode beside Carl, studying a swamp ringed by more of those glowing, weeping willows to our left. The pixies seemed interested in it, but not certain, as if the stench was masking the true scent they had been following. We had rested well, if only for a short time, and had been on the move again after less than an hour. I had wanted to spend some time with Carl. Get a feel for him, because he was a different creature. Literally, and figuratively.

I opened my mouth to speak, but Carl grunted. "Bold son of a bitch, isn't he?"

I followed his gaze to see the Fingering Ginger standing on a hill, holding up his sword again. Then he slammed it into the earth and held up seven fingers. I think. It was more than six, but it was hard to count from this distance.

Then he hauled ass away from us after grabbing his sword.

I turned to Carl, knowing we wouldn't be fast enough to catch him, but feeling like I needed to try anyway. "He looks familiar," Carl muttered, looking frustrated as he stared at the hill.

My breath caught. "Where have you seen him, Elder Carl?" I asked in a curious, but low tone, wanting to hide my own lack of knowledge if he was still savage.

"I don't know. Chateau Falco, maybe?" he said, sounding unsure. He began to click his tongue somehow – because I didn't think his reptilian tongue should have been able to do that – but I snatched his arm.

"Carl?" I whispered.

He glanced at me, frowning. "Yes, Master Temple?"

My heart was racing. Temple. Not Wylde. "You *know* me?" I asked.

"Of course," he said, frown growing.

I let out a breath, beginning to smile. "I thought you were like the others. The girls. Forgotten your humanity…"

Carl's frown slowly shifted to a humorless grin. "I never had any… humanity. Other than what you gave me." He chuckled. "*Now*, I understand why you've been acting so oddly around me. You thought I was like them. My mind clouded…" he nodded to himself, connecting pieces of a puzzle. "I see. You're playing games. Trying to taste the wild while trying to break them of it." He somehow let out a slow whistle. "That's… something. Seems to be working. In a way. At least for them. Any luck on yourself?" he asked, not meeting my eyes.

I started to answer, to tell him I had it under control, but at that moment, he looked up, eyes cold and demanding honesty.

"I… don't know. I want to say *yes*, but I'm not sure. It's hard. Trying to be both."

He nodded. "Well, just pick your favorite. Not that hard. Or be both." He shrugged.

I chuckled, opening my mouth

And heard a roar from the swamp.

I was galloping before I consciously chose to. Because immediately after the roar, I had heard a defiant shout. And a young boy screaming in terror.

My Band triangulated on the scream of their own volition, swooping in from their previous positions to meet behind me in a galloping arrow of blade, claw, hoof, and fang.

And the tip of that arrow was one *Wylde* son of a bitch…

CHAPTER 35

The pixies drifted through the weeping willows surrounding the swamp like lightning bugs, or floating glow sticks. A few more feet and the swamp began in earnest, so I jumped off my horse and hastily threw the reins over a low hanging branch that was wet with a slimy, black substance. The trunk expanded and contracted, as if breathing. I shared a look with Talon, who muttered a response to my unasked question. "It's hibernating. Don't worry."

I didn't even allow that thought to get dissected and analyzed by my brain. I just took it as fact. The rest of my Band tied up their horses, readied weapons, and put their game faces on. Because the shouts and screams still continued, and the roars were louder.

"Lights out," I hissed. The fairies doused their butt lamps and ghosted through the swamp. Tendrils of fog eddied and swirled underfoot, masking safe footing. I called upon Wylde, asking for his guidance. I stared back at the ground, and smiled. A ring of frost slowly drifted from me, encircling my entire group. Talon hissed, cursing about being cold again, and tried to jump back, only succeeding in slipping on the frost and falling on his ass like a fledgling ice skater. I smiled, ignoring his scowl.

The cold ate the fog. I wasn't sure why or how, because I would have chosen heat to burn it away. But we were in the Land of the Fae, and things were different here. Wylde knew this. I snapped my finger softly, and the ice bubbled up, a rough, sandy sheet coating its surface, no longer slick.

Talon hissed at it, on all fours, and scrambled up a nearby tree.

He flicked his tail disdainfully, and then began hopping from branch to branch, scouting ahead. Carl shivered audibly, rubbing his scales. The fan around his neck began to quiver, as if warning away a threat. But no one was around us. I pressed on, and they followed me.

Ashley's braids clinked together softly, but I wasn't concerned about being heard. The sounds ahead would cover our advance. Tory reached down to pick up a club, picking it up in one hand. This feat alone would have earned her an arm in marriage by any of the ogres at the palace. She smiled unsurely at me, and it was a very human smile. Still violent, but human. I nodded one time, holding out my hands like a balancing scale. She nodded back, focusing intently.

Ashley noticed my motion, and began to growl in a low tone, preparing herself, but acknowledging my advice.

I opened myself up to Wylde again.

Because we had a kid to save. A monster to kill. And an unknown third voice just ahead.

Kill, kidnap, or take. Whatever worked. *Whatever was most rewarding to me*, Wylde thought with a hungry chuckle. I let him, nodding slowly, and crept through the swamp.

Smells invaded us, and light died, unable to pierce the thick canopy overhead. Things crunched underfoot, and faint whiffs of decay puffed into the air. It was better since it was frozen, but still atrocious. The ring of frost moved with us, without me thinking about it. Carl studied the ground with a scowl, and I saw flickers of motion as Talon hopped from branch to branch like a ninja Ewok elf. As if sensing my thoughts, I saw his silver eyes glinting in a thin bar of sunlight that managed to pierce the canopy above the branch he stood upon.

We advanced like a single unit, not speaking, merely gesturing towards each other, or sharing a look. But the conversation was clear, even to me, fully partnered up with Wylde. We reached a thicket, and I crouched, knowing the kid was just beyond it. Loud scuffles, shouts, and roars reverberated in the forest as two people fought. I glanced up at Talon. He pointed an arm and waggled his claw in a specific motion. Then he pointed another direction, punched the air twice, and then punched his two fists together.

Kid to the right, ripe for taking. Two warriors fighting.

I nodded, and burst through the thicket, satisfied at the sound of crunching reeds that announced my arrival like the sound of shattering glass.

A pool of murky, oily water surrounded a small island of mud that was covered in decaying trunks, logs, and boulders. I saw a small form pulling his legs inside one of the thick, hollowed out logs near the edge of the water on the island. Then I saw the ten-foot-tall beast of oozing, dripping mud with giant blooms of poisonous fungus and moss growing all over his body. He turned to us and roared, mouth splitting wide to reveal teeth of rotten, splintered bark. Slimy boulders glistened where his eyes should have been, and I noticed a dozen primitive arrows peppering his hide, oozing green, noxious blood. Like pond scum.

And the smell...

Ho' boy.

It was like all the fecal matter and decay in the world had been dumped into this single pond, and that some real asshole of a god had decided to use that substance as clay to make...

This motherfucker. The Shit Goblin.

Tory glanced from the monster to the club in her hand, and then dropped it. She picked up a much larger one, hefting it thoughtfully before nodding. Then a green fog suddenly exploded around her – looking like a sea of desperate claws, all grasping at the air for a taste of freedom before splashing back under the fog with little puffs of green vapor, only to be replaced by more reaching claws.

She pointed a finger, hurling it at the Shit Goblin. It washed over him with absolutely no effect. So, it wasn't a Beast, per se. More like a construct of some kind. Interesting.

Ashley snarled, darting back and forth, side to side on all fours, as if searching for a weakness, not too thrilled to be the only one that would have to use her mouth to fight. With a deeper, frustrated growl, she unfolded to stand upright again, and withdrew two curved daggers – as long as her forearm – and began spinning them in her wrists like little propellers of pain.

The Shit Goblin took a step closer, and then gurgled in anger, spewing feces into the air as he arched his back. And a figure darted into view, having been standing behind him until now.

A woman.

Covered in furs, with eyes of orange fire. She clutched an aged ivory bow, and wore a hooded cloak made of shifting shadows. I could only tell she was a woman by what I could see of the delicate structure of her face.

Oh, and she was familiar.

Tory gasped, and her fog evaporated in a blink.

The Huntress stared at us, lowering her bow in astonishment.

The Shit Goblin backhanded her clear across the pond, leaving him alone with the kid. He sniffed the air, as if trying to find his snack. The Huntress struck a tree, but Talon was there in a heartbeat, shaking her, making sure she was alive. She had landed beside a shaggy stallion made entirely of tree bark and slithering vines. It very briefly reminded me of that Trojan Horse they used as a prop in the movie. Then it made a sound like a rasp filing wood, and stamped a hoof angrily, watching Talon with dangerous eyes. Talon held up a paw, not even looking at the beast, and the Huntress stirred.

Talon leapt away right before her arrow impaled him into the earth. He scrambled up the tree away from the Huntress, hissing and yowling as he fled, complaining about her manners. She climbed to her feet, shook her head to clear the daze, and then placed a comforting hand on the tree horse. Then her eyes locked back on us across the pond as the Shit Goblin stomped the island between us in his search for the kid. I nodded at her one time, meeting her eyes. It took her a moment to nod back, but she did, even if it did look awkward and unpracticed.

Something the Huntress had once said teased me, but I couldn't remember it. Before I could try harder, Wylde squashed it down. He didn't have time to blabber on about the thoughts, memories, and feelings of Nate Temple. Wylde had something to *kill*. That was all that mattered.

The voice persisted, albeit muted, whispering something about Oberon. Something he had said, but Wylde pressed that down, too.

Stop distracting me! he snapped. With an uneasy breath, I listened to his advice.

And I felt Wylde take control.

I was Wylde, Daemon of the Fae. But I was also Master Temple. And I could feel us infecting each other. Adopting traits back and forth. We had both changed, for better or worse.

Tory took a step forward, reaching out an imploring hand to the

Huntress. The archer jerked her head as if shaking away a buzzing bee, and then continued peppering the Shit Goblin with arrows. Tory hurled branches, logs, huge stones, and anything else she could get her hands on. They struck the monster, knocking him off balance, and either firmly wedging in his body, or sailing right through, only for the flowing shit to reform the wound a few moments later.

She continued anyway, serving to annoy him.

Wulfra and Talon also flung blades from a distance, not doing any good, and the Huntress' arrows, although crackling where they struck, seemed to have little effect with each hit.

Elder Carl, on the other hand, was darting from rock to rock, spraying venom at the Shit Goblin, the fan behind his neck rattling and quivering like a hornet trapped in a bottle. Where the venom struck, mud burned away, and didn't reform. Still, there was no way he had enough venom to prevent the monster from killing the kid.

Because the monster had given up on us and was stomping all over the island, shattering each log and hiding place with massive feet.

"My turn," I said, laughing as I lifted my hands to the canopy above.

The trees around us abruptly awoke with screams, as if being skinned alive. I pulled deep, drawing them closer to me, their branches bending, cracking, splintering, and shattering, spraying the oily blood on their bark into the air. Talon dove to the safety of the ground, fur pointed straight up on his back, and panting as he tried to watch them all at once, shaking his head in horror as he spun in anxious circles.

I whispered a word to the trees, and they fought me, not wanting to listen.

I pulled them closer, more branches snapping, roots tearing free from the earth, and their tortured screams replied. The trees finally listened, furious, but accepting. Then, grudgingly, they shot towards the island, latching branches around the Shit Goblin, trapping him.

Then a wave of light pierced the island, growing in diameter as the branches at the top of the canopy began to unfurl, letting the sunlight in. The circle grew wider, and finally touched the trapped Shit Goblin's foot. He squealed like a stuck pig, and his foot hardened like baked clay, then shattered under his weight, causing him to stumble.

But the light kept expanding, striking his knees, his thighs, and on up, until his entire body was struck by the sun. Smoke began spraying out of him, and the rancid smell became a burning fecal smell.

Which was still entirely unpleasant.

Before the Shit Goblin was completely solidified, he slowly swiveled a terrified face my way.

I grinned. "Flush this turd," I said in a calm tone.

The trees snapped back to their original positions, and the Shit Goblin exploded into dried flecks of waste, raining down on the forest and, of course, us.

I looked up to see the Huntress climbing up onto her horse, throwing the kid on its back behind her. I hadn't even seen her snatch him! Then she was galloping away. I snarled, reaching out to the trees to stop her, but they had fallen back asleep, exhausted. I had woken them from their hibernation, after all.

I snarled, but Tory was already racing after her, having picked up a large flat rock to use as a shield. Ashley loped after Tory as backup. Or to save the poor kid. I rounded on Carl. "Get the horses and meet us on the other side!"

He was moving before I had even finished. Just then, one of the pixies zipped right up to my face. "The Hunt comes. Fast."

I nodded. "Talon. Let's get that fucking kid. Now."

I began to run, feeling Wylde slip back into his cave of his own choice. As if bored. I shivered. Not necessarily at the sensation, but at the *lack* of sensation. It had felt so smooth, and he had done it on his own, without me making him.

What if it got to the point that I wasn't even aware who was in charge anymore?

I continued to run, chasing my friends, and hoping Carl was fast.

CHAPTER 36

I came upon a crazy scene, even for me. Ashley watched as Tory and the Huntress fought hand-to-hand. Arrows stuck in a few of the nearby trees, but the bow was now lying on the grass near the fringe of the forest, looking like we were almost out of the swampy area. Following the trail of the kid had caused us to loop around so that I was pretty sure we were angling parallel to the way we had originally fled to the palace, but without climbing a hill, I wouldn't know for sure.

Tory punched and clawed, veins flashing gold beneath her skin, and her thick green fog quivered around her feet, but the Huntress had a cloth wrapped around her nose, to protect herself from inhaling it. To be honest, I wasn't really sure what the fog was. I had seen her control dozens of flavors of Beast without it.

But it hadn't worked on the Shit Goblin, and it didn't seem to be affecting the Huntress.

Then again, the Huntress wasn't a beast. Well, seeing her here, made me reconsider that. She wasn't a Beast, but she wasn't far from it. A wildling. A loner. A survivor. The Huntress used her cloak to catch many of Tory's blows, the shifting shadows trapping, blocking, or parrying her attacks, as if alive. All while the Huntress kicked, clawed, and punched right back. Tory took the blows with no apparent notice, snarling as she fought.

I calmly strolled towards the horse, noticing the kid tied up and struggling on the saddle. Talon held the reins, and although the mount wasn't happy about it, he didn't fight too much. As I approached, he grew very still, turning its acorn of an eye to watch me, even though it didn't turn its head of vines, leaves, and twigs. I held out my hands in a peaceful gesture, and continued to advance.

I clicked my teeth soothingly as I heard pounding hooves from the distance, hoping to all hell it was Carl and not the Wild Hunt. The horse's ears swiveled towards the sound, stamped a hoof made of bark, but didn't try to bolt. I placed a calming palm on the bark-like skin, and the horse visibly shook, as if I had dumped warm water over his back after a long day out in the cold.

And then he sighed.

Talon stared at me thoughtfully, but didn't speak. I carefully reached up, plucked the boy from the saddle, and set him on the ground. His eyes were red and panicked. I placed my palms on his shoulders and stared him in the eyes, careful to make my face look kind.

He stared back, terrified.

Talon chuckled. "You're covered in war paint drawn by blood," he muttered, still laughing.

I frowned. I was? That was new. I remembered seeing it on my arms, but nothing about my face. I stroked my beard with one hand, and then began to smile, nodding. The kid still looked scared, but less so. Now he looked ready to flee, as if placating me.

I shook my head in amusement. "I'm going to get you out of here, kid."

He stared back at me, face frozen in confusion. He had long dark hair, mussed with leaves and twigs, and a long narrow face. He was maybe thirteen years old, but I could have been way off. I wasn't a good judge of those things. He looked like he was about to meet that cruel bastard, the puberty fairy, but hadn't yet been introduced.

When he replied without his voice cracking, I confirmed my assumption. A child, but on the verge of adolescence. "Please… just let me go. I just want to go," he said, eyes glistening with fear, as if he had never known peace. "They're coming. I need to run!" he gasped.

I squeezed his shoulders gently. "Listen, kid. We're not from this place. We're from the real world. And we came here to save you. To bring you back home."

Talon cleared his throat. "They might need a referee. Or some oil," he said, sounding amused.

I turned my head, having forgotten all about the women. They were in various stages of undress, clothing having ripped in their battle.

And they were making out... violently.

Carl grumbled approval as he entered the clearing with a string of horses attached to his saddle. The pixies surrounded the two women, flying in a slowly rotating circle, bathing them in a silvery glow.

To be honest, it looked very romantic. And carnal.

I clapped my hands, and the two froze. They stared at each other, and then jumped apart, panting heavily as they debated fighting or kissing again. The Huntress shot a quick glance at me and froze, face transforming to outrage.

"That boy is mine," she hissed.

"He belongs to no one," Tory snapped right back. "Get your shit together, Huntress."

She stiffened at the words, slowly turning to look at the tiny woman beside her. "It... has been some time since I've heard that name..." She began to walk a slow circle around Tory, staring her up and down, frowning in deep thought. Then, between one step and the next, she froze, one foot about to lift from the ground. "No. It cannot... Tory?" she whispered. Her gaze snapped from face to face, frowning at the rest of us. She sniffed at Wulfra, the Native American Shaman of a bipedal wolf, and gasped. "Ashley..."

She turned to me, shaking her head, not recognizing me. I held up a hand, and a small ball of fire appeared, hovering above my flesh. She took a step back, clutching her throat. "Temple?" I nodded, letting the fire disappear. The kid was staring at my hand in awe.

She dismissed Talon with a disgusted sniff, as if having recognized him long ago.

She stared at the albino lizard warrior. "Your breasts are magnificent," Carl said, his tongue flicking out as if to taste them. He said this while rubbing his sword hilt.

The actual sword, folks. Not his snake.

"Fucking Carl," she said, a faint but genuine smile splitting her cheeks for the first time. Her eyes no longer glowed with fire, and although she looked the worse for wear, it was the same woman I knew, not having changed as much as the rest of us.

"Maybe you want to join us?" Tory asked in a very soft voice. Her eyes were intense, full of passion. But not the passion to fight. To, well... when one girl *really* likes another girl...

I stopped myself from visibly shaking my head. The Huntress had fawned over Tory for quite some time, and Tory had danced that line deftly, still dealing with the loss of Misha.

But perhaps they had found love in this wild place. Not soul deep love. But a taste. A shot of tequila at a busy bar during last call. It was better than nothing.

The Huntress nodded slowly. "I've been here so long," she said in a defeated voice, slowly falling to her knees. "I had given up. Become what I had to in order to survive this place. I retraced my steps, but found no door. There is no escape. I was lied to..."

Her words hit me deep. "Who? Who lied to you?"

She shook her head. "I cannot say... I swore an oath." Her eyes looked up, red-rimmed and hopeless. "I was trying to do the right thing," she whispered.

Tory knelt on the ground beside her, grabbing her shoulders. "You didn't have Nate," she offered, sobbing back lightly. The Huntress broke down, too, crying hard. And Tory comforted her.

I felt suddenly uncomfortable, and I could tell Carl and Talon did as well. I hadn't ever seen the Huntress emotional before. It was... jarring. She had always been so cold and practical. I knew that that part of her was still there, but *this* part was currently unveiled in full force – when I had never known it existed.

I looked up as Tory whispered to her. "I thought you said you would never return here?"

The Huntress nodded. "I meant it. But... I had to—"

The pixies grew suddenly agitated, and Barbie flew right up to me, waving her hands. "Sex later. The Hunt has reached the swamp!"

I jumped to my feet. "What the hell? That fast?"

"They are the Hunt," she responded in a dry tone. "You must flee. They want the child."

I felt the boy squirm beneath my palm, but I gave him a gentle, reaffirming squeeze. "That's not going to happen. He's going home." I turned to the rest of the group. "Mount up. Talon, find us a way out of here. Now!"

Everyone jumped into their saddles, the kid choosing to share my horse. I set him in front of me, so I could keep an eye on him. Also, so a stray arrow didn't hit him in the back before I knew it was coming.

Tory nodded at me, a proud smile on her face.

"We ride," I snarled, whipping the reins as I heard the first sounds of crashing limbs, and sudden horns from a dozen bugles. Or whatever they used.

CHAPTER 37

We didn't bother trying to pace the horses, because the growls, shouts and bellows felt like they were a hair away from swiping our heads off of our shoulders as we galloped. Talon darted down the path, holding up a paw as if to test the air, following some sense of direction even Wylde didn't understand.

We followed him blindly, and I began to think that this would be a great time for him to betray us all.

I realized that these were Wylde's thoughts, not mine. But they had merit. I had no reason not to trust Talon, but since when had that gotten me anywhere?

I called out to the pixies in my mind, but flung out my hand like I was rolling a pair of dice. The kid flinched, looking for a threat. I leaned closer to his ear, my beard tickling his neck, making him jerk with an instinctive, but still nervous, giggle.

"What's your name, kid?" I asked, sensing that the pixies had received my message, and were darting off in pairs, peeling back to race towards us.

"Alex."

"Okay. Alex, I'm Nate. We're going to get out of here, but I need you to listen to me. Trust me. *Only* me. Got it?"

He turned his head, frowning. Then his eyes drifted to my other… friends, and he shivered. "Okay," he said. Very softly.

"Don't be afraid. Fear gets you nowhere. The best way to beat fear is through insanity," I said, chuckling. "No matter how big, strong, and ugly the fear is, and how obvious it is that you don't stand a chance, you *face* it. And you fucking *laugh*. Laughter trumps fear every time."

The kid nodded doubtfully, grunting as the horse jumped over a pile of rocks.

I glanced up, saw that the pixies were almost upon us, and said, "Trust me, kid. No matter what happens, I won't *ever* let you down. Not as long as a breath remains in my body."

I lifted a hand, and the first two pixies raced my way. I sliced open my palm with a small blade at my hip. The kid watched me, frowning as I held it out to him. Then he slowly took the knife, met my eyes, gave me a nervous smile, and said, "Smile at your fears, right?" I nodded in approval. "Okay." He drew the blade across his palm, shallow, but enough to draw blood.

And he didn't avert his eyes from mine as he did. I smiled. "One tough bastard."

He held out his hand like mine, and the pixies darted through our fingers, wiping their wings in our blood as they flew by. Then they continued past us, right towards the Hunt.

"Bleed for me!" I shouted, startling my friends. I held up my hand, showing them my bloody palm. Alex did the same, waving it back and forth. My tribe obviously didn't understand why, judging by the looks on their faces, but they did comply. Soon, we were all holding up bloody palms, and a school of pixies descended down on us, splashing and spinning through our blood, laughing, giggling, and singing as they did.

Then they were past us, looping around the Hunt.

Talon glanced over his shoulder at me, pointing ahead. I saw the familiar golden forest, and groaned. We had nowhere else to go. I saw the massive catnip tree off to our right, but that was a wide-open space and we would be easily surrounded. They would roll over us. The Hunt was in the valley just behind us, likely already racing up the hill. Even at a gallop, we would barely make it inside the golden forest of spidery death before they saw us.

Unless...

I had an idea. Or, maybe Wylde did. It seemed a hybrid of sorts. Him pulling from my knowledge of reading, and me pulling from his knowledge of doing, marrying the two in unholy matrimony. I didn't question it. "Quick! To me!" I shouted.

Within thirty seconds, we stood in a huddle. "Great plan," Talon said, sounding nervous for the first time.

"Everyone touch me."

"I don't like people touching me," Talon argued.

"Really? A group hug?" Tory added.

"Fucking do it!" I snapped, making them all flinch as they sensed Wylde, reverting back to their savage forms. I watched as a film seemed to roll over their eyes, and then they obeyed. Even Talon. Their leader had spoken.

They obeyed.

I heard the galloping of hooves near the top of the hill behind us, screaming and hooting in victory. Wylde grumbled uneasily as he learned exactly how I was intending to pull off his plan, but I ignored him. I lashed out with my power, as a wizard, and did something I was very familiar with. The air cracked, screamed, and wailed in protest at my alien power, and we were ripped into a void, nothing at all like I had intended. The world crashed back into existence and I had a dull buzzing in my ears.

I saw blood leaking from the ears of those around me, and gasped. The world sounded muffled, as if covered in a pillow. And everyone looked a little wild around the eyes. The horses were all dead.

I spun in a dazed circle, wondering what the hell had happened. I had just tried to Shadow Walk…

A silver blur danced in the distance, near the golden forest. I shivered, staring at the hill where the Hunt should have been, but saw no one. The silver blur darted closer, but seemed to be struggling, like a butterfly with a ripped wing.

I frowned. The silver thing looked familiar.

Something about a silver girl that loved sex.

I blinked, and the form was suddenly right in front of my face, a silver woman of perfect proportions, utterly nude, and the size of my palm. I blinked as I watched her open her mouth, trying to tell me something. She had scrapes and wounds, and I saw one of her wings looked broken – shredded, actually.

She touched my forehead, and my ears popped. I gasped in agony, grabbing my ears. She shuddered, and then darted to the others around me, repeating the touch with them. They each hissed, snarled, and shouted as hearing returned to them. Alex sat against the tree, muttering under his breath, shaking his head as he rocked back and forth. He fell over when the silver pixie touched his forehead, but I saw he was still breathing, at least.

I was the first to notice the sound.

And was instantly rewarded with hundreds of dying screams and the sound of clanging metal rattling from the golden forest. The naked winged girl appeared in front of me, and I remembered. "Barbie," I breathed.

She nodded, looking on the verge of death. "They're coming. We sent them into the forest..." she trailed off, face haunted. "They followed us. Followed the smell of your blood. It likely wouldn't have worked if you hadn't disappeared for so long. But there are so many dead. Them... and us..." She let out a sob. "We did our best, Rider. Forgive me..." I nodded numbly. "They're coming now. The survivors. He is with them. And he's not... pleased," she said in a whisper.

Then she collapsed in the grass at my feet, suddenly a full-sized naked woman with silvery skin. She was covered with scratches and wounds. With the color of her blood matching her skin, her wounds looked more like someone had used a soldering iron to melt silver onto her skin. Trembling with the after effects of trying to Shadow Walk in this world, I scooped her up with a groan, almost unable to support her. My leg started to give out, and I felt Wylde step in, muttering angrily to himself as he drew deeply on the earth.

I felt sudden waves of heat rise up within me from the ground, granting me strength as I carried Barbie to the tree. I set her down against the trunk next to Alex, who was still shaking his head, mumbling in terror as the Wild Hunt burst from the golden forest, a swarm of two dozen of the hardest, deadliest nightmares King Oberon had left. The cream of the crop, most likely.

They looked to have spent days in there, and I idly wondered how long I had been gone. Barbie had said that we disappeared for so long. But the sun was still up, and the fight couldn't have taken that long. Even the army of spiders in those cursed trees couldn't have held off the Wild Hunt for too long.

"Wheeee!" Talon suddenly yowled, racing up into the tree and disappearing from view. I blinked, looking up, remembering where we were. The catnip tree.

Motherfucker.

199

"I told you we should have let him finish mating last time..." Carl grumbled from my side. My friends made a line before me, and I knelt close to Barbie, calling upon Wylde for help.

"Wake her. Give her strength. She must look after Alex," I pleaded out loud. Alex didn't seem to hear, and Barbie was fast asleep. I felt my hand reach up to her face, caressing her cheeks, and her eyes snapped open. She gasped as if I had just saved her from drowning. I slowly leaned closer, combing the fingers of both hands into the hair behind her neck, cupping her face as I stared deeply into her eyes, letting her see my soul. My heart.

And I placed a kiss on her lips.

A long, drawn out, passionate embrace, even nibbling her lip as the sounds of death approached on galloping hooves behind us. I let her see my heart through touch.

Because Barbie fed on affection, and my committed, genuine, loving kiss was the equivalent of an adrenaline shot. Not because it was like sex, but because it was *pure* love. She had risked her life for me, and I loved her for it. And I let her know that with my kiss.

She blinked back at me lazily as I pulled away. She licked her lips with a purr, smiling up at me. "No one will harm him," she promised. And then she climbed to her feet to stand before Alex, many of her wounds looking significantly better. Since I was still crouching where I had kissed her, this gave me an excellent view of her posterior, to make sure those wounds were also healed. I decided they were, and flinched as twin curved silver daggers suddenly appeared in her palms inches away from my leering eyes. She laughed lightly, appreciating my attention. The blades ran parallel to her forearms up to her elbow, and three more smaller blades protruded from the hilt and out between each of her knuckles.

Like brass knuckles with razor-blade bracers, but silver. Groovy.

I called upon Wylde. He grumbled in approval of my plan as the sounds of the Hunt pounded up the hill towards our tree, towards my row of friends. The Hunt couldn't see me hiding behind them. I scanned the area, assessing the potential with the sharp, calculating mind of Wylde assessing a battlefield.

I nodded, and began to army-crawl to my chosen spot. As I did so, I felt my body shifting, changing, adapting, uniting with the world around me.

"Distract them as long as possible," I whispered, and my friends all heard, even though they didn't look. Carl's ear holes cocked, tracking my location, but he didn't move his head.

It was time for Art Class.

Art of War, that is.

CHAPTER 38

I remained perfectly motionless as the horde of savages slowed, approaching the base of the tree with revenge in their eyes. Each was lacerated, ribbons of flesh hanging from faces, puncture wounds and slashes in their arms, legs, and sides.

The majority of them were goblins, but I saw an ogre or two. Maybe a troll. I really wasn't sure which was which, since what I thought I had known of the Fae had been so, so wrong.

One of the goblins had a collection of dead pixies tied to a string on his belt. I barely restrained my growl, wondering what had happened to Ebony. Barbie saw the carcasses of her friends, carried as a collection of trophies, and snarled, sliding her bladed forearms together in a soft *whisking* sound.

King Oberon stepped out from behind the giant ogre troll. Whatever. His right-hand goblin, Kaba, stalked at his side, clutching two blades and snarling at the line of my friends. Who snarled right back. King Oberon looked haggard, face pale, and furious. Scratched, but not seriously wounded. But right now, through his anger, he also looked victorious.

"Kill them. Find Wylde. Kill him, too. The child is mine," he growled, staring directly at Barbie.

Still, I didn't move.

But Tory did.

She flung out her hands like throwing two softballs, and a sudden wave of mist rolled over the army, catching up maybe half of them. They instantly went on a killing spree, bashing the brains of their fellow Hunters.

Oberon growled, sending a blast of power straight at her. The Huntress dove in front of it, taking the brunt of the blow, knocking her into the tree beside Alex and Barbie. Tory whipped her head to the side, shocked to see the Huntress do as she had done. Then another blast flew at her, knocking her into the ground. She groaned, and didn't get up. The Huntress was also dazed, unable to move as she blinked at our attackers very slowly, lips moving wordlessly.

Still, I didn't move.

Oberon began to walk laterally in front of my crew, chuckling as he held out his hands, spinning in a slow, triumphant circle. Kaba followed close on his heels, snarling at my friends, a last line of defense for his king. A personal bodyguard. Judging by the way he stalked, those copper blades in his hands weren't just a token. He had earned them. I should have noticed that earlier. I had considered him a secretary, of sorts. Now I had to worry about both of them.

"You've led us on a merry chase, Temple!" Oberon shouted. "But the butcher is here. You've failed. We've waited so long to Invite another Manling to play, but you were a stunning disappointment. Come out and watch your friends die. At least have some dignity."

Still, I didn't move.

Oberon waited until a silent count of three, face morphing into anger as he took a few more steps, trying to get a look at Alex behind my friends. Carl and Wulfra were focused entirely on the horde of monsters. Barbie, on the other hand, stood in a ready stance, slowly pacing to remain between Alex and Oberon.

Oberon pointed as he took another step. "You, child, must die. As much as it pains me to admit. I thought to have chosen Master Temple well, assuming he could save you before I was forced to fulfill my duty." He let out a regretful sigh. "But he failed you. And when duty calls, even I must overlook my feelings. I owed the Queens a favor, and a man cannot refuse a favor owed."

Alex finally leaned out from behind Barbie's exquisite ass to face Oberon for the first time. And then he burst out laughing. Full body heaves, with knee slaps and everything.

Oberon took a threatening step forward, spittle flying from his mouth, right beside a weathered log.

I jumped to my feet, wrapped my arm around his neck, and jabbed a dagger half an inch into his throat. He tensed, suddenly motionless, and Kaba shrieked in terror.

"Drop your blades, Kaba, and step over there," I rasped.

He did, watching as bark, leaves, and catnip pods rolled off my form.

The other Hunters shifted uncomfortably from foot to foot, and for the first time, my friends saw me. I hadn't just covered myself in the disguise. I had *been* the disguise, *becoming* the log.

"How?" Oberon whispered, and I could tell he genuinely had no idea how we had gotten to this point.

"Always appear where your enemy doesn't expect you. At a time of your choosing, at a location of your choosing. And never be forced into a fight," I said, paraphrasing some lessons I had learned from Sun Tzu. Wylde had added some things to it, but overall, it had resulted in the same decision, just with less grunting and hand gestures.

"You *couldn't* have known I would stand here, in this exact spot," he argued, incredulous.

"You were led. And now, you have lost. Due to overconfidence."

"And how was I led?" he asked.

I smiled. "I had her hide your view of the kid. Always rotating just enough to block a good sight of him. Until the end."

"I could have gone the other way, rather than walking this way."

I nodded. "But you didn't. Look, we can analyze this all we want, but guess what, Obie? I've got my stick in your throat." He grew silent after that.

The terrain had been rougher, uneven, and full of debris in the other direction. This had been the direction I would have walked in his shoes, the better to strut victoriously through. Because I knew Oberon. This was a big moment. To best the Manling his brother spoke so highly of.

Pan thought so highly of me that he led me into this trap, betting I could claw my way out.

Pan – Mallory – and I would have words. Soon.

"It seems we are at an impasse," Oberon said, careful of my blade in his throat. "You must make a decision, Manling. Kill or beg forgiveness. Do you dare kill a King of the Fae? Could your mortal mind even imagine the consequences? My people would storm the gates of your world like a tidal wave, rolling through like a plague, burning, pillaging, raping..." he held out his hands slowly, displaying his world. "Until it is like this. Clean. Precise. Honest. Or Darwinism, as you Manlings say." He paused, letting that sink in. "Just know that the moment I die, my soldiers will be upon you, and you will have no more leverage. So, it seems you must beg, tiny Manling," he finished, lowering his hands. "I win."

Kablooie grinned at me, licking his yellowed teeth, no doubt anticipating my punishment – what he would do to me for embarrassing his king.

I let out a breath. "I guess you're right. Killing a King... I hadn't really thought about it like that. That's a big deal. The repercussions would be... climactic." He grunted in response, but didn't move. I pressed the blade into his throat another half inch, relishing his gasp of astonishment. "I guess I've just been so busy thinking about killing a god that I didn't even bother to think how *very* important a *mere* king is. Ah, well. I guess I'm about to find out."

And I very slowly slid the knife into the Fairy King's throat, staring Kablooie in the eyes the entire time. The body dropped before me, gurgling as he choked on his own blood. Then he transformed into a goblin. I paid him no attention, staring Kablooie down.

He stared back at me, stunned.

His shoulders tensed as if finally remembering that he should be running, but a furred figure fell from the tree above, landing directly on top of him, clawing at his face on the way down. Talon stood, yanked Kablooie up to his knees, kicking the back of the goblin's legs as he tried to stand to his full height – because that would have put him head and shoulders above Talon.

And shorter people just hated that.

Kablooie stood motionless, facing me. Then, Talon very carefully extended his claws, revealing inches long claws, and sunk the tips into the flesh surrounding Kablooie's jugular.

If the goblin so much as accidentally passed gas, Talon would sink his namesakes the rest of the way into the flesh, and jerk his hands back, ripping Kablooie's throat out entirely.

"Hey, kitty. Don't you find it weird that even though we just killed Obie that none of his minions came over to squash us?"

Talon yawned loudly, shrugging. "I guess it is kind of interesting."

I nodded, walking towards my friends. "What do you guys think?"

Ashley nodded. "Smells fishy. Like there's a super-secret we're not supposed to know…"

I nodded, snapping my fingers. "That's it." I turned back to Kablooie. "What do you think, Oberon? Because I think we're right. But if you don't want to talk, I'm sure the Devourer will oblige you. He so loves making people do things they don't want to do. A specialty. Well, that and Devouring." Kaba glared at me, the depths of his hatred almost enough to make me gulp. But Wylde was in charge. At least his savageness was, but it was obvious he was drawing on my snark just as much as I was drawing from his primitive side. It was a unique sensation – basically, watching myself be a smartass.

"I wouldn't mind torturing a few of his lackeys, just to be sure," Carl offered politely. The trolls growled, and the goblins snarled, but none of them moved.

"Hey, you!" I said, pointing at one of the two big guys. "You're a hairy son of a bitch. What the hell are you, anyway?"

The creature blinked, not used to being directly addressed other than to be told things like *smash this, rape that, burn that other thing,* and *good boy!*

His eyes flashed to Kaba, and I grinned victoriously. "Troll," he finally grumbled.

I nodded. "Thanks. That was really bothering me for some reason, you know?" He blinked at me, and then shrugged uncertainly. "Now, on your knees. Or Kaba becomes a Kabab," I said.

The troll dropped to his knees in a heartbeat, angry, but desperate. I motioned to Tory. She dipped her head at me on the way by, and waded right into the horde of monsters until she was directly in front of him. "Which one of you tried to attack me? You bastards all look the same."

The troll grinned, glancing at the Huntress who was just now seeming to gather her wits. She turned from face to face, frowning at the situation, trying to get a read on what she needed to do to help. She looked very concerned when she saw Tory surrounded by the Wild Hunt.

Tory nodded. Then turned to the other troll. "Rip his arm off."

The other troll stared at her in disbelief. "Brood no rip arm without—"

He cut off abruptly as Tory kicked him in the face, sending him rolling into the goblins behind him. Then Tory casually grasped troll one's arm, and ripped it from the socket with a sharp motion. He collapsed, squealing and bleeding all over his compatriots. Tory carried the arm with her, hefting it over a shoulder. She reached the Huntress, stared at her for a moment, and then tossed the arm at the woman's feet, a gesture of love as primal as any I had ever seen. A Thank You. A Payment.

An act of love.

The two women suddenly disappeared, and I froze.

Kablooie began to laugh, sounding much different than he had up until now. I turned back to watch him shift into Oberon, still kneeling, and his clothing torn. Even having already guessed this truth, seeing two of my friends abruptly disappear shook me to the core.

Talon's claws suddenly sunk deeper into Oberon's neck, a warning.

What the hell had just happened?

CHAPTER 39

I approached Oberon, satisfied to see him wearing rags, kneeling before me.

"We should probably talk," he said, smiling at me, not even a twinge of concern on his face.

"You should probably be a lot more nervous right now," I said.

Just then, Talon unsheathed his claws, took a step back, bowed his head at Oberon, and then walked past me without a blink. My friends suddenly had their weapons out, pointed directly at Talon. He slowly lifted his arms, placed them on his head, and then sat down on the ground before them in surrender. Barbie was sure to place herself between Talon and Alex, leaving Ashley and Carl to split their attention between the goblins and Talon.

Everyone turned to look at me as if I had the answer to that. But I was engrossed by a sudden revelation as I stared at the submissive Talon. Since we had gone to visit the palace, I couldn't recall ever seeing him with his spear. Ever since our path sent us directly at the Royals...

But I could only process one confusing thing at a time, so I just shrugged at my friends, motioning for them to keep an eye on him.

The horde of goblins quickly dispatched the still screaming troll, and then began to laugh, finally looking back up at my friends. I turned back to Oberon, feeling very cold, and very violent. No more jokes inside of me.

Two of my friends had disappeared, but I didn't know if they had been taken from me, or had found a way back home. Right now, they could be somewhere worse than here, surrounded by very angry Fae nightmares, who wanted revenge for embarrassing their king.

I reached out to Wylde, digging deep. Because I knew this was something I couldn't comprehend.

Talon had released Oberon, fucking bowed, and then walked away only to surrender to my friends. What the hell was that about? If he had turned on me, drawn his spear, and then challenged me to a duel, it would have made more sense. But to betray, and then surrender?

This was a Fae thing, and only a Fae could understand it.

Oberon watched me, nodding slowly as if reading my thoughts.

My voice sounded distant as Wylde spoke through me. "All's fair in war—"

"And love," Oberon finished softly.

"Wylde has no time for such things," I said coldly. "Love is weakness." And I felt a part of me agreeing with that, even though I knew I was just bitter. Because of Indie. Love had been my weakness. And it had broken me. But... love had also healed Barbie a few minutes ago.

"Love conquers all," Oberon said.

"Or swallows you whole," I snapped, thinking of Indie.

He held out his hands, acknowledging my unspoken example. "Love conquers all."

I squinted my eyebrows at him, not wanting to understand, but knowing he was right. True love was strong enough to conquer anything, but it was also strong enough to overwhelm you, eating you alive if given away to the wrong person. Someone not up to your standards.

Then I remembered what he had said when we first met. About only love being able to conquer savagery. And about my friends needing to find a driver to get back home.

Had... Tory and the Huntress tasted enough love to be sent home? Was it that simple? The powerful emotion overcoming their primitive, savage sides? Had Oberon given us the answer in the very beginning of our trial? And was he reminding me of those hints, even now?

If I was right, then he had likely given us answers for the rest of us to get home. I just needed to figure them out. Fast. Before he decided to stop being so helpful.

Oberon climbed to his feet, stretching. He settled a thoughtful gaze on me, as if reading my life story. "This was an Invitation. A challenge. You passed. Barely."

I frowned. "Because I got the kid?"

Oberon shrugged. "Sure."

I waited for more, but nothing came. "Okay, then let us go. And tell me how to kill a god. My promised reward."

"You haven't earned a reward. You passed. Barely," he repeated.

I began to growl. "I got the shoes and saved my friend. And I have the kid."

Oberon watched me. "Perhaps," he said casually.

I glanced back to see Barbie still guarding Alex, and let out a hidden sigh of relief. I met Alex's eyes, and gave him a nod. I had hoped it to be reassuring, but he still looked as terrified as before. I turned back to Oberon. "The Huntress was taken to motivate me. But I almost didn't run into her. I could have very easily missed her."

Oberon shook his head. "No. She was very specifically guided to you. By my Hunters." He looked past my shoulder and I tensed, fearing an assassin immediately behind me, or that someone had nabbed Alex. But no one was there, Alex was fine, and Talon was still on his knees. Then I saw it. A large army of goblins slowly standing from the tall grass around us, totally fresh, not a wound on them.

And they were everywhere. Hundreds of them.

I didn't let fear show on my face, but inside I was screaming. Wylde yanked back control, only leaving me the ability to observe. I struggled, fought, and shouted at him, all in my mind, but it was no use.

And as I realized the futility of it, I conceded. He was right. I needed him. Entirely.

I didn't think the same as these monsters. I needed to become them to beat them. My way had gotten us handily outmaneuvered. I had almost killed us by Shadow Walking, and my trusted cat had betrayed me.

So, I stopped struggling. And... a wave of contentment rolled down my shoulders.

The man that turned back to Oberon was not the same as the one he had been talking to so far. Sure, he was similar. But before, where the king had seen flashes of a different, darker version of me, now he got the full storm. A calm, solid, force of nature, staring down the Fae King with calculating, methodical, hungry eyes.

The burning eyes of a predator. Or a Manling turned Fae.

Which was deadlier – a Manling who had lived a brief life on the Wild Side, and had *chosen* it over all other options available to him.

Oberon's face changed, suddenly cautious, but also... satisfied? "Where are my women?" I snarled, wanting to hear proof of my guess, that they were safe, that love had saved them.

"Love conquers all, Wylde," he repeated in a respectful tone. It would have to be enough.

"We are leaving this place. You will not stop us. Or I will return to bathe in your blood."

Oberon's jaw clenched by reflex at the threat, but he nodded agreement. Not from a position of weakness, but as if the statement only made perfect sense. It would be ignorant to disagree. Uncivilized. "I agree not to retaliate. My request has been fulfilled. The Invitation is withdrawn."

I grew very still, sensing Wylde's sudden apprehension.

Oberon slowly smiled. "That's correct. The Invitation is complete. The challenge over. Now, how, *exactly*, did you propose to leave? To make it home?"

"The shoes," Wylde said uncertainly. "Home." But that was all he had. No explanations.

It was the equivalent of Oberon asking him to explain how a tornado formed.

And Wylde had answered with, "Science," while waggling his fingers mystically.

I focused on the problem, recalling the montage Wylde had shown me when I asked about the heels. I had thought he was showing me visions of safety, protection, love. Which were all facets of what he had been trying to say.

The shoes were *Home*. Safety, protection, and love were all *parts* of a home.

But Wylde was floundering, knowing the answer, but not how to use it. And I had a sudden realization. Wylde needed *me* as much as I needed *him*. Wylde's life was one of *seeing, wanting, taking,* and *doing* – whether it was women or magic. If he wanted a result, he just made it happen, like breathing. It was the way this world worked.

Wylde was limited in this regard. And he knew *Oberon*, not *Pan* – who was just another facet of the same being. Most Fae knew only to fear the

Manlings. Whereas the Royals – the Queens and Oberon – knew that Manlings held something they wanted. Something they needed.

Belief. Which powered their entire world. My mind flew with the possibilities.

The Fae needed humans to believe in them, so they stole our children, replacing them with their own Changelings. That Fae Changeling would influence humans in our world, increasing our belief in the old stories. But I knew power flowed both ways. A balance. So that Manling child stuck in the Land of the Fae? I would bet a few nickels that he also influenced the Fae, poisoning them with his evil Manling ways. And *that* was where the Fae picked up their Manling stories. Just like we picked up their stories from Changelings, perhaps.

Which might just be a weakness. The Fae were addicts, infatuated with us. They *needed* us.

And I had a sudden idea. Why would heels be so important? Out of all the things that could have been used as a key to home…

Then it hit me. I clawed myself out of the depths, begging Wylde to listen. He was so shaken that he accidentally let me. I grasped a sliver of control back from him, rounded on my friends, and pointed at Carl and Ashley. "There's no place like home! Click those fucking heels!"

Ashley gasped, and instantly darted to her horse, scrabbling underneath its bulk to try and reach the shoes still attached to the bridle.

The goblins began to advance, agitated that something was happening with their prey.

But Talon and Barbie abruptly dove into the mix, slicing, screaming, and tearing into the goblins with teeth and blade. And I suddenly saw Talon's spear again, appearing out of thin air. The two moved like miniature tornados, not trying to kill, but simply to maim as many enemies as possible. Wasting their time to kill when so many surrounded them would be instant death. Blue blood flew in the air amidst a cacophony of screams and gurgles.

Carl retrieved the blue pair of shoes, the sun causing the frost to glitter. A goblin carcass slammed into the tree before him, and he jumped, snapping back to attention. He dove to help shift the horse for Ashley. She finally yanked out the pair of flaming red high heels.

But before she could do anything, Carl snatched them from her hands, shoving the blue ones at her. She took them with a bewildered expression. Carl smiled down at the red heels adoringly.

Then they dropped to their asses, strapping on the pumps as fast as possible, but the tide of goblins was rolling closer, despite Talon and Barbie's efforts to hold them back. Carl and Ashley scrambled to their feet, and for some reason, Carl moved much more fluidly in his six-inch heels than Ashley. They grasped hands, clicked their heels together, and shouted at the top of their lungs. "There's no place like home!"

The goblin horde washed over them with the last word, and I feared the worst. But a few moments later, the goblins climbed off each other, revealing only empty space beneath them. I turned to Oberon, arching a brow, not even trying to hide my smirk.

"Pop Culture," he admitted, sounding frustrated. "Well met."

I had been right. Humans infected the Fae, too. But my mind didn't stop there.

My trip had been a challenge. An Invitation... Then I got it. Much like their Changeling business model, the Fae made an adult version. Invitations. But in *that* game, they wanted to bring *us* over, change *us*, and then return us to *our* homes. They wanted us to spread the savage, primitive, wildness we picked up here – and tales of Fairy monsters – among our own people.

But the Invitations hadn't been granted for a long time. It had been granted to those from a different era. Those wizards who lived in a darker period of history – a more brutal period. Adopting the Fae inside them had likely been much simpler for them. Which meant free – or very cheap – energy, to put it in modern terms.

I was willing to bet that a successful Invitation with me would grant them a big old battery to keep their world running. And if the Initiate failed? They got to kill or keep an evil Manling, twisting him into one of their own. Win-win.

And right now, with their most recent Changeling fiasco – they had lost a potential power source. They needed a quick fix, and they needed to save face.

And since they were Fae, they needed to make it *better* than just saving face. They needed to come out *ahead*. It was how they worked. So, they had opened up the Invitation lottery again.

Enter the unluckiest schmuck in the world, Nate Temple.

To *leave*, I needed to accept the Wylde inside of me.

To get their boost of *power*, the Fae needed me to accept Wylde.

Our interests aligned. This wasn't a game. It was a big old con, by the best con artists ever.

Even knowing this, I realized I still didn't have a choice. Realizing the con too late didn't help me. I could only play ball. The game was rigged. No use crying about it.

I knew from experience that we all had that dark presence inside us. We'd had it since our caveman days. You could take a man out of the cave, but you couldn't take the cave out of the man. Hell, we even called our basements man caves. Preach.

The only way out was to become like the Fae. That was why Talon and Carl had adapted so easily. They were already at peace with their wild sides. The Huntress as well.

It was my turn. But first, I needed my key. The third key Oberon had mentioned. Because although it had all been a game, where he would win both ways, he had wanted to be fair, giving me the answers before I had the question.

He had told me that my quest was to find three things. But I was now confident that those three things had been the keys to our freedom, because the heels and the Huntress had been two of the tasks…

And two of the keys home.

He had upheld the letter of the law, pretending to help, while holding us back. He had even prevented Talon from helping. Just like he hadn't told us he would be actively trying to stop us. And he got to stick one to the Queens in the process. Overall, he was one clever son of a bitch. But he was greedy, wanting to get the power for his world, and to beat me at the same time, so he'd made it as hard as he possibly could.

"Greedy, greedy, greedy king," I chastised.

Oberon growled, but before he could do anything, I yanked Alex – the third key – over to me with an extension of power, right as a goblin reached to grab him. Alex squawked in alarm, breathing heavily as he tried to stare in every direction. I snapped my fingers with a whisper from Wylde's magic, and Talon and Barbie disappeared in puffs of smoke, back where they belonged.

Oberon actually snarled in fury. "Never has pride tasted so bitter. I'll admit I dreamt about your failure, but it seems you mastered the Fae inside you. Or adopted it," he added begrudgingly. "Either way, I won."

"I know," I said, bowing with respect. He seemed taken aback by that. "But I'll be back," I promised. "I have a game for you, too." I used his confusion to take one last look at this horrible place. The place Wylde called home. My eyes briefly caught on a familiar face in the distance. A man standing at the back of the second group of goblins. It was Robin Goodfellow.

And I suddenly remembered what had been bothering me. Robin Goodfellow was sometimes referred to as Pan. Or at least, so similar it didn't matter. He grinned, tipping an imaginary hat. Looking a whole helluva lot like a younger Mallory. A thought hit me as I turned away.

"I heard a fable about a white island," I said idly, turning back to Oberon.

He tensed. "And?" he asked, cautiously.

I shrugged. "Just an interesting story. Maybe someone could take care of it for you…"

He nodded, as if seeing me in a new light. "That would be… very considerate."

I snorted. "I don't do *considerate*. You'll pay, and pay well. Or else…" I warned him. "Until next time, Obie," I muttered.

"Be careful with Wylde," the king warned. But I was already stepping out of the Land of the Fae, clutching Alex's hand, ready to impale Mallory with one of his curly horns.

CHAPTER 40

*W*e stepped back into our world with water suddenly crashing over our shoulders, soaking us to the bone. We jumped away instinctively, shivering and gasping. Tory and Ashley were there in a heartbeat, wrapping us up in towels and blankets as they sobbed, laughed, squeezed and hugged us to death. I was sure to keep a hold of Alex's hand, squeezing it reassuringly as these strangers bombarded us, because he didn't yet know they were the same he had met in the Land of the Fae.

I blinked to find Carl lying naked, ass-end up, on the Round Table, which was fully raised for some reason, hovering above the floor. He dipped a claw into the flowing stream of metal, grunted, and then withdrew it, watching the liquid metal drip back into the stream, obviously not burning him, even though it was molten metal. And he still had his crest, which was currently folded back against his neck.

A giant goat grabbed me by the shoulders, bleating, and cheering. I released Alex's hand, reared back, and punched him straight in the nose. The goat flew across the room, shattering one of the marble statues perched in an alcove. The room quieted. Well, Carl roared with laughter, propping himself on an elbow to watch, flashing us with his shiny, scaly ass.

I let out a sniff at the goat, and then encouraged Alex to submit himself into Tory and Ashley's tender loving care. But he shied away from the strange women, stumbling up to the Huntress instead – who was standing before the fire, eyes far away. Alex stared at her back, and then wrapped his arms around her, hugging her hard.

She tensed, lifting up her hands as if allergic to the creature. "Why is it doing this?"

Without missing a beat, Alex's muffled voice said, "Because it likes you. And thanks you."

Tory's heart seemed to melt as she smiled at them. She had a soft spot for kids. And bad girls.

"It's been *hours*," a familiar voice complained. "I thought you weren't going to see what was right in front of you. Again." I turned cold eyes to find Talon the Devourer – not a cat – staring at me from a few feet away. Rather than offering an apology, he dipped his head, and waited.

I stared at him, a torrent of conflicting emotions raging through me.

Nate Temple, the Manling wizard, wanted to kill him. Slowly.

But Wylde? That crazy son of a bitch understood. Completely.

And he loved Talon for his noble actions.

So, I nodded at him. "That was a tough position to maintain. But in the end, you proved your loyalty to all parties." He nodded carefully, as if waiting for Nate Temple to rear his head. The man of absolution. Who never ignored a slight, and repaid it tenfold. At least. "Prior obligation?" I asked. Again, he nodded. "That's why you left the Land of the Fae in the first place..." A proud grin split his cheeks, and he began to purr in approval.

I abruptly scooped up the furry bastard in a big hug, spinning him in a slow circle, enjoying the horrified look on his face.

I finally set him down, enjoying his drunken stumble as he tried to regain his balance.

My friends stared at me, frowning.

None of them, other than Talon, looked as they had in the Fae World. Tory and Ashley both appeared as the day I had met them. Except for their eyes. They twinkled in the corners. Like a hair trigger on a gun.

Ashley nodded, smirking. "I've still got it, Temple. Watch your ass. Especially if you get any ideas about sharing too many stories," she warned playfully, meaning her kiss in the palace.

I belted out laughing, holding up my hands in surrender. "What happens in Fae stays in Fae." The Huntress was actually speaking to Alex in low tones, now, crouched down before the fire. I let them be, but I needed to find a way to get him back home. Pan watched me from the alcove, not bothering to stand as he waited his turn. He knew he was on my shit list.

I continued to ignore him, and turned to Carl. "Dude, put on some clothes. And get your snake off my sacred magical table. I don't want your scales getting in my mystical pool of liquid metal." He grunted, climbing off the table, his manhood catching everyone's attention.

He scowled at the women. "I liked you all a lot better in the other place," he hissed, and then walked over to his pile of leathers to begin tugging them on.

I didn't direct my question to anyone in particular. "Why is my sacred, magical table up?"

Because before my trip, the table had only lifted from the ground when *I* approached it. No one else. I wasn't sure if that was something to do with the round table or if the house had placed its version of a security system on it, allowing only the Master Temple to use the sacred table.

"It lifted up about five minutes before you stepped through the waterfall. It's what let us assume you had succeeded," Talon said.

I sighed, feeling a bit better to hear it hadn't been up when they arrived. I glanced at Talon. "It only used to rise up when I was right next to it. Not across the room near the waterfall. Any ideas?" He grew very silent, basically refusing to tell me what he obviously knew, or else he would have simply said *no*. "Later, then." He nodded in relief. I studied the table and the chairs around it, thinking. Then I turned back to him. "Hey, is this your new look? Or do I still have to deal with your litter box? Because if you can walk, you can damned well use the toilet like everyone else. Anyone on two legs is in charge of their own bathroom duties."

Ashley chuckled.

"It feels nice to be back in my own skin," he said, rolling his shoulders. "But when the need arises, I can become the elegant Sir Muffle Paws."

That could be useful. "What's up with your spear? It took me a while, but I finally picked up on you not using it against the Royals."

He nodded, holding up his hands helplessly. "Part of the obligation," he admitted. Then he snapped the pads of his paw – I had no idea how – and his spear was suddenly in his fist. Tory clapped as he made it disappear again.

I rolled my eyes. "Okay. We need to gather everyone. Figure out what's happened while we were gone. I know it's only been a few days, but I managed to piss off a few of the Greeks before I left. And I have some things I need to take care of before we face them." A lot of things, actually.

"You going to shave first? Maybe shower?" Carl asked, sounding amused.

I turned to look at him, frowning. He pointed at my chin and I reached up. My hand froze. I had a beard. A real one. Longer than it had been last time I checked over there. "Why do I still have this thing?" I said, racing over to the nearby desk that had belonged to the previous Master Temple – the Mad Hatter, Matthias Temple. I yanked open a drawer and pulled out a small mirror I knew was tucked away. I opened it to look at my face and stiffened. War paint covered my face. I moved the mirror down to study my beard.

And for the first time I realized that I still had my coat, but no shirt beneath. Which made the tribal whorls of blue blood on my furred chest very apparent. And savage. My jeans were ripped, too. I turned to the others, frowning. Their clothes seemed the same as the day we had left, but... something was different about them, too, and not just their eyes. Their hair... was longer.

"It's been seven weeks since we last saw you," Pan said in a very careful tone.

I dropped the mirror, shattering glass all over the floor.

"Fuck me..." I whispered.

CHAPTER 41

*T*alon sighed, staring down at the ground. "I had hoped it wasn't nearly that bad."

I groaned, wanting to yell at someone, anyone, but I simply couldn't. It wouldn't solve anything, and I had *known* time was skewed between our worlds. I just hadn't thought it would be anything like this. We had only seen one night and one day. I mentally shook myself.

"Alright. War Council. I need to know what's happened in our absence. Pan, gather my captains and have them meet me in my office in one hour. For your sake," I leaned forward, menacingly, "do it efficiently and expediently, *Robin*."

Then I turned my back on him, satisfied to hear his sudden intake of breath. Everyone else took it as me teasing him – the Robin to my Batman – which was intentional. But I wanted Pan to know that I *knew* about Robin Goodfellow, and that I appreciated his… help. Because even though I didn't know the true depth of Robin's actions in the Fae World, what I had seen had led me to believe that I might have had an unknown ally working in my favor over there. Against Oberon. That didn't appease my anger, but it needed to be acknowledged. He left very quietly.

I faced my Band—

A brief flicker of hesitation flashed across my face, but I banished it before anyone seemed to notice. Friends, not Band. "I'm very proud of you all. You went through hell and back to help me..." I admitted, throat tightening. "Now, go get cleaned up, and meet me in my office," I told them with mock harshness.

"Nailed it," Tory teased.

"Meh," Ashley said, shrugging as she grinned at me.

I rolled my eyes as they began to trickle out. I pointed at Talon. "Get Callie. I need to speak with her. Right now."

"What makes you thi—"

"Don't start, Puss in Boots. I don't have time to skin a cat right now."

Carl burst out laughing. I rounded on him. "Don't start, crossdressing, lizard boy. I saw your eyes when you held those heels," I growled. This time, Talon burst out laughing, and Carl's face grimaced. I waved my hand, letting him know I was only teasing. "Where are the heels, anyway?"

"They disappeared right after we returned," he said regretfully.

I nodded, having figured that to be the case. That they would return to the Land of the Fae. Still, it was nice to be sure. "Hey, is Barbie here?" I asked Talon.

He shook his head. "I think we both went home," he said, enunciating the word. So, she was still in the Land of the Fae. I was sure I would hear from her in the future.

I turned to the Elder. "Run the perimeter of Chateau Falco, Carl. Get a personal read on things. I don't want to be swayed by captains exhausted from fighting. I need fresh, objective... *wild* eyes," I said, turning the command into a compliment.

He hissed, looking grateful as he fingered an ivory blade on his hip. "Permission to kill?"

"Don't draw it out. Kill the enemy if necessary, but I don't need you making a scene. Talk to *none* of our people. Just observe. I don't want your observations tainted by their emotions."

Carl stared at me for a long moment, and I saw Talon doing the same. Then they both nodded approval, but still looked curious about which Nate they were currently listening to.

"I'm Nate fucking Temple, not Wylde," I snapped. "You have your orders. *Move*."

They left. Very quickly.

Which left me alone to think. I needed to talk to Callie. Right now. Because I needed her help. Before anything else happened. If war with the

Greeks was already here, I needed to check on the Armory, to see what we were dealing with.

And now that I was back, I could sense the drain on my power. It was a lot more noticeable. The unfulfilled promise becoming a genuine handicap. Because it had been two *months*.

But another nagging thought kept taunting me. My conversation with War, and him telling me that this fight was not mine. Well, I had done a great job of listening to *that* advice, even though it was a result of an unintentional two-month-Walkabout in the Land of the Fae. But did that mean that even now I should be keeping my nose out of things?

No harm in at least getting an update. But the real shitty part? My friends would likely be excited to finally see me back, hoping that I could now help. And... I might have to tell them that I couldn't.

I ran a hand through my longer hair in frustration, turning around, and almost jumped as I saw the Huntress and Alex standing there, watching me.

"Hey," I said, calming my suddenly racing heart. "I thought you left with the others."

"Alex refuses to leave your side."

I turned to him, smiling reassuringly to appease the anxiety he was barely keeping in check. Then I squatted down, resting my butt on my heels as I balanced on the balls of my feet. "Alex, I won't let anything happen to you. Things here are worse than I had hoped," I said honestly. He continued to stare at me, no emotion in those haunted eyes. Just nightmares. "But it's still a sight better than those sons of goats back there," I pointed a thumb over my shoulder at the waterfall.

Alex let slip a very small laugh, eyes darting to the waterfall as if expecting an invasion.

I held out a hand. "Don't worry. It's not an open door. Trust me," I told him, hoping I wasn't lying. He let out a long, nervous breath, as if trying to regain his confidence and abandon his fear. I let my thoughts focus on the waterfall. Why had I returned *there*? Why had any of us returned that way, rather than at Stonehenge?

This fucking house scared the jeepers out of me sometimes. Every time I found out another secret I wanted to simply burn the place to the ground. What if I had decided to jump into the waterfall one day, and unwittingly found myself surrounded by trolls?

"I have to take care of a few things," I told him, giving him my full attention. "But I trust the Huntress with my life. She's kind of grouchy at times, but she's pretty cool. Maybe she'll show you how to use a bow or knife if you listen to her."

"I want to stay close to you," he whispered.

I held out a hand, intending to placate his anxiety, that I wasn't going anywhere.

Alex bolted into my chest, knocking me on my ass as he hugged me for dear life. The Huntress had tensed, as if expecting an assassination. She actually had a bow aimed at the back of the kid's head.

Then she heard it.

He was crying into my shoulder, and squeezing my neck. "Please don't leave me alone again..." he said, over and over again, voice cracking with fear and laced with sobs and sniffles into my coat. The Huntress withdrew her bow with a guilty look.

I placed one hand on the back of his head, and the other on his back, trying to impart a sense of comfort to him, because I wasn't too familiar with these mysterious non-adults.

But Wylde was. He roared up like a bonfire inside of me, guiding me, empowering me, letting me understand this moment on a level that I hadn't ever considered.

I didn't change anything physically, but my hug was entirely different all of a sudden. I squeezed him, the motion telling him he was safe, that I would protect him, that he never had anything to fear ever again...

That.

He.

Was.

Mine.

The tension in Alex's shoulders washed away, and he was suddenly a limp noodle, still clutching at me, but no longer rigid. As if he had read my bodily cues. In that moment, I realized that Wylde was an okay dude, taking Alex's fear out back behind the shed where he proceeded to beat it into a bloody pulp to show the kid what happened to stupid bastards like *fear*. And to tell Alex that if he ever found he couldn't do it himself...

Wylde would be there to put boot to fucking ass.

Alex finally climbed off of me, looking embarrassed as he wiped his nose. I didn't acknowledge his emotions. Not a smile. Not an empathizing nod. I simply stared at him, letting him know that he was mine.

And that no one ever took something that was mine.

A deep part of me began reminding me of all the times someone had taken something of mine, but I squashed that mouthy little bastard with Wylde's testosterone boot.

"I… can help. Let me help. Somehow," Alex pleaded.

I nodded, scratching my beard in thought. "I always hated it when people looked at me with sad eyes, felt sorry for me, buried me with sweetness and concern," I said absently. "You, too?"

Alex nodded with the typical arrogant look of an adolescent, finding part of his backbone.

I gave him a wolfish grin. "Do you like to play games?"

He nodded slowly. "The Fae liked games…"

I growled angrily, not at him, but at the reference to what he had survived. "Not those kind of games, Alex." I gave him a very level look. The Huntress was watching us thoughtfully, like studying a lecture in college. I gripped Alex's shoulder tightly. "Alex, I want you to promise me something." He nodded, and I took a long, steady breath. "You will never again consider or bring up what was done to you. That part of your story is over. It's time to turn the page. It will not shape the man you will become. At least, not as a handicap. It will only strengthen you. Metal, left too long in the fire, can weaken. But do you know how swords are made?" I asked, treating him like an adult.

He shook his head.

"With fire," I said, smiling. "Just the right *amount* of fire. And it must be *hot*."

He considered that, slowly nodding. "Okay."

"What you went through was just the right amount of fire. Just the right level of heat. You will become a sword, not a weakened piece of metal, am I clear?"

I saw his back straighten, and he looked me in the eyes as he gave me a firm nod.

"That fire is not a crutch. You will not complain about it. Swords do not complain. They become stronger. Better. To make sure that what happened to them will never happen to anyone else. Ever. Again."

A slow, confident smile grew over his face, and I saw the Huntress staring at me as if she had never seen me before. "Yes, Wylde," Alex answered reverently.

I jerked my head. "No, Alex. Nate. My name is Nate Temple." He looked slightly confused, but I smiled at him to let him know I wasn't upset. "In order to save you from the fire, I had to... become a bit like the fire. The people you saw here a few minutes ago?" I asked. He nodded, looking confused. "They were the same people protecting you under the tree. We all had to change... to save you. You're worth it, kid."

The smile and blush that rolled over his face was priceless. "The Huntress is one of the bravest people I know, despite what you saw over there. I trust her with my life, and you should, too. Now, here's the game I was talking about earlier..." And I began to explain what I wanted him to do, giving him something to latch onto in place of his fear. They both began to grin, and then dashed out of the Sanctorum in search of fresh clothing. Tory and her students should be able to help with that. The Huntress wouldn't be leaving his side anytime soon. Coincidentally, this would put Tory and the Huntress together.

Because I was pretty sure I understood one thing about their flight from the Fae. A taste of love had allowed them to leave. The shoes had allowed Ashley and Carl to leave. Talon – being part of the Fae already, could come and go at will. But me? And the kid?

I wasn't entirely sure about that part yet, but I had my suspicions. When I had my feet back under me, I would have Othello start looking for his parents. But I wasn't in any rush. Because dumping him off as soon as I saved him might be the worst thing imaginable. He needed time.

Even if it was in a warzone. But the Huntress would keep him safe.

I headed up to my rooms to clean up, but not before pointedly glancing at the two pairs of beady eyes silently watching me from the third tier high above. They watched me leave, thinking unknown thoughts. Maybe remembering unknown thoughts.

At least to me.

I didn't care. I had a war to fight. Or, at least some people to kill. Three of them, to be precise.

And for some strange reason, this made me deliriously happy. Anxious, even.

CHAPTER 42

I had cleaned up, taken a shower, and scrubbed the stink of the Fae off my flesh. But my mind wasn't in it. Because my mind had been a constant inner dialogue of war. Discerning what Wylde knew, how he might be able to help.

And even though this war concerned my friends, and that they had been fighting it for weeks, perhaps, none of it had hit me on a personal level yet. I hadn't asked if anyone had died, been injured, or how we were holding up. Or if it had even begun.

Who might have already died was irrelevant to Wylde.

Other than their use as an asset. Part of me felt concerned about that, but never for long. Because it was honest. Cold, but honest. We needed to win. And to make an example doing it.

Which meant Indie had to die.

I realized this with a stunned grunt. I turned the water from warm to cold, remembering some article I had read about it helping you, or being good for you.

Also, it felt more primitive. Honest.

The cold water didn't feel good – but honesty rarely did – and that article must have been right on some level, because it did help me. Cleared my head. Woke me up. I didn't deserve a warm, luxurious shower when death was knocking on my front door. And had been for seven weeks or so.

Indie… I thought, placing my palms on the wall of the shower, letting the icy water run down my back, ignoring the shivers it gave me.

This was all her fault. She had been offered a resolution time and time again, and although I had been angry before, furious even, I hadn't decisively put her on the kill list yet, as if subconsciously hoping to see the woman I remembered finally reach out for help.

Because the more I thought about it, the more I realized that things didn't add up. She had told me that the Syndicate had killed her mother, but something about that didn't sit right in my mind. But even if it *was* true, it didn't justify the number of lines she had crossed.

Innocent people had died.

She and her minions had tried to kill my Greek friends.

And then she had taken my Greek friends from me – against their will.

And Ichabod had lied to me. He had taken me out to dinner, pretending to be friendly, saying he didn't know where Indie was. Either he had told the truth, and Indie had decided to wake a goddess of her own, or he had set her up to succeed in case he failed – and he *had* failed.

But had it been some complicated scheme, or had Indie gone rogue?

Because manipulating a broken person was easy. You just had to continue feeding their fears.

I had tried reason with Indie, and it hadn't worked. I was betting that feeding her fears was the only way to get through to her, now. And Ichabod had a Blood Debt against the Syndicate, and would do anything to make good on it. To avenge what they had done to his father so long ago. The Mad Hatter. Matthias Temple.

The one that I had to make a deal with and release from his prison.

I sighed. Talk about a dysfunctional family.

I needed to get my cane back and release the Beast inside it. There were plenty of warnings regarding that. Primarily that it was the worst decision ever considered.

But without fulfilling it, I knew my power was going to be severely impacted. At the worst possible moment. Sure, now I had some attachment to Wylde's version of Fae Magic – but whether that was temporary or not, I didn't know. Also, what were the ramifications of using it? Would it change me? Change my world? Open up the gates between our worlds? Knowing the Fae, there had to be something in it for them.

And, to be honest, it scared the shit out of me.

It was like suddenly knowing how to tap into Quantum Physics…

If Quantum Physics had its *own* Quantum Physics.

It was magic like I had never seen. Nothing like the Maker ability, and nothing like a wizard's ability. It was… like its own force. Not even magic, really. More like tapping into an element that the rest of the world didn't know existed. Like the first army to discover gunpowder. It had always been there, if one only knew how to look.

And using that new discovery had changed the world.

All I had to do was let go of my control, and let Wylde have his way.

Although I knew I needed to maintain our relationship, give and take, I was leery of granting him carte blanche access to my body again. It might become necessary in this war, but that didn't mean I needed to lead with it.

I turned off the water, shivering slightly.

I climbed out of the shower, and began tugging on clothes. Jeans, boots, a random tee, and a quick dab of product in my hair, raking it back with my fingers. It was much longer than it had been before my trip to the Fae. Long enough that I could almost consider doing a topknot.

If I didn't ooze so much manliness that this option was impossible to me.

I felt a smile tug at my cheeks as I left my rooms, heading to my office. I was early. The others wouldn't be there for thirty minutes, at least. Whoever the others were. I hoped none had already fallen, but if they had, I could do nothing about it.

Other than rain such annihilation down on the Greeks that the world would hold their breath, no matter what War had told me.

I would make an example of them. Even if everyone died in the attempt.

This war would be remembered.

But first, I needed to release the kraken – Matthias Temple, the Mad Hatter. Because I had finally understood what the crazy bastard had been talking about with his comments on serendipity and my Invitation.

He needed wild magic, Fae magic, to abscond from his prison.

And guess who metaphorically sported shiny new pointed ears?

This fucking guy.

CHAPTER 43

I sat at my desk, breathing deeply, clutching a book in my lap. It wasn't necessary, but it felt like I may have a little more protection if I held it.

Through the Looking-Glass.

Wylde grumbled in anticipation.

Rather than thinking about it, I let my eyes close. I needed to be quick. The others would be here, soon. I reached through the book, using it as a door, to enter the White World physically.

I opened my eyes to find myself in a familiar white room. Matthias Temple sat in a chair, sipping what appeared to be milk, but I was sure it was actually liquor of some kind. Everything here was white. Even the drinks.

This unjust prison where the Syndicate had sent Ichabod's dad, my ancestor.

And thanks to Obie, I now knew it was part of the Fae World. And that I would be paid for doing him this service.

Since none had apparently gone on their walkabout to the Land of the Fae in quite some time, none had been able to break Matthias out of his prison. But now?

The youngest Temple had received an Invitation, and come back stained with their magic.

Their Wild Side.

Because you couldn't leave the Fae without a burning love for something there, or by adopting their way of life into your heart. Or, if you stole the Queens' shoes.

Which made me chuckle out loud, remembering Carl stealing the red heels from Ashley. Color preferences. For cross-dressing. Fucking Carl. At least they weren't my problem anymore.

Matthias studied me, curious about my laughter. He waved a hand at me. "Is the paint and beard necessary?"

I frowned, glancing down. And blinked.

Not just at his mention of the beard. Because that was growing on me. But the fact that I wore the same clothes I had worn at Chateau Falco. Never before had that happened. I had always found myself here in a set of silver or gray clothing.

Also, I saw the blue painted designs on my chest through the thin light shirt. Like a tattoo. But I had scrubbed my body raw in the shower. I turned to look back at the Mad Hatter.

"My face, too?" I asked hesitantly.

He nodded. Very slowly. And then his face morphed into a huge grin, guessing what the symbols implied, and savoring the hope of upcoming freedom.

"Huh," I said, hiding my concern by walking around the room instead of speaking, letting Wylde get a feel for the place. I could sense him thinking, analyzing, considering, and discarding plans. I let him as I continued to walk, touching a book here, a painting there, encircling the Hatter, giving myself one last chance to change my mind. I was very sure to keep my mind guarded so that Matthias didn't sense this from me. Because he was nosy about things like private thoughts.

But I couldn't think of anything else enticing enough to make him give me the cane.

Force wouldn't work, because although this was his prison, he was utterly in control here, almost able to control the place itself. No matter how powerful I was, he had a freaking palace to back him up. For all I knew, the paintings and chairs could come to life and attack me.

Or he could just *imagine* me imprisoned.

And I *would* be imprisoned.

Because he was a Maker in his prime. One of the most knowledgeable to possibly ever live. His son, Ichabod, was strong, but he hadn't received the training, assistance, and years of study that his father had. In fact, you could say that the reason Matthias Temple had been trapped and imprisoned was *because* of his power, and the threat he embodied to those who wanted to take over that power.

I finally walked back before him. I stared at him, no emotion on my face. Wylde grunted satisfactorily at the situation, then grew very silent staring into the Hatter's eyes. I wouldn't say his silence was concern... but I wouldn't say it wasn't, either.

The Hatter... impressed Wylde. I shivered at that.

Then again, anyone who required a prison this intense kind of demanded respect.

"The cane," I said.

The Hatter held out a hand, and a box suddenly rested on his lap. He carefully opened it, revealing my silver, eagle-headed cane. And the moment he did, the power hit me like a brick. The Beast was... frustrated, to put it mildly.

I reached out a hand, watching as it shook. The blue war paint – Fairy blood – on my arms stood out starkly in this white world. The Hatter watched me, staring through me as if observing Wylde in my soul. "Original terms," he murmured. I nodded, and then he reached inside the box, gently picked up the cane, and handed it to me.

It felt like grabbing a live wire, although it wasn't necessarily painful. It was just... noticeable. Agitated, angry, and demanding. I sent out a thought. *Soon. So very soon*, I promised. *This day, I swear it.*

The buzzing dulled in an instant, and the sensation suddenly changed to satisfaction. Also, I realized that it was sending another sensation at me. Devotion.

Letting me know I had nothing to fear from it.

And... I believed it.

I had spoken with the Beast, and had seen his true nature. He was definitely dangerous, but me promising to grant him freedom had changed things. He looked at me as... family, almost. A younger Brother, perhaps. A younger sibling who had done him a great service.

I just hoped it was sincere.

But it didn't matter. I still had to follow through.

"My turn," I said in a rasping snarl, eager to take something from

Oberon.

Wylde seemed to stretch through me, and…

Well, I don't really know how to describe what he did – what *I* did – but I'll try.

We wove the cosmos: Stardust, dark matter, the core of our planet, mist from dew drops, glitter from fairy wings, troll breath, and zillions of other things. And… it was so damnably *simple*. Not *easy*, but *simple*. We wove those forces together into three perfect ribbons, creating a new force with each of them, something the universe had never seen. And we cackled madly at the euphoria of cutting loose. Matthias sat on the edge of his seat, stunned.

Those three perfect ribbons were born into this white world with the wailing screams of new life, each distinctly different, and piercing.

Light, like we had never believed possible – that of a million suns.

Dark, that seemed to make pitch-black look like a dull gray.

Nothingness, that seemed to want to eat anything and everything… forever.

The three ribbons snapped together in an intricate braid with not a filament out of place.

And like the Hydra, a dozen braids suddenly exploded out of us like new heads, creating spokes of a wheel centered on us – Wylde and me – the hub.

And those braids shattered unseen pillars of finality that encased this White World. The ground shook as a loud gonging sound hammered the air.

Then another, followed by the sound of shattering glass, this time.

I gasped, the crashing and gonging striking louder, deeper, and then I punched the floor with a fist, breaking entirely *through* it. A ripple of force rolled away from the blow, and I could feel the world screaming in outrage and pain. I panted, and power drained out of me like the world was one giant leech attached to my fist.

Then it was done. The drain instantly ceased, and I sucked in a deep breath, feeling Wylde fall over in satisfied exhaustion. I stumbled to my feet, the ground still shaking as I clenched my cane.

Because although my Fae magic had ceased, the chaos had only just begun.

Color splashed over the room. The Hatter's drink was suddenly a greenish hue – absinthe. And then he was washed in colors, too – tan pants, a crimson shirt, and shining black boots.

The color hurt my eyes. I quickly tugged on a pair of sunglasses, tossing an extra pair I had brought with me to Matthias. He squinted, fumbling them before slamming them into place. I shambled over to the window, staring out at a mad world.

White peacocks suddenly erupted into turquoise flashes, and flowers bloomed with all the colors of the rainbow. The ocean pulsed a bluish green, and storm clouds began to roll in on the horizon out of a clear sky.

Great, big, black storm clouds, spinning with red flashes of light, and low, ominous, grumbling thunder – like the roars of some ancient beast awoken from an eternal slumber.

The ocean immediately began rolling over the grass, eating the island around us. I turned back to Matthias, shouting, and even though he couldn't hear me, he nodded, rushing up to stand beside me. We locked forearms, and I closed my eyes, leaving this crumbling prison before it was too late.

The very room collapsed, and we began to fall.

CHAPTER 44

e opened our eyes, panting loudly in a large, silent room. Astonished, startled faces stared back at us. Chateau Falco. My office. The house began to growl a warning, the walls shaking at the sudden intruder, even though he was the previous Master of the place. That held no sway for Falco, though.

"Easy, old girl," he murmured in response. Then he turned to me. He squeezed my shoulders, a tear falling from his eye, and his beard quivering with emotion. "We'll see each other soon, my boy."

Then Matthias disappeared.

I sat down in my chair, clutching the cane in my lap, still breathing deeply.

The book was a pile of ashes before me. Gray, I noticed absently. With flecks of black and white like someone had mixed it with salt and pepper. I shivered, turning to look at the other inhabitants of the room.

Their confusion barely concealed their fury.

Gunnar, specifically. He stormed over to me, chest heaving, cuts and scrapes on his face. I looked him in the eye, and felt the territorial snarl of Wylde looking through me. Gunnar hesitated, and backed down, shaking his head as if at a fly. Then he frowned at me, not speaking, but his lips were a barely-seen compressed line beneath a gnarly, dirty beard. Ashley approached him from behind, placed a palm on his shoulder, and he shivered. He gave me one last look, and then turned away, resuming his place in one of the chairs.

"Any other questions?" I asked calmly.

Everyone stared in disbelief from me to Gunnar, who was now staring off at nothing.

Ashley stood behind him, massaging his shoulders, murmuring into his ears. Mallory sat well back, near the fire, watching everyone. Dean stood beside him, staring at me. Only me. He looked relieved, washing his hands together nervously. I nodded at him. I might have smiled. Maybe.

Tory had the Reds on her lap, stroking their backs, but not smiling. As an evil villain would stroke a pet cat. The Reds had faraway looks in their eyes. As if they had seen too much lately, and that it hadn't broken them, but it had changed them.

Alucard stood behind her, studying those who had entered the Fae Realm with deep, thoughtful looks, as if wondering what had happened to make each of us so cold, so hard, so uncaring. To be honest, he looked a little envious.

I grunted at that. Like a cub staring at the adult lions, telling himself he was old enough to join them rather than staying with the pride. Even though he had no mane. Had never hunted. Had never killed. I shivered, pressing Wylde down. That was his thought, not mine. And Alucard didn't know that any of us would have gladly traded spots with him if we had known what would await us there.

The Huntress stood well apart from the rest, and Alex stood beside her, face entirely blank and mysterious. Occasionally, eyes would drift his way, wanting to ask the obvious, but he would address each look with a vacant stare, directly, face as open as a newborn babe.

And let me tell you, seeing a teenager stare at you with that level of calm was more than unsettling. The Reds would glance at him occasionally, interested, but not wanting to approach.

Or to earn one of his looks.

Perfect.

No one needed to know about him. He was a Regular who had seen too much. This wasn't his war. I mentally reached out to the house. *The boy is my family, guard him as thy own, Falco...*

Alex's head cocked slightly, as if hearing something, and he glanced up at the rafters thoughtfully. This was noticed by almost everyone, only adding to the mystery. He nodded, and said, "Thank you, Falco," in a calm voice. The house purred back.

Even *my* skin tingled at that.

Every other person stiffened in their seats.

I outwardly showed no interest. "What's happened in my absence?"

"Hercules began light attacks a few weeks ago," Raego said, appearing out of nowhere. No one else seemed surprised. Yahn stood beside him, and quickly released Raego's shoulder at my look. So, Yahn had been making Raego invisible. Interesting. It meant he had been using his ability often to so casually use it now. "Peppering the gates. Fruitless attacks, but enough to put everyone on guard. My dragons scout from the skies, nesting on the Eastern front when not flying. They scout in shifts, and anyone getting too close gets free barbecue," he added drily.

"And what has Yahn seen on his journeys across enemy lines?" I asked, staring at the once-cheerful young man. He didn't flinch, merely returned my look. He didn't suddenly look like a badass or anything, but he did look harder. A survivor. A resigned warrior.

"Much—" Raego began, but I held up a finger, silencing him. Then I turned to Yahn, and waited.

Yahn cleared his throat. "Hercules was upset about the picture you took going viral, that you ridiculed him. He gathered his men and began his attack against our gates. Achilles showed up with his Myrmidons as a second faction within the Greeks. I saw Asterion, a smattering of other monsters. Pegasus almost caught me once, but the rest wait. For… something. Callie has helped recharge your defenses at the gates in your absence."

I blinked at that. Callie had… how? That was impressive. "Is it safe?" I asked him, remembering the Nemean Lion Cloak.

He smirked. "Yes. No one can find it. I swear." The room didn't like secret conversations, judging by the shared looks darting around.

"Which goddess?" I asked.

The room grew silent, no one wanting to answer. Finally, Mallory spoke up, in human form. "We don't know."

"I don't think I heard you correctly," I said, voice dropping into a low, angry tone. "We have an army at my gates, and we don't know who leads them? Where is the woman? Or Ichabod?"

"We have seen no god. Indie and Ichabod are also absent."

I frowned. What the hell was going on? "What about the Syndicate? Have we been in contact?"

Gunnar spoke up. "Yes. They've been helping us. What's left of them, anyway."

I turned to him, frowning. "What do you mean?"

"They refused to help or listen. Until a few weeks after you left. Then they appeared out of nowhere, at the gates, between the Greeks and our wall, begging for help. They had systematically been attacked, at the same time. Hunted, they said."

I leaned back in my chair. "Where are they now? They can't be trusted. Not entirely."

Gunnar snorted. "Let me back up a minute for you, Oh Great Leader. You. Left. Us. To. Die."

He lifted a hard eye to mine for a very brief moment, before lowering it again. He was still angry, furious even, but he couldn't meet whatever he saw in my face. I nodded back, letting out a sigh. I cleared my throat, asserting more control over myself rather than letting Wylde do his thing.

"I... was Invited to go somewhere. Invited isn't really the right word. Not to us, anyway. By Invited, I mean I was compelled to go. And whether anyone here believes it or not, it was so I – and those who followed me – would have the strength to help in this fight." But... not to help in the way they wanted. I glanced at the table, looking for a drink, feeling suddenly parched. Dean flinched, dashing from the room with a shamed grunt.

I stood, and approached Gunnar. He tensed, as if expecting me to lash out at him.

I knelt before him, and grabbed his boots, which were torn, scarred, and dirty with stained blood. Which told me that the fighting hadn't remained beyond the wall, or that he had led attacks of his own outside the gates.

"I am sorry," I said. I didn't wait for him to react. "But I cannot win this war for you. I swear it on my power. The war is yours, alone. I have a part in the battle, but the *war* is yours. It is about more than your lives. It's about your determination. This is a siege... against your resolve. This is your crucible. Even though it's a result of what I have brought down upon us. The world is watching, and they're not watching me. They're watching *you*." I lifted my eyes to address each person. "Each of you. All of you. I... wish it were not the case," I added in a cracked voice.

237

They stared back in stunned silence, echoes of doubt filling their minds. I could *feel* it.

Until Mallory spoke up. "He speaks the truth. He has a part to play, but the war itself is about *you* making a statement to the world. Letting the monsters know that Nate isn't the one holding you together, but that you are allies. They already know *he's* scary." His eyes turned hard, glinting with a hungry rage. Like I had seen in Oberon. "Now it's time for them to see how scary *you* are. Without your precious Temple to keep you safe. Nate knew this, and was forbidden to share the information. To *guarantee* that he didn't join in, and to arm him for his own personal battle, an Invitation was... offered to him. One that hasn't been offered in hundreds of years."

That was kind of news to me, that my Invitation had been purposely scheduled to keep me out of the war. I hadn't thought it a coincidence, but it was still unsettling to hear Mallory admit it.

"And now, much like myself and the other gods, Nate must not partici-pate in this war. He has his own tasks to attend," Mallory finished, folding his beefy arms. The unspoken message was loud and clear to me. Mallory couldn't get involved in the war, either. Or Ganesh. They could only watch. Which was kind of humbling to hear my name tossed in with them. With the gods.

Part of me wondered if the gods didn't want to step on the field with a Godkiller running wild.

Me. It was kind of a compliment.

Alucard spoke up. "Sounds about as shitty as things usually go around here. But why does he get free vacation tickets while we are forced to die?"

I felt myself growling, and stopped. Instead, I began to laugh.

I stood to my feet, and grinned at the vampire. "You think you know sunlight, Alucard? Let me show you how wrong you are," and I raised my arms. Beams of light from the open windows suddenly spun in my fingers, where I had taken them away was no longer illuminated, as if I very literally was picking up the beams of light, making the room incrementally darker.

I wove it before him, visible for all to see, and continued to laugh.

Then I made a crown of thorns – made of *light*.

I shot a look at Gunnar. "Or darkness, if you prefer, Wulfric," I said.

And I snatched a shadow off the ground, cast by the remaining beams of light hitting the chair. I picked it up, and it was suddenly no longer on the floor. Gunnar gasped in disbelief. I snapped it out like I was straightening a towel from the dryer, and then tied it into a knot around my shoulders, making a cape. Gunnar scooted back in his chair, but Ashley began to growl at him to remain seated. Gunnar glanced back at her, his lone eye wide, and saw that she was smiling in amusement. He slowly turned back to me, face ashen.

I stood before him, laughing, wearing a crown of sunlight and a cloak of shadows. The crown began to spin above my head, until it was hovering like a halo, and then I grabbed the folds of my shadow cloak, and flung them up in the air, where they stayed, resembling great big wings of darkness.

Alucard wasn't breathing. Then again, he didn't have to.

"My absence was no... *vacation*, Daywalker," I snarled, and then snapped my fingers.

The halo and wings winked out, snapping back to their original locations. That was pretty much the extent of my power after breaking out Matthias. I was still surprised not to find myself exhausted after such a display. Something of that magnitude with my regular magic would have left me crying on the floor.

I cleared my throat. "But I'm still sorry I hurt your trust," I added in a softer tone. "And you have no idea how much it means to me to see you all safe..." I turned my back on them, walking past my chair, hiding a tear as I stared out the large window at the masses of camps. They looked smaller, letting me know that even though none of my close friends had died...

Some people had definitely not survived my...vacation.

Mallory spoke to the room. "Not many survive the Invitation. And if you have any doubts, ask his travelling companions how pleasant it was." I finally turned back to the group. Tory and Ashley nodded distantly, but didn't speak. Which made Gunnar and Alucard all sorts of concerned. "I will say this. Although this isn't Nate's war, he does have a battle, and that battle is vital. And... he never would have survived that battle without surviving his Invitation." I nodded agreement, clutching the cane on my desk. Mallory noticed. But no one else seemed to.

But I wasn't entirely sure anymore what had been so vital about my trip. Was it to get Wylde's help in order to free the Hatter and retrieve the cane? So that I could make good on my promise and have my full wizard's power back?

Or was it simply to *meet* Wylde... because I needed to use his strange magic in order to win... whatever battle I had ahead of me.

I was pretty sure I knew one thing. Well, maybe three things, but the second and third thing would be a personal fulfillment.

One, I was going to kill a god.

Two and three, I was going to kill Indie and Ichabod.

Which was not likely to make his daddy very happy.

The daddy I had just returned to my world.

Yeah, I definitely had a steaming pile of stuff on my plate.

CHAPTER 45

*G*unnar stared at me, stroking his beard. "If all it takes is a beard and some blueberries to do that, I have a sudden urge for blueberries," he said, the beginning of a smile finally coming to his face.

I felt a relieved smile split my cheeks. "It's not blueberries. It's fairy blood. And it won't wash off."

"Oh…" he said, sighing.

I glanced at the lack of monitors on my desk, and a wave of anxiety rolled over me. "Where is Othello?"

Gunnar held up a calming hand. "We sent her to safety. She doesn't need to be here to do her part. Just an internet connection." I let out a breath of relief, nodding.

"Why did the others have to go with you?" Gunnar asked.

Alucard was nodding, wondering the same thing.

I turned to Ashley, wondering if she had picked up on the answer. She finally sighed, and was suddenly Wulfra, complete with her dreadlocks and arm bands. Gunnar jumped to his feet, staring in stunned disbelief.

"That… is hot as *hell!*" he shouted, suddenly wrapping her up in a loving hug. She instantly shifted back, and I knew why. Wulfra wasn't the affectionate type. Gunnar frowned in confusion.

"I… don't think she would like that," she said, frowning to herself. "Or, maybe it's safer to say, she wouldn't know what it meant." Gunnar blinked at her. "But I can let her out later tonight if you want. She would like *that*," she said, grinning suggestively.

Raego burst out laughing, clapping his knees. "Hot damn!"

Gunnar looked to be fighting a grin and a frown at the same time, eager for the experience, but confused by her words. "She?" he finally asked.

Ashley nodded. "It's… like another part of me. A primitive part. I think we all have it…" she shivered. "But that place slams you together with it, face to face, and the test is to find a way to merge with it, or not. If I hadn't succeeded, I either would have died as Ashley, or… become a merciless, bloodthirsty monster. Wulfra," she answered, shaking.

Gunnar gripped her shoulders harder, squeezing them. "I would really like to meet Wulfra, Ashley. But I think I know her already. We all have our monsters," he added with an accepting smile. Then he scooped her up, plopped down in the chair, and set her in his lap, pinching her rear playfully.

Everyone turned to Tory, and the Huntress was suddenly grinning, although no one else noticed it. She sighed, and shifted into her other form – a furkini-clad barbarian, no longer short, and veins of golden light shining through her skin. The Reds stared at her in awe. She flipped back the hood of her saber-toothed gorilla cloak, staring at everyone with hard eyes.

She turned to Raego and said, "Beg for my affection."

And he was suddenly at her feet, begging without an ounce of shame.

The Obsidian Son, king of all dragons, and the most powerful and feared of all colors – black – and he was begging.

Tory grimaced, suddenly shifting back. Raego jumped to his feet, looking very confused.

"It was all I could think to do. You were obviously the strongest shifter here, and I think Gunnar has been through enough."

Raego nodded very slowly. "I need to go check on my people," he said, eyes troubled. Then he left the room. Yahn, not knowing what else to do, followed him.

The room was silent for a full minute until Alucard piped up. "What about the filthy feli—"

"Say it again and die crying in the eternal pits of woe, Glampire," Talon purred from the open doorway. Everyone spun to face him. A five-foot tall Thundercat with an axe-spear stood in the doorway, longer white fur spilling down from his lips to look like a beard. He had a white stain on his chest armor that he was trying to hide. "Talon the Devourer requests a presence with Wylde," he said in a formal tone, glancing at me expectantly. Not Nate. Wylde. He was asking me to prove myself.

I pulled deep, drawing on Wylde. I made a quick flurry of gestures with my hands, followed by a series of grunts. What we had learned in the Fae.

"He speaks ape now?" Gunnar asked the room.

Talon dipped his head at me in gratitude and acceptance, ignoring Gunnar.

"You have bird-shit on your armor," I said, trying not to laugh.

He hissed at me for pointing it out. "Fucking mangy, worthless ravens," he muttered. And this time I burst out laughing. Hugin and Munin had shit on him. Oh god, I loved my life.

Talon cleared his throat angrily, trying to change the topic. "Allow me to introduce Miss Callie Penrose, as requested," he said, holding out a hand and stepping to the side.

"I think one of your birds shit on your pussycat, here," Callie said conversationally, stepping out from behind Talon. His eyes flashed in outrage. "Furball said you needed something—"

Talon hissed, one of his claws suddenly reaching for her throat.

But Callie was a wee-bit faster, reacting as if she had been goading him on purpose.

She had crouched a moment before contact, and crackling blue kamas, like handheld scythes, suddenly uppercut Talon's outstretched arms. She kicked the base of his spear, knocking him off balance, and catching it in a hand as it spun.

Talon gripped the spear tighter, no stranger to combat.

But apparently, Callie had anticipated this as well.

Because one of her Kamas suddenly assisted her initial kick of the spear, bringing it in a full rotation around Talon's arm, twisting his wrist until the base of the spear hit her palms. Then she twisted, jerked down on the base of the spear, and used it as a fulcrum to slam Talon into the ground. He wheezed, blinking up at the axe blade resting at his white-furred throat.

Alucard began a slow clap, muttering, "Did she go to the Fae World, too?"

Callie tapped Talon twice on the chest with the flat of his spear, then brought it back upright to thud the base of the weapon into the floor. She extended her other hand to trade grips with Talon and pull him to his feet. He stared at her for a moment, and then, with a chuckle, accepted her help. He stood before her, nodded in respect, and then glanced at his weapon. "Well met, traveler."

"Well met, Talon. Or Sir Muffle Paws, I presume?" And she handed the spear back to him.

He cocked his head, surprised at her perception. And without an ounce of concern, she turned her back on him, searching the room for me.

She found me, and froze. A hand shot to her chest, and I caught a noticeable shiver, as her eyes seemed to blaze with inner fire. She swallowed, composed herself, and then let herself smile. "I like the new look," she said.

I nodded back. It looked like she had either liked it a hell of a lot more than she had implied, or if I now scared the living hell out of her.

"I need your help," I said.

"You've been gone almost two months, and suddenly you need my help?" she asked. She turned to my friends. "Not even they knew where you were."

I nodded. "We've gone over that," I admitted.

"That's nice. I sure as hell haven't *gone over that.*"

I blinked at her. She sounded upset. "Okay. I'll tell you all abou—"

"Damned right you will. Over dinner. Tonight. Or I walk."

"Deal," I said, wondering why she sounded so angry.

I opened my mouth to probably dig myself into a lot more trouble, but just then, Carl entered. He approached me on silent, stealthy feet, and leaned in close to whisper in my ear, not acknowledging anyone else in the room. I nodded, considering as he spoke, ignoring the looks from the others. He waited for a moment, and then began to back away from me. I held up a hand, and looked at Gunnar, who looked on the verge of demanding an answer.

"I want Ashley to help lead our people. At least as a significant advisor."

His eye tightened, not in doubt of her ability, but wondering what I had heard to make me say that. He slowly nodded, waiting for an explanation.

"Elder Carl, please tell Ashley and Gunnar what you saw, and help her plan. Talon, join them." I turned to Tory. "You are our new Camp Manager. You will work closely with Wulfra and Wulfric to devise battle plans. Coordinate with Raego, the Syndicate, and any other heads of nations or groups. By the way, is the Academy here?" Alucard nodded, frowning at my whirlwind list of commands. "Someone wrap G Ma up with a doily and get her in the talks. See how best to utilize the spell slingers. If you want to see sparks, ask Cindy to do it. She's still in charge of the Syndicate crew, right?"

Gunnar grunted. "I think she has a mysterious boss, but she won't tell us who that is, or if he or she is in their camp, hiding their identity."

I shot Wulfra a look, making a few quick gestures. *Look into it.*

She placed a finger on her ear without a thought, falling into place, even though she still looked like Ashley. Then she realized what had happened, and she stared at me, looking troubled. I made another gesture. *Easy. Marry the two. You know how. Utilize this gift. Like your wolf. Work with it, not against it. And be sure to rock Gunnar's world tonight...*

Her face flushed red, which Gunnar instantly noticed. He shot me a look, and then scowled for good measure. I winked back.

"Huntress, you know what to do." She nodded.

Alucard grunted, one arm draped over the back of his chair, tapping his sunglasses against the leather in a frustrated staccato. "Where do I fall in, and is anyone going to ask who the fucking kid is?"

An arrow slammed into the chair, shattering his glasses. He jumped to his feet, eyes wide.

"Does anyone else want to ask that question?" the Huntress asked in a soft voice.

Alex placed a hand on her bow, stepping forward with a bored, resigned sigh. "I am Alex. Know me."

Then he stepped back, folding his arms.

I tried not to laugh as everyone stared at the kid. "Just to put things in perspective, Alex was in the Fae Side much, *much* longer than any of us..." The resulting silence was brittle.

Callie didn't try to hide her amusement. "I like him. But this place," she said, shaking her head. "You guys," she muttered. "Dysfunctional doesn't even begin to describe it."

I shrugged in agreement as I clapped my hands. "Get to it. Because I think things have escalated." Everyone stared at me, and I nodded. "That's right. Indie – my ex-fiancée – and Ichabod – my crazy grandfucker – are here." I watched the various reactions, all suddenly very hushed. "But I've got a hot lunch date to attend. Or whatever mealtime it is. Part of my personal battle Mallory mentioned," I added.

Gunnar and Alucard shot me curious looks, but seeing Callie scowling at me, their looks shifted to anticipatory grins, waiting for her tirade.

She placed her palms on her tight leather pants, shifting her leather jacket back to reveal a plain t-shirt underneath. I wasn't sure if she typically chose dark clothes to emphasize her hair, or simply because she preferred them.

"Battle? Or dinner? I'm just a feeble-minded woman, and sometimes long talks go right over my head," she said in a low, crisp tone.

I grinned back. "Dinner. Definitely dinner. But I want to *talk* to you about a battle." I extended an elbow, smiling at her. "Let's go see what Dean can round up for some grub. Then I'm going to take you somewhere super-duper cool."

An amused smile replaced her anger at my corny phrase, and she finally took my arm. She glanced down at the cane in my hand. "I guess it's only polite to help a doddering old man walk to dinner," she said, smiling. Alucard began a slow clap. I rolled my eyes. Her fingers were hot to the touch. And it felt nice to be squeezed. I realized physical contact – affectionate physical contact – had been rather lacking on my trip, which made her touch all the more… impacting.

I was grinning as I guided her towards the kitchen, hoping to find my damned butler to see what he could scrounge up without notice. And it needed to travel well…

CHAPTER 46

I held the basket in one arm, and Callie's hand with my own. My cane was tucked through my belt. She shot me a curious look, and then nodded. I winked, turned to the evening sky, and ripped a hole in reality, a great flaming circle erupted before us, revealing a tranquil hill on the other side. Callie gasped.

I led her under the fiery arch, and then let it wink out behind me.

She spun in a slow circle, grinning as she held her hands out. Here, it was a few hours until dawn, but the glowing moon provided enough light. Her white hair practically glowed in contrast to the black leather pants and jacket she wore. Also, the moonlight helped make her look wild, like a sprite.

Like a Fae.

But I knew she was something altogether different from that.

I wasn't sure if she was entirely aware of what she was, but it wasn't my place to tell her. My Angel pal, Eae, had made that very clear. I wasn't scared of the pigeon…

I was respectful of his friends.

I watched her spin about, grinning like a child, and realized I was smiling, staring at the delicate skin at the sides of her neck.

She noticed my look, skipped back up to me, and then grabbed my hand to lead me towards the obvious destination just ahead. Stonehenge.

"Is it sacrilegious to sit in the middle?" she asked, sounding on the verge of laughter.

I shook my head. "I don't think so."

She flashed a pout. "Well, that takes the risk out of it, but we can still have fun."

She led me to the center, let go of my hand, and then placed hers on her hips. "Dazzle me," she said in a meaningful tone, using my words from last time we had spoken.

I chuckled, rolling my eyes. "I've never had a dazzling picnic."

"Then we should try," she said softly.

I looked up at her, wondering. I nodded after a long pause, smiling back. "Okay, Callie."

I set my cane in the grass and opened the basket, frowning down at the contents. "Dazzle me..." I repeated her words under my breath. Then I reached behind me, grabbed my shadow, and unfurled it before us like a blanket. I felt Callie stiffen in disbelief. The shadow blanket nestled into the grass, a good inch thick, and remained after I released it. I ignored Callie as I glanced up at the sky, and reached up as if plucking apples from a tree. I chose four stars, and then brought a small piece of their light down, placing them in the air at each corner of our blanket like I was hanging Christmas ornaments. I leaned back, studied the layout, and then nodded to myself.

I crouched down and began taking items out of the picnic basket. Nothing fancy. Just a meat and cheese platter – freshly cut by Dean – and a few containers of berries. I pulled out the two fluted glasses from their protective case, and popped the cork on a nice white wine Dean had dusted off from my cellars at Chateau Falco.

An 1811 *Chateau d'Yquem*, upwards of a hundred thousand dollars per bottle, these days.

I closed the basket, filled up our glasses, set them atop the basket, and then crawled onto my shadow blanket. I glanced behind me, where my shadow should have been, and saw nothing. Then I turned to meet her eyes, face serious, and patted my shadow for her to join me as I extended one of the glasses to her.

She stared back, stunned. "I'm fucking dazzled," she whispered.

I patted the blanket again, reaching further with the glass.

She joined me, accepted the glass, and leaned back on her elbow, facing me. I did the same.

She was just about as close as she could get.

She was wearing red lipstick, like I had made her wear once for a job in Kansas City. She took a cautious sip of the wine, smiled, and then held it out. "I think I have the wrong glass."

I very carefully switched them, accepting hers and giving her mine, so that the one I held had a faint red mark on it from her lipstick. She stared at me for a second, and then lifted her glass.

We clinked, not looking at our glasses, and then took a sip. I very specifically drank from the lipstick-stained mark on my glass, and she noticed.

"Much better," she said after a long sip, licking her lips very slowly, savoring it.

"Yes, much," I agreed, ignoring the expectant tingle on my lips as I took in her features in the moonlight, remembering this exact scene from the last time I had made her wear lipstick.

"So, this battle…" she began.

"Not yet. I want… to enjoy this," I said, looking at her. Then I reclined onto my back with a loud sigh, staring up at the sky. I could sense the energy pulsing beneath us, from all around us. From Stonehenge. Wild magic.

A door to the Fae.

But that wasn't why I had brought her here.

I had brought her here for one simple reason. Because it was pretty. And peaceful.

The opposite of my life, lately. And likely the opposite of hers, lately.

A gift.

After a moment, she did the same, her side pressing against mine, and we watched the night in silence. She gleefully pointed out a shooting star. Then another.

And just as easy as that, we were a couple of kids, enjoying the world around us. No monsters. No gods. No Fae. Just us. Laughing and pointing at stars, suggesting crude shapes in the clouds, and enjoying each other's company. Our hands brushed against each other a few times, and her body heat was very distracting. I pretended not to notice.

"Nate?"

"Mmm?"

"Why are we here?"

"Where else would we be?"

She propped herself up to look down at me. "Maybe where the war is."

"Thanks for helping with the defenses, by the way."

She shrugged. "Simple enough," she said, sounding very literal.

I sighed, dropping it. "This isn't my war."

"From what I heard, it kind of is. Crazy ex waking up a god intent on destroying all of you and your friends."

I shook my head. "The crazy ex part is right, but they aren't here to destroy me, or my friends. They are here to destroy the Syndicate. I just put us in the middle."

She was silent for a time. "So, now you're just going to step out of their way?"

"Too late for that," I said, shaking my head.

"Then… you're just going to let your friends fight without you? Without the person who got them into it? Against your ex and crazy ancestor? Against a god?"

I sighed, finally propping myself up on an arm. "No. And yes." She watched me, not judging, but genuinely trying to understand. Which said a whole lot about Callie Penrose. She had seen me. Knew I wasn't one to stand by. That I practically *couldn't* stand by when someone was hurting. It was how we had met, after all. And rather than accusing me, judging me, or condemning me, she calmly lay beside me, having a picnic, and waited for me to explain. Because I must have a reason.

"Thanks, Callie."

"For what?"

"Just… being you, I guess," I said, smiling as I felt a large weight lift from my shoulders. Nothing had changed, but knowing one person didn't immediately hate me for my decision took a lot of pressure off me. I don't know why. But me telling her that War had told me I couldn't participate would have removed the responsibility from me. Anyone could nod at that. But without me using an excuse, here she was, talking to me, trusting me, accepting my decision, even if she didn't understand.

Because this whole picnic had been a test. Me testing Callie.

"Here's the gist of it. I can't get into too many details, but I should not participate in the war itself. I can be there at the end, for a very specific moment, but this war has grown in scope and scale. Think about it. Indie, the crazy bitch, woke up a god. Almost a year ago. News spread fast, and everyone feared Armageddon. But nothing happened. And people continued to talk. Hype built. Bets were metaphorically placed. Which means each of my people were analyzed. And each of the Greeks was analyzed. Like one massive game. A Prize Fight."

She nodded slowly, eyes suddenly very intent, not having considered it from that angle.

"And now, it's here. Or very close. And the world is watching, even if most of my people aren't aware of it. Because, you know, we've been hunkered down in my war camp at Chateau Falco. The world holds its breath, waiting to see the outcome..." I said, also seeing everything from a new height, like a hawk drifting over a battlefield.

Wylde was helping me see it.

"It would be very impressive for me to step in, pull out the big guns, maybe even some guns I shouldn't pick up, and take down the threat, right?"

She nodded slowly, transfixed. "You would become a legend," she whispered. "Not that some... many don't already consider you one. But yes, your reputation would explode."

I nodded, staring at her. "And?"

She bit her lip, staring past me, thinking for a long minute. "A bigger army would eventually come, aimed at you, specifically. Using your allies as bait. You wouldn't know who they would attack. Too many targets, and you can't protect everyone..."

I nodded. "Exactly—"

"But if your *allies* fought this war, and made it one hell of a war, *they* would each become legends..." she whispered, eyes widening. "And would no longer be considered targets." She turned to me, excited. "You need them to make this their own. To make names for themselves. To scare the living hell out of everyone that's watching. Rock the bets. Shake the foundations of the world. And it's better to do it against this – although frightening – smaller army than the next, bigger army. It's a big enough fight for everyone to watch, and maybe just big enough for them to beat on their own." She shook her head, stunned. "No, that's not all. You don't need them to do this thing. *They* need to do this. For their *own* confidence. For their *own* protection."

I nodded. "And to truly make them believe that, I need to step down, anger them, infuriate them to some extent. To truly make them believe they need to give this their all. They can't wait for me to come riding in on a... well, that's a figure of speech," I said, changing direction.

"Albeit an accurate one..." she said. Her eyes locked onto the necklace with the wooden disc, as if she could sense it. "You really are a..." she waved a hand, not saying it out loud.

I sighed, then shrugged. "The offer is on the table, but I haven't said *yes*. But times could change. Especially when it's my turn to step into the ring."

Her eyes narrowed. "What is your role in this? What is the battle you said you needed to speak with me about? Who is your target?"

A dark grin split my cheeks. "Me? I get to kill a goddess. And, I'm pretty sure, my ex. Maybe one other person. We'll see."

She nodded. "Your part also needs to be sensational. An example."

I found my grin splitting wider, and turned to her, nodding. "True. But I need your help with something else. I think it's time I go shopping, but the store is currently closed. You and I... share something. Power from another place. Power we don't fully understand, but that I may have more experience in managing."

She nodded slowly, remembering our first encounter.

Because little Callie here was kissed by Heaven. I had my guesses on exactly what that meant, and was pretty sure she did, too, but we didn't bring up that part.

Fact was, her magic would sometimes turn white, a force much more powerful than our typical magic. For example, she could make her flame white, her blades white, her whatever white, where most wizards, when thinking fire, saw an orange ball of flame.

I also had this taint, and mine was related to the damned disc at my throat.

The Horseman Mask the Mad Hatter had made me for my birthday. The one I would wear if I ever accepted Death's offer to ride with him and his Four Brothers.

I had a horse – Grimm, the dark unicorn that had adopted me.

And now I had a Mask – given to me by the Mad Hatter. *Just in case*, he had said.

And the Horsemen had already given me a title, reserved just for me. The Horseman of Hope.

Regardless, I had the white-flavored power, too, and I was pretty sure it had something to do with Heaven interfering, using us as cat's paws. I wasn't sure, of course, because my only source, Eae, wouldn't talk about it. He would actually disappear when I tried to pester him.

But Callie had the same power. Or a similar power.

And I was pretty sure that using Callie as a battery would be enough to kick down the door to my Armory.

"You can't use your own?" Callie asked, frowning, eyes considering my cane very subtly.

"I need your help. It will take both of us. I need your strength to overwhelm the defenses. You and I, combined, can break the door down."

"And why are we breaking the door down?"

I winked at her, climbing to my feet. "To go shopping, of course."

"Sold," she grinned.

CHAPTER 47

*W*e stood outside the giant white tree, Chateau Falco looming over us. I held the cane in one fist, thinking as my eyes roamed the night, idly getting a feel for the various camps.

"This is an odd place to shop," Callie said, glancing up at the glowing tree, smiling at its beauty. Two ravens watched us, sitting beside each other, but not talking. I scowled at them.

They had been oddly absent since my return. Other than shitting on Talon.

"Women. Just give me a minute and we can go shopping, Callie," I said, rolling my eyes.

She laughed as I sat down at the trunk of the tree and crossed my legs. This was the first place I had conversed with the Beast inside the cane. Well, I had imprisoned him.

Dominated him.

And woken up my house in the process.

But I hadn't wanted to do this inside Chateau Falco, and I didn't want to simply hop to some other country and free the Beast. That would be like finding one of Grandpa's old grenades in the attic and then testing it in your neighbor's yard.

Callie watched me in silence, glancing at the cane curiously, but not pestering me.

I closed my eyes, and reached into the cane. The Beast waited in a dark corner, staring at me warily. He watched me for a time, not speaking.

I nodded my head. *It is time.*

The look of relief that washed over his face was profound. He shifted, waiting impatiently.

After a good thirty seconds, I finally spoke again. *So, uh, how do I do it?*

He stared back at me, and then burst out laughing. *You simply wish it.*

I nodded back. *Yeah, okay. Just checking. Um, you're free. I wish it so,* I said lamely.

He shook his head, chuckling, and then stood, brushing off his hands. Then he extended one to me. I met it in a firm metaphysical shake. Not too long or short. Not too strong or weak.

It was a science between us men. The Art of the Handshake.

Then he was simply gone. The cane suddenly felt lifeless in my hands. I opened my eyes, fearing to see hellfire raining down all around me. But nothing had changed. I still heard soft songs at some of the nearest camp-fires, but other than that, nothing.

I patted my chest. "Huh," I said, scanning everything within sight. "That was certainly anticlimactic."

Chateau Falco seemed oddly silent. As if watching me. Hyperaware that something had just happened, even if no one else knew it.

"What did you just do?" Callie asked, sounding concerned.

I climbed to my feet, glancing up at the tree. The two ravens stared down at me, still not speaking. I turned back to Callie and shrugged. "Nothing. Let's go shopping, I guess."

She took my hand, studying me with amusement, and then shook her head, her white hair flicking back and forth, sending me the scent of lavender.

I tossed my cane in the grass. "Won't be needing that anymore."

"Grandpa feels stronger with a pretty flower in his palm?" Callie teased.

I chuckled as I squeezed her hand. "Something like that."

I took two steps, and a bolt of lightning seemed to strike my soul, knocking me flat on my ass.

Not a bolt of *painful* lightning, but a... *pleasant* bolt of power. Something filling my power reserve in an instant. I shook my head with a surprised smile, but the sensation was gone in a blink.

Callie was frowning down at me, holding out my cane. "I think you might still need this."

I laughed, batting it away playfully. She helped me to my feet, still frowning, and she didn't let go of my hand, seeming to grip it tighter, as if to prevent me from falling down again.

I glanced back at the tree thoughtfully.

The branches swayed back and forth lightly, like trees do. But I saw the ravens flapping in the air, off on sudden important business of some sort.

I grunted, and continued after Callie, heading towards Chateau Falco. It wasn't until I reached the door that I realized there was no wind tonight to make branches move.

I let out a soft breath. I had fulfilled my promise, and my power was back. Not that it had drastically been drained or anything, but I had sensed the limit, and it had concerned me. A sudden ceiling on my power, when I knew there was so much more just beyond reach.

And I hadn't wanted to risk hitting that limit at a critical moment.

I had made good on my promise.

I had my power back.

And I was – hopefully – about to go shopping with a stone-cold fox.

If we were successful in kicking down the door.

CHAPTER 48

$\mathcal{W}$e stood before the door to the Armory. Callie, having never seen it, was of course playing with the fishlings. The wolf actually looked interested in risking his hiding spot for a quick pat from the enthusiastic girl playing with his food.

I cleared my throat, and she stepped back, waving goodbye to the fish. "This isn't going to hurt them, right?"

"I don't think so," I said, having no idea.

She folded her arms stubbornly. "I won't hurt the fishies."

I scowled at her. "More than fishies will be hurt if we don't do this. And they're called fishlings. Fishies sounds stupid."

"Fishlings?" she asked, incredulous. "Of all the ridiculous names, that one tops the list." She glanced back at them, as if apologizing for my crude name. "At least *try* not to break the door." Her eyes drifted to the scorch marks on the wall where I had tried just that. "I see the big bad Nate already tried huffing and puffing, but this piggy was too smart."

I scowled. "Fine. But all I have to do to open the door is pet that wolf, and he's having none of it. Used to be a cool guy, but now?" I shifted my scowl to him for good measure. "Jerk."

"It's not his fault. You said there's a spell preventing him."

"I can still be irrationally angry about it. Don't take that from me, Callie. It's what keeps me going when all hope is lost."

257

She chuckled. "Right. Let's do this. What do you need from me?"

"Embrace your power. I don't know if you'll be able to stop me once we start, so we're going to hold hands. If you feel close to burning out or anything uncomfortable, I need you to dig your nails into my palms. Deal?" She nodded uncertainly. I gripped her chin suddenly, gently, but very directly. "Callie... I would never *ever* do anything to hurt you. Not intentionally. That's why I want to hold hands. So you can get my attention. I don't know if I'll be able to sense your limits, or what you're feeling. I'll be too busy directing the power."

She swallowed, and then gave me a tight nod. I let go of her chin, my fingers feeling suddenly hot. She glanced down at my hand for a long moment, rubbing her chin with a light finger. Then she grasped both of my hands, placing her thumbs in my palms for an easy stab.

We both took a breath at the same time, and I drew on my magic. Power raged into me like a flood, enhanced by Wylde calmly adding in his own subtle gifts, strengthening the cord of power I braided. With the cane now just an ornament, my power was *back*. I considered giving this another go on my own, but remembering how it had almost killed me last time, I decided overwhelming force was best. I met Callie's eyes to find her staring at me in awe. I nodded at her, and waited for her to return the gesture before I reached through her.

Power crashed over me like nothing I had anticipated. I actually had to release some of it, not drawing as deeply, almost losing control of my own cord of power. I saw her nose wrinkle in confusion, sensing me take and then give back some of her power, but she didn't stop me.

I began to braid her power into my own, and Wylde suddenly began panting with excitement, grabbing shadows, memories, and feelings from all around us, even from *us*. Pain, love, sacrifice, happiness, loneliness, draining it from us with alien magic. Callie frowned at that.

Then, he began pulling memories from the door itself – from the creatures on the living door. Memories of the wolf groaning as my dad scratched his ears. Memories of terror as a fishling was snatched up by the claws of an owl in the tree. And then the immediate sensation of life as the fishling was reborn into the stream, since nothing ever died on the door. It was one giant circle of life.

And as those memories rolled into the cord, it began to throb, pulse, and expand, the memories feeding it like a steroid.

A patch of wild black thorns erupted around the two of us, and I heard Callie gasp on instinct, growing very still. None of the thorns touched her, but pointed outwards, protecting her, just as they did me. But they did continue to grow – taller, wilder, vines snaking out around us, until it stretched a good five feet out, and as tall as our hips.

I tugged the braid tight, confident no threads were loose, and I touched the door in a polite knock.

No one answered. Remembering Callie's quip about breaking the door down, I spoke, "Then I'll huff, and I'll puff..."

And for the second time, I dove into the wood, but this time I used my braided cord of combined power – the power of two white hats. Or the power of two suckers touched by Heaven.

Callie followed me in, a silent observer, but I felt the moment she began to shake. Not in warning to me about her power, but at the sheer alien nature of the power against us.

Savage magic met us in a unified front, this time, well aware of my previous attempt, and armed to retaliate. In fact, the defenders took on form – a row of wolves – and they attacked in unison, whispering, taunting, mocking, threatening in one incessant wave of emotion.

But this time, I also had Wylde.

He chuckled good naturedly in my ears. *My turn...*

I nodded, still maintaining my control, but allowing him to guide me. The pack of strange wolves, saw a man before them, but with the soul of an ancient wolf. A kindred spirit.

And he began to whisper back. I couldn't hear what he said, but I was glad for that.

The wolves danced nervously, still whispering, arguing, fighting amongst each other, shouting at me, welcoming, attacking, defending, pressing, relenting, but they did this in a quivering mass, as if I was getting a look at the brain of a schizophrenic.

They were scared of the man before them. The man with the soul of an ancient wolf.

Their conflicting emotions raged into a harmony, not cancelling each other out, but joining together into one braided cord, much like mine, but different.

Their cord was grey, flecked with blacks and whites, against our purely white braided cord.

Wylde met this serpent of power with a grin and a tip of his hat, and then…

He did the damn thing.

Like a rain dance, he began to hop about, a mental construct before us, before the door, but also inside the door. By Callie's gasp, I knew she saw the same as I. A wild, savage Nate getting his freak on all by his lonesome, against a serpent of power that was born at the dawn of time.

The cord of power – and the wolves – watched, transfixed.

So, you could say it was a total surprise when Wylde flung out a hand, and our white cord of power launched entirely *through* their gray cord.

It exploded into a thousand shreds of confetti, and the wolves were suddenly gone. We stared into the same blackness I had briefly seen before when trying to break in on my own, like black velvet soaked in blood. Twin eyes stared back from those depths, each larger than us. I'll admit it. Those eyes were terrifying. And, judging by Callie's sharp intake of breath, she agreed.

But old Wylde?

He just cackled with joy.

And started flinging starlight into the darkness.

The great beast didn't quite know what to make of that as the area exploded with light, and this light actually let me see the creature behind the eyes for the first time.

It was the wolf.

The one that I usually had to pet to get into the Armory.

But he was just a puppy. Now, before you think I'm a big meanie for threatening a puppy, you should know that his *shadow* was a great hulking werewolf on steroids. But as Wylde's starlight destroyed the darkness, the shadow shrunk, snarling, screaming, and howling, leaving only the puppy behind, staring at us with cute, loving eyes and a lolling tongue as he panted.

The last of the darkness disappeared with a *popping* sound, and the pup began to wag his tail.

Then, as if made of fog and someone had turned on a fan, the wolf pup collapsed into drifting smoke before disappearing, and a very familiar voice called out.

"Nathin, my host. It has been too long…"

Callie passed out, and I moved too late as she began to fall.

But the bed of thorns around us caught her like the world's softest mattress. Not a single thorn touched her skin, either disappearing entirely or suddenly pointed a different direction. She sunk deep into the nest of deadly thorns, and then bounced back up to me. I caught her, scooped her up, and the thorns evaporated, also like smoke.

We stood in the same hallway.

The door stood before us, and the wolf carving was now pressed against my hip, panting happily at the edge of the now open door.

The Armory was back online, and judging by the welcome...

It was all mine.

Callie murmured in my arms as I carried her across the threshold of my castle.

CHAPTER 49

*P*andora looked much the same as I remembered, if rather wan and pale. But not from sickness. She looked like anyone who had been cooped up in their house alone too long. She stared at me for some time, occasionally glancing down at Callie in my arms with a sad look, and then back to me. She finally sunk to her knees directly before me.

"I tried to lock the doors, but I was moments too late," she said in a soft whisper.

I nodded hesitantly, not knowing where things truly stood. If I could trust her. "Let's get Callie taken care of. Then we'll do a damage report. And talk."

She climbed to her feet, and led us deeper into her home, my Armory.

Wylde liked the fact that I had a beautiful woman locked away in a secret cave, but I ignored him. Pandora chuckled lightly, reading my thoughts.

As always, she glided to a stop in a large room full of couches and chairs with a wall-to-wall balcony overlooking a sandy expanse. I set Callie down on a couch, frowning in concern. Pandora smiled, placed a palm on her head, and closed her eyes in concentration. She opened them a heartbeat later, smiled, and placed a blanket over her. Callie nestled into it with a murmur.

Pandora silently clutched my hand, and led me from the room. I changed her direction slightly, wanting to check something. She didn't object, and we walked for some time before she spoke. "The poor dear is just exhausted. Possibly overwhelmed. You showed her your insides."

I tripped over a bump in the floor, scowled down at the suspiciously flat tiles, and then continued on. I grunted affirmatively in response to her statement.

"That is a lot to take in. For some."

We reached a set of windows, and I casually glanced out of them as we walked. The same otherworldly landscapes filled the openings as I had seen before, and I began to avoid looking at them for fear of remembering them in a future nightmare.

But we finally found the one I had wanted to check, and she paused before I did, sensing my interest as she turned to face me. She grasped my other hand as I stared over her shoulders at a roiling ocean of shifting stone, like mixing concrete with boulders tossed in. No white island.

I met her eyes. "He is free," she confirmed. But she didn't necessarily sound proud of me. Just a statement.

"What happened here?" I finally asked her in a soft voice.

She sighed, studying our surroundings nostalgically, which I found very odd. I began to grow uneasy when she turned back to me, tears in her eyes. "Command me to stop breathing."

I blinked at her. "Pandor—"

"Do it!" she snapped, still sobbing.

"Stop… breathing," I finally said, wondering what this was all about.

Her chest instantly stopped moving. After well over a minute, her face began to darken, and then turn a shade of purple. I grabbed her cheeks, staring at her in alarm as her face continued to darken, and her eyes began to glaze over.

"Fucking *breathe*, Pandora!" I shouted in a panic.

She collapsed to the ground, unmoving. I dove to her side, slamming my ear to her chest. Nothing. I began compressions, remembering my CPR lessons. Wylde began to grow very uneasy inside me, and I felt something changing in the Armory. As if… the place was fading. I continued my cycle, breathing into her mouth frantically as the Armory continued to fade. I struck her chest twice, hard, and she finally gasped, coughing and panting as she rolled over. The Armory suddenly snapped back, no longer fuzzy.

I sat back, confused, stunned, and panting tiredly. "What… the hell was that?" I stammered.

She finally looked over at me, eyes red, throat raw, and said, "Proof of my servitude. I cannot betray you. Literally. Unless you command me to."

Then I realized what this had been. A test. To prove her loyalty. That she hadn't let the Greeks go shopping. I found her staring at me, nodding as she read my thoughts.

"It was the fastest way for you to believe me," she said in an apologetic whisper.

I chastised her for a good thirty seconds, babbling incoherently as I helped her to her feet, and supported her. She simply nodded, eyes downcast, accepting my tirade. "Damn you, Pandora…" I finished, realizing my eyes were misty, now. Realizing I had almost lost a friend.

She smiled up at me. "Is that what I am?" she asked in a hopeful tone.

"Of course, Pandora. I'm… sorry for doubting you." She nodded, and we resumed our walk.

After a time, she finally spoke. "You must be careful, my host." She glanced at my chest pointedly, at the designs painting my skin. "The Wild Side is not for the faint of heart, as necessary as it sometimes is…" She smiled sadly. Knowing what had led me there, agreeing with my choice, but still saddened.

That was the thing with Pandora. She could read your thoughts. Until now, I had held up one hell of a mental shield – instinctively – so that none of my other friends who had the ability could read me. But with Pandora? It was like being around myself. She knew my trials, my tribulations, my choices, and likely their future consequences, hence the sadness in her eyes.

I nodded, unable to speak.

I assessed the hallway – the armor covering a few mannequins, paintings or weapons of all types hanging on the walls, treasured bowls of gems and jewelry sitting on a few tables, and even a cabinet full of vials and potions, neatly labeled with tiny letters that I couldn't read from here.

I didn't step closer, because I didn't want to know what they contained.

I turned to find Pandora watching me again. "Nothing is missing," she said with a smile.

"That's not true," I argued politely.

"The Nemean Lion Cloak of Hercules is in your possession, so I do not consider it missing."

"Oh," I said lamely, not hiding my confusion.

"Hercules was waiting the moment the battle horn blew. If he hadn't been so quick, he never would have retrieved his cloak. That is no excuse for my failure, but I do apologize."

I waved her off her apology. "But how? You're Greek... Shouldn't you be helping them?"

She smiled. "That was a long time ago."

I blinked at her. "Wait, what?"

She nodded very slowly. "Some of us had a choice. Perhaps it is in relation to my new occupation..." she said, holding out a hand to indicate the Armory.

"You're telling me that... what, Achilles and the Minotaur didn't have to abandon me? That they *chose* to?"

She hesitated. "I cannot speak for them. Perhaps they were given a choice, and left you. Perhaps they did not get a choice." She met my eyes. "But I had a choice, and I chose you."

I shook off my anxiety. "Okay. It doesn't really matter. It changes—"

She held up a hand, stopping me. "Let me speak to Wylde."

I blinked at her. "Pardon? Wylde is me. I am him."

She simply held out a hand, capitulating. I sighed and waved my hand in permission, while I prepared to eavesdrop. She closed her eyes and began to nod in agreement to something. Then she was still for a time. I felt Wylde stir within me, but heard none of the conversation. "Hey, speak up, you two."

Pandora opened her eyes, and smiled up at me. That was it.

"Well?" I asked. Then a flurry of thoughts hit me from Wylde.

I almost gasped, translating. "There's a chance..." I swallowed, trying to follow Wylde's thoughts. "That Achilles and the Minotaur *did* receive the choice, that they chose to switch sides... in order to spy..." I whispered at last.

"That is an interesting thought, my host," Pandora said cryptically. I saw the look of warning on her face, and decided that I shouldn't bring up that she had, in fact, spoken with Wylde, who had then relayed the idea to me. Her eyes were far away as she spoke again. "Of course, that thought could be entirely wrong and they could slaughter your friends on the battlefield..." She shrugged. "But a true leader must consider all possibilities, no matter how improbable."

Then I understood her position. She had chosen me, but that didn't mean she could go blabbing secrets. Because... honor. Or maybe an oath not to betray the Greeks. Or… one particular Greek. Achilles. Did it change things? Maybe. Maybe not. But I had the feeling that she wasn't necessarily giving me the answer. She had simply passed on a *third* option since I had only brought up *two*.

The only thing was, I couldn't tell anyone, because if I was wrong, and I told my friends to go easy with Achilles on the battlefield, well, maybe he *had* genuinely switched sides, and he was waiting to gut them like fish. Or my friends would leave him alone on the field, revealing to the goddess that something was very wrong with the battle.

I sighed. "This sucks," I growled. "It doesn't help me at all. It's just another possibility when I was already drowning in them." Because I suddenly realized that her position likely prevented her from giving me answers on Oberon's cryptic comments, too, or telling me which goddess I was facing.

She nodded at me, reading my mind. "My life, my host. My life…" she agreed. "But you should think on Oberon's words," she added. "They were not all lies, as you already learned."

I scowled as we walked in silence for a time, slowly coming back to the room with Callie.

"I would like to honor some of my friends with temporary gifts. They have impressed me during past interactions, but also with their current valor in war." Pandora said conversationally.

I had stopped walking, and a very dark grin began to split my beard. "Okay," I replied.

Her face was studiously blank as she nodded. We soon found ourselves staring down at the sleeping form of Callie.

I scooped her up in my arms and began walking towards the exit. "You have permission to leave and deliver your gifts, Miss Santa Claus," I said over my shoulder. "If you feel so inclined. Also, a friend of mine has hidden the Nemean Lion Cloak. I think it prudent for you to take possession of it again. It really should be kept safe, under your care," I added casually. "But since this war is not mine, I don't need to hear any details about your actions. I trust your judgment, but I do recommend staying on the grounds. I don't think either of us wants the Greeks to steal you."

"Oh, I don't know about that. I can think of one," she laughed lightly, right before the door closed behind us.

I shook my head, grinning. Achilles. The dog.

"Miss Santa Claus…" Callie mumbled, stirring.

"Shhh… Rest. I'll keep you safe until you wake, Callie," I said in a gentle whisper. She nestled closer, hand brushing the disc at my throat.

I almost stumbled, fearing she would be Tasered like everyone else who had tried touching it.

But nothing happened.

I frowned down at her as I continued walking, thinking wizardly thoughts as I carried the unconscious woman to my cave. Wylde grumbled approvingly.

"Pipe down, Wylde," I muttered.

CHAPTER 50

I stood before the gates to Chateau Falco, staring through the iron bars. Idly, I wondered how none of my neighbors had noticed, maybe filed a noise complaint. Then again, it was good that they hadn't. Not many lived near me, but still, this many crazy bastards should have attracted some attention over the past several weeks.

Indie stared at me. Ichabod stood beside her. Both faces were blank. A handful of others fanned out behind them, but a few paces back.

My Guardians lined the walls, great stone griffins. They were linked to Chateau Falco, and would defend it until they were blasted into gravel. This close to the gates, I could feel the power keeping them and the wall safe.

Keeping my people safe. Thanks to Callie keeping the defenses juiced in my absence.

But my stomach roiled as I reminded myself that this wasn't my war.

Well, the two people in front of me were part of my war. Maybe I would be able to take care of that part quickly, and then sit back and watch my friends kick ass without me.

Of course, one of the three people on my hit list was not present. The goddess.

Whoever the flying fuck she was. At this point, I was beginning to grow equally nervous and uncaring. Without the goddess, my friends still had a huge army of monsters to face.

I saw Hercules behind Indie, clenching his club in an angry fist. I could sense his fury hitting me like waves of heat from a fire. He wanted his cloak back. And I had ridiculed him. The war was just an obligation. But retrieving his cloak? Getting back at me? That would be his pleasure.

I kept my face blank, not rising to the bait of his anger, or the anticipatory grin that slowly stretched across his lumpy face, but I did notice his beard was much thicker now, as if he hadn't shaved since I embarrassed him. I turned to Asterion, the Minotaur. He wore the little trident affixations on his horns, designed for war, and clutched a handheld axe in each fist. His eyes were cold, flat, and so dark a brown that they were almost black. It was like staring at a wild animal, one who had never spoken with me over a drink, or ever spoken at all. A creature not even capable of human speech.

A gleaming helm with a tall Mohawk of black bristles indicated another familiar figure. Achilles. I couldn't make out his features beneath the helm, but he wore a matching black cloak over his shoulders. The best way to describe the rest of him was black and gold. It wasn't really gold, but maybe bronze? His helmet, the metal plates covering his black, sleeveless leather armor, and thin plates stamped into the cute little skirt he wore. The skirt was made up of dozens of strips of leather, so he would look particularly cute if he twirled. He wore leather greaves over his shins, and I saw that they wrapped around his heels. Metal plates were also stamped into these. And he wore sandals to match.

He clutched three spears and a shield, and I caught the hilt of a short sword peeking out of the shield, as if held in place by some built-in clip. He stared back, as merciless as a winter storm.

I waved at him, smiling.

Then I turned to Indie, grunted distastefully, and then Ichabod, shaking my head in disappointment as I pretended to search for a third person. I saw Pegasus, a gleaming white winged horse, with an unfamiliar figure on his back. He was young, had long blonde hair, and wore different – but still Greek – armor. He stared back at me with absolutely no indication that he saw anything human. Pegasus still had Bellerophon's bow attached to his bridle, surprisingly enough. And he watched me warily, as if waiting for Grimm to appear.

I sighed, finally approaching the bars, but not daring to open them. "Hey, guys. I came down here to see three dead people walking. But I only see two," I said, casting pointed looks at Indie and Ichabod. "Oh, and where's hathead Grimm? Or any of his brothers, really."

Indie bristled at that. I was, of course, referring to Helmut Grimm and his fellow Brothers Grimm. The ones she had freed from their prison when we last fought.

Indie shot an angry look at Achilles, but he didn't react. Because last time I had seen Helmut, he had been kneeling before Achilles with a spear through his shoulder.

"They didn't make it," she spat acidly. "But I have an army, Nate. And it looks like all you have is face-paint and a beard to scare us away." She smiled wickedly, cradling the stump where her hand should have been. She looked haggard. Tired. Exhausted. And full of vinegar, like an excellent wine gone sour. I ignored the pyramid-shaped stone dangling from her belt in a woven net.

"Meh. But your *army* isn't my concern. I'm only here for three people, remember. My friends can take out the rest of the trash," I said. "I really hope you brought more than these clowns." This time, my gaze settled on Hercules. I paused. "That big ugly one looks familiar. I think I saw him on the internet somewhere, but he was wearing a blue hat and had a dong drawn on his forehead." I leaned closer, studying Hercules intently as his face began to turn purple, veins throbbing. "Oh, it *is* him. I can still see the outline. Hi," I said, waving.

His meaty palm instantly shot to his forehead to wipe at ink that wasn't there. The man atop Pegasus stepped between us, speaking in low tones to the seething Hercules, calming him.

"Where's your mojo?" I asked, turning back to Indie.

She grimaced, both at my tone and the obvious answer. Hercules began to pace behind her, thumping his club into his other palm in a restless drumbeat. "She has better things to do."

"Well, I came here to talk to the person with decision power. Not her flunkies. Let me know when she's free. You know where to find me."

And I turned my back on her. "I will pound you into paste," Hercules roared.

I smiled, and kept on walking.

"Hand over the Syndicate, Nate, or we will have *war!*" Indie shouted.

I glanced over my shoulder, smirked, and said, "Bring it."

I ignored them as I walked away. My friends smiled at me. Just my captains. The faces I wanted the world to remember. Gunnar, Ashley, Alucard, Tory, the Huntress, and Raego. Callie was still sleeping, since we had only just left the Armory an hour ago, but Mallory was looking after her since he refused to get involved in the war.

"Who is the child?" Indie shouted over Hercules. I glanced back to see her frowning thoughtfully. Ichabod looked uncomfortable. Maybe he was realizing that I was protecting *kids* here. What her war would cost.

"None of your concern," I said. "Just another victim of your temper tantrums."

I turned back to see the Huntress was holding Alex back, now. He was snarling in response to her interest, as if trying to prove his prowess – like every teenager everywhere. The Reds stepped out from a nearby tree and spoke to him in low tones, each placing an arm over his shoulders and guiding him away. One did not simply ignore two stunning teenaged girls, no matter how angry one was at the time. The Huntress nodded thankfully at their backs.

The Greeks began taunting me, calling me coward, and other really mean things.

Wylde roared up inside me, wanting to destroy them. *Kill everyone. Salt the earth.* And I was dangerously close to agreeing with him. *Not yet*, I encouraged. I spoke to my friends in a hoarse rasp, still struggling against my anger. "I need to speak to the Syndicate. Now."

Tory nodded. "I'll take you. I'm on camp detail with my students, keeping everything organized."

Gunnar spoke up, holding hands with Ashley. "Nate, a moment?"

"Sure."

He began walking in a different direction so I shot Tory a look, imploring her to wait a minute. Then I caught up to Gunnar and Ashley.

"Thank Pandora for us," he mumbled, not looking back at me.

"I don't know what you're talking about."

He shot me a knowing look from his good side over his shoulder. "Right."

I didn't reply as I continued to follow. I looked past them to see that his entire pack stood just ahead, staring at their Alpha with respect and fierce loyalty. No humans in sight. Hundreds of wolves. Gunnar and Ashley stopped, and I stepped up beside them, not sure what was going on.

Gunnar cleared his throat, and addressed them. "This war is ours." The wolves growled eagerly. Gunnar let the sound die down before continuing. "What I mean to say is that we have recruited, growing our family over these past months. And that this war is literally *ours*. Nate will not participate. He has his own fight to attend. With a goddess. And I need everyone to know that up front. Don't expect Nate to come galloping in to save us. He will be preoccupied." Gunnar paused, roving his lone eye over the crowd, which was now utterly silent. "This. War. Is. Ours!" he suddenly roared, exploding into his hybrid wolf form, a massive bipedal white werewolf. I glanced down. No underoos this time, which was good. More professional for a momentous speech.

The wolves howled. Still seeming a little concerned about his news, shooting thoughtful looks my way, but most seemed to accept the other part with awe. I would be fighting a goddess for crying out loud. They could handle the monsters.

Gunnar turned to Ashley, who was still in human form. He smiled, and then, loud enough for all to hear, shouted, "Ashley Belmont is my Geri! My watcher. My second in command! Obey her!"

The wolves began to dance, hopping back and forth with their front paws playfully, snarling, licking their lips. I saw several – more than several – wolves look decidedly uncertain about this. The newest werewolf in the pack was the second in command? Sure, she was Gunnar's fiancée, but to name her his Geri? That was the most important position outside being Alpha.

I waited, hiding my smile. Geri meant *Ravenous*, which was appropriate, considering what I had seen from her in the Land of the Fae, and what I knew would come next.

Gunnar held out a hand to her. "If you wouldn't mind a demonstration, my love."

"Gladly," she said.

And suddenly, Wulfra stood before the crowd, a savage, menacing wolf with accessories in her hair, and a wild glint in her eyes. The uncertain wolves looked suddenly impressed…

And then *eager*. Those once-skeptics were the very first to howl with pride.

Which was always a good sign. Win over the antagonists, and the rest would become as loyal as you could ever ask.

She nodded back at them.

Gunnar cleared his throat, glaring out at them. "Ashley has tasted the Wild. She has entered, and returned from, the Land of the Fae. A journey only a handful of people could survive. While there, surviving, fighting for her life, and fleeing nightmares that would give our entire pack pause... myself included," he admitted. "She was forced to change in ways we couldn't fathom. I've spoken with her, and quickly realized that this knowledge is an asset in our war. She truly has otherworldly knowledge, and with it, we will rip the flesh from every Greek who raises blade, tooth, or claw against us." The last was a promising growl, an oath.

Ashley nodded. "In this form, I go by Wulfra." The pack stared up at her in awe, because with that name, she became an otherworldly symbol to them, in her own right. Like a superhero. Something to fear, not just another wolf. "This same... gift was granted to Nate, and with it, he will kill a goddess. If that is any indication of what I learned over there." She let that sink in for a good ten seconds. "I submit to Gunnar – even with my knowledge – because there truly is no better Alpha. My knowledge is *war*. But Gunnar far surpasses me in absolutely *every* other aspect. I pass on my thoughts, and his critiques only amplify my newfound knowledge. If I thought otherwise, I would challenge him for control of the pack." She lowered her eyes. "And in so doing, I would fail all of you. But with my... changes, I am best equipped – under Wulfric's authority – to *strengthen* our pack. Anyone who thinks otherwise dies. Here. Now."

And she took a step forward, assessing the pack. Not a wolf moved. And I could sense that quite a few had silently considered that maybe Ashley *should* lead the pack. But her words, and her challenge, had abruptly culled that thought. If a wolf that powerful still chose to submit to Gunnar... what did that say about their Alpha?

Pretty much, that he was a force of nature.

And a good leader employed the best for his staff.

All in all, the pack of wolves had just doubled in strength. And this addition of a Geri that had a new freaking name, for crying out loud, helped them focus on something other than my lack of involvement. They suddenly felt they didn't *need* me. Not with Wulfra and Wulfric at the head of their family.

I murmured under my breath, not moving my lips too much. "Very cleverly done, Wulfric..."

He turned to me, speaking for all to hear. "We will do you proud, Temple."

I shook my head angrily, stepping past him, right in front of the pack. "No," I snarled. "The wolves earn their *own* honor. You will do *yourselves* proud!" I shouted at them, and judging by how they had initially pranced back a step, Wylde had spoken through me, at least using his voice to amplify my words. Adding a bit of savagery to my statement.

Then, the wolves began their hopping thing, snarling, snapping, and howling at random, dancing with energy, ready for war. I nodded at them, turned, and bowed my head to both Gunnar and Ashley. Wulfric and Wulfra. Then I left, heading back to Tory.

So many things to do, so little time.

CHAPTER 51

I followed Tory to the Syndicate's camp. They waited, watching me approach. Cindy stood at their head near a campfire. That wasn't her real name, but she had been representing the Syndicate when I met her, so I had dubbed her Cindy. "This it?" I asked her.

Her face hardened. "Yes. This is all that is left," she answered, studying my face intently, likely curious about the paint and beard. I pretended not to notice.

"And you speak for them?"

"I do," she answered warily.

"Okay. Get packing." And I began to turn away.

Cindy spluttered in shock, taking a step. I saw Tory step between us, veins suddenly pulsing with glowing golden light. Cindy jumped back a step. "That's far enough," Tory warned.

Cindy held up her hands. "We can't just leave. They'll destroy us." She glanced over a shoulder. "What is left of us."

I shrugged. "Not my problem. You've been a thorn in my side for far too long, double-crossing everyone and their brother. You're not welcome here. You're likely to turn your back on us when we need you most. I can't trust you."

Cindy looked desperate, turning to a few of her ashen-faced wizards. "Guestright! What if we claim Guestright! Swear to defend those under your protection. We couldn't betray that without losing a large chunk of our power," she begged, looking sick to her stomach.

I hesitated for her sake, biting back my inner smile. I had needed her to come to this conclusion on her own. I finally nodded. "That might work." I studied the other wizards distastefully, openly sneering at them. They represented all walks of life. Old, young, bald, short, skinny, not skinny, and several obviously international wizards from different countries. "Do this, and I will allow you to remain, fighting where you are told."

Cindy nodded in relief. "We will do as you command."

"You will do as my family commands," I corrected her.

She hesitated for only a moment, and then swore to serve my family for the duration of the war. She shook my hand, and soon, the rest of the wizards lined up. I studied them as they said the words, watching for treachery, and trying to remember each face. None were familiar. Then again, I sensed several disguises woven with magic. This wasn't alarming to me, because I didn't care about their secrets. They were hiding from the Academy, who were camped somewhere nearby. I was watching for treachery in their oath. And maybe this mysterious leader my friends thought was hiding in the mass of frightened wizards. But I saw nothing to indicate that.

Once all had sworn to serve my family, I took Cindy aside, Tory following us.

Cindy looked concerned, even knowing I couldn't proactively harm her after her oath to act as a guest, because we were not bonded together. Still, wizards were sneaky, and I had a reputation for making other wizards look about as sneaky as snails.

The Huntress walked nearby with Alex, showing him how to hold a dagger. They didn't even notice us as they passed, so engrossed in their conversation.

Cindy gasped, clutching her chest. "That's not possible…" she breathed, staring at Alex.

And an icy shiver rolled down my neck as I turned from the departing Alex to Cindy. I grabbed her by the shirt, shaking her. "You *know* him?" I hissed in disbelief.

She was shaking, physically, and snapping her head back and forth, eyes wild as she tried to understand some contradiction in her mind. "The

Changeling..." she whimpered. Then her eyes shot wide and she looked at me with fear.

"He's not the Changeling. He's the Manling," I said, confirming her fear. "But how would you know about that, Cindy?" I asked in a very calm, deadly voice. "Be honest, or your Guestright is void. And instead of letting you go, my people will kill you all where you stand. They think they are safe. Tory's monsters could destroy them in three seconds. All of them."

Tory nodded, glancing back at the wizards who were watching us. They didn't notice the gang of students circling their camp, laughing and joking as they casually walked the grounds.

But each one of them had spent a portion of their life in the ring, where they fought for their life on an almost daily basis. And some of them had only tasted their first free breath at the age of thirteen or so. Thirteen years of fighting for your life, and little more than one year of tasting freedom in a civilized world.

Cindy followed Tory's gaze, and suddenly looked about to pass out, recognizing the kids for what they were. She turned to me, eyes glistening. Much different than the hard-ass I had met a year ago. Then again, she was a survivor of recent genocide. Her people had been hunted. And she was one of the lucky ones. I didn't feel an ounce of pity for her.

"It was so long ago, but I fear it was the first domino." I frowned, and she sat down with a weary sigh. "One of ours was attacked and killed. By a powerful child. We responded in kind, killing the child and his parents, thinking them all a threat. After, we realized the child was Fae."

I let out a whistle. The Syndicate... had accidentally started all of this, pissing off the Fae. First domino, indeed. But this meant another thing. Alex was officially an orphan.

I shook my head, trying to quench my anger. Alex's parents were dead. Shit.

"Ever since that event, things have been... spiraling. First, with you, and your sudden awareness of us, when we had remained hidden for so long. And Ichabod returning." She pointed a finger towards the gates. "And not just returning, but returning to tutor a Grimm! A Grimm you had brought into our world. Then, the Circus. And awakening a god," she waved a hand at the camp in general.

To be honest, that was kind of when my life had really started to go sideways, too. All the craziness amplified beyond my usual demon-hunting, or monster killing. Things had gotten… bigger since I fought the Grimms, met Ichabod, and when Death had brought Indie back from the dead.

I froze, my heart almost stopping at a sudden revelation.

"You didn't really do it…" I whispered to myself. "The Syndicate didn't…" I trailed off, remembering something Death had once said. Everything clicked into place. But I only had one way to be sure. Because this was *huge*, and I couldn't let on that I knew. It had to be a surprise. Even then, I didn't know how to use it to our best advantage.

Cindy stared, bewildered. "I just told you we did. We killed the Fae child," she admitted.

"Stay away from the boy," I warned in a low growl. "Or I will personally kill each of you. Now, go." She nodded adamantly, and began climbing to her feet. "Oh, and just so you know, Ashley and Gunnar are literally family. Obey them." She stiffened, but gave me a shaky nod, remembering her oath to serve my family, not just me.

"Okay," she whispered. She left hurriedly, walking on shaky legs back to her people. They instantly swarmed her, talking in low voices, asking what had just happened. She was broken. Nothing like the woman who had plagued me last year when I had been trying to stop Indie. The smart-mouthed woman who had once worked with my father…

Because my father had been extorted to either join the Syndicate, or come home to find his wife and child murdered. My mom and I.

Which meant there might be a few good people in the bunch, but I couldn't bank on it. Not when weighed against the safety of my friends. My family.

"Right," I said, shaking my head, trying to process my thoughts. "I need you to bring Talon to the tree, now. No one else. Then I need you to arrange a meeting with Ichabod. Grant him a truce. Just him. I need to show him something." Tory frowned before leaving in a hurry after one look at my face. I made a phone call as I walked.

CHAPTER 52

I had ended my call with Othello about an hour ago, telling her what I needed, and had since been lurking around the camp, waiting to see Talon near the tree from a distance. Not spotting him, I had decided to actually go stand beside the tree to wait for him.

Because who knows? Maybe he was doing the same thing. Circling the tree, waiting to approach until he saw me standing there. Like a couple of idiots.

I felt excited and nervous as I approached the tree. I stared up at the branches to find the usual suspects lurking. "Fuck off, Feathers," I shouted up at the two ravens.

"I don't have feathers," Talon griped, suddenly beside me. I managed not to flinch, and turned to him. "Well?" he asked.

"I need you to run an errand for me."

"I'm not very good at errands."

"What if I told you I stole some of those pods from back in the Fae?"

His ears perked up. "You... smuggled Fae catnip?" He scratched his furry beard, then wiped his whiskers really quickly, as if wiping away drool. "I may be interested..."

"There's a burner phone in my office desk. Write a sticky note on it that says 'answer me,' and then answer the call. Follow the directions you receive to the letter." I stepped forward. "As fast as possible. No delays."

He frowned at me. "Is this an Alice in Wonderland fetish? I'm not the fucking Cheshire Cat."

I blinked. "No. But I can't believe I didn't think of that."

He studied me skeptically. "I take it since I am writing a note on the phone, that I am supposed to give it to someone?" I nodded. "Which means I would need to be a cat. Sir Muffle Paws. Otherwise I could simply tell the person to answer the phone." Again, I nodded. "And how would a cat carry a phone?"

"There's a backpack with a unicorn on it in my office."

He stiffened in disgust. "Why on earth would you have such a vile piece of merchandise?"

I shrugged. "Indie got it for you. It's actually a toddler's backpack. She was going to take a picture of you wearing it, before…" I waved a hand at the current situation.

He glared at me. "I will not."

"Oh, yes. You will, Talon." I said, leaning closer. He actually shivered instinctively, and then gave me a curt, begrudging nod. And left.

I checked over my shoulders, and even walked the perimeter of the tree to make sure I was alone. Then, cautiously, I placed a hand on the trunk. It felt the same, even glowed in darkness still, although not as distinctly as it once had. I wasn't sure why, but it still had some juice in it.

I lowered my voice, and spoke. *You in there, pal?*

A great hollowness answered me, and I sighed. It had been a long sho—

Yes, a voice answered, sounding sleepy.

I almost jumped out of my skin in surprise. But now that I focused, the bark did feel warmer where I touched, as if a presence was leaning against the other side.

Is this your new place? And why are you tired? You've been cooped up forever!

Long night, he said with a yawn. I stepped back, frowning at the tree. Then shrugged.

Okay, your life, I guess. Listen, can you find another Beast?

He chuckled. *Oh, yes. That's easy.*

I told him what I wanted, feeling a sudden surge of excitement, equal to my task for Talon.

Before I had even finished telling him, he answered. *Done. Now go away.*

I stepped back from the tree, scowling. Bird shit fell from the tree, narrowly missing my shoes. I raised a fist up at the two ravens, who cackled back loudly. But I did keep moving, just in case they wanted to try again.

Tory called out from a distance. I turned to look at her, and rather than asking her to come to me, and possibly be attacked by the foul ravens, I walked her way. She hadn't wanted to interrupt our conversation. I loved it when people listened.

"He'll be at the gate in one hour. We granted a full truce that he will be safe and unharmed, returned no more than an hour later. The Greeks will be waiting at the gates to accept him."

I nodded. "We'll swaddle him up and hand him back, no trouble."

She watched me, wondering what I planned, but also knowing I wouldn't share.

They were to act as if I wasn't a part of the war. My actions were separate.

They went to war.

And the spoiled little billionaire played his little games.

CHAPTER 53

*T*he gates stood open when I arrived. The greatest of the Greek warriors stood as they had before, watching, waiting, eager. But they didn't move. Indie stood beside Ichabod, arms folded. I saw the pyramid-shaped stone hanging from a net at her hip.

The Hand of God.

And judging by her smile, she carried it around as a trophy, a reminder of power.

Because some of the Greeks also shot her sidelong, carefully controlled looks, as if secretly wanting to shove it down her throat. The Greeks weren't ones to appreciate servitude, unless it was to the god of their choosing.

Take Leonidas, for example. He hadn't liked the friendly proposition to bow down to some strange Persian dude, even if he did claim to be a god in the flesh, or work directly for a god. The Greeks were simple folk. Live their lives, and end any wars.

With extreme prejudice.

Which made me doubly glad that Leonidas hadn't stumbled into this mess.

I hadn't gotten a good look at their bench, but I was pretty sure the big dogs were up here. And that whoever hung back were monsters of one flavor or another. Perhaps a chimera or dozen. Thing was, I wouldn't know unless I sent Yahn out, risking his life.

And...

It wasn't my war.

Only Ashley could make that request. But I had full confidence in her.

I was here for three things.

I held up my arms, spinning in a slow circle, a gesture that I was weaponless. Even though everyone knew wizards didn't need anything to be deadly. We *were* the weapons. Still, it was a gesture of goodwill.

Then I extended my arm out towards my camp, welcoming him.

Indie opened her mouth to speak, but Ichabod ignored her entirely, walking through the gates. The Guardians, my lethal griffin statues on the walls, followed his every step with their eyes. Not attacking, but promising to end any subterfuge with excessive gifts of pain and agony.

Ichabod stepped up beside me, studied me with a curious frown, and then we both began to walk. His eyes danced about warily, as if expecting a betrayal.

"Relax, Ichy. If I wanted you dead, I wouldn't have gone to all the effort to make a temporary truce, and then break it. I simply would have appeared next to you while you slept, sliced your throat, and then returned home to finish my tea."

Ichy's face hardened at the casual threat, but he didn't speak.

"My part in this is to kill three people," I said casually, giving him a blank look. "But that number could become two, depending..."

Ichabod frowned. "I'm not switching sides. I have a Blood Debt against the Syndicate. You standing against that is the only thing putting your people in danger."

I rolled my eyes. "Have you met the crazy lady with one hand? I'm pretty sure I upset her once. Somehow..." I said, scratching my beard.

"Is the paint and beard supposed to impress me? Did you bring me over here to intimidate me? Oh, and another thing. Would you mind guiding me towards the Syndicate camp? I don't want to waste time later, wandering around looking for it. I'm an old man, after all. Get tired easily," he said, grinning like a shark.

Instead of answering, I sighed dramatically, and pointed towards the tree.

He must have thought I was pointing out the Syndicate camp, because he looked downright happy to follow my hand.

But what he saw stopped him in his tracks, his face sagging with emotion in an instant.

Matthias Temple stood there, leaning against the tree. The Mad Hatter.

Ichabod's daddy. And the basis for his Blood Debt. He had sworn to avenge his father for what the Syndicate had done to him.

But...

Here he was, alive and well, leaning against a tree in his enemies' camp. Ichabod was suddenly running, like a boy returning from his first day of school to give his father a hug.

Now, this wasn't the first time they had seen each other in hundreds of years or anything. But it was the first time they had seen each other in *our world* in hundreds of years. Because the Syndicate had banished him, imprisoned him, and for this betrayal, Ichabod Temple had sworn to avenge his father.

Which seemed kind of pointless, now.

They met in a bear hug, squeezing each other like two bros in a gym. I very carefully didn't point out that the Syndicate camp was quite literally fifty or so yards away, in full view of them.

I stood a few feet away from them, giving them a minute. They finally turned to face me, both smiling. Ichabod was speechless, as was Matthias, who looked as if he didn't have a care in the world. He had been broken out of prison, and been reunited with his son.

"Maybe you can reconsider your Blood Debt, now? This whole thing started so you could avenge your father. But... I brought him back. There's no need for this chaos. Innocents will die. And in case you haven't noticed, Indie has genuinely gone psycho. No thanks to you," I added.

Ichabod's happiness slowly faded. "We're well beyond that, now. No matter what you and I want." I continued staring at him, waiting for him to admit what I suspected. I had given him an opening. But he didn't bite.

I opened my mouth to press the issue when I saw Matthias stiffen, eyes snapping wide open.

Then he was blasted into the tree by a bar of light. His chest smoked as he groaned on the ground. Ichabod and I spun in disbelief to see an unknown, nondescript, gray-haired man standing before us. He had sauntered our way from the Syndicate camp, and...

It was one of the wizards who had sworn the oath to me.

My rage exploded at the man's audacity. Now, they all had to die. Part of me grew irrationally excited at that. As if I wasn't currently staring down a powerful wizard who had just taken down a Maker. A wizard who was now staring back at us without a care in the world. Well, staring at Ichabod, mostly.

"Castor Queen..." Ichabod snarled.

And I blinked in stunned disbelief. Wait... the guy who had taken the Syndicate from Matthias over 200 *years* ago? He was still alive?

I didn't get much time to worry about that, because power I couldn't sense as a wizard was suddenly flying all over the place, tearing up the earth in great big swatches of fire and ash. Two Makers going toe-to-toe.

And cheerleader Nate, with no one to cheer on, because, well, they were both bad guys in my book.

But I had a sudden chill as I watched them fling power at each other, fire splashing over shields of water, fiery rain blasting at the other from two feet above his head, shadowy creatures bursting into existence to attack the other from behind, but obliterated without even a glance.

I had sworn Ichabod safe passage while in my camp. If I didn't protect him, the war would start. Right now. And even though that wasn't as much of a concern to me, since the war was going to happen one way or another, I had made a promise.

Son of a bitch. I needed to help the prick. Even though Matthias probably needed immediate help. I glanced back at him, considering casting a protective dome around him, and gasped.

He was gone.

Shit.

Someone tackled me, and I crashed into the grass as fire screamed past where I had been standing. I stared up to see a living serpent of flame, mouth wide, missing me by a foot, but now circling up into the air to attempt another pass.

Alex grunted from beside me, scrambling to his feet. "Thanks," I said. Then I wrapped him up in air, and launched him away a good fifty paces, not even sure how that was possible. But I could sense Wylde's hand, boosting my power with Fae juice of some kind.

The kid bounced, once, twice, then came to a rolling stop. The Huntress snatched him up by a collar, shoving him behind her as she drew her bow, held loosely in our direction, not knowing who to shoot, or what the hell was going on.

I turned just in time to see the serpent sailing straight at Ichabod. He was holding off a dozen different attacks from Castor, and didn't notice the fiery serpent. I tried to grab it, douse it, but it shook off my attempts. Even Wylde could think of nothing to stop it.

So, I grabbed Ichabod by the ankle with a bar of air, and yanked, just as the serpent slammed his jaws shut. I was too late.

The fiery teeth raked across his back, cauterizing the wounds instantly, and Ichabod screamed as I yanked him my way. I threw a dozen different attacks, all projectiles of different kinds, both from my own knowledge, and Wylde's Fae power. Castor cursed, batting a few of them away, and then disappeared.

I rolled Ichabod over, grabbing his face. He was breathing, but in short, shallow breaths, his face a mask of pain. He was unconscious. Not trusting anyone to help me save the enemy, I stood and backed up a few steps.

Then I advanced, rolling over my shoulder across his chest, snatching a pant leg with my lead hand, and then flinging out my other arm as I completed my roll, standing on shaking legs as I held him over my shoulders. Something I had seen in a special ops training video, showing soldiers how to pick up their injured partners in war zones.

The Huntress nodded approval, urging everyone back with loud shouts as I began shuffling as quickly as possible back to the gates. I didn't dare Shadow Walk or use any magic while carrying him. One, because it would hurt him, but two, because it would put the Greeks on alert.

So, I shuffled, trying to jog as best I could. And I realized I was doing this through a corridor of my people – monsters, dragons, werewolves, humans, and the like. Carl jogged parallel to me, snapping warnings for everyone to step back. Because they all had claws out, ready for a fight, not knowing what had happened, thinking that Ichabod had attacked me, ending our truce.

I didn't have the energy to stop them, but Carl and the Huntress prevented them from jogging behind me like a gang, ready to defend me from the Greeks.

Because it was obvious that's where I was heading.

Ichabod groaned over my shoulder as I finally reached the gates, and the waiting Greeks.

"He needs help," I gasped.

The Greeks could have been chewing rocks, or trying to shatter their own teeth. They were silently furious. Without warning, Ichabod was suddenly snatched from my shoulders, and floated on a gentle pallet of air directly in front of Indie. She assessed him with cold, calculating eyes. Then Ichabod sailed back through her camp without her even looking.

She met my eyes, and whispered in the most hateful tone I had heard her use. "You broke the truce. ATTACK!" she screamed, and I snapped my fingers, the gates slamming shut with a resounding clang.

But that was barely heard over the screams, grunts, growls, snarls, howls, and screeches of monstrous Greeks suddenly pounding into the wall that kept my friends safe.

I turned, panting with exhaustion to find Ashley studying me.

She was in full Wulfra mode, and wore a sheepskin over her shoulders like a cloak.

Gunnar stood beside her, in Alpha form, a towering white werewolf on two legs, a combination of man and wolf, his lone eye studying me for injury. He wore a lion cloak over his shoulders. The two looked to be hunting for a bully to bully.

They nodded at me. Ashley pointed a thumb over her shoulder, reminding me to get going. She had a hungry grin on her wolfish mouth, as if stretching muscles, eager to play. She wasn't mad at me. She was excited. Simply reminding me that this wasn't my fight.

I sagged my head, and began jogging past them towards Chateau Falco, unable to meet the eyes of everyone who was about to go to war. I had put them in this, and now they were about to fight a war against battle-hardened Greek Heroes and monsters.

Fucking Hercules, for crying out loud.

And all they saw was me jogging back to the safety of my house.

Even though I knew it was right, I began to cry. Not cry, really, but my face was awash with tears. I made no sound as I jogged, but the tears kept flowing, and my throat felt raw, and my face felt aflame with shame. The shame of letting everyone think I was running, rather than shouting back at them that I had to go fight a *goddess*. And that they could handle a few hundred monsters and Greek Heroes on their own.

But that wouldn't help.

I slowed as war horns cracked the night, deep haunting sounds. Like wails from the pit of Hell. I heard Tory shouting and slowed, searching for her. Not to approach, but to watch. Because letting my friends go to war meant that they could die. I wanted to run around the camp like a crazy person and hug them all.

Which was a very unique position for me to be in.

I finally saw her. She must have noticed me, because she flashed me a quick nod, eyes twinkling with anticipation. Then she turned away, and I saw she was facing a mass of thirty or so kids from junior high school on up, and they watched their school principal give a pep rally.

"Remember all the lessons I taught you! To control yourself, to be in charge, to hold back, and think first..." she shouted, locking eyes with as many students as possible. The crowd nodded, shifting their feet uncertainly. "Forget it," she hissed at them.

As one, their heads jerked up, and the madness I saw made me take a step back. They were kids. But they looked as if she had just promised them all double-chocolate-fudge brownies covered in vanilla ice cream and molten caramel. Some even licked their lips slowly.

"Today is about getting some stuff off your chest. Getting it out of your system. A cleanse, if you want to call it that." Their smiles grew. "Sometimes, a machine must release steam to stay in optimal shape. Times like this are designed for just that... to let off some steam." Like a wave, the children exploded into monsters, all different flavors, sizes, shapes, and colors. Strips of clothing rained down off their sudden hairy, scaled, or armored shoulders. I didn't even know what some of them were. Because the Beast Master I had saved them from had liked to collect exotic monsters, and although I had thought I'd seen them all shift, I realized very suddenly that I was wrong. So very wrong. Or she had been recruiting for her school, Shift, home for wayward shifters with authority issues who lacked impulse control.

Tory glanced back at me for a moment, eyes twinkling, and then she turned to her students. Green fog suddenly coalesced around her as the horns continued blasting, and screams began to fill the night near the gate, accompanied by the sound of crumbling stone. The wall was failing. "Tonight, we bring the terror!" she shouted.

And like a single unit, Tory's berserker horde of monsters descended upon the gates.

I shivered, running as fast as I could in the opposite direction. Because with one more speech like that, I would forget all my promises to stay out of the war. Proud and terrified tears splashed my cheeks as I ran, trying to burn away the nagging feeling that I was running the wrong way.

Wylde gripped my soul suddenly, angrily. I didn't stop, but I did flinch, searching inward. He stared at me, and shook his head one time in disappointment. There was no compassion there. It was the look a coach would give an athlete who didn't have his head in the game.

And it helped. I found my back straightening, and I was finally able to lift my head, watching where I was jogging. I saw Callie in the distance, standing on the steps of Chateau Falco, staring at me. She saw I had noticed her, and gave me a single nod. Then she smiled.

I smiled back, and found myself suddenly running faster. Simply to let out some tension, not aimed towards the house any longer, but past it, towards a sudden ring of fire that erupted near the giant white tree.

Men and women began jumping out of it, landing in fighting stances, like paratroopers touching ground after their flight.

I skidded to a halt, pointing at a familiar face.

G Ma stared back at me, clutching her throat as she saw the designs on my face.

I stalked closer, stroking my beard.

She looked very nervous, but she stood her ground as she spoke. "Where do you need us?"

A hundred wizards, by the looks of it. Perfect. Since Ashley hadn't commanded them anywhere yet, I wouldn't be interfering by giving them a job. "I need a favor from you. No questions. No deviations. You need to do it quickly, and then go help."

She nodded, looking relieved that I hadn't simply killed her.

I pointed behind me, not wanting to attract attention, because although the Syndicate hadn't fled, they looked about to. G Ma glanced over my shoulder, and looked suddenly hungry. "Take them to my dungeons and lock them up. Take enough wizards to guarantee success. You are to lock them all up so they can't use their powers. Then, individually, you are to take them out and make them swear to obey Nate Temple, Gunnar Randulf, or Ashley Belmont. Only." Because I had a sudden feeling that leaving my earlier command open to include family might mean they obeyed Ichabod or Matthias.

She nodded, waiting for more. "You will listen to them take that oath, and verify that there is no possible way for them to sneak around the oath magically. Like throwing their voices, having one wizard use his power to speak for another, and things like that." I took a step closer. "Castor Queen appeared, still alive. A Maker. The previous oath did not hold him."

She shivered at that, face pale. "K-keep them locked up, then."

I held out my hand at the chaos behind me. "We can't afford that. Hercules, and a bunch of other surprises just broke through the wall."

She swallowed. "Okay."

"Be very sure. Beyond sure. Have a circle of wizards testing and verifying each oath. Independently. Then… send them to Ashley Belmont. Your people are also to report to her. At least, those not guarding the Syndicate wizards who fail to convince you of their oath. Keep four of your wizards for each prisoner you keep. The rest go to war."

She grimaced at that. If all the Syndicate were lying, that could mean a quarter of her force suddenly needed to guard the prisoners. But she understood, and nodded.

"Go. Surround them. Now."

And then I began to run, ignoring her shouts about where I could be found. I raced towards the labyrinth, fleeing her words, repeating to myself that I was doing the right thing.

I saw fog eddying around my feet as I ran, pounding earth, and breathing hard. The wooden disc on my necklace slapped my throat as I ran, and the fog grew thicker.

That would make the war harder. Fog was the worst. Hiding friend from foe.

But that wasn't my problem.

I suddenly realized that the fog wasn't just thick, it was all encompassing. I glanced around, and realized it was well over my head, and entirely surrounding me. I couldn't see a thing. I continued to run, trying to escape it, wondering if I had accidentally run into one of the valleys. Or if Castor Queen had returned for payback.

Like I said, fog was dangerous in war. You could get lost. Stumble right upon your enemy without realizing it. I continued to run, holding out my arms for protection, hoping I didn't stumble over a bush.

This was ridiculous. I wasn't anywhere near the war, and we were well within the protection of my home. This couldn't be enemy magic.

Just as quickly as that, the fog was gone, and I stood in a marble pavilion.

Giant columns rose up from a smoothly polished floor, easily fifty feet tall, supporting a ring of marble that connected every column in a perfect circle. The center of the pavilion was empty, and at least fifty feet in diameter. A single marble table sat near the edge to my right, with a pitcher of wine and a lone goblet.

A woman sat on a stool, looking startled to see me. "Be gone," she said.

And before I could react, I was falling, wind whistling in my ears.

CHAPTER 54

I fell for quite a while, and had long since given up on yelling, or shouting, or being afraid.

I studied the stars.

Wylde, on the other hand, had made and dismissed dozens of ideas to try and save us. I knew we didn't have wings, and couldn't suddenly sprout any, no matter what Wylde thought he could do with his freaky Fae juice. And I had no shadows to make a parachute.

But I was oddly content.

I ripped through a blanket of clouds, and sound suddenly struck me. I flipped myself over to stare at the rapidly approaching ground. It was madness. The Greeks had broken down the wall, and Guardians shrieked and screamed as they dove into squads of men, only to be blasted away by wizards on the Greek side. Wizards on my side blasted right back, which meant I had to have been gone a while. Unless they had simply locked up the Syndicate and ignored my command.

The Greeks were shaped in a spear formation, driving right through the center of my property, pressing forward intently, rather than the block formation I had assumed. And they didn't waste time fighting when they didn't need to. They had a purpose. A target.

Me?

How long had I been gone?

Dragons roared through the skies, blasting fire at pockets of flankers that tried to break off from the main body of Greeks, but arrows whistled up into the night sky, ripping through dragon wings, and explosions of green fire erupted into the night, washing the sky with liquid flame, rolling over the backs of any aerial assaults, and despite dragons' immunity to fire...

It seemed they weren't resistant to Greek Fire. Basically, napalm.

Dozens of bodies lay on the ground, but I saw Ashley and Gunnar, back to back, covered in blood as an army of over two hundred wolves darted around them like a school of fish, lashing out at random to hamstring and evade, rip out a throat, and evade.

Blasts of power struck Ashley, but she always managed to turn her back just in time, and whatever power hit that fluffy blanket on her back, reflected right back into the enemy.

The Golden Fleece was just so magically fluffy.

Gunnar on the other hand, looked like a nightmare. He wore Hercules' Nemean Lion Cloak, with the hood up over his werewolf face, looking like the lion had attempted to swallow him whole, and Gunnar was erupting out of his freaking throat.

He also pulsed with power, looking bigger, thicker, harder.

And his blue eye actually glowed as he struck with his claws, sending enemies flying at least twenty feet, or ripping them entirely in half. One poor bastard swung a spear length axe down at him. It struck his back and exploded into toothpicks. Gunnar glanced over his shoulder, snarling, and was suddenly holding the offending shit-stain a good fifteen feet away, gripping him by the throat. He twisted his wrist and the body went limp. Gunnar turned, and hurled him into a trio of soldiers approaching Ashley, bowling them over.

But I glanced over at a sudden motion, not seeing anything in particular, but catching something out of the corner of my eyes. I was much closer to the ground now, and realized I had maybe ten seconds before impact.

An invisible force hit me laterally, angling down, using my momentum to lighten the blow.

Still, it felt as pleasant as being tackled by a random antelope while riding a Power Wheel on a quiet neighborhood street. Claws clutched my torso, but my vision was now swirling from the totally unexpected blow. I glanced down at my body, wondering if he had knocked off an arm.

And I saw nothing.

"Ack! He's stealing my soul!" I yelled.

A familiar voice panted with effort. "Toe-tah-lee saved you, yah?"

Yahn, the candy-painted dragon with chameleon abilities. Meaning he had made us invisible. Or, blended us with the night, camouflaging us with our surroundings. I opened my mouth to thank him.

"Hold on tight!" he shrieked. Then we hit about a dozen bushes in rapid succession, before tumbling and rolling across the grass. We groaned after coming to a complete stop.

I opened my eyes to find my mouth dangerously close to a dark, blonde-haired nipple. "Ack!" I said, jumping off Yahn's chest. He just lay there, unconscious or dead. And very naked.

I let out a breath. My back and, well, my whole body ached, and I was liberally covered in scratches from the bushes. "No one saw. You're still cool," I said, staring down at Yahn. He was still breathing, but didn't move other than that. I nudged him with a boot. Nothing. "Dancing time!" I shouted at the top of my lungs.

He lurched up into a sitting position, eyes wide.

To find me grinning at him. "Master Temple!" he stammered. "We're alive!" he whispered, inspecting his body anxiously.

"Toe-tah-lee," I agreed, holding out a hand. He accepted, and then covered up his naughty bits with both hands, face flushing.

"Can you turn around and stuff?"

"I've got one, too. Your secret is safe," I said. But I did make sure I was in front as I began walking away, practically jogging, eager to enter the—

I skidded to a halt, letting out a sigh. The fight.

I glanced at Yahn. "Go do as you were commanded. Before you broke orders to save my pathetic life." He looked embarrassed, but he nodded. "And Yahn?" he turned, shoulders wilted as if expecting punishment. "Thanks for saving me."

He smirked, and then jogged away. I shook my head, pacing as I watched the fight from a distance. Yahn had changed. Still the same in places, but he was harder. Less afraid.

A product of war.

I sat in the grass, crossing my legs, and rocking back and forth, knowing that if I stood I would run into the thick of things. Wylde kept me company, watching the distant battle through my eyes, and explaining things as he saw it. Some of it was startling, but a lot of it I got on my own. Still, it was very obvious that he saw things much differently than me.

Instead of seeing a person was in danger, Wylde would describe it like Chess. *That trio will be overrun any second, but the attackers don't see the dozen men creeping up over their backs thirty seconds after that.* And *that man is too wide around the eyes. He will break at the first charge.* Or *that woman has fire in her,* pointing at a plump woman carrying a bucket of water between tents, eyes out for danger.

It was oddly academic. Like we were watching old footage from one of the World Wars, or a sports game, analyzing mistakes and successes, learning from them. And I could tell that to Wylde, this was the most invigorating thing in the world.

Even compared to sex.

CHAPTER 55

The Huntress found me as dawn was rising. Well, Carl was leading her to me. She held a broken bow, and was covered in blood. Her quiver had no arrows, and she limped. She looked broken, like her bow.

She looked up at me, and her face cracked. "They took Alex..." and she collapsed to her knees, sobbing.

I raced towards her, my vision pulsing red. Not Alex. His life had already been so horrible. I had just saved him from a hellish existence.

I squeezed her shoulders, ignoring her broken bow. "What happened?"

"It wasn't an attack. It was a surgical strike. To obtain leverage. Ashley caught on instantly, but the wizards showed up too late to help. She didn't have the resources she needed, and with Hercules and that damned golden-haired wonder hurling spears astride Pegasus, they were pinned down. I used all my arrows, and switched to knives, but there were too many."

"Who?" I snarled. "Who took Alex?"

She met my eyes, her own bloodshot. "Indie. And... Achilles."

I stared, dumbfounded. Achilles...

"He could have killed me. Indie commanded him to. But he just looked at me. Sniffed with disdain, and broke my bow. *She's as broken as this bow, now...*" she said, mimicking Achilles' gruff voice.

I turned to Carl, who nodded. "No one could find you. I know that was your intent, but Ashley still wanted to keep you updated. The wizards –

both Academy and Syndicate – have plugged up the gaps, and we can now give them one hell of a fight. But…" He trailed off, looking uncertain.

"What?" I rasped.

"I don't know if you want me to tell you. I don't know if it's what you want. You said you mustn't fight here…" he said, sounding conflicted.

I took a deep breath, reaching out to Wylde. *Guide me. Keep me focused. With pleasure.*

I looked at Carl, and something must have been different in my eyes, because he took an instinctive step back, tightening his lizard lips. His tongue even flickered out uneasily, as if sensing the area between us, uncertain of what he had suddenly stepped into. I nodded. "Proceed."

"She's waiting at the gates, calling for you. With the child. All of them are. She wants an exchange. The Syndicate for the boy."

The Huntress snarled. "Give them to her. Fuck the Syndicate," she cursed.

I considered all my options. No involvement in the war. But my conflict, my battle, was with Indie. And Ichabod. And the alleged goddess who had knocked me out of Olympus or wherever the hell I had accidentally stumbled to.

I opened my mouth to reply, hating myself for it, when my pocket buzzed. I frowned, pulled out my phone, and read the text message.

My heart suddenly began to beat erratically. But I hesitated, focusing on Wylde. He was silent, going over every outcome, and he finally let out a mirthless chuckle. *Do this thing, you cruel son of a bitch.*

I felt my own face smiling, and it must have been a hideous sight, because even the Huntress looked suddenly concerned.

"Let's go see my ex."

~

I sauntered up to the gates, keeping my face calm. My friends watched me, confused. By now, they had all heard I wasn't involving myself in the war, but that I would participate in some small part.

To them, they probably imagined that one small part to be something cosmically violent.

And that moment might just be right now.

The gates were closed, even though the walls had two wide holes on either side of it. No more trust existed between our armies, not with Indie convincing everyone I had broken my truce with Ichabod. Achilles had a few dings and scratches on his armor, and several surface wounds, but overall, he looked clean. But the tips of two spears were bloody, as was his sword.

Hercules, on the other hand, hadn't bothered to hide his war-stained clothing, and from the whispers I had caught while walking through camp, he had tried very hard to get to Gunnar and retrieve his cloak. Even though he was the only Greek to break formation. He smiled at me, but his smile faded as I felt a presence behind me. I glanced back to see Tory and her horde of violent kids – still in monster form – licking their lips at what they considered to be a walking slab of fresh steak.

I didn't bother hiding my smile as I turned back to Hercules. The Minotaur was absent. In shame?

I studied the two humans, Indie and Ichabod. Well, three humans. Indie held the kid before her, gripping him by the hair. He looked dirty and afraid, but unharmed. He also looked furious. Then that fury ratcheted up as he saw the Huntress behind me. Ichabod looked weak, standing beside Indie as if wishing he had a crutch. He wouldn't meet my eyes.

"Well?" I asked calmly. "We were waiting for a real war. Not a toddler trying to steal his superhero cloak back while the rest of your cretins devolved to kidnapping a tiny child."

Indie smiled, and I casually took a step to the side, as if trying to get a better view through the bars on the gate. Then I began to take a few steps closer. Until I was holding the gates in either hand, obviously not a threat. I even leaned casually, propping one leg up on the toes of my boot.

"You break truce with us, and then have the audacity to chastise our actions?"

I glared at Ichabod, who looked angry. At Indie. But he still kept his mouth shut.

"I'm pretty sure you heard exactly what happened. Stop lying to your army. Leading them to believe a falsehood in order to help justify your actions. They are clever men and will see through your ruse. Painting me as something worse than you isn't possible, and deep down, they know it."

She practically quivered at the blow. "Are you saying you have such poor management of your army, that you could overlook such a rebellious act?

Either you broke truce, or you can't control your army. I'll let you pick which one to put on your tombstone."

"I've made it perfectly clear that they aren't my army. I'm only here for... three deaths."

Her face flushed with anger. "We will exchange the child for the Syndicate. All of them. Consider it a favor, since you obviously can't keep them in line."

"They're busy right now. Can we get back to the war thing? We're all rather bored. And although I do despise killing the ignorant, for what you've done, I'll make an exception."

Indie took a step closer, yanking Alex by the hair. He gasped, following on his toes to avoid being scalped. "I will paint your gates with his blood if you don't give me what I want, *right now!*" Indie screamed, spittle flying.

I nodded, glancing to my left. Yahn materialized out of nowhere holding a cell phone. Shouts, stammers, and horrified gasps suddenly rolled over us as everyone who could, turned to look at the screen, and the very beautiful mature woman screaming at Indie in incoherent stutters.

"Say hi to mom, Indie," I said softly.

Indie released Alex's hair as if burned, mouth hanging open. She began to shake her head. "That's... not possible. She's dead."

"Mrs. Rippley," I said, turning. "You are smoking hot for a dead lady," I said, and then turned back to Indie. I thought I heard Achilles chuckle, but his mask made it impossible to tell. And a chuckle didn't mean ally.

"What... the *hell* is wrong with you?" Mrs. Rippley demanded. "He's a *child!*"

Indie suddenly looked twelve years old. Still angry, defensive, disbelieving, but also guilty as hell. "It's not what it looks like," she pleaded before turning to me. "Turn it off. Turn it off!"

"Nah. This is fun. Watching you squirm while your mommy reprimands you."

"Shut your mouth, Nathin!" Mrs. Rippley roared.

"Yes Ma'am," I said, grinning. She wasn't really mad at me. After all, I had been the one person to let her see her daughter after more than a year. Thanks to Sir Muffle Paws arriving on her doorstep.

"How..." Indie whispered.

Mrs. Rippley turned the phone to show Sir Muffle Paws sitting on the floor, lapping up a bowl of cream. As if sensing us watching, he turned, took one look, arched his back, and then ran away in shame. I tried not to laugh. I really did. Which earned another shout from Mrs. Rippley.

"You must have forgotten what Hemingway told you so long ago. After Mardi Gras," I elaborated, watching Indie's confused face. Then I saw it dawn on her, and her lips began to quiver. I nodded. "That she would *live a long life, dying of natural causes*. Something like that."

Indie backed up a step, shoulders shaking, literally having a panic attack. Because while talking to Cindy, I had remembered Death telling Indie that. Trying to make her feel better after her mom had been attacked by one of my enemies.

And you know what? I didn't even feel bad. Not because I'm sadistic. I'm a pretty forgiving guy when it comes to honest mistakes. But cold, rational choices, where one weighed the outcome and decided death and war was a fair price to attain her goals? Nope. The pity train had left long ago. I was actually enjoying this. Letting her look in the mirror and see what everyone else had seen in her for the past year.

What she had refused to see. Refused to admit.

"Let the kid go, Indie. The Syndicate never did anything to you. You were lied to."

She began shaking her head in denial. "But Ichabod. The Fae..."

"What?" I asked, frowning uneasily at the latter comment.

Indie nodded to herself, latching onto it. "He took me there. To that dark place. To help me learn how to handle my Grimm powers." Her eyes shot to Ichabod, pleading. He looked ready to run, but I knew none of the Greeks would allow that. Not because they backed her up, but because right about now, everyone was riveted by the story, and pretty much demanded to know what the hell was going on.

I glanced over at Mrs. Rippley, who was openly sobbing now. Yahn had a satisfied smile on his face. Even though he wasn't familiar with Indie, this war had changed him, and he was watching the cause of his pain suffer.

"I came back... different. The Queens encouraged me. Told me about the evil Syndicate. The Fight Club they ran. The poor children..."

I stood in silence, stunned. I had known Ichabod was an asshat with a shit feather in his cap, but this was something else. I thought he had just lied to her about her mom's *death* – to motivate her to join him. But to take her to the Land of the Fae?

And after that Fae persuasion, Indie had gone to the Circus to take them down because... the Fae had made her see the Syndicate as evil. But at the same time, the Fae had been hounding me, attacking me, to get to Tory, the new Beast Master.

"Indie... did you tell them about us? About our friends? Tory? Alucard?"

She nodded slowly, lost in her own thoughts, but answering my simple question.

I shivered, and felt Tory murmur under her breath, no doubt furious. That was why the Queens had come for us. Once again, because of Indie.

All because I had let her become a Grimm. Something she was never equipped to handle. I had let my love convince me she could handle my world. Like War had warned me about. That small heartfelt choices could have unbelievably horrible consequences.

Indie had believed the Queens. Told them all about us. And she had come back to our world as a heat-seeking missile, locked onto a new enemy. The Syndicate. But the Syndicate was really enemy to the Fae.

Because the Syndicate had accidentally killed one of theirs.

You had to hand it to them, the Fae were fucking *ruthless*.

Alex broke the silence. "I saw them there. They were not... kind. They scared me more than my keepers."

Everyone flinched at that, because most didn't know Alex's story. Not my side, not Indie's side. Ichabod flinched, staring down at the kid in sudden recognition.

"You..." he whispered. Then his eyes shot to me, suddenly very, very concerned. I let a slow smile creep over my face, and gave him a single nod. He looked ready to vomit, understanding that this meant I had gone there, too. And that could mean any number of things.

I heard a commotion behind me, and saw Tory physically restraining the Huntress from storming the gate and taking Alex back herself.

Even though it had been over a year for us, in our world, Alex was likely remembering Indie and Ichabod from only weeks ago. After all, we had seen one night and one day, and had returned to find almost two months had passed. In a way, maybe it was good that Alex's parents were gone. They had likely lost their son years ago, and suddenly having him returned to them, maybe a few months older than when they had lost him... several years ago, could have given them a heart attack, or short-circuited their brains.

Ichabod finally spoke up. "I had no choice. It was the price for our escape. The only way to leave. To use Indie as a blade against a mutual enemy..." he said, almost whispering. "I thought with Indie in agreement, that you would follow, too, Nate. Help me defeat them. But then I saw you had changed, when we went to the Circus. And after that..." he shrugged heavily, looking beaten down, on his last legs.

"How could you possibly justify breaking someone's very *soul*," I pointed at Indie, "to get what you want?" I asked Ichabod, astonished.

"She was such a passionate person, independent. I thought if anyone could survive unscathed, it would be her. But, that passion ended up being her weakness. They fed that passion, fueling her with hatred rather than love. Using her strength against her. No one anticipated this," he held up a hand at the current war. "Not even the Fae anticipated *this*. They just wanted vengeance for the death of their Changeling. I just wanted revenge against the Syndicate for taking my father."

I glanced at the phone, seeing Indie's mother squinting at us, as if trying to make out something that wasn't clear.

"And her? Indie thinking her dead?"

Ichabod stared at his boots, avoiding Indie's stunned glare. "She needed a last... nudge. A final reason to commit to the cause. That nudge was what allowed me to leave that cursed world. It was the price of my freedom."

"*Nudge?* You call that a n—"

"It *is* you!" Mrs. Rippley suddenly shrieked. I turned to see her pointing at... Ichabod. "You... told me I had to go into hiding. That I was in danger. That I couldn't talk to anyone. And you gave me a bag of money so I could quit my job! I loved that job! Nate! I am buying a ticket to St. Louis right this instant! You, Indie, and that man are going to have words. Get that sensible woman, Greta, is it? Yes, Greta. She seems the only intelligent person down there in that lawless state."

"I think we've got it, Mrs. Rippley. You'll be contacted in the morning by a friend. She will help set everything right." I motioned for Yahn to hang up as she began to yell back at me, pressing her face against the phone as if she could stop the call from hanging up.

I stared at Ichabod, shaking my head. Indie was muttering to herself, likely doubting her every decision. That didn't mean she had changed. In fact, it could mean that she was beyond rational, and would be even worse, now. But I had meant what I said. I had a problem killing an ignorant person. They needed to know why they were meeting death. Otherwise, it was murder.

Ichabod had taken Indie to the Fae, to strengthen her. But she had become a monster instead. And rather than fixing it, Ichabod had used it. Fed that monster for his own personal vendetta. He had partnered with the Fae to use Indie to kill the Syndicate.

When I later refused to join up with her on her quest, it had pushed her over the edge. I didn't feel sorry for her. Not really. Although it was a terrible story.

Because I had managed to control my beast. And I had helped my friends do the same. And even if I had felt as vengeful as her while over there, I had never crossed those kinds of lines, done such horrible things, to attain my goal. Sure, I would have done truly terrible things to obtain a just goal, but I never would have intentionally harmed the *innocent*. Because the ends rarely justified the means. Typically, that line of reasoning resulted in exactly this.

For example, I never could have taken out my aggression on an innocent to find my parents' killer. Someone like Alex, who had been the unluckiest son of a— my train of thought evaporated as I noticed him. No one else had. He was reaching into his pocket, and… well, stroking himself. Very enthusiastically.

I heard a few coughs behind me from my people, because he was giving us a show. But none of the Greeks had noticed yet.

Indie noticed the sounds, assuming they were chuckling at her, but she saw that they weren't watching her at all. Her eyes latched onto Alex, and suddenly darted forward, trying to grab him with her missing hand. He evaded, laughing, and kept right on stroking. Indie snatched him up with her existing hand, cursing. She yanked his hand out of his pocket to find him clutching a white feather.

She began to laugh. "Naughty boy. You stole a feather from Pegasus? Now we're all doomed." She said, letting go of him, pretending to be scared. Alex jumped, snatching the feather from her hand. She rounded on him. "It won't do you any good, boy. No matter what you've heard. Stolen feathers don't work. Only a feather freely given can—"

Out of nowhere, Pegasus slammed into Indie, knocking her right into Hercules where she crumpled. He shifted slightly on impact, but didn't stumble. He looked just as stunned as everyone else.

The rest of us watched as Pegasus scooped up the boy and launched into the sky. He flew straight over my protective walls, and dropped down somewhere near the mansion. The remaining Guardians on the wall watched absently before turning stony glares back to the Greeks.

Indie climbed to her feet. "Kill them. All," she spat, eyes solid black.

Hercules suddenly brandished his club. "With pleasure…"

"Game on," I said to myself as I turned away. I had a smile on my face as I began to jog, the Huntress sliding up next to me.

"Did you notice it, too?" she asked excitedly.

I grinned at her. "Sure did. That sneaky little bastard. I wonder where he learned that?"

She scoffed. "He better have a shiny new bow for me, or I'll have his ears."

I told her a few other things, and they weren't as lighthearted, as we sought Alex out.

CHAPTER 56

We found Pegasus grazing near the labyrinth, Carl standing guard beside Alex, like the lizard men that secretly kept the President of the United States safe.

Alex clutched two items in his hands, although I couldn't be sure what one of them was from this distance, the other was obvious.

"A bow!" the Huntress hooted. Then, "Alex, you *clever* little bastard!"

I called out to Grimm, my unicorn, and he was suddenly standing some distance from Pegasus, announced by a great peal of black lightning that was instantly joined by a distant boom. He stood staring at his brother, stamped a hoof, and snorted tiny puffs of smoke from his nostrils. Pegasus dipped his head, bending a knee.

Grimm approached warily, and the two legendary horses walked away, leaning towards each other, speaking in low tones.

I felt Grimm speak to me one last time. *The boy and Pegasus are bonded. No treachery to worry about. He never bonded the other one, who was, apparently, a giant asshole.* I smiled in relief. The kid had a pony.

We reached Alex, who was holding out the bow. The Huntress – after the briefest flicker of hesitation – smacked the bow out of his hand and picked him up, spinning him around in a circle, laughing. "Clever, clever, *clever* little bastard!" she shrieked in delight.

I watched, smiling. I had never seen her so happy. Not in the archery department at a hunting store, and not even near Tory. But around Tory she just looked hungry. I'd probably be alarmed if she looked at Alex like that. But I was betting Tory knew how to sate the Huntress' hunger.

She finally set him down, mussed his hair, and then with shaking fingers, picked up the bow, inspecting it. The wood was exquisite. Black, not as if painted, but as if made from genuine black yew. Intricate carvings etched the surface with designs of horses, flight, and conquest, and the string was as white as snow, almost seeming to glow. Either it was a fresh string, or the hair used to make it was immune to dirt. Looking closer, it almost looked too thin to draw. As if the string would snap. Like a fishing line.

Bellerophon's bow.

The Huntress tested it, and grunted in disbelief, almost falling over. Not from a lack of effort, but from using too *much* effort. She blinked down at it, confused, and then tried again, this time barely pulling the string.

The string drew back as effortlessly as if she was breaking a cobweb, but I saw the wood of the bow itself quivering, as if the wood was holding all the tension, rather than the Huntress or the string. It looked like Alex could draw the thing himself and shoot just as far as Hercules.

"This is the finest bow I have ever seen," she whispered, staring down at it.

Alex beamed proudly.

I stepped in. "Kid, that was remarkable. You used your head, played your hand, and made them see only an angry and scared child." I pointed at his pocket. "Did Pandora give you that?" He nodded, smirking guiltily.

"I tucked it away in my sock." he said. I shook my head in wonder, silently thanking her. Pandora had gifted Alex a freely-given feather from Pegasus from, oh, likely thousands of years ago. It acted exactly like the feather I had for Grimm. An emergency pager, of sorts. Use it, and the horse would appear.

After a few uses, the feather was no longer needed, because you would likely be friends by then, able to call him at will. Bonded. At least that was how Grimm and I had progressed. But remembering Alex going to town on himself in front of everyone, I realized that Pandora probably should have told him how to use it. He could have simply touched it and thought *Pegasus, come to me.*

But what he had done had been *so* much better.

"Did they not search you?" I asked, shaking my head. Anyone should have found it, and instantly feared what it meant. Even Indie.

"Achilles searched me, even patted me down from head to toe and emptied my pockets, but he didn't find it."

"And is that what I think it is?" I asked, trying not to rub my hands together greedily.

He held out a pyramid shaped stone in his hands. "Thought you might want it. She obviously cared about it, keeping it tied to her hip like that. Wanted to at least piss her off."

He handed it over to me. I took it, staring down at it. The Hand of God. The artifact Indie had used to wake up her goddess. The artifact that possibly still linked the two of them together, judging by how close Indie had remained to it. Never letting it out of her sight.

Quick, continuous peals of horns pierced the morning light, and the low drone of shouting voices filled the air. The War had resumed. I needed a better vantage.

"Huntress, Carl, keep him safe. Even if that means entering Chateau Falco and hiding." I turned to Alex. "I can guarantee that if you're seen on the battlefield, that even though you're no longer a bargaining chip, you'll be a high-value target. For stealing Pegasus and pissing off Indie."

Alex looked suddenly ashamed. "I'm sorry. I didn't m—"

"Alex," I said, gripping his shoulders as I leaned down. "That was a compliment. If you haven't pissed anyone off by ten in the morning, you're doing something wrong with your life."

The Huntress groaned, and tugged Alex away from my grasp. "Come along, Carl. Master Temple is a terrible influence. In fact, I should tell you about the time we went to the bank together..." We locked eyes for a moment, and I nodded sadly at the boy. She didn't miss a beat, nodding back. She would tell him about his parents, having heard about it herself right after the fiasco at the gates as we were walking up here.

Carl looked very interested as she continued her story, walking towards Chateau Falco.

I stared out at the war in the distance, which looked like a crazy mosh pit.

But I felt Wylde directing me to specific points, showing them to me in a new light.

The distant formations took on new patterns, and I saw that it was indeed a masterpiece of planning, even though hastily thrown together.

I had picked well with Ashley.

The rest was up to her and her soldiers.

Taking a deep breath, I hefted the stone in my hand, remembering where I had seen one just like it. On the statue marking my mother's tomb in the Temple Mausoleum. She had been holding a pyramid-shaped stone just like this one.

I didn't have time to think about what that could mean, so instead masked the stone with magic, tied it to my belt, and began to jog until fog slowly drifted up around me, taking me to the place I was meant to be.

I still had to take out Indie and Ichabod, but I had a more pressing concern.

A few minutes after jogging through the impenetrable fog, I returned to the marble pavilion. Blue sky surrounded me, and the air felt thin. I saw the familiar table, and the same woman seated behind it. This time there were two goblets, and when she turned to face me, she didn't look surprised.

"Nathin Laurent Temple," she mused. "Godkillers sure are small these days," she chuckled.

An owl fluttered onto the balcony near her table. A great big gray one with a razor-sharp beak, easily three times as large as was naturally possible. Purple feathers mixed with the gray, looking like a parrot had knocked up an owl one night near a certain wizarding school.

It was the owl that finally convinced me.

"Athena," I said neutrally, not dipping my head. For some reason, I wasn't surprised to find out it was her. "You look positively... domestic." She was tall and slender, with blonde hair currently tied back in two plaits down her back. She wore a flowing white toga that was very loose in the front, giving me an Olympian view of Elysium. But I was made of stronger stuff. Godly teats could not sway me.

Athena was considered the Goddess of War, Wisdom, Courage, and a bunch of other things, so I chose my words carefully. Carefully crafted to infuriate her.

Like *domestic*. Not typically attributed to *war*.

Her lips thinned, but she tapped the stool beside her. "Come, sit. I desire a brief chat before I throw you back down to earth again."

"How considerate. Make mine a double. And make it snappy. I want to finish it before your corpse starts to stink, what with all that ichor I'm going to splash on this shining marble floor you just finished cleaning for me," I said, glancing down, ignoring her warning growl.

Then I sauntered up to the table, crossed my legs, and began to drink. This was going to be... interesting.

CHAPTER 57

She watched me for a time, analyzing me, I guessed. Maybe she sensed the Hand of God that was attached to my hip, even though it was invisible. She was a goddess, it wouldn't have surprised me if that was a gift of hers. But it didn't really matter if she knew about it.

I relaxed my shoulders, making myself look bored, content, and peacefully sleepy. Not concerned one iota about sitting next to Athena. As I did this, I drew heavily on Wylde, letting him aid my posture in the same way he would have faced, well, Oberon, for example. How to face an enemy, a powerful one, while displaying a hint of confident arrogance, as if waiting for the right moment to flip over your winning card in a game of poker.

It felt seamless to me as Wylde subtly changed nuances in my demeanor. My face grew more relaxed, and I even crossed my legs as I yawned.

Athena sensed this – not my actual actions – but that something much more important had happened beneath the theatrics. And her eyes grew cold, wary. She didn't speak, but I could feel the hatred and unease radiating from her.

"No grapes? Or olives?" I grunted, sipping my wine.

She sniffed. "Gods do not need these things."

"But you need wine?"

Her lips thinned. "No. I *enjoy* wine."

"Right. Well, can we get cracking? I've got a few other things to take care of today."

She pointed her chin at the railing, and since the table was close to the marble balustrade, I leaned over, staring down. A blanket of clouds hovered hundreds of feet below us, and as I leaned a little further, I realized nothing was supporting our marble pavilion, other than more clouds. I opened my mouth to ask what I should be looking for, because I didn't think the lack of support had been what she was referring to, but as I did, the clouds began to swirl, making a hole in the blanket.

And I saw the war. All of it. As if I was directly above it, close enough to shout down at them. Even though I had walked for quite some time, and was obviously very high above the clouds. It made sense though. Why have your home so far above the mortal world that you couldn't see what was going on with your children.

So.

It was magic of some kind. As I shifted my gaze, the view of the war shifted, so that I could see any particular section with ease, not having to move my head, just my intent. The land obeyed my command. I tested this out, getting a quick layout of the war, per Wylde's guidance, and leaned back, satisfied.

"As I thought it would turn out," I said, happy to see my friends holding and even shattering some of the front lines.

"Such fun, isn't it? Like toy soldiers…" she purred, sipping her wine.

"Except they aren't toys. They're living creatures."

"Ah. Quite right." She waved a hand dismissively. "Semantics."

Wylde had to force me to sit rather than jumping to my feet to grab her owl and beat her over the head with it like a rubber chicken.

"Everyone is watching this," she said distantly, not noticing or caring about my struggle.

I frowned, and then glanced around the pavilion. And my heart stopped. She was right. We weren't alone. I was sure we had been moments ago, or had I just missed the obvious?

A man stood leaning against a column, face concealed by a shadow, idly flipping a coin into the air and catching it. Like a metronome. I saw one of the reflections in his eyes disappear for a millisecond, and then reappear. A wink? Then his body suddenly blurred. He didn't move, but he looked to be… vibrating so rapidly that I couldn't get a clear view. Other than that one wink.

His legs, although a blur, shone with golden light.

Hermes?

I scanned the other pillars and noticed a handful of other odd silhouettes. They all stared back, but for the life of me, I couldn't place them. But they were big. Bigger than me.

A female shape actually hissed at me, and I grinned back. Hera, perhaps? I'd read she was just positively *lovely* to spend time with. As if sensing this thought, her form rippled in agitation.

I caught a flash of silken fabric, utterly transparent, and a stunning mental image that would stick with me until the end of my days. Pale skin shone through the sheer fabric, with not a stitch underneath. I actually felt like I had trailed my hand over every square inch of that body before I even thought to look up at her face.

And my mind stopped.

Wylde grabbed a hold of me and shook me, hard. I groaned, snapping out of it to find Athena leaning towards me hungrily, licking her lips. I had no recollection of what I had seen, other than my memory of the body. I began to consciously recall it, but Wylde stopped me in an instant. *Don't. Trap.*

I gripped the table, and took a deep breath, slowing my pulse and trying to subtly readjust my pants a notch or seven. If even Wylde thought getting his freak on was a bad idea, I could scarcely imagine how dangerous it would be.

Athena was grinning at me. She opened her mouth, but I interrupted her. "I feel suddenly, overwhelmingly, sorry for you." Her mouth clicked shut, and her eyes looked confused. "I mean, if I had a sister like that, I probably would have gone tomboy, too. Started playing with the boys. Less competition. Maybe study up on my books…" I said, as if realizing some deep epiphany.

She actually snarled at me, but I ignored her, staring out at the last figure I had seen. I avoided those silken fabrics, and the amused laughter from that corner of the pavilion as I stared out towards the sky.

And I saw a wild-haired man, white hair whipping in the wind as he leaned on a thick, aged spear of sorts. Two dark, feathered shapes sat on his shoulders, and two monstrous wolves hunkered at his booted feet.

Oh, and he was hovering in thin air about a hundred feet away from the pavilion.

Those birds were recognizable anywhere. Unless there was some other god with feathered sidekicks. And he obviously wasn't welcome on the pavilion, judging by the sharp looks cast his way from the other gods watching my table.

I turned back to Athena and grunted. "Felt like you needed to have bouncers? Very brave."

I actually saw her grind her teeth at that. "They are not bodyguards. They are family. And they don't have a Maker in their pocket like I do," she taunted, eyes flashing.

"Things change," I said, noncommittally. "Toys can be broken."

"They all placed bets, you see..." she offered in an amused whisper.

I frowned. "On who?"

She shook her head. "You'll see..."

I pondered that, swirling my wine. Then I topped off my glass, letting out an annoyed sound that I had to do it for myself. "I'm willing to bet that some of them actually see you for the arrogant brat you are, and are simply here to see you brought down a notch. Maybe six notches." I chuckled, feigning an embarrassed look. "I'm sorry. You Greeks might not know what a notch is. It's like a foot. A form of measurement. So, when I say six notches, I mean—"

"I know very well what you intended, ignorant child!" she spat.

I blinked, looking startled. "I was just trying to be polite. What are we without courtesy?"

"Gods. Olympians."

"Even Gods can fall, cutie-pie," I said, taking a big gulp of my drink. "In fact, there was even a video game about it. This crazy albino bastard killed all of you. Everyone plays it, and... huh. He had these crazy designs painted all over his face and body. Imagine that..."

She rounded, eyes livid. "I'm well aware of that vile trash. I think I shall rectify the world's misperception."

I shrugged. "Not today," I said, glancing over a shoulder. "Unless you want to phone a friend."

"Enough talking. Watch. I want you to see this." I didn't move, not wanting to turn my back on her. She chuckled. "Oh, there would be no fun in that. You'll know when it's time to die."

I leaned over the railing.

And let Wylde watch, listening to his analytical mind decipher what I was seeing.

And... it wasn't looking as good as before.

CHAPTER 58

*I*ndie stood alone, blasting anyone who got too close, but her heart wasn't in it. She looked lost, shaken, and desperate. She stared up at the sky, waiting for her savior, murmuring under her breath.

I knew this, because the sounds of war rolled over us as if we were in it. And when I focused on someone, I heard them over the din. But I heard not a peep from Indie, just saw her lips moving. Maybe she was just saying *mommy* over and over again.

I felt nothing for her. She had brought this on herself.

I turned to see a contingent of Greeks led by Hercules, pounding against a shifting tide of wolves. Wizards stood further back, splashing lone warriors with fire whenever they could, but their attention was mostly taken up by the enemy wizards that I hadn't gotten a clear sight of yet.

I idly wondered if the enemy wizards were members of the Academy sucked away at the last minute by their Greek heritage, simply unlucky enough to be born Greek. It didn't really matter. They were just walking corpses if we did this right.

Right away, I could tell the difference between the Academy Wizards and the Syndicate. It seemed that everyone had sworn, because the number matched the number of Syndicate who had first come to our camp. The Academy stood before them, all hatred momentarily forgotten as they fought to keep the Syndicate alive. With fire, ice, and magic such as I had never seen before.

The Syndicate, although standing further away, dished out plenty of carnage of their own.

It almost seemed like the two groups were competing with each other to kill as many Greeks as possible. And, oddly enough, they seemed to be working together.

A dozen Academy wizards suddenly launched balls of fire up into the air, straight above their heads. But about a hundred feet in the air, those balls suddenly hit some unseen wave of power, and blasted towards the Greeks in a rain of fire, like tennis balls hit by rackets on a serve. Or someone setting up a volleyball for the spiker to come hammer down on the other team.

They were working in concert, and as I thought about it, the move was actually more efficient than each wizard trying to throw their own fireballs. One, because it took effort to cast high and then zip it back down on top of the enemies – which was the only way not to hit your own men – the wall of werewolves Ashley was commanding in a defensive line right in front of them.

But the Greek wizards weren't too shabby, either.

They threw up a wall of water directly before the onslaught, and I groaned.

Athena chuckled, shaking her head.

Then we both froze.

The Greek wizards fell screaming, collapsing, writhing in agony behind the wall of water. Then I saw it. The steam hovered in the air like a dense fog where the fire had blown through, but it wasn't regular steam. It was almost as if it were acid, because the victims had no skin on their faces or arms. I glanced over to the Academy and Syndicate to find them grinning smugly.

Not just fire. My wizards had *expected* the wall of water. And had made their flames acidic, and somehow able to stick to the steam, changing it. Sure, the fires extinguished, but it turned the water to acid, and the shields the Greeks had thrown up to block out steam hadn't protected against a mist of *acid*.

It ate through their shields.

And their flesh.

Athena pounded the table in frustration as she watched a third of her Greek wizards taken out in one fell swoop. I saw them shouting at each other and I knew the mistake wouldn't work a second time. That was the thing in war magic. Often it was sporadic. Attack, fail, attack, fail, new idea that suddenly works, and then the second time is counteracted by the other side. And eventually, you would be a victim to that one successful attack as well.

So, they basically did their best to counter and defend their warriors. With the occasional, epic, lucky strike.

All that to say that chaos and destruction screamed over the heads of the normal soldiers. While they struggled to fight their own enemies with blades, arrows, and claws.

Hundreds of wolves shifted and swarmed, rolling with the occasional bulges in the line, able to speak with each other in their minds, and react to changes much more efficiently than regular soldiers. Hercules made up for this with sheer might, batting wolves aside with his great big club.

Through one of those holes, appeared a lone wolf. Almost as tall as Hercules, and although large, nowhere near as muscular as the Greek Hero. His fur was white, but the splatters of blood kind of ruined that. He stood on two massive paws with the Nemean Lion Cloak draped across his shoulders – the lion head hood covering his own single-eyed glare.

He grinned a wolfish smile, and said in a falsetto voice to the demigod, "Meow."

Hercules roared, face turning bright red.

Then Gunnar was running straight at him. Hercules lifted his club high and tried to bludgeon my dog, but Gunnar suddenly wasn't there. He was at Hercules' hip, slashing with his claws, slicing along his hip bone and tearing the string of his pants.

Hercules snarled in pain, and then his pants fell down.

I burst out laughing. "I didn't think it was that cold out, today."

Athena was now gripping the table in fury, but she didn't respond.

Hercules looked so angry I almost felt bad for Gunnar.

Then Gunnar was suddenly behind him, and judging from Hercules' grunt, he had scored a direct blow. Hercules spun angrily, backhanding his club at Gunnar.

Gunnar didn't move, staring down his death, and I heard Athena begin to laugh.

At the last moment, Gunnar drew back his claws, squeezed them into a fist, and then punched Hercules straight above the elbow. His elbow dislocated with a horrendous *cracking* sound, and Hercules roared in pain as his arm bent the wrong way, his club sailing into a crowd of wolves who had been watching.

Several went down. For good.

Gunnar didn't anticipate the kick to the chest, and I heard ribs shatter as Hercules' huge foot crunched into my best friend's chest, sending him flying. Ashley darted out of nowhere, spun, and let Gunnar hit her in the sheepskin back. He struck like hitting a mattress, and fell to the ground, wheezing, eye closed.

Ashley checked him over, sniffing his bleeding chest where I saw a rib poking out, and then slowly began unlatching his cloak. She set it on the ground beside her, and calmly unsnapped her Golden Fleece. She draped it over Gunnar's chest, and if not for the subtle rise and fall of his labored breathing, I would have thought him dead.

Ashley clasped the Nemean Lion Cloak around her shoulders, and slowly lifted her eyes to stare at the demigod. He had pulled up his pants, and torn off his shirt, using it to tie a makeshift sling to hold his arm close to his body. He didn't have his club any longer, and he turned to look for the fallen Wolf King to finish him off.

Instead, he locked eyes with the Wolf King's Queen.

Wulfra.

And he took a fucking step back on instinct.

I'll say this. I would have actually run away screaming if in Hercules' shoes. And I don't think anyone would have made fun of me for doing it.

She stared at him, not just with the deadly aura that she had picked up from the Fae.

But with the mantle of a ruler. A protector. A famed warrior. A Queen to a fallen King.

She stared at the man who had just severely hurt the one thing she loved more than life itself.

A demon flew down from the skies, surprising everyone as he used human hands to try and snatch up the Golden Fleece from Gunnar. He immediately had a pack of wolves lunging for him, snapping at him.

He took back to the air, flapping great big feathered wings. Upon closer inspection, I saw it wasn't a demon, but a man. He didn't look happy at losing his prize, and circled the air above Gunnar like some massive vulture. A ring of wolves began to circle their king, eyes to the skies now, as well as the ground.

I turned to Athena. She nodded at me.

"Icarus," she smiled. "But you're going to want to see this next part. Not the dog fight."

I turned back to the war, gritting my teeth. What other secret warriors had she scooped up?

Icarus flapped his wings as a trio of dragons suddenly dove towards him, blasting fire at him. Feather boy hauled ass, not wanting to ruin his wings. The dragons pursued, but couldn't keep up, and in turn, they were assaulted by lobs of Greek fire when they tried to chase him over enemy lines.

Against my will, the scene changed, and I found myself above Indie. Ichabod was shouting at her, shaking his hands, pointing at the skies in frustration. Probably wondering where the hell Athena was. I wondered that, too. Was I keeping her in place? Where she was unable to act until our showdown? Some cosmic balance? One with the power to destroy a god forcing the god to confront me?

Or… was Athena simply *preferring* to be up here, finally facing a foe that might be worthy of her interest? Someone worth fighting. A Godkiller.

Neither sounded likely.

My attention suddenly riveted to an older man creeping from bush to bush, sneaking up on Indie and Ichabod as they argued. I hid my smile. Someone was trying to assassinate them. Which would pretty much wipe out the rest of my *to do* list.

The light caught his features for the first time as he glanced up at the sun, no doubt checking to make sure he wasn't leaving a telltale shadow. I had seen him earlier tonight somewhere in the camp, but couldn't place him. A plain-looking, medium build, gray-haired man. I had simply seen too many faces, men ready to give up their lives in this senseless war.

But he suddenly shifted like a mirage, and I gasped in disbelief.

My own face stared back at me. A doppelganger.

And Indie and Ichabod had no idea.

Part of me was surprised, but another part of me wasn't. Because… I had planned on killing them myself when I was finished here anyway.

I heard Athena speak. "Look behind the tree," she said in a too-sweet tone.

I did, seeing another figure hiding behind a tree opposite of the not-Nate assassin, with Indie and Ichabod between them. It was a very sickly-looking Matthias Temple. "Fuck…"

CHAPTER 59

*A*thena chuckled wholeheartedly. "*Fuck*, indeed."

Without any buildup, the two men stepped out at the last second, faces intent on their separate goals. But what the hell was Matthias doing there? I had seen him, still recovering from his prison sentence, unable to hold his own against Castor—

I froze, suddenly remembering. How had I missed it? The man who had changed his appearance to look like me was… Castor Queen. The man who had betrayed Matthias Temple hundreds of years before, stealing and poisoning the newly-formed Syndicate, and banishing Matthias to a life of imprisonment.

Matthias was staring at Ichabod, eyes begging, not seeing the man behind him, so focused on his son. Sensing something, Indie and Ichabod spun to find him standing before them, and entirely different versions of astonishment plastered their faces.

Indie looked suddenly confused and wary, recognizing him, and not knowing friend from foe.

But Ichabod…

In that moment, I watched as Ichabod Temple made his decision. His Blood Debt was no more. His father was back. He had no ties to the Greeks. Indie was on her own.

Matthias smiled in relief, a single tear rolling down his cheek.

That's when Castor Queen – looking like me – blasted a hole in Ichabod's spine from behind.

Indie immediately disappeared with a shout, Shadow Walking to safety.

Matthias stared through the hole in his son's chest to see a man on the other side.

And the face he saw was *mine*, smiling at him. Then I – Castor Queen – disappeared.

And I watched a man's soul slowly wither away and die. Matthias Temple fell to his knees, body racked with pain, agony, and betrayal.

In the pavilion, I began to shake with rage.

Castor Queen… had just made my shit list.

Waves of power began coursing through my body, fueled by Wylde, not knowing what I intended, but strengthening it, empowering it, making it something stronger than I had ever created on my own. A force to kill a god, perhaps.

I ignored Athena's laughter, knowing that if I felt her body even shift towards me, I would end her. And I wouldn't even have to look at her to do so.

Wylde cackled inside me as the beautiful orb of power began to grow, like a volcano about to erupt. I ignored him, too.

I had tried going to Ichabod, to warn him away, to flee with his father. And I knew that before Castor had initially attacked us, that he might have even been ready to make that decision, then. Hell, I had defended him from Castor Queen, after Matthias had been taken down.

But Matthias hadn't seen me *do* that. He had been unconscious, or delirious.

All he saw was that I called him to the tree. Ichabod appeared. Castor Queen attacked. Then Matthias fled and Ichabod was carted away, injured.

But Matthias had come back, to save his son.

And instead?

He saw what looked like me finishing the job I had attempted the night before. But rather than using a proxy through Castor Queen, I had decided to take Ichabod out myself.

The shitty thing was, I *had* intended to kill Ichabod if he didn't abandon his cause. But tonight, he had chosen his family over his feud. His eyes had told me better than words that he was willing to run away with his father, forget the world, enjoy each other after a life of being held apart. *Several lifetimes of being held apart.*

I would have let him walk. Right there. Scratched him off my list of the three people I intended to kill.

Instead? The Mad Hatter, one of the most dangerous people in the world, my ancestor…

Had just watched me kill the only thing that mattered to him, the moment he was about to save him.

Below, Matthias Temple lifted his eyes, and what I saw in them made even Wylde cower.

Then he screamed, and the ground began to smoke around him. He stumbled to his feet, shambled up to his son's body, scooped him up, and with tears streaming down his face, the two disappeared.

"I think I prefer the broken old man over your broken ex-fiancée, anyway." I turned to find Athena staring down at my hand, where a handful of sand was dribbling through my fingers. The Hand of God. I had destroyed it without even realizing it.

Indie no longer had control of Athena.

The Goddess stretched her arms above her head, sighing.

CHAPTER 60

J stood from the table, panting. "All this just to set me up?" I snarled. "Like a coward, you hide behind assassins? I thought you were the Goddess of War. Wisdom. More like pettiness and treachery."

She shook her head sadly, as if pitying me. "All is fair in love and war, my child."

"End this," I snarled. "Just you and me. Enough with your games, Godlet."

She sighed. "Believe as you will, but as much as I loved that little drama, it was not my doing. That is the doing of a man hungry for power. This once-friend of your ancestor. Castor Queen. A Maker. He keeps his cards close, never letting his Beast fully join with him, even after all this time. Extraordinary willpower…" She waved a hand. "But he did this on his own. Why he chose your face as the vehicle can only be answered by him. If you ask very nicely."

I frowned at her. "But you think you're going to kill me, so that wouldn't seem likely."

Her blank face stared back at me, neither confirming nor denying. Instead, she turned her back on me, carrying her goblet with her to the center of the pavilion. "I have always found it odd that after waking from a long rest, oftentimes, all one wants to do is take a nap," she mused, not looking at me. I brushed off the dust from the Hand of God, my mind racing.

What was my situation, now? I pleaded with Wylde for insight, but he seemed wary. He didn't know about the Hand of God, or what I called magic, or gods. What he did was as natural as breathing. One with the universe. It wasn't something to control and dominate, but something to work with. Like one's own arm. You didn't battle with your arm. You simply made it *do*.

Had Indie died from me destroying the Hand of God? Was the war over without Ichabod and her? Or was Athena in full control now, and with a single thought, had she simply killed all my friends? I didn't have time to go look, because now that she was free from the Hand of God and Indie's... partnership – because it was very obvious that it had never really been control – I wasn't about to turn my back on her for one second. But she obviously had no problem turning her back on me, and she had insinuated that I should go ask Castor his motivations myself...

"Wait a minute. You're not going to stop me? You're going to just let me go?"

She turned, suddenly wearing armor. "Oh, don't be ridiculous. I have time to manage a Manling before I go back to bed. Like a bedtime story. Except in this story, the Manling dies."

And the owl, forgotten by me, raked across my back with a scream, ripping skin open, catching my right hand in a talon, piercing a hole clear through my palm. Wylde, as if woken from a deep slumber, roared, and blasted the owl from the air. Charred feathers skidded across the polished marble floor, bumping into the table. I hissed, staring down at my hand.

It was... scratched and bloody, but nothing serious like I knew I had felt. I frowned.

Then I looked up. The other godlings were now openly staring. At me. And at Athena.

Her face never changed. A cold, emotionless mask. Then a helmet of feathers slammed down over her face, like one of those famous Spartan helmets, but fluffier. Still, I knew that even though made of feathers, no blade would break it.

I released my control, nodded back at her as if at a fencing partner, and then cut loose.

I swarmed the helmet with pests, fleas, lice, vermin, and Athena shrieked, screaming and gasping as she struggled to tear it free. I immediately filled the dark space between her cheeks and the feather helmet with starlight, scorching her face with the radiance of a hundred supernovas. The helmet burst to flame, sparks showering the air, and she lurched back gasping, face a charred ruin, oozing golden ichor.

The Blood of a God.

"You should consider retirement. Reminisce about the good old days, while you still can."

She stared back at me with the hatred of Lucifer looking upon God, face a black mask, and hair entirely gone, looking like a smoldering chunk of charcoal. "I will not grow old in bed, but in battle. I am a warrior. We shall see if you are up to the task, Manling."

"Step right up, m'lady. This rogue – although no gentleman – will oblige you," I said, tipping an imaginary hat and executing an overly subservient bow.

She screamed in outrage, and lunged at me. Simultaneously, my mind was invaded by my own memories, and swarmed with a rolodex of facts, knowledge, and learning. Like a speed-read of everything I had ever stuffed into my brain.

Too late, I realized it was an attack. Her fist struck me in the mouth, and I felt my war paint flash with heat as I went flying. I struck the table, but managed to roll away just as the marble slab crashed to the ground, barely avoiding a messy decapitation.

Prime numbers, multiplication tables, philosophical rants, psychological profiles, spreadsheets, and the Periodic Table began reciting over and over again in my mind, competing to be heard over each other, in one symphonic orgy of a nerdgasm.

Memories – scraping my knee in our labyrinth, seeing Gunnar shift for the first time when we were kids, driving my first car, using magic on purpose for the first time, my parents running into my room in the middle of the night to turn on the lights as I screamed about monsters under my bed, a dozen first kisses, my first heartbreak, and my first funeral – all zipped through my mind, scraping me raw.

I shook my head, dazed from the blow, and exhausted as my own mind fought my body.

I sought the emptiness inside of me, barring out all thought, and desperately gave in to Wylde, my pure self. He scooped me up like he was driving past me on a motorcycle on a long, winding road on a summer day, not a care in the world as he mentally cruised through her attack.

Because he didn't have any of that useless stuff in his head. No memorization of asinine facts for Athena to bombard him with.

And he was a solitary sage, a creature of silence. When not in war, he sat alone by a fire and relived his memories *himself* – with the same tenacity many in our world watched reality TV.

So, the second phase of her attack didn't bother him, either.

Athena's boot slammed into the place where I had been lying, to find me suddenly standing beside her. I struck her with the exact opposite of wisdom, pulling deep from the brief look I had seen of that other goddess – the one I presumed to be Aphrodite. Pure lust and emotion rolled over Athena, halting her in her tracks as she began to shake her head as if at an army of gnats. Because she was the virgin goddess, and had no idea how to deal with this new sensation.

Then I yanked the traits from another nearby god – Hermes – infusing her with his penchant for trickery and deceit. Basically, dosing her with an overwhelming sense of paranoia – because Hermes was known to con his fellow gods in favor of mortals. And I let her imagine this, that he was here simply to watch her fall to one of his elaborate schemes – and lose a war to a mere mortal. And that the reason Aphrodite was here was to celebrate with me, afterwards.

Then I connected her to Wylde, that creature of pure instinct. He lived by memory, sure, but it was more of a supreme understanding of the world around him. Like a Zen warrior monk.

He couldn't comprehend her gathering of useless knowledge. He simply accepted what he saw, and utilized it.

That was his core. His heart of fire, of passion, of conquest. Not just war, but a wild sense for domination that was very literally infused into his blood. He didn't worry about how far away a star was, or how many people worshipped him, or how hot something needed to be to melt.

He saw the world in pictures and video.

Knowing that something melted if too hot. And froze if too cold.

How hot or how cold? Didn't really matter. He simply knew it, as if one knew his heart needed to beat to stay alive. He didn't know how many beats per minute that was. Why would that matter? He just knew that it needed to beat.

The mix of sensations dominated her.

"What... is this?" she gasped, furiously slapping at her burned cheeks, laughing, shouting, and giggling in random outbursts as lust, paranoia, and wildness fought for dominion of her treasured mind.

"Life, toots." And I throat-punched Athena, which I have to admit, felt pretty damned cool.

I felt cartilage crunch as she flew into one of the pillars, cracking it. Dust rained down on us, and for a minute, I feared the whole thing might collapse. But it steadied, and other than crumbling chips of stone, the pavilion remained.

"Silly Godlet, life is for mortals," I muttered to the tune of that cereal jingle.

I briefly touched my face, wondering why my mouth wasn't full of broken teeth where she had hit me. But my face was unharmed. I pulled my hand away to find blue chips of dried blood, and stared. The war paint was flaking off, and... it must have been an armor of sorts. But... only against a god?

Athena was scooting away on her rear, no more armor. Her toga was ripped and torn, flashing skin here and there, and I felt Wylde growl with interest. I knew I was leering as I approached her, and judging by the terrified gasps from her lips, she sensed my thoughts as well.

She tried to attack again, but I batted it away easily. I used my shadow to tie her arms together, and then rolled the lust I had felt for Aphrodite into a ball with silken whips fraying out from the edges, like a tattered ball of yarn.

I set it to spinning directly before her, so that the threads of lust struck her in steady slaps.

She groaned in pleasure, while struggling to scoot away at the same time, knowing it was an attack of some kind. She flopped onto her side, then her stomach, and tried to crawl away.

Wylde very much liked this new development.

I grabbed her by the back of the toga, and ground my knee into her spine, arching her back to hear me as I spoke directly into her ear. "End... this..." I gasped, struggling against Wylde's surge of emotions, because he had only one thing on his mind right now, and it wasn't for a family film's audience.

Aphrodite must have been enjoying herself, judging by the climactic moan I heard a few columns away. I didn't look, using all my mental strength to dance that line between Wylde and myself. I needed him, but I couldn't let him *become* me. I still had things to do.

And I was pretty sure his idea of a good time would not be appreciated by the other attending gods. At least what I had in mind could be justified. A fight to the death.

"Take me, Elpis..." she gasped.

Wylde almost overwhelmed me at that, suddenly animalistic at hearing her begging in such a specific statement, because her words could be taken in multiple ways. Aphrodite did her thing, very loudly, again, as if urging Wylde on. I held onto my control by a hair, knowing what Athena had truly meant, even if she had said it in a way that appealed to Wylde, the one she knew had to be in control.

So even though she wanted this over with, she was still playing games, trying to make me lose my inner struggle with Wylde.

Take me... as in, kill me. But according to Wylde, *take me* meant something entirely different.

Also, she had called me *Elpis*...

The Greek word for *Hope*...

She groaned, struggling against the lust whips still hitting her. I shut them down instantly.

She gasped as the pain from her injuries suddenly replaced my whips. "Grant me what I wish, Manling... What I hope for..."

To die in battle.

Wylde roared up within me, and I used that surge – although for different goals entirely – to snap her neck. Somehow, she managed to utter one last thing before her soul fled her body.

Thank you...

Wylde roared in outrage, storming back into his cave, snatching up three women on the way as he shouted incoherently. A ring of power exploded around me, not physically altering anything, even though it should have incinerated every biological atom at contact, but a spiritual blow, that helped knock Wylde back, solidifying my line of control. I gasped, panting, not really understanding, until that point, how close we had been to merging.

I had killed her, and in return... she had saved me. From myself.

I stared down at the dead goddess at my feet, then slowly lifted my eyes to the watchers. Aphrodite was openly... enjoying herself, but I only saw this through my peripheral vision, not letting myself get a full look at the open wares she was proudly displaying. "Abstinence kills," she purred, laughing. I shook my head. *Poor taste*, I thought.

Hermes nodded at me, and – although still a blur – I saw his face for a very brief instant, and it looked understanding, not vengeful. A *thank you* for giving his sister what she had asked for. A clean death from a worthy opponent, rather than Wylde's idea of a victory dance.

I knelt by her side, and bowed my head. No warrior wanted to die in times of peace. They wanted to go out swinging. Well, true warriors. The ones that fought for the joy of fighting. Not those protecting something or defending something – although they were also warriors.

I'm talking about those who truly enjoyed the *art* of war. Sons and daughters of battle.

I thought about calling Charon, but hesitated. I had just killed one of his upper-level managers. Obviously not his boss, but someone above him, for sure. I glanced at Hermes, frowning. The blur nodded, and suddenly appeared immediately beside me, feet flashing golden with a unique whispering sound like a mechanical hummingbird.

"Always so messy," he murmured in a surprisingly normal voice, nothing that made my ears instantly bleed.

"Thanks for the coin that one time," I said, not looking up, fearing he would break my mind with some godly strength in my current state.

When I did dare to look up, he was gone. So was Athena, and not a drop of Ichor remained.

I propped myself up, still slightly dazed from the mental onslaught Athena had used. Echoes of calculations, passages, quotes from books, and other random facts still whispered in my ears. And the memories.

But I had stuff to do. I climbed to my feet, turning towards the entrance.

But it was gone. I frowned, spinning in a circle to find that the pavilion had no exit. Aphrodite began to clap. I slowly turned to face her, sure to use only my peripheral vision to see her. Still, that was enough to almost make me collapse into a puddle of drool.

I actually found strength in the lingering aftereffects of Athena's attack, using the useless facts to keep me distracted from the goddess of lust, allowing me to focus and be rational.

I sensed her pouting. "You're no fun. I'm sure I could help you find a way to pass the time while your blood cools. I've never bedded a Godkiller. Makes a girl downright forward."

"Girl or hussy?" I said in a faint whisper.

Without missing a beat, she said, "Darling, I can be either, or anything else you desire... You already warmed me up, so I'm ready to—"

I gagged her with my shadow, stuffing it deep into her mouth, wrapping it around her head, and then binding her hands and feet. Without looking at her.

I stared down at my hands, shocked at the sudden flurry of motion, and wondered how the hell it was possible with Wylde still angry at me.

No one wants an easy kill... he muttered angrily. *If I can't get what I want, I won't let you have it either...*

I blinked. Wylde had just... cock-blocked me? I began to laugh, turning my back on Aphrodite. Well, that was something. He had just saved me by trying to be petty.

A few of the silhouettes around me clapped, but when I turned to look, they were all motionless, vague forms again, no way to tell who they were. No way to know if I had just killed their daughter or sister. If I had just hogtied their daughter or sister. I also ignored the sound of bags of coin being tossed my way. The gods liked to pay their debts, having lost their bet.

I muttered to myself as I stalked up to the balustrade, wondering how the hell I was supposed to get home. But Aphrodite had been right. My blood was too hot at the moment. And even though Athena was dead, the war wasn't mine to fight. And if I had been down there right now, I probably would have just ended it with one self-sacrificing blow to shake the world to its core.

But one thing kept me sane. Either Indie was dead, or I would get to go kill her soon.

Punish her for what she had wrought. But if she was dead, and Athena was dead, and Ichabod was dead, maybe the war was already – or soon would be – over.

CHAPTER 61

J stared down at the war, shifting my eyes constantly, but it was chaos. I didn't see Hercules or Ashley, but I did see Gunnar still surrounded by a pack of wolves, as if I had only just looked away for a moment.

Less wizards remained, and their attacks and defenses had less impact. Wolves and Greek soldiers fought more out of habit than anything, looking bored and confused. But the aerial fight had ramped up.

Dragons flew through the air, blasting fire at hideous flying naked chicks. I grimaced. Harpies. Like mutant women, covered in scales or balding patches of fur, bellies distended as if pregnant, and birdlike talons for feet.

Icarus batted his feathered wings, commanding the harpies from above, using some of them as a shield to guard him from the dragons as he directed his army. The harpies were fast, and didn't hesitate to sacrifice their own for a kill. And there were a lot of them.

Still, it was obvious that Icarus was the might behind them. They were berserkers, and without the brains, they would be run to the ground.

I saw a flicker in the air, moving fast, but when I turned to look, it was gone. I stared harder, and then, almost at the edge of sight, I saw the flicker again, much closer to Icarus, now. I blinked. Yahn? What hope did he have against a horde of harpies, even with his invisibility?

As if sensing this, the harpies began to sniff the air, sensing that something was wrong.

As one, they all looked up at one specific point, and Yahn materialized, shouting, flapping his wings as if to retreat in fear. Suddenly seeing him appear, they swooped after him with horrifying shrieks.

And didn't notice that he had momentarily – while still invisible – swooped past their line of defense and delivered his payload.

I – being high above them – saw it perfectly clear, and stared in stunned disbelief.

Because Alucard was flipping through the air in a tight ball of golden sunlight, like that videogame of the hedgehog, but made of sunshine.

Rays of light spun around him as he flipped, and struck Icarus like a lightsaber, slicing and melting and burning his wings in a heartbeat.

I grinned as I recalled the Greek's story.

He had flown too close to the sun and his wings had melted, casting him back down to the earth. And Mr. Porcu-shine must have remembered, because the day-walking vampire had some freaky ability after biting Tory once. Not only was he immune to sunlight – the best gift ever for a vampire – but he had pretty much turned into a battery, getting his powers from direct sunlight.

And... he could use those beams of light as a weapon, on occasion.

I watched Icarus' wings burn, flare up, and vaporize.

And he fell.

Right into Tory's horde of monsters, who stared up at the sky with open mouths.

They caught him like a pit of lions would catch a raw steak, and ripped him to shreds. His screams abruptly cut off, to be replaced by much more disturbing sounds. Alucard flung his arms out and golden wings flared out behind him, letting him glide to the ground in safety. I remembered him having black wings of a sort when he had been a blood-drinking vampire, but his sunshine wings were new to me. He resumed the battle as if nothing had happened, tearing into a section of Greek soldiers. Seeing he was safe, I backed out, searching for Achilles. I had seen very little of the famous warrior.

But I couldn't find him.

I began to grow frustrated. I glanced back at the pavilion, but still saw no sign of an exit. And Aphrodite – no doubt skilled at bondage – had escaped my shadow restraints and was gone.

But I did see Hugin and Munin watching me from a nearby balustrade. Their master was nowhere to be found, but I saw the other gods were still hanging around, keeping me company. "Hey, birdbrains. Know when I can leave? Or how?"

They cocked their heads as if unable to understand me. I needed to know what was happening down there. To get some insight. Sure, I could see it, but without Wylde's help, I was having trouble deciphering if we were winning, or if it was even close to over. And as much as I wanted to, I didn't dare let myself go down there while the battle was raging.

War had made that perfectly clear.

My actions might help win the battle.

But it would end in misery, and my friends would lose the war.

This was their moment to shine. To make a name for themselves. And I was stuck watching.

An idea came to me as I saw someone pacing by the labyrinth, searching for something.

"Hey! You two. You like pranks, right? Grab the furball for me. Bring him up here. Preferably without a word of explanation and against his will."

Even though beaks couldn't smile, they managed it, and they were somehow able to understand my words again, the shitheads. They dove straight down, wings flared back as they pierced the clouds, moving like meteors. I turned from the war, and scooped up the dust from the Hand of God. Then I righted the table, which amazingly hadn't broken, and refilled the glasses with wine. Because there was a pitcher perched on the balustrade.

I scowled at the gods hiding nearby, but none of them moved. I tipped my hat in their general direction, because obviously, one of them had brought out a fresh pitcher when I wasn't looking.

Then I scooped up Athena's goblet and refilled that, too. I was just topping it off when I heard the yowling, spitting, hissing sound.

Ever been on your back porch one night and it sounded like someone was being murdered or skinned alive? Then, you soon realized that it was just a tomcat in heat?

Well, Talon sounded like that. But unhappier.

I grabbed a glass and watched as Hugin and Munin flapped up past the balustrade, carrying a very angry Talon. He swiped and clawed at the black talons gripping his shoulders, but they must have been made of steel, because I saw only sparks where he struck, and the ravens didn't seem to be overly bothered by it. Oddly, they accidentally flew too high, bumped his head on the marble ring high above, and then mistakenly dropped him.

He cursed, but landed on his feet, glaring up at them.

He lowered his eyes, saw me, and froze.

"Where is your war paint?" he whispered nervously.

I touched my face, scrubbing it. I glanced at my fingers but saw nothing. I glanced down at my arms and chest and also saw none of the blue paint. I looked back at him and shrugged.

He slowly approached, eyeing the other glass, licking his lips. He snatched it up and took a long drink, eyes furtively scanning the pavilion and columns.

"How are things?" I asked, staring back down through the clouds at the war, chin resting on my crossed forearms as I leaned over it lazily.

"Is that…" he asked, sounding as if facing away from me.

I didn't turn around. "Yeah. They're voyeurs. Like to watch. I tried talking to them. Only one of them wanted to do more than talking, but the others are as silent as a tomb. Stuffy club."

"Maybe we should just leave? Before they…" he trailed off, not knowing exactly what to say.

"Can't. Not supposed to help. Bad things will happen if I jump in too early."

He was silent for a few seconds. "Are we expecting company?" He sounded very nervous, likely turning from one of the watchers to another, wondering which god was in charge.

"Oh, the god thing? I took care of that already. She thanked me at the end. You know what's crazy? I think she actually wanted to die…"

"Who?" Talon whispered.

"Athena. You're drinking from her cup, by the way. I didn't wash it yet, but I did wipe—"

The mug crashed to the marble floor, and I glanced back, smiling. Talon was staring at me. "You spilled your drink." I waved him to pick it up. "Go on, then. Get a refill. Join me. No one likes to drink alone." And I turned back to the war, watching the senseless death below.

"I don't think you ever needed to go to the Fae World," he said after a long silence. I heard him refilling his cup and then he was standing beside me. His stupid velvet boots had masked his approach. I felt him watching me as he continued. "I think it might have been hiding inside you all along," he said.

I nodded tiredly. "Yeah, I wondered that, too..."

"So, Olympus," Talon said slowly. "This is it?"

I shrugged. Then propped my chin up enough to take a drink. "I think this is just a set of bleachers they use. To watch us. Like a soccer match."

He grunted distastefully. "Well, how do we get back? When you're ready, anyway."

I sighed. I had considered that while watching the battle, and didn't like my options. "The door leading up here was over there. Haven't seen it since, though. Any ideas?"

I didn't see him beside me so turned around. He was walking the perimeter of the pavilion, and I noticed that we were now alone. The gods had left. Did that mean it was time? Hugin and Munin still perched on the railing, ignoring us, watching the world below.

Talon finally returned, shrugging as he leaned out over the marble. "I don't see a way out."

I grunted. "Option tw—"

"Look!" he gasped, suddenly staring down at the war.

I turned, and really wished I hadn't.

"Talon... how long have I been gone?"

He hesitated. "Grimm saw you an hour ago. I only just returned from Mrs. Rippley's care."

I nodded woodenly as I stared down at Indie, and the hulking man standing beside her.

CHAPTER 62

*I*ndie stood before the giant white tree, looking like she had been woken up from a deep sleep, or escaped as a refugee in a boat with dozens of people over the recommended capacity.

She looked sickly, crazed, and desperate.

Hercules stood beside her, arm functional, and clutching his club. She had healed him.

Ashley stood between Indie and Gunnar, who was still surrounded by a ring of wolves. I saw his chest moving, and let out a breath of relief. Still, Ashley couldn't stand a chance against Hercules after Gunnar had nearly died. Even with her abilities from the Fae.

No one appeared to have informed Ashley of this.

Because Indie was pointing at Gunnar, and screaming for Hercules to destroy him. "Kill his best friend and the coward will return!" she shrieked.

My fingers began to tingle, as if I was holding a live wire.

I needed to get down there. It was time. I could sense it.

I roared, and everyone below us looked up, the entire war halting for a moment as if they had heard me. The columns began to crumble at the explosion of sound, and the very floor began to shake. Crackles of lightning danced around my fingers, and I knew it wasn't *my* magic.

This was... something else. I gripped the marble balustrade, and the marble simply disintegrated as if made of dried sand. Hugin and Munin squawked as the balustrade around the entire perimeter began to fall way like dust in the wind.

A flash of light made me look down to see that wild designs were actively painting across my body, as if watching an artist tattoo me in fast-forward.

Except they weren't blue. They were gold.

Like the Ichor that had spilled from Athena.

My eyes felt hot, and I stared back down, ignoring the protesting groans of the pavilion behind me, ignoring Talon's horrified shouts, warnings, and urgings that we must flee.

The ravens cawed as well, but I had eyes only for the war. The general fighting had halted, and both sides were silently forming an arced line of flesh opposite the tree, surrounding Ashley and Hercules as they began to square off, less than a dozen paces from each other. The Nemean Lion Cloak around her shoulders made her look much bigger. Imposing. Like some nightmare demon from the darkest forest in the world.

I roared again, and the pavilion rocked. Talon fell on his ass, sliding up to my boots. The marble ring high above fell, crashing around us in explosions of sand and broken chunks of marble, as if my initial touch had weakened most of it, and the last shout had shattered the bonds holding this place together.

The place wasn't going to hold.

Option two, then.

"I will show them fear in a handful of dust," I whispered, releasing a fistful of powdered, Olympian marble.

I grabbed Talon by the neck, grinned at his face from inches away – which looked to be suddenly illuminated by a flashlight – and then hurled him out into the open air. "Save him," I commanded the Ravens in a voice that was much too calm for how I felt. They dipped their heads, and dove after the yowling cat.

I stepped up to the edge, let out a cackle and jumped head first toward the war.

The pavilion exploded behind me with a great concussive boom that I could hear over the screaming wind howling in my ears as I flew straight past Talon, arms tucked into my body for maximum aerodynamics.

I watched, helpless to go any faster, as Ashley and Hercules began to fight…

Hercules came in swinging, hammering his club into the ground as he approached, making great big divots in the dirt as he did. Ashley didn't move a muscle, waiting for him without fear.

Hercules' face grew stormy, and he dropped the tactic, going straight for the kill. He swung the club down at Ashley's face, and still, she didn't move.

As if choosing to sacrifice herself for love, to make a point. Like those iconic pictures of a girl placing a flower in the barrel of an enemy rifle.

But Ashley wasn't calling the shots. Wulfra was.

She caught the club with one fist – as strong as Tory had ever been – and yanked it past her, using his momentum to tug the lumbering Hercules off-balance.

And right into the clawed uppercut that struck below his jaw. Her claws tore through flesh, squeezed, and ripped away his lower jaw in a fountain of blood. He bellowed in utter shock, but she kicked his foot out from under him, sending him sprawling on his mauled face as he skidded past her.

The armies stood like statues. Stunned.

Then she spun, tossed the bearded jaw bone, and pounced on him, digging into his back with violent swipes of her claws. Blood flew and Indie shrieked in outrage, commanding him to get up, commanding everyone to help him kill Ashley.

Hercules finally flung her off him, but no one else moved, stunned at the savagery of the brief encounter.

I continued to scream through the air, trying desperately to move faster, but also terrified about how I was going to land. One great big splashy-splat wouldn't help anyone, least of all, me. But I had a few more seconds to make my final decision on that front, because I really didn't like the options that kept coming to mind.

Gunnar began to stir, but the wolves held him down, knowing he would only kill himself by trying to stand – let alone fight – in his current state. The broken ribs could puncture his organs, causing internal bleeding. Still, he struggled against them, only able to watch as his fiancée fought the demigod.

And that was what concerned me.

Hercules wasn't just a monster. He was a demigod. I had watched Athena – after her skull had been roasted – still fight me without too much discomfort.

So, how much of that power carried on to the demigods? And was Indie about to heal him, keeping him in perfect shape while Ashley burned away everything she had? I knew one thing. Without the cloak, Ashley wouldn't have been able to stop that first blow. And she had given Gunnar the Golden Fleece to keep him safe from further attack.

Taking strength over protection. Which meant she was vulnerable.

And going against a guy who had been tried and tested by the gods, and had come out on top.

As if dismissing his obvious injuries, Hercules turned, snarling at Ashley, his chest a fan of blood. Then he came in close and began to box, using his sheer mass to throw her off balance.

She was fast, and although strong from his cloak, her body couldn't take the blows. She stopped trying to defend herself – the cloak was no good for that – and began countering, using her speed and strength to try and outpunch him. I saw her ears lay flat as she laid into him, dodging, bobbing, weaving, and striking every time. She used pressure points, particularly the one by his right shoulder. Every three strikes found one blow – at least – to the exact same spot, and his strongest arm slowly began to grow limp, useless, leaving him open to even *more* attacks.

But before that began to work, he had landed a handful of good blows on her, and she was hunched over, face matted with blood.

I was so *close*. Almost there. I gripped the necklace in my fist, debating, remembering seeing the Horsemen and their true forms, but fearing that I wouldn't know how to use it in time. With a curse, I let go of the coin and called Grimm. *Now.*

The reply was immediate. *I can't fucking fly anymore!*

Well, talk about poor timing… I was maybe a hundred feet above them, now.

The Mask, you fool! Don the MASK!!

With no time to second-guess, I tore the disc from my necklace, and slapped on my Mask. I felt it latch onto my face with a thousand velvety fingers, and horns blared in the distance, great, belting trumpets. Everyone jolted at the sudden sound shattering the relative quiet of the duel. I had time to shiver in anticipation of the world's biggest cannonball fail before I heard Grimm.

Yes…

Black lightning hammered the earth in one explosive divot behind the ring of soldiers, causing Hercules to flinch, but Ashley didn't even blink. I heard the snapping of wings from Grimm's back a millisecond before he caught me. I struck him hard, struggling to wrap my body around his torso, hoping I bounced off into something soft and not pointy if I failed. The wolves, maybe.

Grimm faltered, regained balance, and swept down lower behind the great white tree, and I managed to get a better hold on him. But it wasn't graceful.

Everyone was so transfixed by the fight, and the two sudden explosions of sound that they didn't even see the temp Horseman dangling from the flying fucking death unicorn. Or at least they were looking the wrong way. Where the bolt of lightning had struck from Grimm's arrival, but we weren't there. We landed just behind the great white tree, and I hid behind my unicorn.

Like a boss.

Alucard was hiding near the trunk of the tree, out of view of the armies, and staring at me in utter disbelief, but I ignored him, staring down at my hand with a frown. I was holding the goblet of wine from the pavilion and... it still had wine in it! No wonder I hadn't been able to grab onto Grimm properly. I glanced up at the sky, wondering if this was Hermes' idea of a laugh.

I stared over Grimm's back as Ashley ducked her head at a full-armed punch from Hercules. Almost too quickly to see, she used that motion to stab her claws straight through the same pressure point she had hammered relentlessly. I knew this, because she sunk up to her forearm into his chest. In desperation, he tried to grab her with his good hand, to choke her to death, but she yanked her arm out, and then sliced the offending hand clean off with her claws.

He grunted, and collapsed to his knees.

Ashley wobbled as Hercules fell onto his back. She slowly turned to the crowd, and snarled in victory. I noticed Alucard still staring at me, horrified as I finally walked out from behind Grimm, ready to complete my *to-do* list. I shoved the wine goblet at him, and whispered, "Hold my wine for a minute. And watch *this*." I didn't even wait for a response, ignoring the stammering whimpers from the Daywalker as I stared at Indie's back.

Which was when she attacked.

A spear of darkness hammered into Ashley's kidneys and out of her chest right as I took my second step. I heard Gunnar howl and everyone turned to stare in disbelief at the cowardly attack from Indie.

Which meant she was literally the only one who didn't see me stalk up behind her, grab a fistful of her hair, and stab her in the kidneys three times in rapid succession. I glanced down to see a single, black thorn in my fist, as long as my forearm. It dripped crimson as I stared at it.

No one moved as she fell to the ground at my feet, and the light around me pulsed like a disco ball from my new tattoos. I stared down at her, watching her grunt, squirm, and try to crawl away, still not knowing what had hit her.

"Hey, Indie. I figured it was time we saw a counselor. You know, to talk about our relationship problems…"

And I slowly followed her as she tried to crawl away.

CHAPTER 63

*T*he crowd was now a wall of pale faces, and a dozen or so even ran away in horror as they looked upon me. Many were Tory's students, but I saw a few Myrmidons – the bravest of the brave – slip away. The Huntress had a very firm grip on Alex, and was standing beside Tory and her monsters, well insulated against any up-close surprise attacks. Pegasus stood within one step from Alex, too, forming a wall of flesh against any *long-range* attacks.

The blonde-haired, silent guy I had seen astride Pegasus stepped out, shoving Greeks out of his way. "Get out of my way! Don't you know who I am?" he snapped, earning many cool glances, but no return arguments. He finally broke through and pointed directly at me. But he didn't look at my face.

Either he hadn't seen it yet, or he was refusing to acknowledge it. Judging by the fear on every *other* face, I assumed the former. I smiled at him, but I didn't think the Mask relayed such emotions.

"Where is your honor? Attacking a woman from behind! Rally, you foo—"

An arrow tore clean through his throat, but it had been aimed at an upwards angle so that the arrow flew high into the sky. I glanced over to see the Huntress kneeling with her new bow, having slipped out from the crowd for a moment.

"That Jason prick was also a fucking asshole," Pegasus snorted, which earned a few chuckles.

Jason? As in, Jason and the Argonauts? I wondered, idly.

Some nodded at the Huntress, but attention soon riveted back to Indie – who was still crawling away, gasping, too overcome with pain to simply Shadow Walk – or maybe she was too exhausted to flee, having used up all her power in the battle.

Gunnar had been carried up to Ashley, consequences be damned, and there was no way in hell anyone was getting through the ring of wolves protecting them. His wolves placed him down, and then lay her head in his lap. She gasped at the movement, and Gunnar's voice cracked in disbelief as he cried out against his will, his wolves suddenly whimpering and whining.

Everyone thought she had been dead. But I now knew that the only reason she had survived this long was a result of her healing abilities as a shifter. But I had no gift for healing.

"Get Pan! NOW!" I roared, and the majority of the crowd physically flinched to cover their ears. But I saw a dozen wolves suddenly barrel through a section of bodies in their haste to obey my command and get Pan.

I watched Ashley shakily reach a claw into her belt pouch, and then hand Gunnar a blood-soaked piece of paper. He accepted it, but his eye never left hers, cradling her face with one paw, and stroking her ears with his lethal black talons.

The only other sound was the whimpers and dragging scuffle of Indie trying to escape.

I took two steps, and stomped down on her knee, casting a blanket of magic over her so we wouldn't hear her cry out. But her back arched up in agony. I kept my boot on her knee, pinning her in place. I didn't even glance down at her as I did this, my eyes locked onto Ashley, praying, begging, hoping for her to survive long enough for Pan to arrive.

He appeared in a blur, eyes scanning the somber faces until he locked onto Ashley. He gasped, and dove for her with fingers outstretched, because as long as he could touch her, she had a chance. His fingers touched her knee and they both simply disappeared.

Poof. Gone.

Gunnar snarled in anger and confusion, and then shot me a calculating look. He winced upon seeing my face, but I shrugged in response to his unspoken question. I had no idea. Indie squirmed underfoot again, but I

344

didn't have time for her yet, so I ground my boot, still masking her tortured screams. I felt her reaching for her power and began to laugh as I squashed that, too.

I don't know how.

I just simply made her *not*.

Then I laughed again. Why was I wasting energy standing on her? I left her pinned to the earth with wild, savage, whispering powers, and turned to look at Gunnar, holding out my hand towards Indie, offering him my prize. Like I would have done in the Land of the Fae. *Take my kill, Brother*, it said.

Gunnar stared at me in utter silence for about a full minute.

Then he tried to stand, and collapsed with a groan.

I was suddenly standing beside him, reaching out a hand that was no longer flesh, but rough, uncut diamond claw. Not like a rapper's necklace, or anything, but like the raw diamonds found in a mine – surrounded by coal, and yet to be polished – with the hope of a glimmer underneath all that grime.

White and Black.

Blending the line between both shades.

Gunnar reached up a tentative paw and finally touched me. He gasped, his lone eye shooting wide as his chest began to crack, pop, and writhe where Hercules had kicked him.

I crouched down, eager to maintain contact.

He began to shake, squirm, and howl, still in full wolf form.

His wolves did not like this – not one bit – unsure whether the scary, diamond-fleshed dude was hurting or helping.

And they began to move, circling around me. I felt a sharp tug on my shoulder blades, and diamond spikes slammed into the earth around me in a protective cage. I glanced over to see that those spikes furthest from me were longer and taller – and that each spike was connected to one horizontal bar of the same, rough, diamond-like substance as my new claws.

Which was sprouting from my shoulder blades. Like a skeletal pair of wings.

Gunnar began to whimper like a kicked dog, thrashing in agony.

I slowly swiveled my head to find Grimm smiling with his razor sharp-teeth... at Pegasus. As if to say, *What's up now, bitch?*

Gunnar suddenly lurched upright, gasping as he flung his arms at me in a loving, brotherly embrace that has been passed down from generation to generation since time immemorial.

Around my throat.

I let him.

His forearms began to shake, and I saw his missing eye slowly reforming into a stone-like chip, as if he was wearing a cheaply bedazzled eyepatch. The same as my claws and wings. His face went slack as he stared up at me, mouth moving wordlessly. I don't know what the hell he saw, but his fingers slowly began to loosen.

I grasped his wrist with one of my claws, preventing him from withdrawing. With the other claw, I slowly began to remove my mask. "I accept your judgment, Wulfric," I whispered. "I should have been here sooner."

He stopped me with a look, his stone eye flashing with the diamond underneath. "Is it still... you?" he asked in a rasping tone.

I nodded. "Yes."

He let out a long breath, and then yanked his hand from my grip. He used the other to press the mask back onto my face. "Then my best friend is going to help me find my fiancée."

I was glad he couldn't see my face, because he would have known that I had very dark thoughts on that matter. Not that I didn't trust Pan. He got here as fast as possible, being prevented from involving himself in the war. But the fact that he had *disappeared*. Because I was almost confident that I had seen the beginning of Ashley's last exhale before they vanished.

The shock alone caused by traveling like he had would have been enough to severely complicate *any* minor injury, let alone while she was knocking on death's door.

But I nodded. Because I would help him. And if we found Ashley dead, we would resume this conversation. I tried to stand, but Gunnar yanked me down beside him, shoving a folded piece of bloody paper at me. There was a hole in the corner where Indie had stabbed Ashley.

My diamond claw shook as I read it.

Gunnar,

If you're reading this, I am gone. But you need to accept something. I chose this. Not Nate.

You're stubborn enough to blame him, no matter what the facts tell you. So, I hope my words will achieve better results. He would never do anything to hurt you. Not ever.

346

Seeing him in the Land of the Fae was... a revelation.

He risked his life, countless times, to keep us alive, to save a kid, to get us home. And he saved me from myself. That place changes you, and doesn't let you give up. He helped me remember my human side, what I valued above all else...

You, Gunnar. My stray, one-eyed mutt. Wolf King. Lover. Best friend.

You may wonder why you're reading this, assuming there's some big conspiracy. That I knew I came here to die... But nothing could be further from the truth. The fact is, after a few of our more notorious skirmishes with monsters, I began writing these letters. Just... in case.

Because no matter what happens, in Nate, you have a better friend than anyone could ever ask for. He's not perfect. He's even an asshole, at times. Arrogant, conceited, and hot-headed.

But I think you know the truth about Nate, too, whether you have admitted it or not...

He is all those things so we don't have to be. He wears those faults on purpose. Giving us something to lash out at, a target for our rage when the bad guys seem too strong. When the monsters are too scary. When all hope seems lost.

He lets himself become a punching bag for our fears. Taking our beatings as we point out his faults and call him out on his failures, giving us the chance to feel tough again, to regain our confidence, to rebuild our self-esteem. Because we know that the monsters fear him.

And if we can stand up to Nate, we must be strong enough to stand up to the monsters, too.

Because by standing up to Nate, we've already done what the monsters couldn't.

So, cherish him, like I do. He is your brother. Your family.

He's the man we need. But he also needs you. Without you he's a broken bike, missing a wheel, and I think the world is going to need a bike soon...

With all the love in the world,

Ashley Randulf.

Tears struck the paper, and again, my gaze focused on the hole near the corner. My entire body began to shake, and my diamond-spiked wings began to rattle, stabbing into the earth in a steady drumbeat. I slowly lifted my gaze to find my best friend staring back at me. He gave me a single, slow nod, and my heart threatened to break. He... didn't hate me.

"We'll find her," I promised. "I know a few guys who owe me favors. Even if I have to go down to the Underworld myself."

"Not without me, you won't," he warned, standing to his feet. I accepted his paw, the one with the family rune on his wrist, and climbed to my feet. I handed him the letter, and yanked the spikes of my wings from the ground as I slowly turned to Indie.

"She ripped the letter. I think she needs to answer for that," I rasped.

"Agreed," Gunnar growled, stepping up beside me.

Not a soul tried to stop us as we stalked up to the wide-eyed Indie.

My ex-fiancée.

I glanced at Gunnar. "Trust me for a minute," I whispered. He nodded after only the briefest of hesitations.

CHAPTER 64

I released my magic and flipped her over with a boot. She stared up at me and immediately gasped. "Who…"

"You've performed unspeakable crimes, leading hundreds to their deaths, with never a care for anyone but your own revenge," I said, loud enough for all to hear. "You never cared for your men. Never cared for those you commanded to die. You are not the woman I once knew. Or… you never were the woman I *thought* I knew…"

Her face scrunched up in confusion. "Nate? Is that you? I had hoped…" she choked, coughing up blood.

I reached down towards her chin and she flinched instinctively. I wiped away the blood with one claw, my diamond skin seeming to soak it up. "But you did this by falling for a lie. A great injustice was done to you, and you handled it abhorrently. For the woman whom Nate Temple once pledged to marry, the woman she should have been, I grant you this one hope for atonement." I felt Gunnar stiffen beside me, and mutters began stretching back through the crowd.

She began to nod vehemently. "Please. I'll make up for it. Somehow. I will—"

"Tell *them. Beg them. They* are the ones you guided to war. *They* are the ones you must apologize to. *They* are the ones you should hope to earn forgiveness from."

And she began to do so, begging, pleading, offering herself in any way available. I watched her eyes as she spoke, and knew her words were genuine, heartfelt. She had literally been duped, and the rage of thinking her mother had been killed had started a war. She hadn't remembered what she had been told, that her mother would live to a ripe-old age and die of natural causes. To be honest, I had almost forgotten it, too. It felt like years ago, and with all the chaos, it had been easy to accept the terrifying story of her mother's murder when she had first told it to me…

I glanced around thoughtfully. Right here, in fact. This was where she had first told me about her mother being killed by the Syndicate. Before she had woken up a goddess.

I turned back to her, again, focusing only on her eyes. I didn't listen to her words, I listened to her eyes, and waited until I saw it.

That glimmer of… Hope.

And Oberon's words whispered in my ears. *Only savage hope can quench a heartflame…*

And then I extinguished Indie from the world of the living. No bells, whistles, or fancy magic. I simply stabbed her through the heart with one of my diamond coated wing-spines. I gripped her chin as she struggled to breathe, but spoke loud enough for all to hear.

"I will take all Hope from this world. All hope for the wicked. All hope at forgiveness. Crimes will be judged. Apologies – even if heartfelt and true – shall not outweigh the crimes. Examples will be made. Only terror will remain… for the guilty."

And the light winked out from her eyes.

I stood, brushed my claws together with the sound of rock grating on rock, and stared out at the stunned crowd.

I took off the Mask and it shifted back into the familiar wooden disc I had grown partial to. "That felt so good. I can't even…" I admitted softly, shaking my head. "But that's not why I did it. I meant every word." Then I met several eyes in the crowd. "You've been put on notice. Tend to your wounded." I turned to Gunnar. "You up for commanding them?" I asked in a soft tone.

He nodded, his stone eye glinting, and turned away, belting out orders for our men.

And I turned away, walking towards the tree. I saw an umbrella sword leaning there where Indie had left it. I hadn't even seen she had it. I fought the momentary sensation that struggled to hit me, and snatched up the blade. It hadn't been hers. I walked over to Alucard, who was shaking his head slowly. Not in recrimination, but in sheer shock. Overwhelmed.

I handed him the cane he had let Indie borrow so long ago, and retrieved my goblet. I downed it, and said, "Thanks."

Then I sat down, taking everything in.

"Mind if I take charge of the Greeks?" a familiar voice asked.

I turned my head to find Achilles staring at me from a few paces away. He still wore his crested helmet and armor. Asterion stood beside him. The Minotaur dipped his head, looking concerned.

"Where were you?"

"Playing that stone-game he's partial to," Achilles answered, pointing a thumb at Asterion.

I just stared at them, not understanding. But I nodded in response, because someone had to take care of the Greeks. To get them out of here before hotheads decided to pick up where they had left off.

Achilles dipped his head, and then he was off, shouting at the Greeks, establishing the chain of command, and ordering his men to drop weapons – yes, even their favorite ones – and depart the property with hands on their heads. "Meet at the usual spot," he growled. I heard the sounds of blades, spears, shields, and even helmets striking the ground, and then an organized, submissive retreat.

When Achilles stepped back up, Asterion finally settled down into a cross-legged position across from me. He wore the fighting gear I had seen him don a year ago. When he had stood on my side against Indie. Achilles no longer had a weapon, but his helmet was within reach. He sat down beside Asterion, and the two shared a long look.

"Your beard is... formidable," Asterion said uncomfortably.

I just stared at him. How many had he killed? How many of those who had once trusted him, befriended him, had died by his blades.

Achilles grunted. "Well, I don't feel like playing tea-party princess. I want to thank you for not joining the field sooner."

My lip curled back in a sneer. "So that you could kill more of my people without recrimination?"

He dipped his head, accepting my anger. "My blade never left my scabbard. My spears did," he admitted. "But I didn't kill anyone, and I only fought as a last resort. When I found out Indie was going after the kid, I made sure to lead that attack to keep him safe. Obviously, that put me in the thick of things, but you can ask around. None died by Myrmidon blade."

I frowned. Asterion nodded. "I tasted no blood this day, either."

Then I remembered what Achilles had said. About playing a game. "I don't understand."

"If you had entered the field, we would have been forced to meet you in battle. Since you did not, we were able to... not participate," Asterion said in a gentle tone. I frowned harder, not understanding. As soon as Athena had called the horns to war, all my Greek friends had disappeared. Why, if not to join their brethren, their goddess.

"I made a deal with War before the other one showed up," Achilles said.

I almost jumped to my feet. "Ares! Are you *shitting* me? I've got him to worry about?"

Achilles held out his hands in a calming gesture. "No, the true God of War. The one who doesn't need to add the word *god* before it..." he said, meaningfully.

I flinched. The... Horseman? Achilles slowly lifted an arm to point to my right. A red-haired young man stood a hundred paces away, looking familiar, but definitely not like War. He held up a circle in his fist, and I froze. The man from the Land of the Fae. The stranger who kept appearing with a handful of fingers in the air, as if trying to tell us something.

"Weeks," I murmured under my breath as he began to approach, suddenly understanding.

"Yes," Achilles said. "He was trying to warn you about the time slippage in the Land of the Fae. How many weeks you'd been gone. He couldn't speak with you, and couldn't gesture to you in an obvious way. So he chose that form, and sent you curious motions from a distance, getting as close to breaking the rules as possible."

The man finally reached us and sat down, watching me. "I couldn't very well use Morse Code, although I did think about it. Not that Wylde would have understood," he added with a dry chuckle, suddenly transforming to his usual scarred self. The other two didn't flinch, so they either still saw the same man, or they were used to him changing appearances without warning.

I stared at him. "You spoke with me. Before I left..."

He nodded. "And got yelled at for it. Even though I hadn't broken any rules."

I nodded, turning to Achilles. "You made a deal with War, and... that trumped your oath?"

Achilles looked uncomfortable. "Well, there's no need to start using dangerous words, or anything, but my oath to War would trump Athena, had it been discovered. And I would have likely been murdered on the spot. But... since we obeyed Athena, and she only touched down that one time..." he shrugged guiltily. "I didn't do as good of a job as I should have with the boys. Shit happens," he added with a roguish grin.

I turned to Asterion. "And you?"

He shifted, fingering his beaded Buddhist necklace. "I was placed under Achilles' command. Somehow," he added, looking guilty as shit, but not elaborating. "Bad management all around. Then Hercules, the big idiot..." he added, shaking his great big horns, "was never meant to lead men. Never even realized how poor of a job Achilles was doing. Then again, no one wants to question Achilles too closely."

Achilles grinned at the compliment, and then leaned forward. "That stunt with the selfie. Did you know it went viral?" he chuckled. "And the hat! Make Greece Great Again!" he bellowed, slapping his knees. He actually wiped a tear from his eye. "He was so mad about that he could hardly think straight. Believe it or not, that had as much of a factor in this win as anything else. If he had been paying half the attention to our army as he was about the number of shares and likes that stupid picture was getting..." he trailed off, still laughing.

I smiled sadly, glancing at his corpse. "He fought well. In the end."

Achilles looked surprised to hear me say it, and then sick to his stomach at the thought of Ashley. "Not well enough. To think, a mortal killing one of history's greatest legends... That deserves a ballad," he said, folding his arms. "Especially now," he added in a sad whisper.

My golden tattoos must have faded, because I no longer felt them, and I wasn't casting light on them. Asterion spoke, his low tone rumbling in my chest, and I realized I was simply staring at the ground, exhausted. "The world is close to a tipping point, and more people believe in the Horsemen than the old Greek Gods. It's why the gods like their Makers. To help people remember who they once were... and still are." He brushed his sausage fingers dramatically, as if wiping away filth. "Well," he continued, glancing over at the fallen bodies behind me. "Problem solved. Even a temporary

Horseman was able to kill a god. So, what does that say about the *full* Horsemen?"

War didn't say anything, and neither did I. I hadn't used my Horseman power on the god. We both knew it. Even if Achilles and Asterion seemed to think I had.

But telling them that would only make them fear me more.

My throat was suddenly tight. War gripped me by the arms, respectfully and protectively, and pulled me to my feet. As a brother would. "We should take a walk. Talk. About... things."

I nodded, waving absently at Achilles and Asterion.

CHAPTER 65

*W*e walked to the other side of the tree, towards the Huntress and Alex. Pegasus and Grimm stood apart from the humans, convinced of their safety now that the Greeks were gone. I would need to fix the wards and the wall, and get Dean to help with the injured since we no longer had Pan to help.

So many things to do.

"You kidnapped the Huntress," I said absently. "To make sure I was preoccupied."

War nodded with a sigh. "I knew it was the only way Tory could make it back. And the only way to get you to go. Knowing a friend was in danger."

I nodded tiredly, remembering our talk on the roof. He had pretty much apologized in advance, I had just been too thick to realize it at the time.

"That's twice you've donned the Mask, now. To borrow the power. Maybe third time's the charm?" he asked, chuckling.

I sighed. "How pissed are the others?"

War turned to me, frowning. "Why would they be pissed? Death practically set up the Pay Per View so we could all watch." He pointed a finger at the sky, and I saw a small portal staring down at us. Three cloaked figures gave me proud nods before it winked out.

When I turned to look back at War, he was gone.

I let out a frustrated sigh, ignoring Wylde's dry chuckle in the back of my mind. He had been quiet since Athena. Either pissed or otherwise occupied with his flock of cavewomen.

I continued walking, heading towards Alex, fearing the conversation ahead, but knowing he needed to talk. He looked sad, despondent, and although not too young, he looked like a little boy at the moment. A little boy who had lost his mommy.

I mentally prepared myself for the tough conversation, and tried to come up with a solution. Did he stay here, now? Did Tory look after him? I didn't want to treat him like a package, handing him off to whoever would—

I saw a flash of light to our right, and I reacted without thinking, jumping in front of Alex on instinct, since the Huntress was fidgeting with her bow. A bar of light hammered into my palms, scorching, burning, and...

Doing none of that.

I was simply imagining what it felt like, because as I stared down, I realized I felt nothing. The bar of lethal light struck my palms, and... that was it.

I shoved, and the attack slowly receded.

A feral howl answered me, and I finally looked up to see Matthias, eyes dancing with bloodlust, spittle flying from his lips as he began to shout. "I will take EVERYTHING from you! Freeing me, only to murder my son, *before my very eyes!*"

His power trebled, and my arm began to shake, my palm crackling and sizzling.

It was the palm with the brand on it. The Temple Family Crest. And although I could hear it burning, I felt nothing. Sweat began to pop out on my forehead as I groaned, pressing back against his Maker's power, my ancestor's power.

The power of a grieving father.

Willing to kill his own descendant.

I pressed back, and his eyes grew wilder. Then, several more bars of power formed around his head, and immediately lanced past me, right over my shoulder.

And struck the Huntress. One of her arrows flew true, hammering into Matthias' stomach before she was knocked backwards a good thirty feet, dropping her bow. Alex was screaming.

I was screaming. "YOU WILL NOT HAVE HIM. ALEX IS MY FAMI-LY!" I roared, and suddenly the unicorn and winged horse, Grimm and

Pegasus were airborne, circling the Maker with lethal intent, even if it cost them their lives.

I took a step, feeling as if my soul was ripping away, pressing back his attack. He snarled, hissed, and screamed. I saw people running our way, wolves rolling over the hills, dragons circling the skies, but knew they would be too late.

Although I felt no pain, my soul was dying. I could tell.

But that didn't fucking matter.

Alex needed me.

And I'd be damned before I let anyone hurt my kid.

As I held his beam of power at bay, I began grasping at the shadow cast by the giant white tree behind me. It was massive, and my mind began to splinter as I tried to manipulate it. But ever so slowly, it shrank, and a great hovering blanket of shadow slowly formed above our heads. Matthias' face turned pale upon seeing it.

"This isn't over, boy. Not by a long shot. Breaking you will be fun. My new life purpose. You and Castor Queen will die in agony," he promised. And with a thunderous *crack*, he disappeared.

I collapsed.

I realized I was whispering out loud. "It wasn't me, Matthias. It wasn't *me*..."

Someone gripped my face, and they were crying.

CHAPTER 66

*T*he sensation of many bodies crowding me woke me. That unexplainable sense of being trapped. My eyes shot open, and I tried to jump to my feet, but I was pinned down.

"Easy, Nate, easy. You're safe. Friendlies here. Just a protective barrier," Gunnar said in a gentle tone.

I finally looked around to see Tory holding the Huntress' head in her lap, sobbing. She was breathing, although she looked to be in great pain. Someone was clutching my chest, and I glanced down to see Alex openly weeping as he clutched onto me.

I settled my hand on his head. "Easy, kid. No one's going to hurt you. No one is going to take you away. Ever again."

His terrified eyes turned to me, and the smile that suddenly bloomed on his face was so emotional that I felt tears dripping down my cheeks. Unconditional love. Amazement. Fear. Family.

I nodded back in answer to the feelings painted on his face.

And he began to cry, clutching me even tighter. "You saved me," he whispered.

I gently moved my thumb in his hair in soothing circles. "You saved me, Alex. In that other place. Just as much as I saved you. If not more," I said. He clutched me tighter, and I continued to repeat my promises, even as I acknowledged them to myself for the first time. He had a home. And that home would keep him safe. I had risked my soul to save this kid, and it had felt so natural. So instinctive. So primal. *Thanks for that, Wylde...*

"Let's go home," I finally said, thumbing my palm thoughtfully. It felt fine. Healthy skin, although calloused with the Temple Family Crest branded into it. But it wasn't a blackened stump. "Chateau Falco has grown accustomed to youthful life roaming her halls. I want to introduce you to her, Alex."

He looked up at me. "I would like that, Master Temple. Very much."

I grimaced. "Let's stick with Nate."

"Yeah, the other thing sounded weird," Gunnar agreed. "And you need to rest up."

I nodded up at him, smiling as I studied his stone eye.

He shrugged in answer, so I left it alone for later. But I knew why he wanted me to rest up. We had a damsel to save. Well, a wolf queen.

Which could be... interesting.

If she was still alive.

I felt a pleasant jingle in my pocket and smiled. The pouches of coins from the pavilion. Someone had made sure I got what I had earned.

A fistful of Olympian gold. I chuckled, shaking my head as I walked home with my family.

~

~

*N*ate Temple returns in **WAR HAMMER**... *Turn the page for a sample!*
Or **get the book ONLINE!**

SAMPLE: WAR HAMMER (TEMPLE #8)

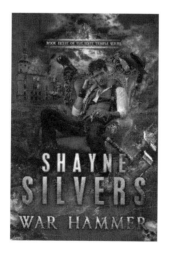

I glanced over my shoulder at the fidgety vampire. "Ready?" I used the microphone built into my helmet to speak to Alucard. My visor was up, but our helmets were connected via radio.

Alucard sighed. "I guess so." His voice sounded tinny since we were so close to each other.

I turned back to the front door, repositioning myself slightly on the back of the idling ATV. "Yahn should be out any minute. I texted him five minutes ago. Be ready to floor it."

"There are so many ways this can go wrong," Alucard complained.

"It's just a little fun. Calm down," I scolded him, rolling my eyes. "Is everyone else ready at the tree?" I asked.

He grunted. "I think so. I still don't know why we're doing that either. It will be fun, sure, but don't we have more important things to do?"

I grunted. "I *know* we have more important things to do. But we can't *do* them yet. Things like this will keep everyone's attention occupied so we don't kill each other out of sheer boredom."

"If you say so," he muttered. At least he sounded mildly interested in our upcoming fight. But he was such a drama queen sometimes, especially of late. The sun shone down on us, and it was surprisingly warm outside for this late in the year. Underneath Alucard's melancholy, I could sense that the weather had perked him up a little. Being a Daywalker vampire, he still had instinctive fear of sunlight, even though it now gave him power. He didn't need blood anymore, just a dose of UV to power up. Still, some old habits were hard to break.

The front door of Chateau Falco – my mansion – began to open, and I grinned as a figure stepped into view. My target was Yahn, and he was about to be hazed into my family – a welcoming rite of passage – since he had done so much to assist during the war with Indie and her Greeks.

I glanced down, the motion awkward with my helmet, and pressed the buttons on all three of the leaf blowers beside me, which were aimed directly at the door. As each kicked on, thick clouds of blue powdered paint – which I had packed inside the tubes of the leaf blowers – launched directly at the open doorway, pelting the unsuspecting dragon. I let out a triumphant cackle as I stared at the cloud of paint. "Take that, *Mr. I'm so cool because I'm invisible and stuff!*" I mocked in my best high-pitched Swede impersonation. "Welcome to the family!" I hooted, turning off each leaf blower – now empty of their payloads.

As the leaf blowers powered down, I heard a very different sound than I had anticipated.

Not the feminine shriek I had expected from Yahn, but two feral snarls of outrage. One a spitting hiss, and another a deep, foreboding growl. My stomach clenched, and I didn't need to see through the cloud to realize I had made a very, very big mistake.

"You're dead!" Gunnar roared, just as Talon screeched, "I'm going to kill you!"

"Alucard, go, go, GO!" I snapped, kicking the leaf blowers off the back of the ATV and grasping onto the cargo bars at my hips.

"Shit! That's not Yahn, you fucking lunatic!" the vampire said, shifting the ATV into drive.

"Fucking right, it's not!" Gunnar snapped, lunging from out of the cloud of colored paint to tackle me, his fancy new eyepatch glittering in the sunlight – because the werewolf only had one eye. His usual glorious, long blonde hair was now completely blue, as was his entire body, transforming him into the world's buffest, tallest Smurf. As he took his second step, he hit the trip-wire I had set up with make-shift grenades of more powdered paint. Three massive *booms* overpowered his shout in an explosion of green paint that blasted the area like mortars had just struck my mansion.

The silence was deafening, and even Alucard hesitated as we both stared at the shifting cloud.

"Wow! Like, totally rad. Paint party!" I heard Yahn call out cheerfully from beyond the open doorway, apparently having been behind Gunnar and Talon, thus escaping the hazing I had carefully prepared for him.

I heard a pair of very low, menacing growls.

"Fucking GO!" I reminded Alucard at the top of my lungs. The vampire slammed on the gas right as Gunnar emerged from the cloud of smoke, and our tires squealed on the driveway. I cackled triumphantly as Gunnar fell short, a massive, green and blue vision of murder. "See you at the tree!" I slammed my visor down, just in case Gunnar saw fit to shoot me from a distance.

"What the fuck, Nate?! I thought you were trying to get Yahn?" Alucard hissed into my earpiece.

"I was! I thought you told everyone else to be at the tree already!" I argued, watching as Gunnar decided to run after us, much faster than most humans could. He hadn't changed to his werewolf form, because that would leave him naked during our upcoming game at the giant white tree that dominated the grounds of Chateau Falco, my ancestral home.

And paintballs wouldn't feel good striking naked flesh.

Talon wasn't far behind, silver eyes glinting in the sunlight as his were-cat-like form tore up dirt and leaves in his pursuit of absolution.

"The wolf is slightly unhinged, if you forgot, and Talon is a certifiable psycho. He was much better as a housecat. And in case you forgot, cats *hate* getting their fur dirty. Why didn't you check who it was, first?" Alucard growled into his headset.

Talon had been disguised as a Maine Coon the entire time I had known him. Up until I decided to take him to the Land of the Fae, which had been when he revealed that he was much more than just a talking housecat. He was now a bipedal werecat warrior – imagine a Thundercat from that kid's cartoon – and he went by the name Talon the Devourer. The only other thing I knew was that he was the Fae version of a killing machine.

I shrugged. "I was too excited. It didn't even cross my mind because, you know, everyone else was *supposed* to be waiting at the tree!" I shouted over the sound of the engine.

Alucard grunted noncommittally. "Don't try to blame this on me." I stared off into the distance, noticing that the laborers working on the wall surrounding my property had paused to stare at the sound of explosions and the clouds of colored smoke wafting through the air. Also, they were likely wondering why three figures were now chasing an ATV across the grounds. I waved at them, and they quickly resumed work, probably not sure if one of the helmeted figures was the man who had hired them.

We skidded up to the tree to see a bewildered assortment of people staring at us, already decked out in their paintball gear. Two of them were teenaged girls, creeping ever closer to that mystical age when they presumed the world would be handed to them on a platter – eighteen. They were stunningly attractive red-heads named Aria and Sonya, but we just called them the Reds – both for their hair color and their color of dragon. They could use mind control, like all shifter dragons, and their crimson irises flashed in the daylight, their horizontal pupils contracting as they stared past me, shaking their heads. "What the hell was that?" they shouted in unison, studying the still-present cloud of smoke drifting near the entrance to the mansion, and the two figures tearing after us. Yahn jogged behind them, grinning excitedly.

The bastard. He had no idea how much time I had secretly put into setting up that trap.

Alex was leaning against the trunk of the large white tree, shaking his head in disbelief, not sure if he should be smiling or seriously concerned about the monsters racing our way. He was tall, dark-haired, and broody, but he was also wildly naïve at times. We had saved him from the Fae not

too long ago, the prisoner of one of their fabled Changeling operations –
where they kidnapped a human child and switched it out for one of their
own. They got power from this, and I still hadn't verified how long Alex had
been a prisoner, but we were slowly nursing him back to mental health,
showing him that not everyone was a monster.

Basically, letting him be a kid again.

In a way, I had kind of adopted him, because his parents had been
murdered.

I very bravely repositioned myself so that the ATV was between me and
the approaching psychopaths. Yahn ran after them, faster now, but still
grinning like a big idiot – enjoying himself.

But the two ahead of him were not enjoying themselves. They wanted
revenge.

Gunnar, the alpha werewolf of St. Louis, and Talon, a seriously deranged
cat-man from the Land of the Fae. Both were very, very good at killing
things that annoyed them.

"Nate, why did you paint-bomb the two most unstable beings here?"
Aria asked, grimacing at the two rainbow-skinned nightmares.

"And why, oh why, did you *let* him do this, Alucard?" Sonya, her sister,
added.

I still hadn't decided which was their most dangerous forms – as red,
fire-breathing dragons, or as two mind-controlling teenaged girls. And they
had Alucard – their stand-in dad, since their mother had been killed –
wrapped around their fingers.

Alucard grimaced. "He was trying to get Yahn, but Gunnar and Talon
came out first."

"Well, that sucks," Alex said, uneasily. "They're not *really* going to kill us,
right? They look pretty serious…"

"Play it cool, Alex," I said, backing up to stand beside him. I leaned
closer, verifying the Reds weren't watching. "Channel four," I told him,
tapping the side of my helmet to switch to a different frequency. He did the
same, plopping his helmet down over his head.

"This it?" he asked into the headset, his voice carrying over the commu-
nications channel.

"Yep. Let's make sure Alucard is ready. I don't think Gunnar is going to
want to give us any time to set up."

I cocked the pistol in my hand and – without warning – shot Alucard in the back of the helmet. He shouted, spinning to glare at the Reds. They instantly pointed at me, laughing inside their helmets. Alucard turned to glare at me, and I waited until the Reds weren't looking to flash him four fingers and then tap my helmet.

I couldn't see through the visor on his head, but I bet he wore a frowny face…

~

Get your copy of WAR HAMMER online today!

~

Turn the page to read a sample of **UNCHAINED** - Feathers and Fire Series Book 1, or **BUY ONLINE**. Callie Penrose is a wizard in Kansas City, MO who hunts monsters for the Vatican. She meets Nate Temple, and things devolve from there…

(Note: Callie appears in the Temple-verse after Nate's book 6, TINY GODS… Full chronology of all books in the Temple Universe shown on the 'Books in the Temple Verse' page.)

TRY: UNCHAINED (FEATHERS AND FIRE #1)

The rain pelted my hair, plastering loose strands of it to my forehead as I panted, eyes darting from tree to tree, terrified of each shifting branch, splash of water, and whistle of wind slipping through the nightscape around us. But... I was somewhat *excited*, too.

Somewhat.

"Easy, girl. All will be well," the big man creeping just ahead of me, murmured.

"You said we were going to get ice cream!" I hissed at him, failing to compose myself, but careful to keep my voice low and my eyes alert. "I'm not ready for this!" I had been trained to fight, with my hands, with weapons, and with my magic. But I had never taken an active role in a hunt before. I'd always been the getaway driver for my mentor.

The man grunted, grey eyes scanning the trees as he slipped through the tall grass. "And did we not get ice cream before coming here? Because I think I see some in your hair."

"You know what I mean, Roland. You tricked me." I checked the tips of my loose hair, saw nothing, and scowled at his back.

"The Lord does not give us a greater burden than we can shoulder."

I muttered dark things under my breath, wiping the water from my eyes. Again. My new shirt was going to be ruined. Silk never fared well in the rain. My choice of shoes wasn't much better. Boots, yes, but distressed, *fashionable* boots. Not work boots designed for the rain and mud. Definitely not monster hunting boots for our evening excursion through one of Kansas City's wooded parks. I realized I was forcibly distracting myself, keeping my mind busy with mundane thoughts to avoid my very real anxiety. Because whenever I grew nervous, an imagined nightmare always—

A church looming before me. Rain pouring down. Night sky and a glowing moon overhead. I was all alone. Crying on the cold, stone steps, and infant in a cardboard box—

I forced the nightmare away, breathing heavily. "You know I hate it when you talk like that," I whispered to him, trying to regain my composure. I wasn't angry with him, but was growing increasingly uncomfortable with our situation after my brief flashback of fear.

"Doesn't mean it shouldn't be said," he said kindly. "I think we're close. Be alert. Remember your training. Banish your fears. I am here. And the Lord is here. He always is."

So, he had noticed my sudden anxiety. "Maybe I should just go back to the car. I know I've trained, but I really don't think—"

A shape of fur, fangs, and claws launched from the shadows towards me, cutting off my words as it snarled, thirsty for my blood.

And my nightmare slipped back into my thoughts like a veiled assassin, a wraith hoping to hold me still for the monster to eat. I froze, unable to move. Twin sticks of power abruptly erupted into being in my clenched fists, but my fear swamped me with that stupid nightmare, the sticks held at my side, useless to save me.

Right before the beast's claws reached me, it grunted as something batted it from the air, sending it flying sideways. It struck a tree with another grunt and an angry whine of pain.

I fell to my knees right into a puddle, arms shaking, breathing fast.

My sticks crackled in the rain like live cattle prods, except their entire length was the electrical section — at least to anyone other than me. I could hold them without pain.

Magic was a part of me, coursing through my veins whether I wanted it or not, and Roland had spent many years teaching me how to master it. But I had never been able to fully master the nightmare inside me, and in moments of fear, it always won, overriding my training.

The fact that I had resorted to weapons — like the ones he had trained me with — rather than a burst of flame, was startling. It was good in the fact that my body's reflexes knew enough to call up a defense even without my direct command, but bad in the fact that it was the worst form of defense for the situation presented. I could have very easily done as Roland did, and hurt it from a distance. But I hadn't. Because of my stupid block.

Roland placed a calloused palm on my shoulder, and I flinched. "Easy, see? I am here." But he did frown at my choice of weapons, the reprimand silent but loud in my mind. I let out a shaky breath, forcing my fear back down. It was all in my head, but still, it wasn't easy. Fear could be like that.

I focused on Roland's implied lesson. Close combat weapons — even magically-powered ones — were for last resorts. I averted my eyes in very real shame. I knew these things. He didn't even need to tell me them. But when that damned nightmare caught hold of me, all my training went out the window. It haunted me like a shadow, waiting for moments just like this, as if trying to kill me. A form of psychological suicide? But it was why I constantly refused to join Roland on his hunts. He knew about it. And although he was trying to help me overcome that fear, he never pressed too hard.

Rain continued to sizzle as it struck my batons. I didn't let them go, using them as a totem to build my confidence back up. I slowly lifted my eyes to nod at him as I climbed back to my feet.

That's when I saw the second set of eyes in the shadows, right before they flew out of the darkness towards Roland's back. I threw one of my batons and missed, but that pretty much let Roland know that an unfriendly was behind him. Either that or I had just failed to murder my mentor at point-blank range. He whirled to confront the monster, expecting another aerial assault as he unleashed a ball of fire that splashed over the tree at chest height, washing the trunk in blue flames. But this monster was tricky. It hadn't planned on tackling Roland, but had merely jumped out of the darkness to get closer, no doubt learning from its fallen comrade, who still lay unmoving against the tree behind me.

His coat shone like midnight clouds with hints of lightning flashing in the depths of thick, wiry fur. The coat of dew dotting his fur reflected the moonlight, giving him a faint sheen as if covered in fresh oil. He was tall, easily hip height at the shoulder, and barrel chested, his rump much leaner than the rest of his body. He — I assumed male from the long, thick mane around his neck — had a very long snout, much longer and wider than any werewolf I had ever seen. Amazingly, and beyond my control, I realized he was beautiful.

But most of the natural world's lethal hunters were beautiful.

He landed in a wet puddle a pace in front of Roland, juked to the right, and then to the left, racing past the big man, biting into his hamstrings on his way by.

A wash of anger rolled over me at seeing my mentor injured, dousing my fear, and I swung my baton down as hard as I could. It struck the beast in the rump as it tried to dart back to cover — a typical wolf tactic. My blow singed his hair and shattered bone. The creature collapsed into a puddle of mud with a yelp, instinctively snapping his jaws over his shoulder to bite whatever had hit him.

I let him. But mostly out of dumb luck as I heard Roland hiss in pain, falling to the ground.

The monster's jaws clamped around my baton, and there was an immediate explosion of teeth and blood that sent him flying several feet away into the tall brush, yipping, screaming, and staggering. Before he slipped out of sight, I noticed that his lower jaw was simply *gone*, from the contact of his saliva on my electrified magical batons. Then he managed to limp into the woods with more pitiful yowls, but I had no mind to chase him. Roland — that titan of a man, my mentor — was hurt. I could smell copper in the air, and knew we had to get out of here. Fast. Because we had anticipated only one of the monsters. But there had been two of them, and they hadn't been the run-of-the-mill werewolves we had been warned about. If there were two, perhaps there were more. And they were evidently the prehistoric cousin of any werewolf I had ever seen or read about.

Roland hissed again as he stared down at his leg, growling with both pain and anger. My eyes darted back to the first monster, wary of another attack. It *almost* looked like a werewolf, but bigger. Much bigger. He didn't move, but I saw he was breathing. He had a notch in his right ear and a jagged scar on his long snout. Part of me wanted to go over to him and torture him. Slowly. Use his pain to finally drown my nightmare, my fear. The fear that had caused Roland's injury. My lack of inner-strength had not only put me in danger, but had hurt my mentor, my friend.

I shivered, forcing the thought away. That was *cold*. Not me. Sure, I was no stranger to fighting, but that had always been in a ring. Practicing. Sparring. Never life or death.

But I suddenly realized something very dark about myself in the chill, rainy night. Although I was terrified, I felt a deep ocean of anger manifest inside me, wanting only to dispense justice as I saw fit. To use that rage to battle my own demons. As if feeding one would starve the other, reminding me of the Cherokee Indian Legend Roland had once told me.

An old Cherokee man was teaching his grandson about life. "A fight is going on inside me," he told the boy. "It is a terrible fight between two wolves. One is evil — he is anger, envy, sorrow, regret, greed, arrogance, self-pity, guilt, resentment, inferiority, lies, false pride, superiority, and ego." After a few moments to make sure he had the boy's undivided attention, he continued.

"The other wolf is good — he is joy, peace, love, hope, serenity, humility, kindness, benevolence, empathy, generosity, truth, compassion, and faith. The same fight is going on inside of you, boy, and inside of every other person, too."

The grandson thought about this for a few minutes before replying. "Which wolf will win?"

The old Cherokee man simply said, "The one you feed, boy. The one you feed..."

And I felt like feeding one of my wolves today, by killing this one...

∾

Get the full book ONLINE!

∾

Turn the page to read a sample of **WHISKEY GINGER** *- Phantom Queen Diaries Book 1, or* **BUY ONLINE**. *Quinn MacKenna is a black magic arms dealer from Boston, and her bark is almost as bad as her bite.*

(Note: Full chronology of all books in the Temple Verse shown on the 'Books in the Temple Verse' page.)

TRY: WHISKEY GINGER (PHANTOM QUEEN DIARIES # 1)

*T*he pasty guitarist hunched forward, thrust a rolled-up wad of paper deep into one nostril, and snorted a line of blood crystals—frozen hemoglobin that I'd smuggled over in a refrigerated canister—with the uncanny grace of a drug addict. He sat back, fangs gleaming, and pawed at his nose. "That's some bodacious shit. Hey, bros," he said, glancing at his fellow band members, "come hit this shit before it melts."

He fetched one of the backstage passes hanging nearby, pried the plastic badge from its lanyard, and used it to split up the crystals, murmuring something in an accent that reminded me of California. Not *the* California, but you know, Cali-foh-nia—the land of beaches, babes, and bros. I retrieved a toothpick from my pocket and punched it through its thin wrapper. "So," I asked no one in particular, "now that ye have the product, who's payin'?"

Another band member stepped out of the shadows to my left, and I don't mean that figuratively, either—the fucker literally stepped out of the shadows. I scowled at him, but hid my surprise, nonchalantly rolling the toothpick from one side of my mouth to the other.

The rest of the band gathered around the dressing room table, following the guitarist's lead by preparing their own snorting utensils—tattered magazine covers, mostly. Typically, you'd do this sort of thing with a dollar-bill, maybe even a Benjamin if you were flush. But fangers like this lot couldn't touch cash directly—in God We Trust and all that. Of course, I didn't really understand why sucking blood the old-fashioned way had suddenly gone out of style. More of a rush, maybe?

"It lasts longer," the vampire next to me explained, catching my mildly curious expression. "It's especially good for shows and stuff. Makes us look, like, less—"

"Creepy?" I offered, my Irish brogue lilting just enough to make it a question.

"Pale," he finished, frowning.

I shrugged. "Listen, I've got places to be," I said, holding out my hand.

"I'm sure you do," he replied, smiling. "Tell you what, why don't you, like, hang around for a bit? Once that wears off," he dipped his head toward the bloody powder smeared across the table's surface, "we may need a pick-me-up." He rested his hand on my arm and our gazes locked.

I blinked, realized what he was trying to pull, and rolled my eyes. His widened in surprise, then shock as I yanked out my toothpick and shoved it through his hand.

"Motherfuck—"

"I want what we agreed on," I declared. "Now. No tricks."

The rest of the band saw what happened and rose faster than I could blink. They circled me, their grins feral...they might have even seemed intimidating if it weren't for the fact that they each had a case of the sniffles

—I had to work extra hard not to think about what it felt like to have someone else's blood dripping down my nasal cavity.

I held up a hand.

"Can I ask ye gentlemen a question before we get started?" I asked. "Do ye even *have* what I asked for?"

Two of the band members exchanged looks and shrugged. The guitarist, however, glanced back towards the dressing room, where a brown paper bag sat next to a case full of makeup. He caught me looking and bared his teeth, his fangs stretching until it looked like it would be uncomfortable for him to close his mouth without piercing his own lip.

"Follow-up question," I said, eyeing the vampire I'd stabbed as he gingerly withdrew the toothpick from his hand and flung it across the room with a snarl. "Do ye do each other's make-up? Since, ye know, ye can't use mirrors?"

I was genuinely curious.

The guitarist grunted. "Mike, we have to go on soon."

"Wait a minute. Mike?" I turned to the snarling vampire with a frown. "What happened to *The Vampire Prospero*?" I glanced at the numerous fliers in the dressing room, most of which depicted the band members wading through blood, with Mike in the lead, each one titled *The Vampire Prospero* in *Rocky Horror Picture Show* font. Come to think of it…Mike did look a little like Tim Curry in all that leather and lace.

I was about to comment on the resemblance when Mike spoke up, "Alright, change of plans, bros. We're gonna drain this bitch before the show. We'll look totally—"

"Creepy?" I offered, again.

"Kill her."

~

Get the full book ONLINE!

MAKE A DIFFERENCE

Reviews are the most powerful tools in my arsenal when it comes to getting attention for my books. Much as I'd like to, I don't have the financial muscle of a New York publisher.

But I do have something much more powerful and effective than that, and it's something that those publishers would kill to get their hands on.

A committed and loyal bunch of readers.

Honest reviews of my books help bring them to the attention of other readers.

If you've enjoyed this book, I would be very grateful if you could spend just five minutes leaving a review (it can be as short as you like) on my book's Amazon page.

Thank you very much in advance.

ACKNOWLEDGMENTS

First, I would like to thank my beta-readers, TEAM TEMPLE, those individuals who spent hours of their time to read, and re-re-read Nate's story. Your dark, twisted, cunning sense of humor makes me feel right at home...

I would also like to thank you, the reader. I hope you enjoyed reading *WILD SIDE* as much as I enjoyed writing it. Be sure to check out the two crossover series in the Temple Verse: The **Feathers and Fire Series** and the **Phantom Queen Diaries**.

And last, but definitely not least, I thank my wife, Lexy. Without your support, none of this would have been possible.

ABOUT SHAYNE SILVERS

Shayne is a man of mystery and power, whose power is exceeded only by his mystery...

He currently writes the Amazon Bestselling **Nate Temple** Series, which features a foul-mouthed wizard from St. Louis. He rides a bloodthirsty unicorn, drinks with Achilles, and is pals with the Four Horsemen.

He also writes the Amazon Bestselling **Feathers and Fire** Series—a second series in the Temple Verse. The story follows a rookie spell-slinger named Callie Penrose who works for the Vatican in Kansas City. Her problem? Hell seems to know more about her past than she does.

He coauthors **The Phantom Queen Diaries**—a third series set in The Temple Verse—with Cameron O'Connell. The story follows Quinn MacKenna, a mouthy black magic arms dealer in Boston. All she wants? A round-trip ticket to the Fae realm...and maybe a drink on the house.

Shayne holds two high-ranking black belts, and can be found writing in a coffee shop, cackling madly into his computer screen while pounding shots of espresso. He's hard at work on the newest books in the Temple Verse—You can find updates on new releases or chronological reading order on the next page, his website or any of his social media accounts. **Follow him online for all sorts of groovy goodies, giveaways, and new release updates:**

Get Down with Shayne Online
www.shaynesilvers.com
info@shaynesilvers.com

facebook.com/shaynesilversfanpage

amazon.com/author/shaynesilvers

bookbub.com/profile/shayne-silvers

instagram.com/shaynesilversofficial

twitter.com/shaynesilvers

goodreads.com/ShayneSilvers

BOOKS IN THE TEMPLE VERSE

CHRONOLOGY: All stories in the TempleVerse are shown in chronological order on the following page

NATE TEMPLE SERIES

FAIRY TALE - FREE prequel novella #0 for my subscribers

OBSIDIAN SON

BLOOD DEBTS

GRIMM

SILVER TONGUE

BEAST MASTER

BEERLYMPIAN (Novella #5.5 in the 'LAST CALL' anthology)

TINY GODS

DADDY DUTY (Novella #6.5)

WILD SIDE

WAR HAMMER

NINE SOULS

HORSEMAN

LEGEND

KNIGHTMARE (TEMPLE #12) — COMING SOON…

FEATHERS AND FIRE SERIES

(Also set in the TempleVerse)

UNCHAINED

RAGE

WHISPERS

ANGEL'S ROAR

MOTHERLUCKER (Novella #4.5 in the 'LAST CALL' anthology)

SINNER

BLACK SHEEP

GODLESS (FEATHERS #7) — COMING SOON...

PHANTOM QUEEN DIARIES

(Also set in the Temple Universe)

COLLINS (Prequel novella #0 in the 'LAST CALL' anthology)

WHISKEY GINGER

COSMOPOLITAN

OLD FASHIONED

MOTHERLUCKER (Novella #3.5 in the 'LAST CALL' anthology)

DARK AND STORMY

MOSCOW MULE

WITCHES BREW

SALTY DOG

CHRONOLOGICAL ORDER: TEMPLE VERSE

FAIRY TALE (TEMPLE PREQUEL)

OBSIDIAN SON (TEMPLE 1)

BLOOD DEBTS (TEMPLE 2)

GRIMM (TEMPLE 3)

SILVER TONGUE (TEMPLE 4)

BEAST MASTER (TEMPLE 5)

BEERLYMPIAN (TEMPLE 5.5)

TINY GODS (TEMPLE 6)

DADDY DUTY (TEMPLE NOVELLA 6.5)

UNCHAINED (FEATHERS... 1)

RAGE (FEATHERS... 2)

WILD SIDE (TEMPLE 7)

WAR HAMMER (TEMPLE 8)

WHISPERS (FEATHERS... 3)

COLLINS (PHANTOM 0)

Printed in Great Britain
by Amazon

60392440R00232